MOLLY GREEN has travelled the world, unpacking her suitcase in a score of countries. On returning to England, Molly decided to pursue her life-long passion for writing. She now writes in a cabin in her garden on the outskirts of Tunbridge Wells, Kent, ably assisted by her white rescued cat, Dougie.

Also by Molly Green

The Dr Barnardo's Orphanage series:
An Orphan in the Snow
An Orphan's War
An Orphan's Wish

The Victory Sisters series:
A Sister's Courage
A Sister's Song
A Sister's War

Wartime At Bletchley Park

MOLLY GREEN

avon.

Published by AVON
A division of HarperCollins*Publishers* Ltd
1 London Bridge Street
London SE1 9GF

www.harpercollins.co.uk

HarperCollins*Publishers*
1st Floor, Watermarque Building, Ringsend Road
Dublin 4, Ireland

A Paperback Original 2022
1
First published in Great Britain by HarperCollins*Publishers* 2022

This trade paperback edition published by HarperCollins*Publishers* 2022

ISBN: 978-0-00-851855-4

Typeset in Minion Pro, 11/14pt by
Palimpsest Book Production Limited, Falkirk, Stirlingshire
Printed and bound in the UK using 100% renewable electricity at
CPI Group (UK) Ltd

MIX
Paper from
responsible sources
FSC™ C007454

To all the men and women who worked in the 'enigma' that was Bletchley Park. It's been widely acknowledged that the codebreakers brought about the ending of the war by approximately two years, thereby saving thousands of lives. The work, especially that performed by the women and girls, was mundane and tiring, the constant changing shifts causing havoc with their health. What's more, they were rarely told any details about any event they'd played a part in, nor how vital their work was in the war effort, but now their secret is out we can thank them profusely for what they uncomplainingly achieved.

It's also been officially recognised that the geniuses of Bletchley Park created the world's first electronic digital computer, the forerunner to our modern computers, namely, Colossus. At appointed times a facsimile of Colossus can be seen in action at Bletchley Park, as well as the National Museum of Computing in Block H – both I can unhesitatingly recommend.

PART ONE

Chapter One

1st September 1939, London

Dulcie Treadwell, firmly grasping the handles of her two carrier bags, pushed through Peter Jones's exit onto Sloane Square, glad to be out of the stuffy department store. She glanced about her. A window cleaner on a ladder outside one of the shops whistled as he spotted her. She looked up and grinned. Two young mothers pushed their prams past her, chatting together, taking no notice of their babies howling. A bus rumbled by and a man rushed after it, grabbing the rail to haul himself onto the platform. A perfectly normal London scene. And yet a strange stillness hung in the air. A waiting. An expectation. She felt she could almost cut it with a knife.

It had been a hot, dry fortnight. Dale, as she preferred to be called, stood on the pavement, enjoying the heat of the morning sun on her face, the carrier bags brushing her legs. Anticipation fizzed through her at the thought of showing off her new dress and shoes to Jane and Rhoda at the tea dance on Sunday – her twenty-first birthday. Thrusting out her hand to grab the attention of a taxi coming towards her, she stepped into the road. Annoyingly, it sped by. So did the next one.

Dale crossed the road and made her way briskly towards Eaton Square. She became aware of a strong male voice from an open window of one of the houses she was passing. She slowed down. What was going on? She shouldn't eavesdrop, but they ought to have shut the window. Then it dawned. Of course. It was the wireless. Probably some sports programme. She gathered her pace, but the same voice followed her from more open windows. Why had everyone got the volume up so loud? She glanced at her watch, wondering if it could be the news. Everyone listened avidly these days, still hoping war could be avoided. But if it *was* the news, it wasn't the right time of day, so it must be a special announcement.

Perhaps she'd catch the last of the broadcast if she hurried. But from the next house came the sound of sobbing. Then someone inside banged the sash down. Abruptly stopping and stepping back, she felt someone from behind collide into her.

"Ere, mind where yer goin", an irate woman's voice reprimanded her.

'Oh, I do beg your pardon. I heard someone crying in that house and wondered if they needed help.'

'I think yer'd best mind yer own business, miss', the woman said, glaring at her, "fore yer start causin' more accidents.' She ambled off.

Dale stared after her, then looked back at the house. She could still hear the sobbing even through the now-closed window. Dale hesitated, then shook her head. She should take that woman's advice – it was none of her business. She strode past the next row of houses.

And then her attention was caught by the words '. . . signed by the King', voiced by the same wireless newsreader, followed by a few more words, then the snippet '. . . general mobilisation . . .'

Her pulse raced. She quickened her footsteps. She needed to get home to switch on the wireless. Find out what was happening. More snatches of the report floated down from the windows:

'. . . Mr Chamberlain's statement . . .'

'. . . hostilities along the frontiers between Germany and Poland . . .'

The rest of the sentence was muffled by crackling. Her heart in her mouth, Dale began to run, trying to keep up with the newsreader before the broadcast ended.

The last words she heard before she turned into Charlwood Street rang in her ears:

'. . . Great Britain and France are inflexibly determined . . .'

Dear God, is this the news we've all been dreading? A war with Germany?

Her fingers felt thick as bananas as she fumbled to unlock the front door. She rushed into the sitting room, threw her bags down and switched on the wireless. Foot tapping with impatience, she waited a full half minute as it warmed up. But all that was playing was some light music. She'd missed it. Damn! The next news wouldn't be until one o'clock. But surely Mother would have heard it. She'd probably be in the kitchen listening to the wireless while she was preparing lunch.

But she wasn't there.

'Mother, where are you?' Dale called.

And then she heard a muffled sound from above – like someone groaning in pain. She took the stairs two at a time, almost slipping on the rug outside her mother's bedroom. Without knocking, she flung open the door – took a step back. Her mother was bent over her dressing-table, her head buried in her hands, sobbing hysterically.

It must have been the news bulletin. Her mother had

5

been through the trauma of the Great War only twenty years ago. The shock of a new war would be even worse for her generation. Dale rushed to her side, then gently prised her mother's hands away from her face. 'Did you hear the whole thing?'

Her mother raised her head, her eyes red with weeping.

'Where have you been all this time?'

'I went shopping,' Dale said. 'You knew that.'

'You shouldn't have left me – today of all days . . . the most terrible news.'

'I know,' Dale said. 'I heard snatches of it from open windows as I walked from Sloane Square.'

Patricia Treadwell shook her head. 'What are you talking about?'

It was Dale's turn to be puzzled. 'From what I could catch, I think the Germans must have invaded Poland, which means *we* now have to declare war on Germany.' She gazed at her.

'It's not that at all.' Her mother's expression was dull. 'I haven't switched the wireless on ever since that letter came this morning.'

Dale's stomach gave a sickening lurch.

'What letter? Who from?'

'From your father.' Her mother fished out a handkerchief and blew her nose. 'I don't know where to begin. It's all so dreadful.'

'Just say it.' Dale's patience was beginning to wear thin. Then a frightening thought struck her. 'Has he had an accident?'

The words choked in her throat. Her father had only recently gone to Scotland – he was rather vague on exactly where, or how long he'd be gone. All he'd said was he was going to join a team who were experimenting on tracking

6

weather by radio. Apparently, it was all rather hush-hush, but a vital development if there was to be another war. Although Dale had no idea what he was hinting at, she was secretly proud of him.

Her mother stared at her for a few moments with unfocused eyes. Then she shook her head. 'No. No, nothing like that. I wish it were.'

'What is it, then?'

Patricia Treadwell set her teeth in her lower lip. 'He's not coming home when we expected him.'

Mother tended to be overly emotional and even erratic, Dale reminded herself, especially since she'd been going through what her friends called in an undertone 'the change', where apparently women of a certain age succumbed to mood swings.

'Does he have to stay longer in Scotland for his work?'

Patricia shook her head again. 'No.' The word seemed to come from deep down within her.

'Is he ill?'

'He's far from ill.' Her mother's voice was harsh.

'Then what—'

'He wants a divorce!'

She couldn't have heard right. Dale stared at her mother. She could see her mother's chest rise and fall . . . hear the hiss of her jagged breath as she struggled to get her words out.

'Wh-what did you say?'

'You heard,' Patricia replied, bitterly. 'He's met someone in Scotland and asking me if I'll divorce him. Well—' she glared at Dale '—he's got another think coming if he thinks I'll let him go to some floozie.' She blinked rapidly.

Dale's mouth went dry. Shockwaves rushed from her throat to her stomach. Was it true that her beloved father really *had* met another woman? It didn't seem possible. He'd only been up there a couple of months. Mother could be difficult, heaven knew, but she and Dad seemed to rub along – well, mostly anyway. But all this time Dad must have been needing more from his wife. But a divorce . . .

She swallowed hard. A divorce was so final. Surely he'd want to discuss something so important – so devastating it would change all their lives – by coming home first and talking to his wife before making such a decision. But no, he'd simply written her a letter. No wonder Mother was in such a state. She must feel wickedly betrayed. And so do I, Dale thought bitterly.

'I've given him the best years of my life, supporting him when we were young and had no money. Taking that switchboard job in the war so he could train to be an engineer.' She paused, her eyes flashing. 'Do you think I wanted to do that? No. I did it for him. Gave up my own life so he could fulfil his. And how does he repay me? He goes off with another woman – I expect she's younger than him and that makes *him* feel young. He says she makes him happy.' She squeezed shut her eyes as though trying to ward off the images that were making her so upset. '*Happy!*' Patricia spat the word. 'Being married and having children is a responsibility – not a guaranteed path to happiness.'

'Mother, you're in shock.' Dale put an arm round her trembling shoulders.

'To think all this time he was sleeping with her and I knew nothing about it. How could he?' She began to weep.

Dale's insides churned as she stood helpless, dreading to hear any more intimate details. She waited until the sobbing subsided. Her mother looked up, tears still streaming down her face.

'And if I set him free and he goes to this woman, what

will everyone say?' Without waiting for her daughter to reply, she added, 'I'll be the only divorced woman in the street.'

'Who cares about the street and what people think?'

'I do.' Patricia threw her a furious glance. 'Everyone will be whispering behind my back. Saying I couldn't keep hold of my husband. Don't you remember poor Mrs Kingsnorth in Beaufort Street? The neighbours who she always said were so friendly ended up not speaking to her and she had to move right away. And *he* was the one playing away, but everyone blamed *her* for not being able to hold on to him. She let herself go, they all said, so it was her fault in their eyes.'

'They weren't proper friends and the gossips aren't worth tuppence,' Dale said crisply. 'And *you* haven't let yourself go. You always look lovely.'

It wasn't exactly the truth. Her mother had gained some weight and these days rarely bothered to dress up. She'd had the same hairstyle ever since Dale could remember. Maybe when she'd calmed down, Dale would suggest a trip to the hairdressers for a more up-to-date look. Not today, though. She'd get her head bitten off.

Dale handed her a fresh handkerchief. 'Come on, Mother, dry your tears. I'll go and make a pot of tea and you can tell me what he said.'

Dale went downstairs and put the kettle on and was setting out the tea tray when her mother appeared.

'Go and sit down and I'll bring this through,' Dale said as she poured milk in the jug and put a few biscuits on a plate. She carried the tray to the sitting room where her mother sat staring out of the window. She handed Dale the envelope.

'You can read it. I thought it was to tell me he'd finished the job and was coming home.' Her hand flew to her mouth to stifle another sob.

9

'Let me just read it before I say anything,' Dale said, removing the two sheets of notepaper. As usual he'd just written yesterday's date and 'Edinburgh'. They had to use a PO Box number when they wrote to him. Part of the hush-hush, she supposed. Quickly she skimmed the contents all the while chewing her lip. Her father sounded dead serious.

'How dare he sign "Yours"?' Her mother's voice rose.

'I suppose it's habit,' Dale said. She could understand her mother's fury. It was a meaningless, cruel signing off. She hardly dared look up. When she did, she was shocked. Her mother's eyes were steel, her mouth set in a thin line.

'*Claudia.*' She lifted her eyes to the ceiling. 'What sort of a name is that? He even said I've always been a good wife and mother . . . and *faithful*,' Patricia's voice droned on. 'He forgot to mention *that*. Oh, how could I have been such a fool?' She looked Dale in the eye. 'By the sound of it, you won't be able to go on any more shopping sprees. But I know one thing – I'm *not* selling the house. I'm not having the neighbours say I've been turned out of my own home.'

'I'll have to get a job that pays more than a junior reporter.' Dale's heart hammered in her ears. Was this the chance she'd been waiting for? To do something more stimulating than covering garden fêtes, children's parties, church jumble sales . . . She'd tried so hard to put herself forward for the serious news, but her editor, Mr Franklin, wouldn't hear of it.

'I never did like you taking that job,' her mother was saying. 'Why don't you become a secretary? You could get a job with someone important and earn a lot more.'

'No, I don't want to sit behind a typewriter all day typing up dreary reports by some ghastly boss, or worse, being forced to sit on his lap while he's giving dictation.'

Her mother gasped. 'Surely they don't do things like that.'

'Don't they? It's what happened to Lucy. Her boss said

he'd sack her if she didn't. She had to do what he said because she's got three brothers and a sister to take care of since her dad walked out.'

Oh, God, I've said the wrong thing.

Patricia kept her eyes fixed on her daughter's.

'You see what happens when the man leaves home. Just like your father. Leaving us to fend for ourselves. Oh, Dulcie, I don't know what I'm going to do.' She broke down again, then, dabbing her eyes with a handkerchief, she looked up at Dale. 'What were you saying about Germany when you first came in?'

'I think they've already invaded Poland. Maybe there'll be a news bulletin on the vision set.'

'I was watching something earlier on,' Patricia said, sniffing. 'They were taking us on a visit to the zoo – it made a lovely change from news – and I was really enjoying seeing the animals – when suddenly the picture vanished. No sound. No nothing.'

'I'll try it again.' Dale turned the knob, tapping her foot as she waited for it to warm up. 'Hmm.' She twiddled the tuning knob. 'It can't be the electricity,' she said finally, 'because the lamps and the wireless are working. The BBC must have switched it off for some reason. But they ought to have said something beforehand – unless the set itself has gone wrong.' She turned it off.

'*Everything's* gone wrong today.'

'But this is serious, Mother. If we're in for another war it will change our lives drastically.'

'Your father has already changed *my* life drastically,' her mother flashed. 'Don't forget I'll have a war *and* a divorce to contend with.' She gazed at Dale and her expression became resolute. 'Thank God I've still got you living at home. You'll be such a support to me.'

Dale's heart sank. She couldn't leave Mother to face the future on her own. She'd have to think of something that would give her a decent living close by. But what? And with her mother so upset, how could she enjoy her special birthday with her friends at the Grosvenor Hotel the day after tomorrow at their Sunday afternoon tea dance? Could she even go?

Chapter Two

'We need to keep the kitchen wireless on,' Dale said as she ladled out the soup. 'They're bound to repeat the whole thing several times today.'

They didn't have long to wait.

'This is the BBC news special at one o'clock,' the announcer's voice was grave, giving an account of what had happened today with the invasion of Germany into Poland and the almost immediate bombing of Warsaw.

It was all too horrifying to be real.

'Poor Poland,' Dale said.

'Yes, poor Poland,' her mother repeated. 'And it will be us next. We said we'd go to their rescue if Hitler marched in.' She looked at Dale in despair, as though for the first time taking it in. 'Haven't they learnt anything from the last one? It's only twenty years ago since it ended. All those young men wiped out or left with broken bodies so they'll never find work again . . . leaving heartbroken families and friends. Do they really want to risk another one?' Her voice became shrill.

Dale's thoughts tumbled over one another.

We let the Nazis walk into Czechoslovakia six months ago without a murmur. We'll have to honour our pact to help Poland so that will definitely mean war. Dad's in Scotland with his other woman so it will be down to me as far as Mother's concerned. I'll be trapped.

'Mother, you know Jane and I are supposed to be going to the pictures this evening,' Dale said after the two of them had finished an unusually quiet supper and they were in the sitting room.

'I should have thought that's the last place you'd want to go after what's happened today,' Patricia Treadwell said. 'We haven't even got the blackout curtains up. The newsreader said they have to go up this evening.'

'We can do it tomorrow.'

Her mother frowned. 'Are you sure the cinemas will be open? They're talking of closing the theatres and cinemas once it starts – which could be any moment.'

'Surely not without an announcement.' Dale got to her feet.

Patricia sat in her chair, staring ahead of her. 'I don't know why you have to go out.'

'If I don't, Jane'll think I've had an accident. They're not on the phone so I can't let her know. But after the news today I doubt we'll want to sit in a cinema. We'll probably just have a natter in a Lyons.'

After listening to her mother the whole afternoon about her cheating father and his mistress, Dale was desperate to get away and pour out everything to her closest friend.

Patricia, her cheeks stained with tears, looked round. 'You'll be the death of me, Dulcie, the way I worry about you.'

'There's no need to worry – I can take care of myself.' Dale pecked her mother on the cheek and flung on a light summer jacket, then rammed on her hat. Pushing down a flicker of guilt, she said, 'I won't be too late but don't wait up.'

Entering Victoria underground station, Dale bought her ticket and stood on the escalator as it took her down to the platform for her train. The platform was crowded from one end to the other with children, mostly in pairs and holding hands, their teachers keeping them in disciplined lines. For a moment she was puzzled. There were too many to be on a school outing. And then she spotted they were all carrying small suitcases and little cardboard boxes slung across their chests – the gas masks everyone was talking about. Of course. The evacuation of the children had started. Poor little kids. One of them bumped into her.

'Say sorry to the lady.'

'Sorry, miss.'

Dale looked at the tear-stained face. A little girl, no more than six or seven. Dale swallowed hard. Even before any announcement it looked as though they were already at war.

After changing at the Embankment for the Northern line to Leicester Square and another packed train, she was thankful to be outside and in the square, her mind still reeling at the thought of thousands of children being torn away from their parents, most of them not understanding what was happening, going who knows where.

Lost in her thoughts she walked towards Shakespeare's statue, their usual meeting place. Moments later she heard Jane call her name. She turned to see her friend come running up, smiling. The two friends kissed and linked arms.

'Glad you made it,' Jane said. 'I tried to ring you from a phone box before I started out, but the lines are jammed. Apparently, everyone's phoning to find out what's going on. And they've closed the cinemas.' Jane's nose wrinkled at the audacity of the cinema management.

'I suppose it's a new government ruling. We're bound to get quite a few of those.'

15

'It'll be miserable if they stay shut when we're at war.' Jane pulled a face. 'Oh, Dale, isn't it awful about Poland?'

'Dreadful. It's hard to believe.'

'I feel so sorry for those people.' Jane picked up an empty cigarette packet and threw it in a nearby bin. 'Did you know the blackout's going to be strictly enforced as soon as the sun sets this evening?'

'No, I didn't. All Mother said was that we hadn't got our blackout curtains up yet and I said we'd do them tomorrow.' She glanced at her watch. It was five past seven and the sunlight was already fading.

'Did you bring a torch?' Jane asked.

'No.' Dale tutted in annoyance. 'Did you?'

'I put one in my bag when I heard about the blackout tonight but I can't imagine how we'll be able to find our way in the dark without proper lights. I bet there'll be traffic accidents.' She glanced at Dale. 'Why don't we get a cup of tea and have a natter, then call it a day. You haven't brought a torch and I don't want you to fall over.'

'I suppose you're right,' Dale conceded, 'though I was looking forward to seeing *Jamaica Inn*.'

'So was I,' Jane said. 'But nothing's going to be the same with the news today.' She paused. 'Look, there's a Lyons.'

'Tell you what, Jane,' Dale said, 'let's have a hot chocolate. Goodness knows if we'll still get it if we really do go to war with Germany.'

The two friends found a table by the window and Dale immediately plunged in.

'Will you join up?'

'Yes. In fact, I went to the recruitment office this morning.'

'Gosh, you haven't wasted any time. Which one?'

'The WAAFs.' Jane took a sip of chocolate. 'And you? Do you think you'll do the same?'

'To be honest, it doesn't really appeal,' Dale said. 'If there's a war I really want to stay and report it.' She scuffed her chair closer to the table and lowered her voice. 'But all the while my boss refuses to let me cover anything important, I can't see much chance. If I was a man I wouldn't have this problem. That's what's so frustrating. If I can't do that, I don't know what on earth I'm going to do. I'm not qualified for anything.'

'What about your German? That ought to come in jolly useful now. Maybe you could work in intelligence, or something.'

Dale grinned. 'What – as a spy?'

'Maybe,' Jane chuckled. 'Seriously, I bet there's some kind of important war work you could do. You'll think of something – or something will just turn up.'

'Well, while I'm waiting, why don't we go for seconds,' Dale grinned as she gestured towards the two empty mugs.

As it began to get dusk, she noticed Jane glance out of the window several times.

'We should go.' Her friend pulled out her purse.

'I'll pay.' Dale glanced at the bill. It wouldn't break the bank but as her mother had warned her, she must start being more careful about money.

Outside, Jane said, 'Let's hope they won't keep the cinemas shut for long.' She gave Dale a brief hug and kissed her cheek. 'And fingers crossed we *don't* go to war with Germany.'

'Yes,' Dale said. 'Fingers crossed.'

But she knew as she uttered the words, they were futile. The children in the Underground already being evacuated plainly told what was about to happen. It would only be a matter of weeks – maybe only days – before Chamberlain made his announcement. She just hoped it wouldn't be the day after tomorrow.

As soon as Jane disappeared in the crowd Dale felt strangely alone, trying to take it in that they were on the brink of war. She'd heard stories from her mother about the last one and they were horrifying. Men dying from all sorts of diseases as well as injuries in mud-filled trenches. The newspapers said this war would be different and would affect civilians more. That was the frightening part. How would everyone cope? How would *she* cope?

Dale stood for a few minutes in a daze. As usual the square was crowded with people, probably bent on getting home now there was no entertainment. Dogs on leads barked. A mother reprimanded her toddler for trying to escape her grip. Everything appeared almost normal, but she should take Jane's advice and go home before the city began its blackout.

And then it hit her. She might be off-duty but this was something to go down in the history books and her chance to write a serious report for the newspaper. People who hadn't ventured out for the evening would have no idea how it would feel to witness their city suddenly plunged into blackness. And *she'd* be the one to tell them. At present the square was ablaze with lights, looking like fairyland, and she realised she'd always taken it for granted, just as everyone around her. How was the council planning to do it? Would they all be turned off at the same time? She must get her facts straight. Quickly she checked her handbag. Yes, there was her notebook and pencil.

Dale looked around. Where would be the best place to watch whatever was going to happen? Maybe one of the bridges? She frowned. Westminster Bridge. It would only take her twenty minutes if she hurried.

As she approached the bridge, people were already lined along the footway. She stepped onto the bridge and walked halfway along, keeping an eye open for a space, but everyone seemed to have had the same thought.

Ah, that looks promising – between that chap and the lovey-dovey couple.

'Excuse me.' She tapped the couple. 'May I squeeze in?'

The couple completely ignored her, but the man on the left half turned and nodded.

'Sure.' He moved a fraction over.

Dale jostled into the narrow space.

''Ere. Mind where yer puttin' yer feet,' the girl from the couple said sharply.

'I'm sorry.' Dale smiled apologetically but even in the growing dusk she saw the girl's eyes flash with annoyance.

'Thank you,' she said to the man to her left, acknowledging the few extra inches of space he'd given her.

'Sure is a significant day,' he said, turning his head towards her. 'You've come to see the show.' He said it as a statement rather than a question.

Nice face. And voice. Soft accent. American? Canadian?

'Yes,' Dale agreed. 'Though I'm not certain I'd call it a show. More like the beginning of a nightmare.'

'You're right, unfortunately.' He peered over the side of the bridge. 'But it'll be quite something to tell the folks back home – the night all the lights went out in London.'

She couldn't think of an answer that wouldn't sound trite. Instead, she merely nodded in agreement and took out her notebook. She wrote the date and time, then waited.

People were talking and gesturing but the man next to her stood quietly, his right shoulder almost touching hers. The courting couple on the other side were kissing as though there was no tomorrow, murmuring endearments whenever they stopped for breath. For some reason it irritated her. Were they really that uninterested? Then it struck her that maybe for them there would be no tomorrow. The young man could be called up and who knew what would happen to him? Maybe no tomorrow for herself either, Dale thought grimly, craning her head towards the sky as though any minute now the Luftwaffe would appear and strike them all. How ridiculous she was being. Shifting her feet a little further to the left to give the courting couple more room, to her embarrassment she felt the man's presence even more acutely. He was going to think she was sidling up to him. She quickly bent her head to her notebook and jotted down some notes.

The sun began to dip over the Thames. Nothing happened. Dale felt the first chill through her summer jacket and shivered.

'Aren't those lights flickering in the distance?'

He'd spoken so softly she'd had to tilt her head closer to hear him. He lightly patted her arm and pointed.

'I don't see anything.' She was aware now that her shoulder was pressing against his. She fancied she could feel the warmth of him. She couldn't move. It would look too obvious – as though he would think she was aware of the contact. Or worse, that she'd even manoeuvred it on purpose.

Concentrate, Dale. You're here to write a report so your readers can picture the way it happened – just as you're about to witness.

The waiting was interminable. She dreaded London being plunged into darkness, yet nothing could stop it. There was no sound from anyone on the bridge except the couple next to her, cutting into the mood with their chatter. Idly, she wondered what an American was doing in England on the brink of war.

As though he knew she was thinking of him he turned

20

to her. Their eyes held for long seconds. Dale looked towards the river again, thankful for the brim of her hat so he couldn't see the sudden heat rushing to her face.

'Here it goes,' he said.

Mesmerised, she watched as the first brightly lit area was snuffed out. Then another. And another. And yet another. One by one, bit by bit, London was falling into an inky hole.

'Only one part left now,' the man said quietly.

Dale drew in a sharp breath.

'That's it, then.' He said the words flatly and Dale was sure he had the same empty feeling that she did.

Those historic moments had taken less than two minutes.

'I was wondering how they were going to do it.' Dale rubbed her eyelids, hardly believing she'd witnessed something so depressing. She'd had no idea she'd feel quite this upset, but it was horrible. Her beloved city would be submerged in a blackout every night for heaven knows how long. Maybe years if the last war was anything to go by. There wasn't even a streetlamp left to illuminate the bridge, just pinpricks of light on the boats on the Thames, and behind her the already dimmed headlights of motorcars and taxis and buses. Thank goodness it wasn't yet completely dark. She tried to swallow but her mouth was too dry.

Tears pricked the back of her eyes. Then without warning they began to fall down her cheeks.

'It's a rotten business,' he said, turning to face her. 'Do you feel as bad as I do?'

She sniffed, then brushed the tears with her gloved hand, hoping he couldn't see enough to notice.

'Please don't cry.' His voice was warm now with concern. 'Next thing you know, you'll have me crying, too.'

She couldn't help smiling as he pressed a handkerchief in her hand.

'Thank you. That's very kind of you.' She wiped her eyes and without thinking, put it in her jacket pocket.

'I was wondering—' there was a hesitation, then he cleared his throat '—if perhaps you'd like a drink. I know I could do with one.'

He stood about the same height as herself in heels, yet he seemed taller.

She hesitated. It appeared to be a genuinely friendly invitation, but she was conscious of her mother waiting for her at home.

'I'm sorry, I really can't,' she said. 'Someone's expecting me.'

'Oh.' His brow furrowed. 'Then I'm sorry, too. He's a lucky guy.'

She wouldn't correct him. But he *did* sound truly disappointed. Would another hour really hurt?

'Dale Treadwell,' she said, impulsively.

'Does that mean—?'

'Yes, but just a quick cup of tea and it'll have to be on the way home. Maybe a Lyons Corner House. There's one near here.' She paused and looked at him. 'I think I'd better know who I'm having this cup of tea with.'

'Glenn Reeves, at your service, ma'am.' He tipped his hat. 'You're sure you wouldn't like something a little stronger than tea?'

'I won't tonight, thank you.' She stopped. Damn! He must think she was angling for him to ask her out again. Flushing with annoyance at herself, she stole him a glance.

But though his eyes flickered he simply said, 'Okay,' and crooked his arm, inviting her to slip her hand through the space.

How badly she wanted to take his arm. But she pretended not to have noticed the gesture as they walked back along the bridge. She wouldn't give him any hint that this was anything more than a polite acceptance on her part, having shared such a moment. Resolutely keeping her head bent, she tried to feel where her feet were stepping, inwardly cursing for not bringing her torch.

As they were about to cross the road her foot twisted on the edge of the pavement. Dear God, she was going to fall over! But immediately, Glenn grabbed her and pulled her back.

'Are you okay?'

'Yes. I don't know what happened. I know this area so well.'

'Walking and driving in the dusk is just as dangerous as the dark, and now we've got no lighting it's impossible. Here . . . take hold of my arm.' When she hesitated, he chuckled. 'I won't bite, you know.'

'I should think not.' The words sounded stiff, which she hadn't meant.

Inside the café it was very different. Blackout blinds were already down and table lamps cast a soft glow, making the room feel cheerful and cosy. Waitresses, affectionately known as Nippies, rushed to and fro, juggling trays of food and drinks to the many hungry customers, who were talking non-stop. One of the waitresses smiled as she sailed by, the tray held above her head.

'Table over there.' She nodded to one almost in the centre of the crowded room. 'Someone'll be with you shortly.'

It wasn't the best spot for a quiet chat, Dale thought, as she led the way, but it would do.

Glenn helped her off with her jacket and removed his hat, hooking the items on a nearby coat stand. He turned to her. 'I was wondering . . . would you think me too fresh if I asked you take your hat off, too, so I can see your face properly?'

23

She did as he asked, flushing a little at his last words.

'Are you sure you wouldn't like something to go with your tea?' he asked as he joined her at the table and a Nippy handed her a menu and hovered with her order pad.

'I know you can't stay long,' Glenn said, 'but perhaps you could be tempted with one of those sweet rolls – I believe y'all call them buns – with real butter. This fake stuff's not for me.'

'What, you don't like marge?' Dale chuckled.

He grimaced. 'So that's what it's called.'

'Would that be two currant buns then, sir?' the waitress asked, with a hint of impatience.

Glenn looked up. 'Oh, pardon me, ma'am.' He turned to Dale. 'You're sure you couldn't eat something a little more substantial?'

'I had supper already, though I couldn't eat much after hearing about Poland.'

The waitress gave a discreet cough.

'I believe it will be just the two buns with real butter, and tea for the lady and a beer for me.'

'Another war's been on the cards for a long time,' Glenn said when the waitress disappeared. 'Trouble is, Chamberlain believed Hitler's signature was a genuine sign that he wanted peace. But he's never come across anyone like Hitler before. I guess no one has.'

For the first time she could study him properly under the lights. Corn-coloured hair, a generous mouth that quirked at the corners and startling blue eyes that questioned hers. She gave a mental jolt. It was as though she almost recognised him. And then he smiled.

What a beautiful smile . . . and that attractive cleft in his chin.

24

Chapter Three

Time drifted as Dale listened to Glenn's warm southern accent. She liked the way he leant forward over the small table as he asked her opinion on the day's events, his lapis-blue eyes meeting hers as he attentively listened to her answers.

'Where are you from?' she asked eventually. Before he could reply she said, 'Oh, I realise you're an American . . .' He didn't correct her, so she continued, 'although your accent isn't the same as ones I've heard in American films.'

'I'm from the Deep South . . . Ge-or-gia . . .' He drawled out the words in an exaggerated fashion, making her laugh. 'Are you familiar with where the different states are?'

'I'm not exactly sure.'

She felt annoyed that she didn't know. All they'd learnt at school were the marvels of the Empire coloured pink in her atlas, taking over what seemed to be most of the world.

'Well, now, you won't have heard of my town,' Glenn said. 'It doesn't have more than five hundred folk.'

'Only five hundred? We wouldn't even call that a village – it'd be a hamlet.' She grinned. 'What's it called?'

'Warm Springs. Not too far from Atlanta – the capital of Georgia,' he added. 'We might not be big but we're famous for two things. One is that its mineral springs are supposed to be healing.'

'Is that how it got its name?'

'Not really. It used to be called Bullockville after a huge land-owning family by the same name—' He broke off. 'Say, are you really interested in all this?'

'Yes, I am. Go on.'

'Okay. Well, Bullockville was changed in the Twenties by the other thing the town is famous for.'

'Which is?'

'Our President Roosevelt. He renamed it when he made it his home. It's where he lives when he's not in The White House.'

'Oh.' She sent him a mischievous smile. 'Well, that *does* put you in a different light.'

'I hoped it might. Impressive, huh?'

'Especially if you tell me you hob-nob with the President when he's there.'

'Of course. We're good buddies. He's always asking for my advice.'

She joined in his laughter.

'Why are you in London when we're on the brink of war?' Dale suddenly thought to ask.

He hesitated for a split second. 'I'm kinda on vacation.' She frowned. 'What you Limeys call "holiday".' He took a swallow of beer.

'What do you mean, Limeys?'

'What we call the British,' he said with a grin. 'The name came from your sailors not getting enough vitamin C on board ships, so they got scurvy. When the medical folk realised what was happening, they suggested they take lime juice on board.' His grin widened. 'You British call us all Yanks whether we're Northerners or Southerners.'

'Is there a difference?'

'Sure is. Where I'm from we're Rebels – a throwback from the Civil War.'

But all the while Dale enjoyed their conversation, his teasing, their laughter, she couldn't help thinking he was only here on holiday. He'd be going back to America. To this little town of Warm Springs. Maybe very soon. She felt a stab of something more than disappointment.

'What do you do for a living?' he asked.

'I'm a reporter for *The Kensington Evening Post*.'

'Sounds exciting. You must really see life in that job.'

'That's what I thought when I trained. But I never get sent to anywhere exciting. Apparently, I'm too fragile to deal with anything meaty. It's always the men who are chosen to go.'

'The war may quickly change that.' Glenn's tone was sympathetic. 'They're gonna need women to fill some of the men's jobs.'

'If there's a war . . .'

'Not if – it's *when* . . . and very soon, going by today's news.'

Dale bit her lip. 'I'd want to do my bit but my mother's just had some devastating news. She's going to need my support. I don't have any brothers or sisters and my father's away working so there's just me.'

'I'm sorry,' Glenn said. 'Do you want to tell me about it?'

She hesitated. If she told him the truth, she'd feel disloyal to her mother. And yet she felt she could tell him anything. He'd probably even give her some practical advice.

'What is it, Dale?' He covered her hand with his own. The touch of his skin sent an electric shock up her arm. 'I promise it will never go any further.'

'I know. But not now.'

Did that sound forward?

He gave her hand a light squeeze.

'If you ever want to confide in me, it will never go any further.'

Eventually, Glenn said, 'Didn't you mention someone was expecting you?' He gave her that same warm boyish smile. 'Not that I want you to go.'

Dale glanced at her watch. To her horror it was nearly ten o'clock – not much different if she'd watched the second showing of the film. She jumped to her feet.

'I didn't realise it was so late.'

'Whereabouts do you live?'

'Pimlico.'

'I'm not familiar with it. But may I see you home? There's sure to be a taxi.'

She hesitated for the merest fraction of a second. What would be the harm? Only her mother not approving.

Picking up strange men, she could hear her mother saying. But Glenn didn't feel strange. She could have talked to him all night. But to be on the safe side she wouldn't take him right to the door.

'I was going to walk.'

'Even better. I'll have your company for longer.'

A warmth ran through her.

Once outside he said, 'It sure is dark out here. I can't even see my hand in front of my face. I didn't think to bring a torch.' He paused. 'You'll have to stick very close to me.'

Even if she couldn't see it, she was sure he was grinning.

'So long as you know it's only for safety purposes,' Dale said with a laugh.

'Well, of course. I wouldn't dream it could be otherwise,' he chuckled. 'You'd better lead the way as I have no idea where I'm going.'

'We'll walk along Millbank, but it won't be as pretty without the twinkling lights.'

'We'll have to imagine them,' he said, feeling for her hand.

She'd tucked her summer gloves into her handbag in the café as though she'd known all along this is what he would do, but the sudden contact of his skin with hers sent her blood fizzing. She matched his stride, but he didn't say anything. She was glad. She didn't want to break the spell of walking in the strange blackness with this unknown American, her hand held firmly in his, as though it were the most natural gesture in the world.

'Are you warm enough in that thin jacket?' he asked after a few minutes. 'I can lend you mine, if so. I'm not at all cold.'

She laughed. 'We'd look a right pair with you only wearing a shirt and me wearing a man's suit jacket.'

'If anyone can spot us in the dark they're welcome to make a judgement,' he chuckled, stopping to remove it. 'Here . . . slip your arms in.'

Wearing his jacket, she could smell the scent of him. Warm. Masculine. A whiff of tobacco that wasn't unpleasant.

They continued in silence, turning away from the river onto Vauxhall Bridge Road. Every now and again Glenn gave her hand a little squeeze as though to assure her he was still there. All too soon she stopped in her street – unfamiliar in the complete darkness. No lights shone from any window now everyone had to comply with the new blackout rules.

'This is where I live.' Dale's voice was flat.

'We're here already?' He sounded as disappointed as she was.

''Fraid so.' She turned to him in the dark. 'It's been lovely,' she said, now feeling awkward they were going to say good-night. What would he expect from her? Would he kiss her?

Would she mind if he did? Part of her said an emphatic *Yes, I would mind* – after all, she'd only known him three hours – but the other part thrilled with possibilities.

'And I enjoyed this evening better than any I've had in a long time—' Glenn broke into her thoughts '—which is strange when you consider it's been one of the grimmest with the news of the Polish invasion – and knowing what that will bring – and then all the lights going out in this wonderful city.'

'I feel the same,' Dale whispered, though why she was whispering she had no idea.

'May I see you again?' he said. 'That is, if the person expecting you isn't a serious contender.'

Dale laughed. 'I'm not sure whether my mother would consider herself as a serious contender or not.'

Glenn chuckled. 'She might be a more serious contender than a boyfriend.'

He was probably closer to the truth than he realised.

'I'm engaged tomorrow and can't get out of it,' he continued, 'but I might be able to get some time off the following day . . . Sunday.' He paused. 'That is, if you're not doing anything.'

'I'm supposed to be going to a tea dance in the afternoon – at the Grosvenor Hotel with some friends.'

'Maybe I can see you there. Are you on the telephone?'

Dale swallowed. If her mother picked up the receiver first . . . For some reason she wanted to keep him a secret. But he was waiting.

'Yes.'

'Can you write it on a piece of paper – that notebook you were busy with on the bridge?'

She removed his jacket and handed it to him and while he was putting it back on she took out her notebook and hurriedly formed the letters and numbers as best she could, then tore the sheet out.

He carefully folded the piece of paper in two and put it in his jacket pocket.

'I'll wait to see you inside.'

'No, don't bother. I have my key.' She stood opposite him, every nerve in her body alert. 'Thank you again,' she said to his shadowy silhouette.

What now? Oh, what now?

A light breeze wafted between them. He stepped closer.

'Dale . . . I don't know about you but now I've met you I don't want to let you go.'

'I don't want you to,' she stuttered.

'You're so lovely,' he whispered. 'I knew it when we were standing on the bridge, even though I couldn't see you properly. And then in the teashop you were even more beautiful than I'd imagined.'

He took her by the shoulders and kissed her forehead, then lightly brushed his lips against hers.

'Thanks for a swell evening, but your mama is probably worrying about you so I'd better let you go before I get carried away.' He gave her shoulders a little squeeze. 'Good night, Dale.'

Without another word he turned and abruptly walked away. Her lips tingling from the touch of his mouth, she stood watching as the broad-shouldered figure vanished into the night.

Dale stood for several minutes savouring those last moments. Wishing she still had her hand in Glenn's, she groped her way along the railings to her front door, hating the thought of going inside, breaking the spell, being questioned about the evening. Her mother wouldn't rest until she'd heard every detail.

31

Reluctantly, she put her key in the lock.

In the sitting room there was just one side lamp on. Luckily, the room was at the back of the house so the light wouldn't show from the road. First job tomorrow was to put up the blackout curtains. But where was Mother? She must have gone to bed early. Dale breathed out, relieved that she wouldn't have to answer a load of questions. But her heart dipped when she heard her mother calling.

'Is that you, Dulcie?'

'Yes. I'll be up in a little while.'

Dale put the kettle on to make a hot water bottle. Even though the hot summer was only just drawing to a close, the solid Victorian building always struck her as chilly. Now, especially, she sought comfort. She poured in the water and tightly screwed the top, then went upstairs. She'd hoped that in the ten minutes she'd taken, her mother might have fallen asleep, but the light was still on under her door. After tucking the water bottle into the cold bed, she swiftly undressed and donned her pyjamas, then cleaned her teeth in the wash basin, all the while trying hard not to analyse too much what had happened just minutes ago. She picked up her hairbrush and pulled it through her long golden-blonde hair, counting to fifty, trying to calm herself. Twenty, thirty, forty, fifty . . . She threw the brush down, even though her mother insisted it would only shine at a hundred strokes, but the movements had only made her more on edge. She'd never in her life felt so attracted to a man, so comfortable with him, so interested in what he had to say. But she mustn't dwell on it any longer until she'd said goodnight to her mother and was back in the privacy and quiet of her bedroom. With a deep sigh she knocked on her mother's bedroom door and went in.

'The cinemas were definitely closed this evening until

further notice,' her mother said as she put down her book and removed her glasses, 'so why didn't you come home straightaway? I was worried to death when it got dark and I couldn't see the neighbours' lights on in the blackout. I don't suppose you remembered to take a torch either. They said on the news that London was now officially in the blackout and everyone should prepare themselves – it could last some time if the country goes to war. And goodness knows how long that would be. The last one . . .'

Dale's head was too filled with Glenn to follow her mother's repetitive account of the Great War. The way his eyes twinkled, his lips . . . She wasn't aware that her mother had broken off and was staring at her.

'As you didn't see the film, why are you so late?'

'Jane and I went to a café and then I thought I'd go to one of the bridges and watch the blackout take place.' Dale gave a little shudder at the memory. 'It was riveting and horrible at the same time.'

Much as she tried to push away the image of Glenn, she could almost feel the warmth of him standing close to her on the bridge. His shoulder against hers. Desperate not to let her mother guess anything momentous had happened to her, she tried to suppress the surge of blood rushing to her face. But too late.

'Why is your face red?'

'Is it? I suppose it's because it's warmer in here than outside – the sudden change of temperature.'

Her mother's gaze was unwavering as she sat up straighter. 'Did Jane stay to watch the lights go off?'

Dale hesitated. The interrogation she dreaded was happening.

'Not the whole time,' she said, hoping the half-truth would suffice.

'But *you* stayed. Hmm. Yet Jane couldn't even stay two minutes. Because that's all it took apparently to turn them off.'

'I got chatting with one or two people.' Dale was becoming irritated. 'I wanted their opinion. You know it's what I have to do in my job.'

'But you weren't working today.'

'I know, but we were told you always have to keep your ears pricked. And keep a notebook. This was too important to let slip by, so I'll be writing a report for the paper. I'll let you read it when I've finished . . . if you're interested.'

Her mother nodded absentmindedly and took a sip of water. 'Anyway, I'm glad you had a nice time. Goodnight, Dulcie.' There was a tremor in her voice.

Dale hesitated, then went over to the bed and kissed her mother's tear-stained cheek.

'I'm sorry you had a rotten day with that letter from Dad,' she said. 'I don't know what to say about it. Maybe not very much until he comes home and talks to you.'

'Home!' her mother spluttered. 'He's found his new home in Scotland.'

'It might not be quite like that. Try not to get upset if you can help it. Things will work out, I'm sure.' She paused. 'Goodnight, Mother. Try to sleep. That's the best thing if you can.' She shut the door quietly behind her.

Wide awake in bed, her hot water bottle held between her feet, she lay on her back, linking her hands behind her neck. Poor Mother. What a shock that letter must have been. Guiltily, she realised she'd only just begun to absorb the main message – her beloved father wanted a divorce. All that on top of the invasion in Poland and a war between Britain and Germany which now looked inevitable. Then meeting Glenn.

Lying in bed, Dale self-consciously drew one hand away from her neck and touched her lips, imagining she could

34

still feel that brief kiss. Her stomach fluttered. She'd never felt like this about anyone. And she couldn't admit to anyone, not even Jane, how she felt. It was too fragile. Anything could happen. She pressed her three fingers to her pulse as she'd been taught in First Aid classes. It was beating too fast. Her mind was tumbling and spinning; the harder she tried the less she could make sense of what had happened to her.

Breathe slowly and deeply. Steady your breath.

Unconsciously, her lips parted. She could feel the thud of her heart in her eardrums. It was all so sudden. Overcome with the intensity of her emotions she bolted upright in the bed. She had to stop this. She reached for her book on the bedside table, but she couldn't concentrate even on the first sentence. Frustrated, she dropped it on the floor.

She might as well admit it. In one short evening she'd fallen head-over-heels in love with Glenn Reeves.

Chapter Four

Dale awoke early. Blinking, she sat up and glanced at her alarm clock. Quarter to five. Too early to get up. She lay for a few minutes thinking about last night. And Glenn. She closed her eyes, reliving their meeting on the bridge. What if she'd done as Jane suggested and gone home straightaway? She would never have met him. She certainly wouldn't be waking up like this – his face as clear as though he were there before her. A quiver caused goose pimples to travel up her arms.

Then she shook herself. She was being perfectly ridiculous, acting like a schoolgirl with her first crush. She'd get up and make a cup of tea. Clear her head.

Going through the motions of putting the kettle on and making a pot of tea brought her back to reality. She took the tray into the sitting room and flicked through yesterday's newspaper she'd had no time to read. It had been printed too early to mention the invasion. That would be in all today's papers. She sipped her tea and chewed a digestive biscuit. Oh, for a cigarette. But her mother frowned on her daughter smoking, and she'd definitely smell it the moment she ventured downstairs.

Dale's mind was still as jumbled as it had been last night. How was her mother going to cope with the letter from

Dad? Her nerves weren't strong at the best of times. Would she go to pieces? She'd certainly been emphatic that she'd never grant him a divorce. Dale sighed and sprang to her feet. She couldn't dither around. She had to get the report written and impress her boss.

The smell of her father's favourite tobacco lingered in the air as Dale opened the door to his private study. Last year, while she was attending night classes to learn shorthand and typing, she'd asked if she could set up her typewriter in the room and practise when he wasn't there. Reluctantly, he'd agreed. He'd always regarded his room as strictly private but now he was in Scotland enjoying a new life, she couldn't see he had much say in who occupied the room any more.

She sat down at the table by the window and removed the cover from her typewriter and rolled in a piece of paper. Putting her elbows on the desk she thought for a few moments about how she should tackle the report.

Just write it as it comes – from the heart.

She began to type.

On the evening of Friday, 1st September, after the news we were all dreading hearing of the German invasion into Poland, Leicester Square looked almost normal, except that the cinemas were closed. As usual, London was lit up like a fairground, its lights as dazzling as any firework display. A young courting couple paid little attention to the river as they kissed and murmured sweet nothings, eyes only for one another. Did this momentous occasion that was sure to go down in history not give them any cause for dismay? But it was mostly a curious crowd of Londoners who lined up on the footway of Westminster Bridge at dusk, watching what was to be a spectacle in reverse.

Dale lifted her hands and hesitated. Should she pick Glenn

out as another spectator or keep the focus on the lovebirds? Just thinking his name made her spine tingle. She licked her lips and continued, not knowing exactly where her fingers would alight as she pounded the keys.

It was as though a giant hand was operating enormous light switches. One by one, a brightly lit area, then another, was snuffed out as easily as a candle, leaving what looked to the spectators like black holes. Even the courting couple hushed as they turned their heads towards the Thames. Another piece of London disappeared. And another. Finally, the last bright area was extinguished. It was over in less than two minutes. The only light that could still be seen was the sudden flare of a match as someone lit a cigarette.

On the bridge people turned away. Still no one spoke. The only sounds were shuffling footsteps as they made their way slowly back along the bridge, immersed in their own thoughts, no doubt of the horror to come.

Then a girl's voice, her sobs catching at her words, broke the eerie silence. 'Oh, Jamie, what's goin' to happen to us all?'

Dale paused. That looked about the right length. She reread it while it was still in the typewriter, satisfied it encapsulated yesterday evening's atmosphere, then removed the sheet of paper and carefully folded it and tucked it into her handbag. It didn't matter that she'd been given her first precious time off since she'd started three months ago, often working ten hours a day, six days a week. She'd go in this morning as soon as the building opened and put it in front of the editor.

He'd give her a quick glance, then bring his glasses from his forehead down to his nose and quickly read through her report.

'Well done, Miss Treadwell,' he'd say, looking up with a pleased expression. 'I think we can safely ascertain that you can be sent to cover some of the more . . . shall we say, difficult situations.'

'Thank you for your faith in me, Mr Franklin,' she'd answer.

Grinning to herself at this imaginary scene, she put the cover back on her typewriter and took the stairs two at a time to run a bath.

Dale could hardly contain her excitement as she stepped into the main office just on half-past eight. As usual the room was full of swirling smoke. Only Bill looked up, his smile broad when he saw her.

'I thought you were off until Tuesday.'

'I was . . . *am*,' she corrected herself. 'But I witnessed London being blacked out last night and wrote a report. I'm hoping Mr Franklin will approve.'

'Good for you, getting some practice in.' Bill gave his half-lazy smile.

'Oh, I didn't do it for practice. I'm hoping he'll use it.'

Bill raised his eyebrows. 'I see.' He paused. 'Do you want me to have a look at it before you show Franklin?'

'That's kind of you, Bill, but I need to let him see I'm serious and can produce work fitting for the occasion without any help.'

He nodded. 'He's in. Might as well strike while your iron's hot.' He gave her an encouraging smile.

'Wish me luck.'

Before Dale knocked on Mr Franklin's door she glanced through the glazed top half. As usual, he had his shirt sleeves rolled up and the top button of his shirt undone, making the knot of his tie crooked. He was rifling through a stack of paperwork, cigarette hanging from the corner of his mouth. She hesitated. Maybe she should come back when he was less busy. But it was too late. He'd already looked up and seen her, waving at her to come in.

'Well, Dale, nice though it is to see you, what's brought you in?'

'I was on Westminster Bridge last night,' Dale began. 'I witnessed the blackout, so I've written a report.'

Franklin leant precariously back in his chair, gazing at her with his piercing eyes. 'Did you now?'

She handed him the sheet of paper and as he read, she kept her eyes glued to his face, though it was impossible to read his expression. After a couple of minutes, he handed it back to her.

'You need to talk to Bill.'

'Why?'

'He's got more time than I do to teach you how to write this kind of report – one that's publishable.'

Dale swallowed. 'I'm sorry, sir, but I don't know what you mean.'

'I mean it's not written how a report should be written.' His chair creaked as he brought it upright. 'The public want facts, not these asides about courting couples – flares of matches, sobs catching at words.' He looked straight at her. 'This sentimental twaddle is nothing to do with the bloody lights in London going out permanently. *That's* the real core of the story.' He leant towards her and she drew back. '*That's* the reason why you women don't get sent to cover the *real* news.' His voice softened. 'Look, Dale, you've only been here five minutes. You're still learning. So get Bill to show you *his* report. You might just learn something.'

So Bill had already written one.

Somehow, she had to make Franklin understand that she'd written the piece exactly as she'd witnessed it and what she'd felt at the time. She cleared her throat.

'Mr Franklin, I wanted to show how some of the people were reacting, wrapped up in their own lives, not really appreciating how we'll all be affected once the war starts. I thought it would get to the hearts of the readers when I mentioned individuals like the courting couple—'

'I'm busy, Dale. Now run along like a good girl.'

He bent his head over his papers. She was dismissed.

Humiliation making her cheeks burn, Dale marched out and went back to the main office. Her nerves on edge, she winced at the sound of a dozen typewriters clattering in her eardrums as she strode to her desk. Usually, she loved being part of the buzzing, noisy office but not today. The sooner she was out of this place, the better.

Bill glanced over.

'What happened, Dale? You look upset.'

'Apparently, you wrote about the London blackout, only yours was a short, clean report and according to Franklin, mine was a load of sentimental twaddle – his exact words – and—'

'Let me see yours,' Bill interrupted, holding out his hand.

Dale hesitated. But what did it matter now? She opened her bag and handed it to him, watching his expression as he read it.

'Hmm.' He looked up and peered at her through his thick lensed glasses. 'You've gone for the human aspect which I hadn't acknowledged. But I see now, reading your account. And it's good . . . very good indeed.'

'I just wrote it straight off without thinking any of that,' she said, suddenly wanting to give him a hug of gratitude.

'Trouble is, it's more suitable for a women's magazine.'

She gulped. 'Can I see yours, Bill?'

He gave her the carbon copy. She read it and looked up. 'It's to the point, which is what Franklin obviously wants,

41

but it's not my style. Besides, I'm earning no more than when I was a trainee three months ago.' She hesitated. 'Thing is, Bill, our circumstances at home have changed over the last day or two and I need to earn more money than the pittance I'm getting here.'

'Why don't you let me put in a word for you to Franklin? Ask him to give you a chance and that I'll take it upon myself to teach you how to write a report that he'll print.'

'No, Bill. Don't speak to Franklin on my behalf. I have to fight my own battles.' She saw the look of disappointment on his face. 'But I will take up your kind offer as long as I'm here.'

'That's settled then.' Bill hesitated, his warm eyes full of concern. 'You know, Dale, it wouldn't be the same without you around.'

She knew he had a soft spot for her. He occasionally asked her if she'd like to go out one evening to the pictures, but she always made an excuse. He was a dear, but that was all.

She rose to her feet.

'See you Tuesday, then,' Bill said.

'Mmm.'

She'd already made up her mind she'd telephone in that she wasn't feeling well and not show up until Thursday, when Glenn would be going back to America. For that lapse she'd work twice as hard and stay late if she had to, to make up for it. She'd be glad to do that to help take her mind off him – even if it meant putting up with Franklin.

Chapter Five

Dale and her mother had almost come to the end of a morning's work putting up all the blackout curtains when the doorbell rang. Her arms ached from doing most of the actual hanging.

'I'll get it.'

She sprang up, glad to have a few minutes' break, and opened the door to a young lad in smart post office navy-blue uniform. A beam of sunlight bounced off his peaked cap and onto the handlebars of his bicycle, flung against the wall.

'Mrs Treadwell?'

'That's my mother.'

The boy nodded and thrust a brown envelope into her hand.

'Telegram for your mother, then, miss. Just sign here.' He handed her a small book where her mother's name and the address had been entered.

Blowing out her cheeks Dale shut the front door and walked slowly back to the sitting room.

'Who was it, Dulcie?'

'A telegram – for you.'

Her mother slowly blinked. 'I don't want to open it. It's bound to be bad news. You open it.'

Dale picked up a knife from the table and slit open the envelope.

'Read it out, please.' Her mother's voice shook.

PATRICIA AM COMING HOME LATE PM FOR DULCIES BIRTHDAY STOP WE NEED TO TALK STOP HARRY

Patricia Treadwell closed her eyes as though trying to digest this latest piece of news.

'I don't want to see him,' she said, finally. 'He's only making the effort because of your birthday.'

'I don't think that's the only reason, Mother. He says you and he need to talk. You have to face him. And the sooner the better so we all know where we are.'

'I know where I am,' her mother snapped. 'In my home, and I'm not leaving it. Nor am I intending to divorce your father.'

'Try not to make any plans before the two of you talk.'

'No, before the *three* of us talk,' corrected her mother. 'This involves you as much as me. Your life's going to change, too. And I need you there to support me. Unless, of course—' she looked directly at Dale '—you're on your father's side.'

'It's not fair to drag me into it. It's private – between you and Dad. He won't appreciate my being there either.'

'I'm not interested in what your father appreciates or doesn't.' She paused. 'He certainly doesn't appreciate his wife, that's for certain,' she added bitterly. 'And I intend to tell him just what I think of him. But I'm not waiting up. Tell him I'll see him in the morning.'

Dale glanced at her mother, taking in the drawn expression and eyes that were red with weeping. Her chest tightened. Dad had let them both down in the most

44

humiliating way possible. How *could* he risk losing every-thing he'd worked for, for another woman – more than likely younger – he thought he'd fallen in love with? No wonder her mother was bitter.

'Mother,' she said softly, 'I'm angry too. But attacking him won't help.'

'I put Dad in the front bedroom last night,' Dale told her mother when she took her a cup of tea next morning. 'Was that all right?'

'I don't much care where you put him,' Patricia said, taking the first sip. 'Is he awake?'

'No. I'll leave him for a bit longer.'

'Sit here a moment, Dulcie.' Her mother patted the bed. When Dale tentatively sat on the edge, she said, 'I hope you'll back me up in this.'

'Mother, I've said before – it really has to be a private discussion between the two of you. But before he goes I shall have a word with him myself.'

Her mother brightened. 'Do you promise?'

'Yes.'

A sigh escaped her mother's lips. Then she gave a small sad smile.

'Happy birthday, dear. That little packet is for you.' She gestured towards her dressing table.

Dale opened the tissue paper to find a pair of cotton crocheted gloves.

'They're beautiful.' She looked up at her mother. 'Did you make them?'

'Yes. They'll look just the ticket with your new dress.'

'They're perfect. Thank you, Mother.' Dale kissed her cheek.

*   *   *

Dale spent the next half an hour in the sitting room listening to some music quietly playing in the background while her mind flew in all directions. Her parents had married during Dad's last leave in the Great War. Dale bit her lip. Is that all there was in such a commitment? Getting wed. Having a child. Then meeting someone else and calmly telling the other you want to bring it to an end?

She startled when her father boomed, 'Happy birthday, darling. Congratulations! Today you've got the key of the door.'

'Thanks, Dad.'

He studied her. 'You know, you take after your mother in your colouring, but you're more like me in your ways.'

It was the last thing she wanted to hear. Deliberately not answering, she switched off the wireless.

'How's your reporting going?'

'Not that well.'

'Oh? Why's that?'

She quickly filled him in.

'Please don't discuss it with Mother. She's worried enough already. But I need a job that pays better *now*.' She gave him a steady look.

'You realise Friday's news means we could be at war any day now? So what will you do? Join up?'

'With your bombshell to Mother about a divorce, I certainly can't leave her on her own to face it.' She gazed directly into her father's eyes.

'She's stronger than she lets on,' her father said, looking away after a second or two. 'How did she take it?'

'She feels betrayed – and I have to say, so do I. You really shouldn't have written that letter out of the blue. It was cruel.'

He looked away and took his pipe from his pocket. 'I

46

felt the sooner she knew, the better it was. Get the worst over with.'

'No,' Dale said. 'You weren't thinking of her. You were taking the easy way out by not facing her.'

Her father let out a deep sigh. 'Your mother and I haven't been happy for a very long time. Once she gets over the shock, she'll be relieved to be rid of me.'

'It's not that simple. And I'd better tell you, Dad, she's not going to give up the house easily.'

'I don't think it will come to that, but I wanted to warn her it was a possibility.'

'Not in Mother's book, it's not. And I'll tell you something else – if you do make her sell, it'll destroy her.'

'Nonsense. She's got more gumption than that.' He drew his brows together. 'You know, darling, you mustn't let any decision of mine stop you doing what you want to do. Now we're at loggerheads with Germany, you'll want to do your bit for the war effort, just as your friends will. Your mother's not an invalid. You must live your life.'

'Just as *you* have, Harry,' Patricia said as she came into the room.

Harry rubbed the back of his neck. 'We have to talk sometime, Patricia.'

His wife glared at him. 'I'm going to make breakfast.' She disappeared.

Her father caught Dale's eye and grimaced.

'I think you might be right,' he said. 'It's not going to be that easy.'

Dale felt a rise of anger.

'Why did you think it would be?' she snapped. 'You've told Mother in a letter you've fallen in love with another woman. What do you expect her to feel? She's devastated.'

'She doesn't love me any more. She hasn't for a long time.

She tolerates me because she doesn't want to lose face. I can't live like that any longer. Not when I know what it's like to be really happy.' He studied her. 'Talking of being happy, Dale, there's a new sparkle in your eyes. I thought so last night but I was too tired to say anything. It must be a man. Am I right?'

Dale put her hand to her face to stem the hot flow of blood. She nodded.

'Is he in the forces?'

'No.' She gave a sigh. 'Look, Dad, I don't want to talk about him. I've only just met him.'

'Be careful, Dulcie. Don't let your heart rule your head.'

As yours apparently did. Dale clamped her lips together.

Chapter Six

When Dale had finished the bacon and eggs her mother had made, she scraped back her chair. Rising to her feet, she collected some of the dirty dishes.

'You need to get to work, Dulcie,' her mother said. 'I don't want you being late because your father's deigned to come and visit.'

'It's Sunday. I'm off today.'

Patricia clicked her tongue. 'I don't even know what day it is . . . though I do know it's your birthday,' she added with a wan smile.

Dale gave her a hug. 'It'll work out all right, Mother. I know it will.' She paused. 'I'm going for a walk to give you and Dad a chance to have a serious talk.'

The sun was already warm as Dale walked briskly towards St James's Park. A real Indian summer. She stopped a moment, breathing in a deep lungful of air, noticing the trees still had their green leaves, giving no hint that autumn was only just around the corner. Borders of colourful flowers and shrubs met her eyes wherever she looked. Cyclists rode by, ringing their bells at a bird or squirrel in their path, couples walked arm in arm, and an elderly couple passed her, nodding and saying, 'Lovely morning.'

Dale watched as they tottered along – still holding hands at their age. It must be wonderful, though such a contrast to her parents now. She wondered what Glenn was doing and her heart contracted. He might be trying to telephone her at this very moment. She was so sure there'd been something special between them. Or had it all been imagined? Maybe it was only those moments shared on the bridge, the atmosphere charged with tension, that had made things seem more than they were.

It didn't even feel like her birthday, Dale thought, as she wandered along. Any day now they were bound to announce that Britain was at war with Germany – hardly conducive to getting into the party spirit.

She bought a copy of the *Sunday Express* at one of the kiosks. In the park she chose a bench in the sun and sat down, opening the paper to the Appointments page. She ran her fingers down the columns. Accountant, engineer, electrician, bricklayer, heavy duty driver . . . they all wanted male applicants. Dale frowned. Where were the female vacancies? Oh, here they were: child minder, housekeeper, secretary, library assistant, teacher . . . She didn't fancy any of them.

Leaning back on the bench, she closed her eyes, trying to block out her immediate problem of finding another job where she'd be appreciated. But more than likely all newspaper editors were like Franklin where women reporters were concerned. Her mind replayed the scene in his office. Yes, she thought, she might have to try something completely different.

Curbing her temper, she turned the page to the cryptic crossword puzzle. Her pencil poised, she read the first clue: *It's simply all the rage.* She couldn't help a smirk. If they were all that easy, she'd be done in five minutes, she thought, as she pencilled in *anger.* Quickly filling in more clues, she remembered how her father had once told her he could complete crosswords in his head. When she'd challenged him to prove it, he'd filled in the squares at top speed, taking hardly more than a couple of minutes. Grinning with triumph, he'd tossed over the answers in the following day's newspaper. Every single one was correct.

Now, closing her eyes for a full minute to work out a particularly difficult clue, she stifled her irritation at her feeble attempts and after some minutes she gave up in disgust. She couldn't concentrate when all she could think of was her parents arguing with each other.

Sighing, she rose to her feet. It was time to go home.

As soon as Dale walked into the hall, she could hear her parents' voices. Puffing out her cheeks, she stepped into the sitting room. In an instant she tensed against the atmosphere. Her father stopped talking and looked towards her.

'There's been an announcement on the wireless,' he said. 'The Prime Minister Neville Chamberlain is going to address the nation at quarter-past eleven.'

Dale glanced at her watch. It was nearly time.

'I'll make a pot of tea,' she said. 'I have a feeling we're going to need it.'

Dale brought in the tray and handed her parents tea, offering them biscuits, but they both declined. She took a couple and settled down close to the shelf where the wireless perched.

Finally, Chamberlain's defeated tones came through the speakers.

'I am speaking to you from the Cabinet Room at 10 Downing Street. This morning, the British Ambassador in Berlin handed the German government a final note, stating that unless we heard from them by eleven o'clock that they

51

were prepared at once to withdraw their troops from Poland, a state of war would exist between us. I have to tell you now that no such undertaking has been received and that consequently, this country is at war with Germany.'

The three of them looked at one another.

'That's it, then,' Harry said. 'Another bloody war. More young lives lost. And I'm considered too old to fight.' He blew his nose loudly. 'Bloody Nazis.'

The announcer said a few words followed by a peal of church bells. Then there was a series of Government announcements, although Dale barely took them in. After a few seconds' pause the National Anthem played and she and her father automatically rose to their feet while her mother still sat, her jaw open in disbelief, then burst into tears.

'Now, now, Patricia, don't get yourself all worked up,' Harry said, putting a hand on her shoulder. 'We'll all come through this.'

Angrily, she shrugged him off. 'It's not just the war,' she choked, 'though that's bad enough. It's what you've landed me with on top of it. I don't know how I'll face everyone.'

'You've got Dale.'

'She has a right to her own life,' Patricia said unexpectedly. 'She can't stay with me for ever.' Patricia glowered at her husband. 'Can you believe it's our daughter's twenty-first today – the same day as war's declared? But she's been looking forward to the tea dance this afternoon and I don't want us to spoil it for her.'

'I'm not sure if I should go now,' Dale put in.

'Don't talk nonsense, dear. Of *course* you're going. We're at war. Everything's changed. It'll be like nothing you've ever experienced before. Just go and meet your friends. Who knows when you'll see them all again?'

*   *   *

Dale gave a deep sigh as she pinned up her hair, then changed her mind and snatched out the kirby grips. She glanced at her watch. She should be there by now. The girls would wonder what had happened to her if she didn't soon get a move on.

Half-heartedly, she slipped the new dress over her head and pulled up the side zip with none of the excitement she'd felt in the department store when the saleslady had paid her extravagant compliments. She cast a critical look in the standing mirror. The dress, royal blue with a bold pattern of deep pink and gold flowers, had a sweetheart neckline, and the skirt showed off her slim calves to perfection. Her glance dropped to her feet. The gold peep-toe shoes made her long narrow feet appear elegant and feminine. She sent a clownish grin to the mirror. No smear of red lipstick on her teeth. All right – she was as ready as she was ever going to be.

She really had no enthusiasm for the tea dance or her birthday or even seeing her friends. If only Glenn had rung. He should have rung by now, the way he'd sounded so keen to have her telephone number, though he'd mentioned he couldn't see her yesterday. Surely he hadn't got another girlfriend. The idea made her stomach churn. But he'd told her he didn't want to let her go. So was it all a load of what Americans called 'sweet talk', said in the heat of the moment? Not that she'd had any experience of Americans, but she'd watched plenty of their sentimental films.

Well, she wasn't going to hang around like some starry-eyed little innocent, waiting for him to ring. She'd had enough of that with Chris Taylor two years ago. A devastatingly handsome man who'd swept her off her feet and dumped her as soon as she refused to go all the way with him.

But Glenn's not like that, her inner voice said.

'How do you know?' Dale spoke aloud.

Angry with herself for being hoodwinked yet again she shouted goodbye and slammed the door behind her, then flagged down a taxi.

Pushing through the Grosvenor Hotel door she could hear dance music and people's laughter. They seemed oblivious to the news they'd only heard a few hours ago. Yet there was no point going in if it was to sit all afternoon with a miserable expression. Squaring her shoulders, she painted on a smile and showed her ticket to the woman at the door.

'Now we're at war we require everyone who enters to sign in at reception with their name and address,' the woman said in a bored tone as though she'd repeated it a hundred times already.

Dale added her details to the large open book, already filled with dozens of names – but not Glenn's. She handed her ticket to the same woman, who directed her to the double doors through which music was floating.

Most of the tables were unoccupied but the dance floor was packed with couples, very few of the men in uniform, jostling one another as they sought a space to practise their steps. Trying to look casual, Dale cast her eye around for her friends.

'Over here, Dale.'

Jane and Rhoda were smiling and waving to her at a nearby table, laid up with cakes and sandwiches, where two men were sitting. Oh, no. She wasn't going to play gooseberry for anyone. But she'd have to say hello to them at least. The two men stood up as she reluctantly approached.

'Happy birthday, Dale,' Jane said, jumping up to kiss her cheek. 'We were getting worried. We thought you weren't coming.'

'I nearly didn't.' She removed her new lacy gloves and laid them on the table.

'Well, this could be one of the last chances we'll get together, so we'd better make the most of it,' Rhoda said, kissing Dale. 'Happy birthday, but sorry it's not the best day to celebrate it now the war is official.'

'Oh, a birthday indeed,' one of the men said, giving Dale a wink. He was tall and good-looking and knew it, was Dale's immediate impression, his dark hair smoothly in place, courtesy of Brylcreem. 'Keith Underwood. Delighted to meet you.' He held out his hand.

Dale politely shook it, then wished she hadn't already peeled off her gloves as he brought it to his lips in the manner of some Continental gigolo and kissed it, his eyes boring into hers.

Dale drew back. Keith Underwood was just the kind of man she disliked. She wasn't one scrap bowled over by him. If there was one favour Chris Taylor had done for her it was to warn her against being taken in by a smooth operator.

'I'm Mick Baker.' Keith's companion was short and stocky with sandy hair. He brushed the crumbs from his mouth before thrusting out a dimpled hand. 'Happy birthday.'

'Thank you.' Dale took his hand briefly. It was sticky from the cake he'd been eating.

'I'll just go and get a drink' – *and wash my hands,* she almost added. She looked round. 'Anyone else for a top-up?'

'It's your birthday so let me do the honours.' Keith immediately pulled out a chair. 'You sit down. Now what will it be?'

'Thank you. A bitter lemon would be nice.'

'Nothing stronger?' Keith pressed.

'No, thanks.'

Mick jumped to his feet. 'Ladies?' He held up his glass.

'Not for me,' Jane said. 'I'm feeling a bit squiffy already.'

'You need to eat something, Jane,' Rhoda said, her green eyes fixed on Keith. 'I'll have another gin and orange, please.'

Mick nodded and followed his friend to the bar.

'Isn't he gorgeous?' Rhoda beamed, tucking into an egg and cress sandwich.

'What, Mick?' Dale laughed. 'I wouldn't have thought he was your type at all, Rhoda. He wouldn't reach your neck.'

'You daft thing. You know jolly well who I mean.' She closed her eyes. 'Keith's a lovely dancer,' she said dreamily. 'By the way—' she opened her eyes '—you look wonderful in that dress, Dale.'

'Yes, it's beautiful,' Jane said. 'Did that clever mother of yours make it?'

'No. Peter Jones. And these.' Dale stuck her feet out.

'Oh, they're fabulous,' Jane cried. 'You've been on a shopping spree by the look of it.'

'I couldn't resist them. But they cost as much as the dress.'

'Whatever you paid, they're worth every penny,' Rhoda said, her eyes gleaming.

It was good to be with the girls but every time the door opened Dale looked up. Just in case . . .

Keith and Mick returned with drinks in hand.

'There you are,' Mick said, handing Dale her bitter lemon and Rhoda her gin and orange.

Keith raised his glass. 'To three beautiful ladies,' he said, taking several gulps of his beer. 'What would we chaps do without them to keep us on the straight and narrow?'

Dale squirmed. 'Don't include *me* in that assessment,' she said tartly. 'My time's worth more than worrying about keeping men on the straight and narrow, as you call it. They need to start taking responsibility for themselves.'

'Oh, dear.' Keith looked at her with a mockingly apologetic smile. 'Have I upset you?'

'Not at all,' she said, aware of her friends' eyes on her. 'I'm just too busy for that kind of nonsense.'

'Oh.' Keith gazed at her with even more interest. 'What do you do – if I'm permitted to ask, that is?'

Mick chuckled, then lowered his head when Dale threw him a glare.

'Dale's a reporter,' Jane explained. 'She's always after a story so be careful what you say. You could see your name in print for the wrong reasons.'

Keith smiled and drew his chair nearer to Dale. 'Oh, what paper?'

'I doubt it'd be one you'd read,' Dale said tartly.

'You're right on that,' Keith said, not seeming at all offended. 'I pride myself on never reading a newspaper, but I think it's marvellous you ladies doing men's jobs—' he caught her glare '—and doing them jolly well,' he added hurriedly.

'Please don't patronise me.' Dale gave him a cool look.

Keith blinked. 'It was a compliment.' He hesitated, as though not quite so sure of his ground. 'Look, why don't we have a dance?'

'I don't dance.'

'But Dale, you—' Rhoda quickly closed her mouth as Dale nudged her under the table.

Keith stood. 'You don't have to worry about it. Just follow me.'

'Go on, Dale.' It was Jane. 'Do you good to relax a bit.'

Maybe it would. She took Keith's outstretched hand. As he led her on to the floor, something made her glance back towards the door.

Her heart stood still. Glenn Reeves was walking in.

To Dale it was as though someone had switched on a thousand fairy lights.

Chapter Seven

Dale saw Glenn's eyes sweep round the room. He was searching for her. She knew it. For a few seconds she didn't know what to do: whether to pull her hand away from Keith or try to steer him over to the other side of the floor. Glenn was alone. But he'd think she was with Keith. He'd think their evening hadn't meant anything to her except a chance encounter that had passed pleasantly enough as they'd both shared the disbelief that London had plunged into darkness. Nothing more. And then he caught her eye. He was too far away for her to read his expression, but she tried to let him know by the smallest shake of her head that Keith was nothing to her. Glenn turned and walked towards the bar.

Feeling lightheaded, Dale stumbled over Keith's large feet as they began to move round the dance floor.

'Oh, I'm sorry.'

'Good thing you warned me you didn't dance,' he said, bending his head and smirking, the sickly smell of his Brylcreem wafting over her face.

She bit back a retort. She was known for her ballroom dancing, but she wasn't going to let *him* know. How badly she wanted to see where Glenn was sitting. If only she could break away from Keith's grip. She stuck out her jaw. She'd finish the bloody dance, then go and find Glenn before he came over to their table. Introducing Keith and Mick would be the last straw.

Oh, the relief when the dance finally ended.

'She's not as bad a dancer as she lets on,' Keith said to the others when they were back at the table.

Rhoda gave a shriek of laughter.

'Why? What's so funny?'

'Oh, nothing,' Rhoda smirked.

Where was he?

Dale didn't dare move her head. It would be too obvious. But then a shadow fell over their table.

'Hi,' he said casually, looking round the group. 'I'm Glenn Reeves, from the US. I thought I'd check out a real English tea dance.' His quick glance at Dale was no more than he gave the others.

What was he playing at? Why didn't he let the others know he knew her?

'Sit yourself down,' Keith said. 'The more the merrier.' He shook Glenn's hand. 'Keith Underwood,' then he pointed to Rhoda. 'That's Jane and next to her is Rhonda.'

'Other way round,' Rhoda said, thrusting her hand out and treating Glenn to one of her best smiles. 'And it's Rhoda.'

'I'm Mick Baker.' Mick shifted his chair to make a space.

'Thanks for the invitation, but I wouldn't mind a turn on the dance floor first.' Glenn turned to Dale and this time he smiled. 'No one's introduced *you.*'

She'd play his game. 'Dale Treadwell.'

'Then would you care to dance, Miss Treadwell?'

Dale's heart lurched. At least she'd find out why she hadn't heard from him.

Not daring to look at Jane and Rhoda, and aware Keith was watching her, she rose to her feet and took his hand. That same electric shock rushed up her arm.

He led her onto the dance floor. The small band resumed. A waltz. One of her favourites – the 'Blue Danube'. A lovely long piece of music, she thought happily.

Let him be a good dancer.

'Love the dress,' he said softly as he slipped an arm around her waist.

'Thank you. I bought it especially for my birthday today.'

He raised an eyebrow. 'You didn't mention birthdays the other night.'

'Oh, you *do* remember you've met me before, then?' Dale raised her eyebrows.

He grinned. 'I wanted it to be our secret.'

His words gave her a jolt of recognition. She'd thought the same when they'd parted that evening. She could feel the pressure of his fingers through the thin dress material. Her entire back quivered. She placed her left hand on his shoulder and he took her other hand firmly in his as he expertly guided her around the floor.

Instinctively, she followed him, her steps matching his exactly. Stealing a glance, she remembered how they were on the same level now she was in heels. She liked his sun-streaked fair hair. She liked the cleft in his chin. She liked the startling blue eyes . . . Everything about him made her mouth want to smile. But she still wanted an explanation. He caught her looking at him and grinned, bringing her hand to his chest.

'What is it?' he asked, his voice muffled in her hair.

She couldn't speak. He pulled her closer.

She shut her eyes. She never wanted the music to end. Everything had felt so wrong – the Polish invasion, Dad asking Mother to divorce him, Franklin sneering at her work, war on Germany declared on her twenty-first birthday – but now, everything felt so right. It was as though she were floating on a cloud. When the music finally stopped her feet seemed to have a will of their own. Glenn gently squeezed her hand as they moved a few more steps.

'I hope you enjoyed that as much as I did,' he said, not taking his arm away from her waist.

'Mmm, yes,' she said, dreamily, then teased, 'but I expect that's down to you not being at all a bad dancer.'

'All the Fred Astaire and Ginger Rogers films I've watched must have finally paid off,' he chuckled. 'I suppose we'd better be getting back to your friends.'

'My friends are Jane and Rhoda,' Dale said. 'I've never set eyes on those other two until this afternoon. They were already sitting at the table when I came in.'

'That tall dark one – he seems to have eyes only for *you*.'

'Then I'd better get back to him.' Dale kept her face straight.

'I suppose he's what you would call good-looking.'

'Is he?' She smiled. He sounded a little jealous. 'I hadn't noticed.'

'Hmm. I don't believe it.' He briefly kissed her forehead. 'It's noisy here and I want to talk with you, so shall we go? Just say goodbye and leave them to it?'

For some reason Glenn's question sounded quite daring.

'Where shall we go?' she asked.

Glenn put his hand lightly on her back as he led her through the dancing couples, most of whom were standing close together waiting for the band to strike up again.

'We'll think of somewhere.'

There was no one at their table. Dale saw Jane dancing with Mick but no sign of Rhoda and Keith. Jane gave her a huge wink over Mick's shoulder and nodded towards Glenn with her thumb up. Dale couldn't help smiling.

'Your friend seems to approve,' Glenn said as he helped

her on with her jacket, 'but your admirer looks to have disappeared.'

'How fickle men are.'

'Not this one.' Glenn's tone was suddenly serious.

'I'm glad.' She picked up her handbag.

Outside Glenn flagged down a taxi.

'We'll go to the place I'm staying,' he said. 'And before you think I'm out to seduce you—' he grinned '—we'll keep downstairs in the lounge like decent folk.'

'Now I'm disappointed.' Dale's smile was mischievous as she climbed into the back of the cab.

'Don't tempt me.'

'Where to, sir?' The driver twisted his neck round.

'The Lansdowne Club, Fitzmaurice Place.'

'Right you are, sir.'

So Glenn belonged to a club. How was that possible when he was only here on holiday? And then she remembered that slight hesitation when she'd asked him what he was doing in England. And how deftly he'd switched any further questioning on to herself. Not that she thought he was trying to hide something – no, it wasn't that – but there was the distinct feeling he wasn't perhaps being so open with her as she'd been with him.

These and many other unanswered questions were still running through her head when the taxi driver drew up outside an imposing building with its rather austere façade.

Glenn paid the fare, then took her arm and led her up the step to the front door where a doorman opened it to allow them through.

Dale's eyes widened as she looked around. The interior was in the distinctive style of Art Deco with its huge arched windows and sleek curving forms, the afternoon sunlight catching accents of chrome. The lounge was crowded with military personnel with not one woman in sight. There was a constant sound of chattering and glasses chinking. She wouldn't feel comfortable walking in there. She turned to Glenn.

'It doesn't look as though women are allowed.'

'Actually, this is one of the very few clubs in London that allows women as members, never mind just visitors.'

'Oh.'

'I think we should go to one of the members' rooms,' he said. 'We need to talk.' He looked down at her feet. 'Are those gorgeous shoes comfortable enough to walk up five long flights of stairs?'

'Surely there's a lift.' She hesitated. 'But didn't you say we'd be downstairs?'

'I did, but it's far too noisy. The members' rooms are on the fourth and fifth floors, bedrooms on the third. We can take the elevator to whichever floor you fancy.' He grinned.

She felt the blood rush to her cheeks.

'The fifth will do,' she said, hating herself for sounding so prim. For goodness' sake – she was twenty-one. Two of her other friends were already married with babies. She swallowed.

Glenn opened both lift doors and Dale stepped out.

'Straight ahead and then to the left,' Glenn said.

No one was in the room though there was the whiff of recent cigarette smoke and . . . Dale wrinkled her nose . . . a faint smell of perfume. At least it was a sign of *one* other woman.

'This is more like it.' Glenn took off his jacket and hung it on the back of one of the chairs. 'Come over here, Dale, and take a look at the view.'

She dropped her jacket over Glenn's and walked over to the enormous bay with its floor-to-ceiling windows. It was dizzying – as if she were flying, even though she'd never been in an aeroplane.

He put his arm around her waist and drew her close to his side, his shoulder gently pressing hers. The contact comforted her. She forced herself to look ahead, rather than at his profile, and gasped. The whole city was spread before her.

'Pretty impressive, huh?' Glenn said. 'Even though it's not yet dusk you can pick out St Paul's Cathedral.'

'It's amazing. I've never seen London from this height.'

They stood for a minute or two, and though Dale's eyes were fixed on the view, her longing for him grew in intensity until she thought she would burst. As though he felt the same, he turned her towards him and traced his finger along her jaw.

'Dale, you're beautiful. Did I ever tell you?' His voice was deep.

'You did when we walked back to mine on Friday,' she said, smiling.

'Then I'll tell you again. Darling Dale, you're so very beautiful. I'm crazy about you.'

'But you didn't ring yesterday when you said. You told me you couldn't see me so I thought it might be a girlfriend.'

He shook his head. 'There's only one girl for me and she's standing right here.' He lightly stroked her cheek. 'It was work. I wanted to call you. But I couldn't make head nor tail of the telephone number you gave me. You wrote the numbers on top of each other. So I checked 'Treadwell' in the phone book and called all four in Pimlico but the first three were wrong numbers and the last one, the line was dead. Luckily, I remembered you were going to a dance today at the Grosvenor Hotel.'

A warmth flooded through her. He hadn't given up.

'And then when I came in and saw you dancing with that good-looking guy, I was so sure he was a boyfriend you'd conveniently forgotten to tell me about that I nearly walked out.'

'But—'

He stilled her mouth with his kiss.

She didn't want it to end. Almost faint with longing she held on to him, her arms around his neck, stroking the back of his head, parting her lips under his . . . warm, tender, inviting . . . until she felt the tip of his tongue, heard his breath coming in short, jagged gasps. A flood of desire gripped her as he kissed her for the second time.

'I mustn't—' He pulled away. 'Dale, I'm sorry, but I don't know what you've done to me. I'm not just crazy about you – I think I've gone and fallen in love with you. It's ridiculous. We hardly know each other. But nothing else seems to matter – the only thing I need to hear is that you feel the same.'

She blinked. She'd wanted him to feel the same way as she did, but now he'd voiced the words it was real. It was wonderful but bewildering that something so momentous had happened so quickly, leaving her insides weak. Desperately, she tried to gather her thoughts.

'I'm rushing you and it's not fair. You don't have to answer. But I wanted you to know how I feel. Come and sit with me.' He kept his arm around her as he walked her towards one of the sofas.

The smell of leather wafted into her nostrils as Glenn settled her on the sofa, piling cushions at her back and one behind her neck, then sat beside her.

'This feels very luxurious,' she said, desperate to relax but so aware of him. How close he was. 'How are you able to be a member of an English club when you're only here on holiday?'

He hesitated, then cleared his throat. 'I'm not exactly on vacation.'

She swung to face him. 'Really? Then why are you here? Isn't it a strange place to visit especially when England's been on the brink of war with Germany for months?'

'You're right. It *is* an odd time to come here.'

'Go on,' Dale said quietly, a feeling of dread creeping round her heart.

'I'm a foreign correspondent based in Chicago. But in radio rather than journalism . . . still, a job not dissimilar to yours.'

It didn't sound at all like a junior reporter, especially her own job with all its restrictions.

'I can't go into any detail.' He smiled when he saw her frown. 'Don't worry, dearest, it's all above board. I have to report how things are with the ordinary folk – their attitude, how they adjust to new circumstances, the impact of food rationing if, no, *when* it happens as it did in the last war – that sort of information.'

For some reason Dale felt peeved. It was as though his boss had sent Glenn to spy on them.

'I'm sure we'll cope . . . as we did in the last war while we were waiting for the Americans to come to our aid,' she added coolly.

He gave a half smile. 'No, no, I don't mean the British. We all know back home about the British stiff upper lip – their indomitable spirit. No, I only wish it *was* here so I could see you more often.'

Dale's stomach tensed.

'Then where—'

'Germany,' he said. 'To be precise . . . Berlin.'

66

Chapter Eight

Dale's blood ran cold. She wasn't prepared for this. Not Berlin. She'd seen clippings on Pathé News, making her sick with fear as Hitler ranted and raved to tens of thousands of cheering Germans. She remembered last year her disbelief on reading in the newspaper of the night when the Nazis' rage against all Jews went out of control as they smashed the windows of Jewish-run businesses, dragging the owners from the premises to heaven knows where. The Gestapo, who had the reputation of being the evil, murderous secret police of Nazi Germany, and who had organised such a heinous crime, called it *Kristallnacht*. No! Her mouth went dry. She licked her lips and tried to swallow but she couldn't. Not Berlin. She couldn't bear to think of Glenn in the same city as such a madman.

'B-but they're now our enemies,' she faltered.

'Britain's, but not America's, in Hitler's view. Not yet, anyway.'

Dale's mind was spinning. Then a bubble of anger arose.

'Look at me,' she hissed. Ignoring his raised eyebrows, she said, 'You told me you were on holiday here. That's clearly not true. What exactly are you doing in London if you're supposed to be in Berlin reporting on ordinary German people's lives – which, you should know, I don't believe? Please don't treat me like a child. I want the truth.'

Glenn's eyelids lowered such a tiny fraction she wondered if she'd imagined it. Then he smiled and ran his fingers through her hair.

'I'm afraid I can't, my love. Let's just say I've got to see some VIPs here in London before I go into the lion's den.' He stopped playing with her hair and his face became serious. 'Believe me, it's safer if you don't know too much. Let's just leave it at that. I wouldn't want to drag you into anything that could get you into trouble.'

Dale was silent. Then a thought struck her.

'How can you travel to Germany from here?'

'I can't,' Glenn admitted. 'I'll have to go through Switzerland. Once I get to Germany, being an American, I'll be fine.'

A lump grew in her throat. She knew there was nothing she could say that would make any difference. He obviously had a top-secret job to do and she could tell by the determined look in his eye that he would see it through.

'It doesn't sound fine at all – it sounds highly dangerous.' She choked on the words.

He pulled her more firmly to him. 'Listen. You and I are two of a kind. If there was danger, you wouldn't run away from it any more than I would.'

'I haven't had to face danger . . . not yet, anyway.'

'You've got plenty of guts. You could've gone home when London went into the blackout. But you didn't. Your instinct was to get the story.'

'There weren't exactly bombs raining down.'

'Maybe not – but you didn't know that.' He stroked her arm but she flinched.

'How long will you be gone?' Her tone was flat, as though she couldn't dredge up any more emotion.

He didn't answer for several moments. Then he turned to her and brought her chin round to face him.

'Tough question,' he said. 'It's doubtful we'll be given any leave. It depends upon what our government plans to do. But when – not if – America enters the war, we'll be booted out.'

'And I'll never see you again,' Dale said fiercely. 'Why did you let this happen when you knew? You tell me you love me in the space of two days, and now you're leaving. For how long? Years, if it's anything like the last one.' She choked on the last words. Hot tears rolled down her cheeks and she did nothing to stop them. 'Why didn't you tell me the truth straightaway?'

'Dale, don't be upset. I can't stand it if you cry.' He reached for his handkerchief and tried to dab her face but she turned her head away. 'You wouldn't want me to be any different.' When she didn't answer, he sighed. 'Listen to me, Dale.' He took her arm. 'It's a way of playing my own small part in all this horror Hitler's unleashed. America will need convincing. Roosevelt has told the people more than once that he doesn't want to go to war. That he's not going to endanger the lives of our young men and women. But he may very well have to in the end. Britain can't go alone – she'll need allies. Until then, America can give them the backing. We have the resources.' He paused. 'And you know something? You're the kind of girl who'll want to play a part in the war yourself – no matter how difficult.'

She only half heard his words. All she could think of was that she was in love with this man and now he was going far away and she might never see him again. She jerked from his grasp.

'When are you leaving?'

Briefly, he closed his eyes, then looked at her. 'In three days. They're letting me have those days to have a look round London, which I've never visited, and I can't think of anyone else I'd rather be with to show me.' He gave her a tender smile. 'I want them to be a very special three days. Do you think your boss might give you some time off, so we can have those days together? To see London, to talk, to share a meal, a glass of wine . . .' He paused, his blue eyes anxious. 'I just want to be with you, the girl I love – that's all.'

Three days. Just three precious days. Dale closed her eyes. It was nothing – no time at all – and yet it would have to be everything. But what if he'd told her he loved her just to . . .?

Unbidden, Chris Taylor, her last boyfriend from two years ago, sprang into her mind, digging up the ghastly memory of how he'd told her he loved her, then wheedled and cajoled and tried so hard to persuade her to let him make love to her when they'd gone back to his flat one evening. But her inner voice had whispered he was a cad and he couldn't love her at all if he acted this way. To Chris's fury she'd said she wasn't sure she loved him and had pulled away. He'd been angry, saying she'd led him on. She'd wrenched open the bedroom door and run down the stairs, heart pounding, knowing she'd made a lucky escape.

But Glenn wasn't Chris. He hadn't mentioned anything of the kind. But it didn't stop the warmth from rushing to her cheeks at the thought of being with him in every way.

'What's wrong, Dale?' Glenn's voice brought her back to the moment.

Dale's mouth was dry. She licked her lips.

He was watching her, his eyes full of love and concern.

'Tell me. You know you can tell me anything.'

'I was just . . .' She trailed off, then made herself look at him. 'Would you expect anything more from me?' She swallowed hard.

Glenn's brow furrowed. 'Do you mean you're worried

70

I might try to seduce you?' He held her gaze and she nodded miserably. 'Did something like that happen to you?'

How had he guessed?

She nodded. 'I once had a horrible experience, and I wouldn't want to go through anything like that again. It was a shock because he was supposed to be in love with me.'

'He wants to hope I never set eyes on him,' Glenn said, anger coating his words. He kissed her forehead. 'You won't have that worry with me. Just the two of us enjoying each other's company is fine by me. I love you and want the best for you – always. So don't you forget it – okay?'

She was feeling dizzy. Her body tingled. She'd always dreamed of the first man who would make love to her. Who would he be? What would he look like? She lifted her face and met his gaze. He smiled. That wonderful lopsided smile, his face already familiar. She knew for certain who the man would be to make her a woman. He was sitting right next to her, as dear to her as though she'd known him all her life, and yet as thrilling as someone she knew nothing about but wanted to learn everything.

'Okay.' She smiled a little shakily. 'I won't forget.'

'I think we deserve some sustenance after all that,' he said, giving her a tender smile. 'I don't think you got a chance to sample the afternoon tea, as you British call it, at the Grosvenor, so we could have an early supper, though we'll have to go downstairs to the dining room – if we can stand being around other people, that is.'

She laughed. 'I'm too hungry to worry about other people.'

'Then let's go.'

In the dining room Dale was cheered to see a few women at the tables, bringing lively chatter, laughter and the clinking of glasses. It was as though everyone was determined to enjoy what might be their last time together in such a happy atmosphere before they were split apart by the onset of war. Dale was thankful she was wearing her new dress and shoes, although she was conscious her outfit was modest compared with the other women whose jewellery glittered and sparkled on the deepest of cleavages.

The head waiter approached them. 'Table for two, sir?'

'Thank you.' Glenn stepped aside to let Dale walk in front.

When they were settled at a table and the waiter had put a large damask napkin on Dale's lap, then Glenn's, and handed them both a menu, Glenn said:

'Choose whatever you fancy, darling.' He gazed at her. 'Do you mind if I call you "darling"?'

'No,' she said immediately. 'I like it.'

'Good. Then at least *that's* settled.' He grinned at her, revealing a crooked lower tooth.

It only enhanced his attraction, she thought, as she smiled happily back.

Chapter Nine

'I'm intrigued that such a modest-looking building in a regular road is where your Mr Chamberlain will decide how the war will proceed,' Glenn said the next day as they stood outside 10 Downing Street. 'When you compare it to the White House.'

'Yes, I've seen the White House in the papers,' Dale said. 'It looks very impressive but Number 10 is much bigger than it looks. It goes a long way back and has something like a hundred rooms. And anyway, we Brits are not so flamboyant as you Americans.' She gave him a teasing smile.

They walked over to the Houses of Parliament and Big Ben, hand in hand the whole way.

'I'm going to take some pictures of you,' Glenn said, opening the camera he had slung round his neck. 'Give me that gorgeous smile of yours.'

'Let me take one of you,' she said, when he'd taken a few.

'Better still—' He broke off and stopped a passing figure.

'Pardon me, sir, but would you mind taking a picture of my girlfriend and me?'

The man glanced at Dale, who smiled at him, then took the camera from Glenn, who put his arm round Dale.

'Ready?' the man said. 'Say cheese.' He took the photograph and handed the camera back. 'Hope it comes out.'

'Much appreciate it,' Glenn said as the man nodded and hurried away. He turned to Dale with a grin. 'Where are you taking me next?'

Dale glanced at her watch. 'It's nearly lunchtime.' She paused. 'Shall we stop for a bite to eat?'

'I can't think of anything better,' he said, pulling her towards him and kissing her, right there on the pavement, oblivious to curious stares.

'Kissing you is like floating on a cloud,' he said. 'Something I've never experienced before.'

She wouldn't tell him she felt the same. It might dilute the magic.

The following day it was Tuesday and Dale walked with Glenn along the Serpentine, enjoying a never-before feeling of playing truant from the newspaper office. She swallowed a flicker of guilt that she'd told Bill at the office she wasn't feeling very well and how concerned he'd been.

But immediately her mind switched to Glenn. He'd organised a modest picnic from the hotel which they'd devoured by midday. After feeding the ducks they sat on the grass in the sunshine, talking quietly. Dale leant against a tree, her hands behind her head, her troubles melting away as she watched Glenn light a cigarette. He sent her a rueful smile.

'You can't believe the country's at war, can you?' He waved his hand towards the lido where hundreds of people were bathing.

'I know.' Dale paused. 'If this is war, then it's not as bad as I feared.'

'I doubt it will stay this calm for very long.' Glenn looked at her. 'Shall we go for a cup of tea?'

'You're so enthusiastic over everything British,' Dale said, rising to her feet and carefully folding the greaseproof paper from the sandwiches. 'Even our tea.'

'I'm learning your British ways.' He kissed the tip of her nose. 'Truth is, it's only because the coffee here is so bad—' he chuckled '—but your tea is just great.'

'Good job you added that, or I'd be really cross.'

'How could you ever be cross with me?' he grinned, taking her in his arms and kissing her swiftly on the lips.

Tomorrow – and then it'll be over.

Dale swallowed hard. She mustn't spoil it by letting him see she was anything but happy. And she was happy – deliriously so. But it wasn't going to last.

Glenn looked at her. 'What's the matter, sweetheart?'

'N-nothing. Except, well, how will we stay in contact? You won't be able to send me a letter through the post from Germany now we're at war.'

'I'll think of a way. There *will* be a way,' he said emphatically. 'And I want you to remember one thing. Whatever happens, however long it takes, I will come back to you.'

That was all very well, but he'd be in the thick of things. Hitler's headquarters was in Berlin and no doubt the Air Force would be bombing the daylights out of it. Her eyes pricked with unshed tears.

'So just think about now.' He ran his finger along her jaw making her face tingle. 'Isn't it wonderful that we're in love and together, enjoying London. Don't think about what *might* happen, darling. Just love today – this minute, this hour, with me, knowing we have tomorrow. It's probably more than a lot of folk have right now.'

She nodded. She couldn't speak. He was right. No one knew what was going to happen. She only hoped London was prepared for any punishment Germany was about to dish out to them.

'Shall we go, my love?'

'I don't think I can walk much further in these heels.'

'Do you want to go to the club and relax? Maybe have an early supper and go to the movies? Two sitting-down things to do. Does that sound like a plan to you, sweetie-pie?' he drawled, and she knew he was trying to cheer her up.

Dale couldn't help laughing. 'Yes, it does. It sounds a wonderful plan.'

Glen flagged down a taxi.

'What about the fish?' Glenn said as he looked up from the menu in the club's dining room.

'Perfect.' Dale smiled at him and he twinkled back. She wanted to pinch herself. How had she been so lucky to have met such a lovely man? 'Tell me about your home.'

'There's not a lot to tell,' Glenn said, taking a mouthful of white wine. 'Atlanta is much hotter than here – it's about ninety-five degrees now. We usually have much milder winters than I believe y'all do here, and spring comes early.'

'So you don't work in Warm Springs, then?'

'Good God, no. There's nothing to do there. I used to rent a flat in Atlanta when I was studying journalism, but my folks are still in Warm Springs. They wouldn't leave if you paid them. That's where they grew up – where they met. And where I went to school. It's a cute little town but you can't make a living any more so practically all the college kids have left, which is a shame ... but I guess that's progress.' He looked a little wistful.

'What did you like at school?' she asked.

'History,' he said, immediately. 'And your Shakespeare. We used to put on a play once a year. I loved it.' He twinkled at her. 'And you?'

'I liked language and literature, too. And I used to be pretty good at German.'

Glenn raised an eyebrow. 'How's that?'

Dale took a sip of wine. 'My mother had an Austrian maid, Ursula Fassbender, for quite a few years. I think it was the only kind of position she could find when she came to England, but I realise now how educated she was. She taught my mother German and would tell her about Vienna and going to the opera and the wonderful orchestras.' She paused. 'At that age I desperately wanted to understand what they were talking about so I asked Frau Fassbender to teach me. She made the city sound so magical I decided that one day I'd see it for myself.'

Glenn looked at her, a serious expression flitting across his face. 'You said you *used* to be good at German.'

'I was. The trouble is if you don't speak it regularly you soon forget it.'

She went quiet. Whenever she'd asked her mother if she still heard from her maid who'd become a friend, her mother would say she didn't know her latest address, or simply change the subject. But that was years ago. A shiver crawled down Dale's spine. Was it possible she was Jewish? Had she gone back to her country? She only remembered that one day Frau Fassbender hadn't been there and her mother had said little, only that she'd miss her. She vowed to ask her mother what had happened.

'Hmm.' Glenn fiddled with the salt and pepper pot. He glanced up. 'I hope your German will never be needed . . . because if it does—'

'—it means we'll have been invaded,' Dale finished with a shudder.

'Let's don't talk about it.' Glenn wiped his mouth with the napkin. 'What movie are we going to see?'

She knew he'd changed the subject on purpose. Their time was precious. It was wasted talking about things they had no control over.

'They're showing *Wuthering Heights*.'

'Merle Oberon and Laurence Olivier,' Glenn said immediately and grinned. 'An American Hollywood movie.' He looked at her. 'I bet you've read the book.'

'Yes, I have. Not at school, though. We weren't allowed. It was considered too risqué for fourteen-year-olds,' Dale finished with a self-conscious laugh. 'Far too much passion.'

Glenn leant towards her and lightly tapped under her chin. 'So now you're twenty-one you think you might be ready for some passion?'

'Depends on who's offering it,' she said, grinning.

'May I put my name down?'

Dale couldn't help laughing. 'You may – but I'm not sure what good it will do you.'

'Only that it'll make sure no one is in line behind me – not now . . . not ever.'

His eyes were intent upon her, reaching into her soul. Her laughter faded as she held his gaze.

'You don't need to worry about that,' she said without thinking.

'I don't?' The blue of Glenn's eyes intensified.

'No.'

'Why not, Dale?'

Tension crackled the air.

'Because . . . because I think I love you, too,' she said in a rush.

A smile spread almost disbelievingly across his face. 'Oh, darling, I hoped you did. I thought you did, but it's made me so happy to hear you say the words. And you know I love *you*, dearest Dale.' He paused. 'Dale's an American name for a guy. Did you know that?'

'No, I didn't. But it's not my real name. I named myself Dale when I was four.'

He took her hand and kissed the palm. 'Then what *is* your real name?'

She hesitated. Few people knew it outside her family. She'd never liked it. It always sounded old-fashioned.

'Dulcie,' she said, reluctantly.

'Dulcie,' he repeated, still holding her hand. 'But that's a beautiful name. I love it. Dulcie dearest. Darling Dulcie. It flows perfectly.' He studied her. 'Are you always known as Dale?'

'Yes. Except for my mother and my teachers.'

'Then it's even more special. I'd like to call you Dulcie. Do you mind?'

'No.' The way he'd pronounced it had sounded like poetry.

'If you're ready, Dulcie, shall we go?'

Glenn had chosen the back row, renowned for courting couples. She'd felt a little awkward, but he'd led her there as though they'd been reserved as special seats just for them. After helping her off with her jacket, he took off his own, and laid both across his knees, then loosened his tie. Dale was aware of his every movement. She noticed how his white shirt showed off the broad shoulders to perfection. Just a whisper of cotton between him and his skin . . .

She swallowed hard. Dear God, how she wanted this man. Her whole body tingled with unfamiliar desire.

'Can you see all right?' Glenn's face was close. 'If not, I don't mind if you have to move closer.'

'I'll wait and see who sits in front of me,' she whispered back teasingly, willing her heart to stop pounding.

As it was, a petite lady and her equally short husband took

the seats in front just as the picture house plunged into darkness.

'I can't see a thing,' Glenn said, and she could hear the grin in his voice, 'so I'll just have to move closer to *you*, if that's all right.'

'I'm not sure you're being totally honest,' she said, smothering a giggle, 'but I'll give you the benefit of the doubt.'

'Thank you kindly, ma'am,' he drawled, his fingers possessively closing over her hand.

She couldn't concentrate on the film. Every sinew in her body was aching for him. The passion Heathcliff showed for Cathy on the screen in front only served to inflame her. This uncontrollable need to be with him, part of him, body and soul. Just at the point where she thought she would burst, Glenn turned her chin towards him and kissed her. She twisted in her seat, her hands feeling the warmth of his skin beneath his shirt, the taut muscles, her fingers now laced round the back of his head, awkwardly pulling him even closer in the confined space as his kiss deepened, thrilling her, until she thought she would faint.

'Dulcie. Dearest darling Dulcie.' His voice was almost a groan.

She undid one of the shirt buttons and slipped her hand onto his bare skin. She felt it quiver under her fingers.

'Shall we go?' He said the words against her lips.

She didn't speak – couldn't. Instead, she took her hand away, fumbled to do up his shirt button, and removed her jacket from his lap. Scrambling to her feet, she threw her jacket on and quickly made for the exit.

The manager opened the door for them. 'Film wasn't to your taste, then,' he said with a smirk.

'I guess we weren't in the mood,' Glenn returned as he allowed Dale to step in front of him.

'That's a shame. It's been very popular so far, especially with the young ones.'

Dale choked back a giggle. Once outside, she breathed in the London air as though she were at the seaside.

'That manager was a cheeky devil,' she said, still laughing, as Glenn took her arm.

'He knew exactly why we were leaving. That we couldn't keep our hands off one another.'

'How do you know that?'

'He only had to look at us. You all flushed and your hair a mess. Me with half my clothes torn off by this incredibly beautiful temptress . . .'

'Stop it! Were we really that noticeable?'

'Anyone could tell at a glance we're madly in love and can't wait to be somewhere private. And that's exactly how I feel.' He paused. 'Do you?'

Dale bit her lip. 'Yes, I do, but—'

'But what?'

'Nothing.'

'Dulcie, I'm fine with whatever you feel comfortable with. All I want is for you to be happy . . . to enjoy every moment we have together. Is that agreed?'

She nodded. 'It's agreed.'

'Good. Then shall we go back to the club? At least there's a chance of some privacy.'

'Can we just walk?' she said. 'It was a bit stuffy in there.'

'Mmm. I must admit things were getting hot in more ways than one.' He grinned as he took her arm.

Dale's mind was racing on their almost silent walk to the Lansdowne Club. What should she do? She stole a sideways glance at him. He'd be gone after tomorrow. She might never see him again. She was twenty-one. A woman. But an inexperienced one. Her heart beat faster. If he asked her, she would.

But Glenn didn't ask anything. Instead, he ordered coffee, which one of the waiters brought to them in the foyer, and proceeded to speak of his family. He was the eldest of three – Lamar, his brother, only eighteen months younger than himself, and Cindy, his sister, who was still at school. Glenn was the only one who had moved away from the family farm. His parents sounded loving and proud of their children and Dale suddenly longed to meet them. To be drawn into their family, their way of life. A complete change from crowded, rushing London. Inwardly, she pulled herself up sharply. She was being ridiculous.

Glenn paused and put his cup down. 'Am I boring you?'

'No,' Dale said emphatically. 'I want to hear everything that concerns you.'

'But you're very quiet. Not like you.'

She stared at him.

'Are you sure you're okay?'

She nodded. Before she could change her mind, she said very quickly, 'Only that I'm thinking how much I want you to make love to me. Now. In your room.'

Glenn's eyes widened a fraction.

'Dulcie,' he said quietly, 'I have a feeling this is your first time. Am I right?'

'Yes,' she whispered.

He leant towards her and took her hand. 'Are you sure, darling? *Really* sure?'

'Yes.'

'And you won't ever regret it?'

'I'll regret it if I don't . . . if *we* don't,' Dale said firmly.

Glenn stood and held out his hand.

'Then, Dulcie, my love, shall we go?'

*　　*　　*

It was only the second time she'd entered a man's bedroom. That first time with Chris . . . She forced the horror from her vision. Glenn pulled down the blackout blind and switched on a side light. He took her in his arms.

'You're not to feel under any pressure at all.' He kissed her, then held her a little away. 'And if you want me to stop at any time you must tell me. I won't be offended at all. I mean it.'

'All right.' She looked towards a door to the right-hand side, half open, showing a bathroom. 'May I have a quick tidy up?'

'Of course. Take as much time as you like.'

Feeling as though she were in a dream, Dale stepped into the bathroom. Glenn had left it neat from this morning and she wondered if he'd prepared it, hoping, or if he was generally a tidy person. She stared at herself in the mirror above the sink. Her hair was a mess. She'd worn it up today, but several stray locks had escaped the kirby grips and combs she'd so carefully put in place that morning. She should try to do something with it, but she was too over-wrought, too much in a hurry to bother. Her eyes looked unnaturally bright in the dim light and her lipstick had almost disappeared from so many kisses in the cinema and just now. She couldn't help smiling and the woman in the mirror smiled back. Would she look any different after . . .?

She gave a shiver of anticipation and entered the room. Glenn was sitting on the foot of the bed. He turned and looked up at her.

'Are you sure you want this?'

'Yes,' she said.

He held out his arms. 'Then come to me.'

She slowly walked over to him . . . sat next to him.

He turned and kissed her, this time so softly, so tenderly,

then one by one he removed her grips and combs so that her hair fell to her shoulders. For a few seconds he swept up a handful and buried his face in it, murmuring something, though she couldn't distinguish the words. Slowly he began to undress her. She thought she'd feel embarrassed, but she didn't – not at all. She only knew she wanted him with all her heart. Her breath came in quick gasps as she stood naked in front of him. Then she saw him swallow hard.

'You have the most beautiful body,' he said thickly. 'It goes so perfectly with your lovely face.'

He helped her under the sheet and quickly undressed. There was a minute's pause, then he slipped under the sheet and lay on his side so he was facing her, folding her in his arms, her breasts flattening against his chest. Then she felt the weight of him on top of her, and not knowing whether it was his or her own heart thudding, Dale instinctively wrapped her legs around his body.

'It may be a little uncomfortable,' he whispered, 'but I'll be as gentle as I can.'

Involuntarily, she let out a cry from the brief shock of pain . . . and then she forgot. Forgot about pain, forgot about the rules that she was supposed to be married to do this, forgot he was going away and she might never see him again . . . All that mattered was that Glenn loved her and was proving it to her in the most intimate way he could, stopping to kiss her neck, her mouth, her breast, and whispering how much he loved her.

'I love you, too,' she said. 'So very much. With all my heart and soul.'

Dale awoke and for a few seconds couldn't think where she was. Then she felt him stirring beside her. She raised herself on her elbow, watching him, fascinated by him. His fair hair flopped onto his forehead, his golden lashes softly touching his cheeks. He looked so young asleep. Hesitantly, she put her hand out to touch his face, running her fingertips down his nose, along his jaw, tracing the shape of his eyebrows, caressing his bare shoulder, then separating the golden hairs on his chest. That was the moment he opened his eyes and smiled lazily.

'You've been studying me.'

'I couldn't help it.'

'Come here, you wicked woman, and make a closer examination.' He pulled her on top of him.

Chapter Ten

An hour – maybe two hours – later Dale somehow managed to tear herself from Glenn's arms and quickly dressed. She'd insisted he was to stay in the club so he'd ordered a taxi to take her home.

We have tomorrow, darling. Another wonderful day ahead of us.

She'd turned his words over and over in her mind in the cab as the driver steered through the pitch-dark roads. When he drew up in Charlwood Street she stepped out and handed the driver a ten-shilling note.

'Already settled, love,' he said with a wink, and drove off.

She hadn't wanted to think beyond tomorrow when who knew how long it would be before they saw one another again. Now, bursting with euphoria that she was in love and was loved in return, she put her key in the front door, but it opened before she could unlock it.

'Where've you been, Dulcie?' her mother demanded. 'I've been worried to death. Do you know it's almost midnight?'

'I told you I was meeting a friend after work,' Dale said, hating to pretend she'd been at work all day, even though she told herself it was only a fib to shield her mother. 'We didn't realise the time.'

'Presumably this friend is a man?' Her mother sent her

a stern look. 'And please don't lie, Dulcie. I'm not stupid. You're not all flushed-looking over Jane or some other girlfriend.'

'Yes, I have met someone,' Dale admitted.

'Why don't I know about him?'

'I haven't known him an awfully long time,' Dale said. 'But Mother, I really like him . . . a lot.'

Her mother looked at her sharply. 'Don't say you've fallen in love with him.' When Dale didn't answer, Patricia continued, 'That's where it all goes wrong. They're all charm until they get their own way. Then it's goodbye and on to the next. And if he's in the Navy he'll have a girl in every port.'

'No, Mother. He's not like that. I think . . . I know you'd approve. We do love each other, but he's going away the day after tomorrow.' Her eyes were bright with unshed tears. 'His work is part of the war effort.' She wouldn't tell her mother Glenn was American. That would set off another negative train of questions.

Patricia pursed her lips. 'I've brought you up to be a good girl but falling in love can put paid to common sense and any stupidity will live with you for ever. Just remember that.'

Dale was silent. She knew what her mother was hinting. Glenn had protected her from the possibility of getting pregnant, but she wasn't going to explain that to her mother. Their lovemaking was their own private affair.

'I'm twenty-one now, Mother,' she said, putting on a bright smile. 'Officially a woman with the key of the door.'

'I don't care if you're fifty, you're still my child,' Patricia said firmly. She looked Dale in the eye. 'I presume he has a name.'

'His name's Glenn Reeves – and please don't worry about him, Mother – he's a gentleman.'

'I hope he is for *your* sake, or it will end in tears.'

She glanced over. What did her mother mean? Dale realised how little she really knew her parents.

'Mother, you've not told me how you left it with Dad. Whether the two of you have come to any decision about the house and—'

'I've told him flatly I'm not moving,' her mother snapped.

Dale gave an inward sigh. 'What about the divorce?'

'I've thought about it. My pride tells me not to hang on to someone who no longer has any feelings for me, so I've told him I'll divorce him. Then the sordid part begins. He has to give me proof he's having an affair. I really don't want to see—' she took in a jagged breath '—any photographs or . . . that woman.' She began to weep.

'Oh, Mother.' Dale was swiftly at her side. 'Don't cry. He'll regret it one day and ask you to go back.'

Her mother looked up with bloodshot eyes. 'Then he might get an unwelcome surprise.'

Dale was thoughtful for a few moments. 'You know what, Mother. I think you should get a job. You're a marvellous cook. There could be someone out there who would love you to cook for them. A nice rich widower.' She chuckled but her mother remained silent. 'Seriously, why don't you think about cooking professionally? It would give you some financial independence.' She touched her mother's shoulder. 'What do you think?'

'I think not.' Patricia drew in her mouth. 'Going out to work as if we were paupers. Whatever would your father—'

'Dad's got no say in the matter,' Dale said firmly. 'It would get you out of the house and give you an interest.'

'No, Dulcie, I don't want that sort of interest, thank you very much. Looking after some old boy who wets himself and dribbles down his chin.' She shuddered. 'No, that's not how I see my future. Besides—' she stared at Dale '—who'd look after *you*?'

'I'm perfectly capable of looking after myself.'

'Not on your earnings,' her mother returned.

Glenn cursed as the telephone rang. Who the hell was calling at this time of night – or rather morning? He had just switched out his bedside light after thinking about Dulcie for the last hour since she'd left. Meeting such a wonderful girl on a bridge in London while watching the blackout take place had been unbelievable – like a scene from a movie. And then having her show him around London. He couldn't wait to set eyes on her again in just a few hours' time. At the thought of spending another whole day with her, his pulse raced. All he knew was that he'd fallen for her hard and fast.

Sighing, he leant across to pick up the receiver.

'Sorry to disturb, old boy, but I'm afraid there's been a change of plan,' came the clipped, though not unfriendly, tones of Stephen Markham, his British contact.

Glenn braced himself as he sat on the edge of the bed.

'Are you dressed?'

'Yes,' Glenn lied.

'Good. You have exactly fifteen minutes to pack a bag. I'm sending a car for you. A plane will be waiting to take you to Switzerland. From there you will catch a train to Berlin – all as previously arranged, but you have to go *now*!'

No! Glenn gripped the phone so hard that it hurt. After a moment, he opened his fingers and let the handset clatter onto the cradle, feeling as if he'd crawled out of an elevator that had torn itself from its bearings and plummeted to the bottom of the building. In a few hours Dulcie would be waiting for him on Westminster Bridge.

They'd planned their last day just wandering wherever it took them. He closed his eyes. What would she think? What would she do? At first she'd be worried. Then angry, thinking him a jerk for standing her up. And then it would strike her – he'd said he loved her just to get his way with her. It was all a lie, she'd think. And she would never forgive him.

He groaned as something hit him between the eyes. She'd been going to give him her address and write her telephone number clearly this time. Now, he had no way of contacting her to explain.

Sick to his stomach, Glenn rapidly dressed, then lit a cigarette. If only he could tell her the truth – that he was not just a war correspondent, but was also working for MI6, and would be passing information from Berlin back to London. But if she knew that she'd be even more worried about the added risk. He took a few drags of his cigarette, then viciously stubbed it out.

Damn it all to hell! But what was the point of cursing? There was a war on. And war didn't play fair.

He flung some clothes, a couple of books and his empty notebooks, a pair of extra shoes and a few toiletries into his travel bag, grabbed his jacket and the bag and headed for the door. He gave a quick glance behind him, seeing in his mind's eye his beloved Dulcie lying on the bed, her golden-blonde hair spreading over the pillow, smiling at him. His throat ached as he took in a jagged breath. Dear God, how he loved this English girl. And how he hated leaving her with no message to say why.

But he had a job to do. His mouth pulled tight, he resolutely opened the door and shut it quietly behind him.

The following morning the weather had turned. It was colder and had begun to drizzle, but to Dale the city sparkled.

Nothing escaped her. She noticed a little dog trotting joyfully by the side of his mistress, a newspaper boy whistling as he cycled past, the smell of warm yeast wafting from the baker's . . . If this was being in love, she wished everyone she passed could feel the same. She smiled at anyone who caught her eye as she hurried along to their agreed meeting place on Westminster Bridge for nine o'clock. It was Glenn's idea. He wanted to stand in the exact position he'd stood only five days ago when they'd first met.

They'd planned to visit St Paul's Cathedral and take the rest of the day off to wander round Covent Garden and maybe have a peep inside the Royal Opera House.

I wonder if he likes opera.

Maybe they could go the next time they met . . . when he came back from Berlin. She brought herself up sharply. *The next time.* How long would they have to wait? Months? Years? But she mustn't allow herself to be pessimistic. If she did, it would set a gloomy tone for their last day.

Glancing at her watch she saw she was eight minutes early. It was raining harder now. Compared to the other night there were only a couple of dozen people walking along, their heads bent under their umbrellas. She hadn't bothered to bring one as she always ended up either losing it or nearly poking someone's eye out with one of the spokes. No, she was safer with just her hat, although it was beginning to feel rather soggy. What a shame they hadn't arranged to meet in one of the cafés, where it would be warm and dry.

The minutes passed. It was now five past nine. Ten past. Quarter past. Twenty-two minutes past. She told herself he wasn't the sort to be unpunctual. But it was only a feeling. She didn't really know. The rain was beginning to slide down the inside of the collar of her raincoat. Nearly half-past. She was beginning to feel uneasy. Had something happened at work to delay him? Had he had an accident? Fear rose in her throat. How would she know if he was ill or injured? He'd come soon – she was sure of it.

But he didn't. The minute hand on her watch relentlessly moved on. Surely if work had stopped him coming, he'd ring. If she went home, Mother would say he'd phoned. Then her stomach gave a sickening lurch. She'd never rewritten her telephone number for him. Or her address. Importantly, how she could get in touch with *him* when he was in Berlin? They'd been going to write all those details down today. Frantically, she pounced on one thought and then another. Maybe he was at this minute trying to retrace his steps and they'd just missed each other. Maybe if she went home right now, she'd bump into him.

She'd give him ten more minutes.

The ten minutes passed. And another five. It was only then that reality hit her between the eyes so hard, so sharply, so persuasively, it nearly knocked her off her feet. Glenn had tricked her with his Southern charm by telling her he loved her, he wouldn't do anything she didn't want, they'd go at *her* pace, he wouldn't expect anything of her she was uncomfortable with . . . all lulling her into thinking what a gentleman he was. He'd been putting on an act to have his way with her. Using her. Then discarding her.

She closed her eyes and bit down hard on her bottom lip. This was his way of saying goodbye. A coward's way. Just like her father. He wouldn't have to see how hurt she was and feel any guilt.

What a fool she'd been. What a blind, stupid fool!

Shaking with fury at herself, with him, with her mother who had so correctly forecast what was bound to happen, Dale turned back, head bowed, not knowing how she managed to reach the other side of the Thames, her vision was so blurred with a mix of rain and bitter tears.

A motherly-looking middle-aged woman coming from the opposite direction stopped her. 'Are you all right, love?'

Dale stared but couldn't register what the woman was asking.

'Um – I . . .'

The woman touched her arm, her grey eyes warm with compassion. 'There are only two possible reasons for your tears, my dear. And I can see those are not tears of joy. The other reason is that you're crying over a man. And believe me, they're not worth it. You'll know that when you're my age.' She patted Dale's arm and nodded as though for emphasis, then walked briskly past.

Dale gazed after the woman's retreating back. Angrily, she blinked back her tears.

Even another woman – a stranger – could tell. He was never coming. He'd never intended to.

PART TWO

Chapter Eleven

July 1940

'There's a letter for you on the rack,' Dale's mother said one day in the kitchen after Dale returned from work.

Her heart leapt. *Glenn.* After ten long months he'd finally found a way to contact her.

Dale rushed to the hall but her heart dropped as she removed the typed envelope and glanced at the postmark. It was simply 'London SW1'. Clumsily, she slit it open with a pencil and opened the sheet of paper. It was from Whitehall. The Foreign Office.

She blinked. *What on earth . . .?* Not understanding, she felt her hand tremble as she walked back to the kitchen and read the letter.

Dear Mr Treadwell,

She rolled her eyes at the 'Mr' and read on.

We are writing to congratulate you as one of the six winners in the recent crossword competition organised through the Daily Telegraph.

'Oh, my goodness.' She looked up at her mother, her eyes wide. 'I've won a crossword competition in the newspaper!'

'I didn't know you'd gone in for one. Why didn't you mention it?' Her mother waited for a reply.

Bill at work had spotted it.

'Look at this,' he'd said as he handed her the *Daily Telegraph* one day when she'd been feeling as though nothing would ever be right again. 'It's a crossword puzzle competition. I've seen how quickly you do them every day in *our* paper. This one's more cryptic but I bet you could do it.' He looked at her and grinned. 'First prize for completing in under twelve minutes is a hundred pounds.'

'When Dad went to Scotland my mother cancelled the *Telegraph* so that's why I do them here.' She sent Bill a sheepish look. 'I used to compose them when I was a child and my comic – *School Friend* – printed them. I got half-a-crown for each one.' She chuckled. 'That was good money in those days.'

Bill grinned. 'There you are, then. If you win, that will be quite an increase.'

Dale was brought back to her mother's next question.

'I wish you'd told me. You do leave me out of things, Dulcie. When was all this?'

'About a month ago.'

She wouldn't mention to her mother that she'd nearly changed her mind and decided at the last minute not to go. By the time she'd told herself she'd nothing to lose, she'd been late at the *Daily Telegraph* offices in Fleet Street.

The woman on the front desk had frowned.

'Your name?' she barked.

'Dale Treadwell.' Dale plopped into a metal chair on the back row, making a horrid scraping noise.

'Right, Miss Treadwell, if that's *everyone*—' she threw a

glare at Dale '—then perhaps we can begin.' She glanced at a wall clock. 'But not until I give the word. You have twelve minutes. Then when I say "Stop" you will put your pencils down immediately.' She gazed round. 'If you finish early you are to stay quietly in your chair so you don't disturb the others. Is that clear?' Her eyes had alighted on Dale.

Dale gritted her teeth.

'You may turn your paper over,' the woman had ordered.

Dale wrinkled her nose as she became aware of her mother still wanting to know why she'd not mentioned the competition. 'I wonder if anyone completed it faster than me.'

'The trouble with you, Dulcie, is you're so competitive. What does it matter?' Patricia paused, then asked, 'Is there a prize?'

'A hundred pounds,' Dale said, her eyes still fixed on the letter. 'I just did it for a bit of fun.' Her eyes dropped to the next line.

A postal order is enclosed as your runner-up prize. You were second in nine minutes and thirteen seconds.

Dale felt in the envelope and pulled out a small slip of paper. She turned it over and to her astonishment found it was made out to her for £10. She hadn't won first prize. But still . . .

She laughed. 'I've won ten pounds, Mother. Somebody beat me, but at least it's a good indication that I'm pretty good at crosswords.' She looked at her mother. 'We'll have a slap-up meal in a nice restaurant with this—' she waved the postal order '—and I'll put the rest away.'

'You'll do nothing of the kind,' Patricia said. 'You know I don't care about eating out in restaurants. But I'll make something special this evening to celebrate. I'd better look up some recipes.' She disappeared.

Dale went back to the letter.

We have vacancies for a particular type of work as a contribution to the war effort and we think you might be suitable. This will not be publicised or advertised. With that in mind you should not discuss this letter with anyone, including your immediate family.

Please let me know if you are interested and if so, write giving brief details of your background, education, hobbies, etc. Please send to the address above and we will arrange an interview.

I look forward to hearing from you.

Yours faithfully,

J. P. Duckworth

Foreign Office

Her mind flew. What did it mean . . . *a particular type of* work? And why had the letter come from the Foreign Office? Did it mean they would send her abroad? To spy? Her mind raced. If that was the case, she'd have to turn it down because she couldn't leave now Dad had dropped his thunderbolt.

She looked up in a daze. Despite all the possible obstacles a thrill shot through her. It looked very much like she was being given the opportunity to do something special, although where crossword puzzles came into it, she hadn't the foggiest. If only she could discuss this with her father. He might have been able to cast some light on it. But now her father had made his decision to break away from the family. She shrugged and tucked the postal order into the letter and put them back in the envelope, then suddenly remembered Glenn saying that he was sure she would play her part in the war effort, no matter how difficult. Momentarily, she closed her eyes, the familiar longing for him engulfing her. Would he say that this was her chance?

A fortnight later Dale shut her front door and hurried towards one of the busier roads where she'd have better luck in hailing a taxi. She felt the first spots of rain. Two cabs passed – both occupied. Darn it! This morning was one of those times when she wished she'd borrowed her mother's umbrella as soon as she'd noticed the dark clouds. The drizzle turned into a shower and she dodged under a shop awning, a curse escaping her lips to think she'd spent twenty minutes pinning her hair back into a fetching half up, half down style. It was going to be ruined. Well, at least she was wearing a raincoat. Others, caught like herself without umbrellas, hurried by, their heads lowered as the rain became more insistent. Dale put her head out only to see a third taxi pass, then miraculously it slowed down just beyond where she'd been sheltering to stop and let out the passengers. She dashed to the front of the cab and flailed her arms outside the windscreen. The driver grinned and nodded.

'You're lucky,' he said, half turning to her when she'd settled in the back seat, then glancing in the mirror before he drove on. 'Everyone wants a cab in this weather.' He gave a wide berth to a horse and cart, then said, 'Where yer goin', love?'

'King Charles Street,' she said a little breathlessly.

'Oh, very posh. Watcha doin' there? Gettin' yerself a job in Whitehall?'

Dale gave a start. She'd been warned not to disclose anything to anyone. 'Oh, just meeting a friend,' she said casually.

He chatted all the way about how good it was that

Chamberlain, the appeaser, had finally resigned and they'd now got a decent prime minister with fire in his belly.

'Just what the country needs,' he went on. 'Churchill might not be everyone's cup of tea but he's more'n a match for that little sod, Hitler. And that speech he made. Moved the missus to tears, it did.' He half turned again, and Dale wished he'd keep his eyes on the road. 'Did you hear it?' Before she could answer he rattled on. 'About giving his blood, sweat and tears.'

'Don't forget the "toil"', Dale said, hiding a smile.

'Yeah, that, too.' A bicycle pulled out in front of him. 'Bloody idiot. 'Scuse my French, but is he tryin' to kill himself?'

Somehow, the driver's lively manner as he continued a non-stop commentary on the way Churchill had miraculously got almost all the troops from Dunkirk back home to Blighty, and he was the only man with any guts to face up to bloody Hitler, restored her faith that they really would win the war, despite the latest awful news that the Germans had invaded Jersey. *Would it be us next?* Imagine those horrible jackboots marching up and down in London. Dale shuddered as she looked out of the window, thinking not for the first time how strange it was that there were hardly any children and few young men about. She swallowed. How long would it be before they all returned?

During the last week the papers had been full of the RAF battling over Kent skies, desperately trying to keep the Luftwaffe at bay, and there were distressing articles about pilots, some only nineteen or twenty, being shot down. Now, everyone was on edge, waiting for the inevitable invasion.

'Nearly there now, miss.' The taxi driver cheerfully broke into her thoughts.

Dale's stomach fluttered. She licked her lips but her mouth was so dry she found she couldn't swallow. This was ridiculous. Even if she wasn't suitable, they couldn't shoot her. She wondered what Glenn would say if he knew she was on her way to an interview with the Foreign Office.

Gloom threatened to sweep over her. She'd thought her tears had dried long ago, but now she had to squeeze her eyes shut to stop them falling. The same little inner voice that had told her countless times he could have had an accident, he could have been ill and sent back to America, he could be just as upset as she was, continued to whisper that she would hear – one day.

Relieved when the driver pulled up in King Charles Street, Dale stepped out.

'That'll be three-and-six, miss.'

She gave him a shilling tip. He was worth it.

'Thanks, love. Enjoyed the chat.' He roared off.

'Look out, missus,' a small plump man said sharply as he ducked to avoid Dale.

'Oh, I'm sorry,' she said, her mind still on Glenn.

She *must* put that episode out of her mind. It hadn't meant anything to Glenn – just a pleasant interlude to pass the time before he was sent away. No matter that she'd given herself to him, body and soul. No matter that she still loved him. She had to face it. Get used to it. He was never coming back to her. At this moment she needed all her will to concentrate on what lay ahead.

She paused for a few moments to gaze up at the magnificent buildings of Whitehall, then negotiated the first pile of sandbags outside the Foreign Office as she approached the armed guard standing in front of the right-hand archway.

'Good morning,' Dale said.

He nodded. 'May I see your identification?' She handed

103

him the letter from Whitehall. He looked at it, then said, 'You may register at the reception desk.'

She showed her letter to a second guard who pointed her onward.

Dale gasped as she stepped into a majestic hall. Surreptitiously, she glanced up at the vaulted ceiling, the magnificent staircase. Trying to look as though she was not in the least perturbed by all this grandeur, she walked sedately over to the desk, where a young man in a dark suit noted her name.

'You'll be seeing Major Barking,' he said. 'Take a seat.' He jerked his head towards a row of plush visitors' chairs.

Dale watched with mounting curiosity at the people who came and went through the doors. She looked at her watch. Twenty past twelve. Major Barking obviously didn't bother about punctuality. She noticed a girl of about eighteen, smartly dressed in navy, go up to the reception desk and speak to the young man. He caught Dale's eye and said something to the girl. She looked round at Dale and giggled.

Dale felt she was being scrutinised. The butt of some joke. She was about to leave in disgust when the girl came up to her.

'Miss Treadwell?'

Dale stood. 'That's right.'

'Will you follow me, please?'

Dale was conscious of the sound of both pairs of heels as they clacked across the marble floor and into a passage until they reached a series of closed doors.

The girl looked back to where they'd just come from. In an undertone, and as though someone might be ready to pounce on her for any indiscretion, she said, 'Don't take any notice of Major Barking. His barking's worse than his biting.' She looked at Dale and giggled. 'D'ya get it?'

Dale nodded and smiled weakly. 'Thank you for enlightening me.'

The girl nodded and gave a timid knock.

'Enter!'

'Your noon appointment, Major Barking.'

Without looking up, the man behind the desk said, 'Thank you, Brenda. Show Mr Treadwell in.'

Brenda winked and closed the door quietly behind her as Dale stepped further into the room. The open sash window didn't disguise the smell of recent cigarette smoke.

For a few moments Dale stood there, her raincoat dripping. She glanced round at the shelves full of books, the papers and files strewn on the desk where Major Barking was making notes on a large jotter. She cleared her throat. He looked up, then removed his glasses and raised an enquiring eyebrow.

'Who are you? I'm expecting Mr Dale Treadwell.'

'*I'm* Dale Treadwell.'

'Really? Hmm.' He looked closer at her. 'By the name on your letter I thought you were a man.' He sounded put out, as though he'd been hoodwinked.

'Oh, I'm sorry. I always go by Dale. My real name's Dulcie. Does it make any difference I'm a woman . . . sir?' she added quickly with a smile.

He ignored the question as he studied her. By the length of his body above the desk he was tall, with a narrow face and long-fingered hands. The seconds ticked by from the clock on the wall behind her. She became uncomfortable under the penetrating gaze. Had she sounded rude? Had she lost her chance of working at something that sounded far more interesting than her current job? Something valuable towards the war effort, though she couldn't think what. She shifted her feet, then her eye

105

strayed towards a gun on the far edge of his desk. Her smile wavered. Why did he have a gun on his desk? Was this normal or had he just used it like a prop in a theatre to disconcert her? She licked her lips, then drew herself up.

'Right, Miss . . . er . . . Miss Treadwell—' he narrowed his eyes at her '—you'd better take a seat. Can I offer you a cigarette?'

'Um, no, thanks.'

He nodded.

'Just as well. Bad habit.' He lifted one from a silver cigarette case, and without consulting her, lit up.

Dale pulled out the visitor's chair and set it close to his desk. She hesitated, then removed her raincoat. She wouldn't show him she was intimidated in any way by the sight of his gun. There was a long silence. She crossed her legs and forced herself to look at him directly. Unsmiling, he barked out questions, and she bit back a nervous giggle, remembering Brenda's words.

'Do you speak German?' He inhaled, then blew the smoke in a stream over the top of Dale's head.

'Reasonably. We once had an Austrian maid, Ursula Fassbender. She knew very little English so she used to talk to us in German, and I liked answering back in German because it sounded so different – I suppose it was a bit of fun for a child.'

'How old were you at the time?'

'Seven, maybe eight.'

He clicked his tongue, either with disappointment or impatience, she couldn't tell.

'I asked her to give me lessons, so she did when I came home after school. She was with us until I was about fifteen, then one day she wasn't there.'

He tapped his fingers impatiently on the desk.

'But you read and write in German?'

'I did. I'm afraid I haven't kept it up much since she left.'

'Do you ever read German books?'

Dale shook her head. 'Not really. Except *Der Kleine Prinz*,' she said, smiling to overcome her embarrassment. 'I read that in German.'

'Ah, Antoine de Saint-Exupéry. You understood it?'

'Yes. It wasn't difficult.' She suddenly remembered. 'Oh, and I do like Goethe's poetry . . . and, um, Hermann Hesse.'

'Hmm.' Major Barking tapped a long ash into the ashtray, then looked at her properly for the first time.

'*Bitte, sprechen Sie mir auf Deutsch.*'

Dale hesitated. '*Was soll ich den sagen?*'

'Anything,' he answered abruptly in English.

Dale licked her lips. It had been several years since she'd spoken German. Racking her brain she opened her mouth, praying something clever would come out. But nothing happened.

'I can't think—'

'When did you start doing crossword puzzles?'

'Since I was a child. I—'

'*Auf Deutsch, bitte!*'

She took in a breath, then began to tell him about her enjoyment of crosswords – she couldn't remember the word for 'puzzle' so she used the English word – and how she actually made them up as a child and they were printed in her comic every month. The major's expression didn't change. His head remained tilted to one side, constantly dragging on his cigarette as he listened intently, occasionally inter-rupting with another question. By the end of the session, she was mentally exhausted. She'd somehow managed to dredge up the words to give him detailed enough answers, but it had been a strain.

'What about your father?' he asked in German.

'He's in Scotland,' Dale said in English. Her brain was exhausted. 'He's an engineer. Something to do with radios. My mother and I aren't absolutely sure. He says it's hush-hush.'

'Hmm. I think I can guess.' He stubbed out his cigarette. She opened her mouth to ask him but he held his hand up. 'Your German's not bad though your grammar leaves a lot to be desired, but that's presumably the fault of the maid who taught you. However, you have a certain flair which could be useful.'

Does he intend sending me to Germany as a spy?

Her mind reeled.

'And you keep up with the war news, I imagine.' It was a statement.

'Oh, yes. I'm a reporter. I have to. But I'm interested anyway.'

He leant forward, all attention. 'On a newspaper?'

'Yes. The *Kensington Evening Post.*'

He snorted. 'Hmm. I would have thought you could do better than that.' He gave her another penetrating look. 'Why did you answer the crossword competition in the *Daily Telegraph?*'

'Because it's my father's newspaper.'

'Do you read it?'

'When I get the chance.'

He nodded and jotted some notes on the pad, then glanced up. 'I imagine you can type.'

'Yes . . . and shorthand. I came top in both on my course.'

'Hmm.' He regarded her with what seemed like a grudging respect. 'Well, you're probably wondering what you're here for.'

108

Dale sat entirely still, waiting for this man with his cigarette and terse manner to speak. What on earth would he say?

'But before I go any further, I must ask you to sign the Official Secrets Act.' He passed over a document.

Dale hesitated. 'Before I sign, Major, I'd like to know what I'm actually signing for.'

'You're signing for never breathing a word about what I am about to tell you. So before I give you any explanation I need you to sign and date it.'

She did as she was told, remembering to sign her name as Dulcie.

He glanced at her signature. His mouth tightened a fraction, but he didn't comment. Instead, he looked right into her eyes with his own steely ones.

'This is the most important document you will ever sign, Miss Treadwell. If we offer you a job and you give any *hint* of gossip or discussion about the work with *anyone at all*, you'll be severely punished with no recourse. That could mean imprisonment for up to thirty years . . . or worse.' He threw a glance at the gun.

Dale's eyes followed his. Her scalp prickled. She took in a steadying breath.

'Not saying a word goes for your family, your friends—' his eyes never left her face '—and includes the boyfriend. Presumably you have one?' His expression forbade her to deny it.

She fought a bubble of anger. How dare he make any assumption at all when she'd only been in his office for less than half an hour. It was none of his business whether or not she had a boyfriend. Glenn's face slipped into her mind and she shook the image away.

She swallowed hard. 'I don't have a boyfriend and I *can* keep a secret.'

'I hope so.' He stared at her. 'We have to defeat Jerry at all costs. We're looking for men and women to work as a close-knit team in a top-secret location. It requires patience and long hours cooped up. It's vital work which will shorten the war.' He caught her in his stare. 'Shall I go on?'

'Yes, please,' Dale said. Unconsciously, she tilted forward, every nerve alert to what he might tell her.

'Your German, limited though it is, will doubtless be useful. And we're interested in journalists as well as a host of other skills.' He lit another cigarette, then looked at her. 'Do you play chess?'

She shook her head. Would this be the deciding factor? Her heart thudded in her chest as she kept her eyes fixed on him.

He drew on his cigarette.

'Well, you seem to have the kind of brain for cryptic clues in crosswords.' He exhaled a stream of smoke in Dale's direction. 'Unusual in girls.'

'I'm nearly twenty-two,' Dale retorted. 'Hardly a girl.'

'Same goes for women,' he said, irritatingly.

Not another one. Why do men always assume women aren't as clever?

She took a deep breath.

'So, Miss Treadwell, if I offered you the job right now, would you accept?'

Faces flashed before her, all with different expressions: her mother's worried look, Dad's approving nudge.

She opened her mouth before she changed her mind. 'Yes.'

Major Barking nodded and made another note, then picked up the telephone receiver and snapped out an order.

'Oh, Major . . .?' Dale began when he'd put down the receiver.

'Yes?'

'What will my salary be?'

He allowed a pause before he spoke. 'Two pounds ten a week. Out of that is your rent wherever you're billeted.'

Disappointingly, it was only five shillings more than she was already earning. But this sounded as if she'd be much closer to the war. Her heart began to beat fast.

'What town would I be working in?'

''Fraid we have to keep it under wraps for the time being.'

'Well, I'd need to tell my mother my postal address. She'll be on her own if I've left home.'

'If we offer you a job, then all the information you'll need will be sent to you. If that's the case you won't have much notice – could be only two or three days – at most, a week.'

'I can be ready.'

'Then that'll be all, Miss Treadwell.' He pressed a button on his desk, then stood and came round to her side of the desk.

Dale rose to her feet and gathered her raincoat. 'Thank you, Major.'

'Just one thing,' he said, his eyes on her face. 'I think you might very well have a place with us – that is, so long as you learn to think before you open that pretty mouth of yours.'

Damned cheek.

There was a knock at the door and Brenda appeared in the doorway.

'Can you escort Miss Treadwell back to reception, Brenda, and see that she's signed out.'

'Yes, sir.'

'Thank you for your time, Major Barking,' Dale said, her voice cool from his last remark about her mouth. She forced herself to meet his eyes, the image of his gun she was sure he'd deliberately put on the desk in front of her growing large in her mind. What if something slipped out unintentionally? There was obviously no punishment they would discount.

For a fleeting instant she wondered whether she was getting into something she'd later regret. Then she pulled herself together. This was war work. Doing her bit. For all his manner, Major Barking seemed to think she might be useful. She'd have to prove to him his judgement of her was correct.

As though he'd tapped into her thoughts, for the first time he gave her a smile as he held open the door for the two women to pass through.

Dale hurried straight to the café where she and Jane had arranged to meet afterwards.

'Well,' Jane said, rising from the table as Dale walked in. 'Did you get it?'

'Can we order tea first?' Dale said. 'I really need one.' She shrugged off her now sodden raincoat and folded it over the back of her chair.

Jane poured the tea, then raised an eyebrow. 'So? Spill the beans, then.'

'I can't,' Dale said. 'I had to sign the Official Secrets Act without even knowing what my job would be, or even where I'd be working. I was warned if I give even a hint of where I'm going or what I'm doing to anyone, including family, I could be severely punished – thrown into prison – even shot.'

Jane chuckled. 'Don't be so melodramatic, Dale.'

'I'm not,' Dale said, stirring a lump of sugar into her tea. 'If I tell you I was interviewed by an officer in full regalia and a gun on his desk – I think deliberately to scare me – you might get a clue as to what I've gone through.'

Jane's mouth fell open. 'Blimey!'

Dale took a sip of tea. 'I haven't even been offered anything yet, but I get the impression the work – whatever it is – is vital for the war effort. I'd like to get involved – I need something to get my teeth into. To take my mind off—'

'You're not still carrying the torch for that American?' Jane interrupted, looking over the rim of her cup with narrowed eyes.

'If you mean Glenn, no, I'm not,' Dale shot back. 'And I don't want to discuss him.'

'It's only that—'

'Stop!' Dale raised her voice, the palm of her hand up towards her friend. 'No more . . . please.'

Jane stared at her.

'All right, if that's how you want it. I just thought I might be able to help. We've been friends for ever so you should know you can tell me anything and it would never go any further.'

Dale swallowed. How could she have been so horrible to Jane? Someone who'd always been loyal to her, stuck up for her when she'd lost her temper, giggled together from when they were children. They were more like sisters than friends. She went to take Jane's hand but instead knocked over the small jug of milk. A sharp-eyed young waitress flew over to clean the table.

'From what you've told Rhoda and me,' Jane said when the girl had mopped up, 'it sounds as though he was just an American passing through, and you were both infatuated. But maybe it's time to meet someone else.'

Dale shook her head. 'It wasn't infatuation.' She wiped her eye with the edge of her napkin. 'I was so stupid, Jane. I let him— Oh, you don't want to know.'

'Oh, Dale, don't say you let him make love to you.'

'I did,' Dale said miserably. 'I'm twenty-one, for Pete's sake.

Supposed to be an adult but I was a bloody virgin still. I loved him and he said he loved me. It seemed the most natural thing in the world. We were supposed—' she choked '—supposed to see one another the next day before he was sent off to—' She stopped herself in time. His going to Berlin was confidential information. 'Well, sent off on his next assignment.'

'Hmm.' Jane studied her. 'I suppose you never know by looks alone.'

'I was the one who suggested it,' Dale said flatly.

Jane raised a surprised eyebrow. 'Really? Well, then, he might have been genuine.' She paused. 'What did he do? You've never said.'

'He's a broadcaster for one of the Chicago stations.'

'Do you know which one?'

Dale shook her head.

'You know, Dale, I'm wondering if something's happened you haven't thought about, and he's still trying to get in touch with you.'

'Jane, can we change the subject . . . please?'

Chapter Twelve

Euston Station was not the freshest smelling place on Tuesday evening, just five days later. Trying hard not to inhale the fumes from the huge beasts thundering in, smoke and steam belching from their engines, or groaning their way out of the station, Dale half ran up the platform gripping her suitcase. She'd crossed her gas mask and handbag over her chest but at every step she could feel them thumping against her. The gas mask was just one more thing to think about. They'd been handed out as soon as the war started, but apart from the one time she and Mother had practised putting theirs on, when Dale thought she would suffocate in the attempt, and the revolting rubber smell had stayed in her nostrils for days, she frequently forgot to take hers with her. Today should have been one of those days.

The station was heaving with servicemen from all the forces, some of them waiting on the platform for their train, embracing their wives and girlfriends, others pouring excitedly out of trains which had just arrived, frantically looking for friends and family. At a distance, their uniforms made them all look the same, as though they were soldiers in a toy box. But close up so many of them looked even younger than herself. What would happen to them when the action really began? It didn't bear thinking about.

The blasted traffic had been worse than she'd expected, especially as she hadn't left herself nearly enough time for a relaxed journey to the station. Her taxi driver had tried hard to dodge the worst of it but he'd often struggled to get through. But it wouldn't have mattered how much time she'd allowed herself, she knew she would be on edge until she arrived at this place called Bletchley where she was to spend the next months – maybe years – and had it explained what she was to do. She didn't even know where she'd be billeted. All she had was a brief letter in her handbag telling her she would be met at Bletchley station, where she'd be taken to Station X, and a postal address she could give to her mother and father, and only her friends she could completely trust – dear Jane and Rhoda. Box III c/o The Foreign Office. That was it.

If only she could have let Glenn know how to reach her . . . but he was in the past now. Her eyes pricked with his memory, but she immediately reprimanded herself. She had a job to do and she was damn well going to do it.

Now, as she stood waiting on the platform to board the train, a figure deliberately placed himself in front of her.

'I was before you,' she said crossly as she addressed the middle-aged man in a pin-striped suit. He ought to have better manners at his age.

To her chagrin he immediately raised his hat and stepped to the side. 'Sorry, miss. You seemed so preoccupied I thought you were meeting someone.'

She seemed to be cross all the time lately. Irritable with her mother. Furious with her father. Angry with herself. She smarted as she remembered Major Barking's insinuation that she might not be able to keep her mouth shut.

Dale battled her way through the train's already packed corridors, filled with people sitting on their cases. A tall soldier clad in khaki slid open one of the compartment doors.

'I'm just leaving to have a cigarette. You're welcome to have my seat.'

'What – just for five minutes?' Dale said.

'Nah. You can keep it. Pretty girl like you shouldn't have to stand.' He waved her inside.

'Here, love.' Another soldier patted the empty seat beside him. 'I'd rather have your company any day than old Shorty out there.'

Dale smiled. 'Thanks.'

'Can I put your case up on the rack?'

'How kind. Thank you.'

'Whereabouts are you off to?'

'Bletchley.' As soon as she said it, she shivered. But if he was going further, he'd see for himself where she got off. He didn't strike her as tucking away that piece of information to report her.

'Listen for the conductor to call it out,' he said. 'With all the signs being taken down, we have to rely on hearing our station announced if we don't recognise it.'

Some seventy-five minutes later the train slowed down.

'Bletchley. This is Bletchley.'

The soldier pulled her case down. 'Excuse us, mate. This young lady needs to alight.'

Holding her case, he slid back the compartment door to the corridor, then pulled down the sash window to grab the outside handle. The door swung open and he jumped down the step and set her case on the platform, with Dale following.

'Good luck,' he said, giving her a wink.

'You, too. And thank you.'

He gave a mock salute and hopped back onto the train,

hanging out of the window to wave goodbye as the train pulled away.

She felt almost as though her best friend had vanished, leaving her all alone on the wide deserted platform. Dale blinked as she eyed the stretch of dismal grey concrete. Bletchley didn't appear to be anyone else's destination. She waited five minutes, then heaving a sigh she walked towards the exit and bumped into a tall lanky young man.

'Oh, I beg your pardon,' he said, doffing his cap. 'Larry Burton at your service. I'm from the Park. Sorry I'm a few minutes late. Are you Miss Parsons or—?'

'I'm Dale – Dulcie Treadwell, and I've been told to report to Station X. Or should it be Station Ten?'

He looked puzzled. 'We call it Station X – what BP stands for.'

'BP?'

'Bletchley Park – or just "the Park".' Larry glanced at a small sheet of paper. He tutted. 'I'm supposed to be meeting you and a Miss Sonia Parsons.' His eyes travelled the length of the platform and raised a disappointed expression to Dale. 'Did you notice any other female on the train who looked as though she was bound for Bletchley?'

'No.' It seemed a rather pointless question. 'They were nearly all soldiers and I was the only one who got off.'

The young man shrugged. 'It doesn't look as though she's coming so we might as well get going.' He took her case. 'Right. The motor's just outside.'

The first thing she noticed was a high chain-link fence on the side of the tracks topped by circles of barbed wire. She felt her heart pump in her chest. Another reminder of the war, though thankfully the Germans hadn't yet started any bombing. But that could all change overnight.

Unconsciously, she crossed her fingers, praying her mother would keep safe.

Larry Burton put her case in the boot of a shabby black car and opened the passenger door. When she was settled, he started the engine.

'How many miles is it?'

'No more'n a few minutes' drive,' Larry said, 'so you can register you've arrived and then I'll take you to your digs if it's no further than the town.'

'I don't know where I'm billeted,' Dale said. 'I haven't been told anything.'

She was beginning to feel nervous that it was already getting dusk and she had no idea where she was. Or, for that matter, where was Miss Parsons?

Larry chatted away but she was too tired and distracted with her thoughts to give him anything more than monosyllabic answers, thankful he didn't seem to notice. The motor's engine sounded loud through the quiet countryside, passing small, neat fields, some with cattle who had already bedded down for the night. Larry's foot constantly pedalled the accelerator as though he were playing a piano – badly – then every few seconds pushed down hard on the brake as he rounded the bends in the narrow lanes.

'Here we are.' He pulled up at a pair of imposing iron gates where an armed guard stepped from the brick sentry box, glanced at Larry's identification paper and waved him through.

The motor's tyres crackled and crunched up the gravel drive. Dale narrowed her eyes against the gloom, trying to get a view of the front of the house, partially obscured by trees, one of them an enormous Wellingtonia. A few wooden outbuildings and cottages were scattered around the main house.

119

'This is it,' he said as he hopped out and opened her door, then retrieved her luggage.

She arranged her gas mask and shoulder bag straps back across her chest as he went in front with her case. She was only a few yards from the entrance when it happened. One moment she was fine, looking up at the sprawling Victorian mansion, the next she was spread out on the gravel, her bare hands splayed as she used them to protect her face.

'My goodness, what happened?' Larry Burton was instantly by her side.

'I must've caught my heel in the gravel.'

'Can you walk?'

'I think so,' she said, a little shakily.

'Here, take my arm.'

She grabbed his thin arm, surprisingly strong, and felt herself being hauled up.

'Take a few deep breaths.'

She gasped at the sudden pain shooting up her leg as she tried to take in some air.

'Where does it hurt?'

'My foot.'

'You'd better hang on to me.'

It felt as if someone was stabbing her foot with a knife and twisting it. Gratefully, she clutched his arm as she limped towards the solid arched entrance.

Larry rang the bell. After a pause the door opened. A woman in tweed skirt and cardigan, her brown hair scraped back in an unbecoming bun, stepped forward. She couldn't have been more than forty.

'Ah, you're—?'

'Dulcie Treadwell.' The pain in her foot was making her head swim.

Larry, who was still gripping her arm, spoke up.

'I'm afraid she's just fallen over so she needs to sit down.'

'Oh, bad luck.' The woman gave her a sympathetic glance. 'You'd better come straight to the sick room. Is it your ankle?'

'It's my foot.'

'Well, Nurse will sort you out.' She paused. 'By the way, I'm Mrs Jones, in charge of registration. But don't worry – I'll do it on your behalf, now I've seen you.'

'I'm sorry to be a nuisance,' Dale said, miserably.

'Can happen to anyone,' Mrs Jones said briskly. She glanced at Larry. 'Where's Miss Parsons?'

'No idea. She didn't turn up.'

'Hmm.' Mrs Jones frowned. 'Well, I expect we'll hear from her sooner or later.'

With Larry on one side and Mrs Jones on the other, each firmly taking one of her arms, Dale limped along a vast panelled hall where people were hurrying to and fro, clutching piles of papers. A steady hum of voices and the whir of machinery emanated from closed doors. In a side corridor, when Dale thought she couldn't go another step, Mrs Jones led her into a small ward, smelling strongly of antiseptic, with only one occupant, a young woman about her own age, who was sitting on a chair by the side of her bed. She looked up from her book.

'I've brought you a companion, Isobel,' Mrs Jones said.

'Oh, dear, what's happened to you?' the delicate-looking girl asked.

'She's twisted her foot,' Mrs Jones said. With Larry's help she took Dale to the adjacent bed and sat her on the edge, then gently lifted her legs and swung her onto the bed. 'That'll take the pressure off.' She glanced at Isobel. 'Where's Nurse Bull?'

121

'She's in the kitchen where she keeps the medicines,' Isobel said. 'She'll be back in a tick.'

Dale's foot was throbbing. She could feel her stocking tighten against the swelling. *Please, God, don't let me have broken anything.*

'I'll go and get some ice,' Mrs Jones said. 'Thank you, Larry. We'll let you know when the next recruit comes in. Let's hope it will be Miss Parsons.'

'Thank you, Mr Burton,' Dale managed before he and Mrs Jones disappeared. She turned to Isobel. 'Stupid thing to do. I'm so cross.' Then she remembered her manners. 'Well, I know you're Isobel. I'm Dale Treadwell.'

'Isobel St John.' The girl put out a slender hand across the gap. 'And in case you're wondering if I've got anything catching, I'm here for some Beecham's Powders. I've got my monthlies and they do seem to help but I forgot to bring any.'

Dale wasn't used to someone she'd only just met speaking so openly about Aunt Flo, as she and her friends called it. She was about to murmur something sympathetic when a plump woman in an ill-fitting nurse's uniform burst in.

'Here you are, Miss St John.' She held out a couple of small packets, then stopped abruptly as her gaze fell on Dale. 'Oh, a new recruit. What's the matter with *you*, then?'

Dale recoiled.

'This is Dale Treadwell, dear Nurse Bull, needing your kindest attention.' Isobel looked up and treated the woman with what looked like an insincere smile. 'She's sprained her foot. Mrs Jones has gone to get some ice.'

The nurse pursed her lips. '*I'll* be the one to decide if ice is required,' she said, sounding distinctly peeved. 'And I'm certainly not surprised you twisted your foot,' she added as she took up a chair and set it next to Dale's bed. 'Those high heels are more appropriate for a party.' She grimaced at the sight. 'Roll down your stocking, please.'

Dale was about to say something when she remembered Major Barking's offensive comment about thinking before she opened her 'pretty mouth'. She closed her lips tightly and unhooked her stocking suspender, swearing inwardly at the sight of a ladder already running from her knee. She tried to bend forward to roll it down, but the act of bringing up her injured foot caused her to gasp.

'Do you think I've broken anything?'

'Let me have a look.' Nurse Bull took Dale's leg and firmly placed it on the lap of her broad starched apron. 'Bruise is already coming out,' she said, triumphantly, using a thick finger to feel round the area as Dale winced. 'I'd better give you the same as St John. That should stop the pain.'

She was interrupted by Mrs Jones carrying a small aluminium bucket.

'Ah, there you are, Nurse Bull,' she said, holding out the bucket. 'Ice for Miss Treadwell's foot.'

'Thank you for your trouble but I'm fully able to take care of my patients.'

'That's as maybe,' came the unruffled tones of Mrs Jones, 'but the sooner the ice is applied, the quicker the swelling will go down.' She ignored Nurse Bull's flinty glare and turned to Dale. 'Is anything broken?'

'I doubt it,' Nurse Bull chimed in, 'as she wouldn't have been able to bear any weight on it at all. She'll have to stay here in the sickroom,' she added triumphantly, 'so I can keep an eye on it.'

Just my luck to be under her observation.

'I think that's the answer,' Mrs Jones said, relief coating her words. She glanced at Dale. 'I'll leave you to it, then. I'm sure you'll feel better in the morning.' She vanished.

While Nurse Bull busied herself getting Dale and Isobel some water to dissolve the powders, Isobel said:

'Can I make you a cup of tea? I'm having one.'

'That would be heavenly.'

A few minutes later Dale sipped the tea, hot and soothing, but the pain had wiped out all her energy. She gave a groan.

'Poor you,' Isobel said, swallowing the powdered water and pulling a face. She looked at her watch. 'Oh, I'd better get back to the Hut.'

'The hut?' Dale questioned. 'Do you mean you live in a hut?'

'No, it's where we work.'

'But it's so late.'

Isobel chuckled. 'Not for me. My shift is four 'til midnight.'

'That sounds awful.'

'Not so awful as the midnight to eight in the morning. That's the killer one.'

Dale wondered what shift she'd be given. As though Isobel read her thoughts, she added, 'We take it in turns, one particular shift for a week. Three shifts cover twenty-four hours. It does nothing for your digestion when you find yourself eating dinner at three in the morning and the next day when you change shifts you're back to normal.'

'Does everyone work in the hut?' Dale asked.

'No. Some are in the main house – boffins, mostly. There are quite a few Huts – with a capital "H".' She grinned. 'They're larger than they sound and can accommodate a whole team. Some of the workers sleep in them as well – in a curtained-off room.'

Dale gave an inward shudder. It sounded ghastly – like a school dormitory. Then she shook herself. It was *war* that was ghastly and from what she'd seen on Pathé News, people in countries that had already been invaded were

124

having a shocking time. She vowed not to grumble again, even silently.

'What sort of work do you do, Isobel?' she asked curiously.

Isobel's jaw dropped as she stared at Dale in horror.

Dale's cheeks burned as it dawned on her. Not here even five minutes when she was asking a stranger to breach the Official Secrets Act. She could have kicked herself. Wishing she was anywhere but in the sick room of Bletchley Park, she quickly said, 'I'm sorry, I shouldn't have asked.'

'No, you shouldn't.' Isobel's expression was serious. Then it relaxed into a smile. 'Just be glad it was me you said that to, and not Nurse Bull. She'd have had you for mincemeat.'

After Isobel had wished her good luck and disappeared, Dale remained on top of the made-up bed, looking round the sparse ward with its drab colouring, the exact shade of nicotine, and the disinfectant smell. She felt bewildered. She'd been plucked from everything she was familiar with and dropped into a world where nothing made sense. Living, sleeping and working in huts, not allowed to say what you were doing, not knowing where she was to be billeted, her first night in the sick bay, Sonia Parsons not turning up, a dragon of a nurse . . .

Dale sighed. She'd said she wanted to take up the position. And even though she'd had no idea what she was in for, she'd jolly well have to grin and bear it.

Chapter Thirteen

'Here, put this ice bag on your foot,' Nurse Bull said. 'Hold it there until I tell you.'

Dale dutifully did what she was told as Nurse Bull bustled about, smoothing bedspreads and plumping pillows on empty beds.

Busy doing nothing, Mother would say.

After a quarter of an hour Nurse Bull strode over.

'Right, that should be long enough.' She took the bag. 'Just rest with your feet up.' Glancing at Dale, she said, 'You'll be wanting something to eat, I suppose.'

At the mention of food, Dale realised how hungry she was.

'That would be lovely, thank you.'

She hadn't eaten anything before setting off. It had been too upsetting leaving her mother, even though she'd assured her she would phone as often as she could and write regularly. And when she had time off she'd go and see her. But her mother had simply shaken her head and kissed her, then stood at the door to wave a tearful goodbye.

Dale looked up as Nurse Bull put a tray of food in her hands.

'That should do you,' she said. 'Then after you've eaten, the best thing for you is to get undressed and have a good

126

night's sleep. Your foot should be a lot better in the morning. Well, it'd better be – you're not much use to us if you take time off as soon as you arrive.'

'Thank you, Nurse.' Dale only just managed a neutral tone.

'I'll be next door then, doing some paperwork.'

Dale removed the cover from the plate, which disclosed two fried eggs, a sausage, a heap of baked beans and two rounds of toast. She'd never be able to eat all that. But ten minutes later, she'd wolfed the lot. Feeling a little more like herself, and although her foot was still throbbing, she decided to try putting her weight on it. It was the wrong thing to do. She gave a sharp intake of breath at the wrenching pain. Maybe it was best to take Nurse Bull's advice after all.

A sound like water swishing on the shore awoke her. Sleepily, Dale opened her eyes, wondering where on earth she was. More swishing noises directed her gaze over some freshly made beds to the window, where Nurse Bull was opening the second pair of curtains with a flourish.

She'd made it to Bletchley Park. But she'd only got as far as the sickroom. Still, the sun was already up and she felt more refreshed than she had for ages – since . . . She shook herself, refusing to let her mind fill in the image of Glenn. Instead, she deliberately turned on her brightest smile.

'Good morning, Nurse.'

Nurse Bull turned round. 'Ah, there you are.' She looked at her watch. 'You've slept for nine hours and twenty minutes!'

It was almost an accusation. Dale decided to ignore the comment.

'What time is it?'

Nurse Bull consulted her watch again. 'Seven minutes after eight.'

Dale put her legs over the edge of the bed, bringing Nurse Bull over.

'Let me look at that foot first before you put any weight on it.'

Dale stuck her foot out. The woman bent low and surprisingly gently took hold of it. She pushed Dale's toes down, then back up again.

'Does that hurt?'

'Not much . . . well, maybe a little.'

'And this?' Nurse Bull slowly turned the foot from one side to the other.

'Ouch.'

'Yes, I thought so. The bruise has come out but most of the swelling's gone down.' She glanced at Dale. 'Let me see you walk.'

Dale gingerly took a few steps. Her foot felt sore but nothing like the pain of yesterday evening.

'You won't be able to get those on.' Nurse Bull nodded to the offending shoes. 'Have you brought anything more sensible?'

'I've got a flat pair in my case.'

Dale found her light brogues in her shoe bag and slipped one on her left foot, the good one. The other pinched her but she wouldn't let the ogre know.

'They'll be fine,' she said. 'I really want to get started today – and of course find my digs.'

'Best get washed and dressed first. I'll show you to the bathroom.'

By the time Dale was ready and on her way from the bathroom to the ward, a short, plump young woman with merry eyes and wearing a smart navy-blue suit waylaid her.

'Miss Treadwell?'

'Yes.'

'I've been asked to take you to Jumbo – I mean Commander Travis,' she quickly corrected herself, 'right away, if your leg is up to it. He's the Deputy Director. He likes to see all the new recruits.' She paused. 'I'm Ruth Robins, by the way.'

Dale walked by the side of Miss Robins along what looked like the same dark panelled passages of yesterday evening, then up a sweeping staircase, each step causing Dale to wince. Miss Robins looked at her curiously but said nothing, knocking firmly on a door.

'Enter!'

'I'll leave you to it,' Miss Robins said, and scampered back down the staircase.

Dale took a deep breath and walked in.

A stocky figure – presumably how he got his nickname 'Jumbo', Dale thought, hiding a smile – he was dressed in civilian clothes and seated at a large, immaculately laid-out desk writing notes on a large pad. Thank heavens there was no gun. He looked up briefly with a neutral expression.

'Take a seat, Miss Treadwell.' Without pausing he continued, 'I understand you're fluent in German.'

'I'm not fluent but I have conversational German.' Dale felt a prickle of apprehension. Was he about to test her? 'But I still don't know what you want me to do.'

'All in good time. You'll be working in Hut 6 – probably the busiest one. Bletchley Park has been set up to intercept and crack German codes.' He paused, his eyes fixed on hers.

A shiver ran across Dale's shoulders.

'I'll leave Mrs Wilcox to explain the machine you'll be working on. The main thing is, whatever you're told, whatever work you carry out, you are not to discuss it with anyone else at the Park except the people in your own Hut. Never forget you've signed the Official Secrets Act. Any questions, see Mrs Wilcox – and if she's not around, or you deem it extremely important, then report to *me.*' He looked at her, his eyes alert. 'Is that clear?'

'Yes, sir.'

A frisson of anticipation raced through her. She couldn't wait to start.

'I'm sure you'll soon fit in.' He glanced at her leg. 'Were you limping when you came in just now?'

'Yes,' she admitted. 'I stupidly fell over on the gravel just outside the entrance when I arrived yesterday evening.'

'Hmm.' He looked directly at her. 'Did you report this to Nurse Bull?'

'She, um, looked after me last night.'

He gave a slight smile. 'Good.' He picked up a small sheet of paper from his desk and handed it to her. 'Your billet. It's a private house in the town. I'd rest that foot of yours today, and your duties can start tomorrow morning.' He frowned. 'Any questions?'

There'd be no point. He obviously wasn't going to say anything at all about the 'duties' he'd mentioned.

'I don't think so.'

'Get someone to drive you to your billet as it'll be a bit of a trek with your leg.'

'Thank you . . . sir.'

He nodded. 'You might find it useful to get yourself a bicycle.'

Without waiting for an answer, he went back to his desk and picked up the telephone receiver. She saw herself out.

Nurse Bull was nowhere in sight when Dale collected her case from the sick room, and she made her getaway as quickly as possible. There was no one about – she imagined everyone was already at work – when a girl with pale blonde hair abruptly pushed past her as Dale tried to reach the front door.

130

'Excuse *me*,' Dale said.

'Oh, sorry,' she said, 'I'm in *rather* a hurry. Just arrived and have to register.' She stepped aside and glanced at Dale. 'Do you have any idea where that would be?' Her accent was moneyed, as though she was used to servants running at her beck and call.

'I think you have to see Mrs Jones first to register,' Dale said. 'Well, she's the one I saw yesterday evening, anyway.'

'That's when I was supposed to be here, but I had no way of letting anyone know.' The girl rolled her eyes. 'My train was held up for hours. We just sat there. No food or drink. The dining car had long closed. Good thing Mummy had the forethought to pack me a full lunch box.'

Dale blinked. 'Would you happen to be Sonia Parsons?'

The girl's eyes widened. 'Good gracious. Are you psychic?'

'Everyone was looking for you,' Dale said bluntly. 'The chap who was meeting us at the station yesterday evening, and Mrs Jones.'

'And there was me trying to find a taxi this morning but no luck, so I had to walk.' Sonia giggled. 'Thank goodness I managed to bunk in with three others in their digs, though it wasn't the most comfortable night in one room. I won't tell you where the fourth one slept.' She giggled again.

Sonia Parsons sounded a right little madam. Feeling mean, Dale hoped she wouldn't be working in the same Hut.

'Well, you're here now.' Dale stuck out her hand. 'Dale Treadwell. Pleased to meet you.' She noticed the girl's hand was long-fingered, smooth and white, with bright pink varnished nails.

'You already know *my* name.' Another giggle.

She's enough to drive anyone crazy. How on earth did she get recruited?

'I do hope we'll be working near one another,' Sonia said. 'Have they told you where you'll be?'

'I'm not starting until tomorrow so I'm not exactly sure.' Dale paused. 'But I don't think we're supposed to ask one another anyway.'

'Surely *that* can't be a secret.' Sonia's china-blue eyes were wide.

'Probably better to be safe than sorry,' Dale said briskly. 'Anyway, let's go and find Mrs Jones.' She looked round, her eyes lighting on a familiar face. 'Oh, there's Isobel.' She waved.

'Have you found your digs yet?' Isobel asked as she hurried over.

'No, I'm just on my way.' Dale stepped aside. 'Let me introduce you to our missing colleague, Sonia Parsons. She needs to register.'

'I'll take you,' Isobel immediately said, looking at the girl. 'It's in the library. You need to get it done so you can start straightaway.'

'Oh. I thought I'd get a bit of a breather first.'

'Not at BP you won't. We need all the help we can get. It's gone bananas here.'

When the two of them had vanished, Dale drew breath. She retrieved her case and made for the front door again to see a man in running shorts, panting heavily. She watched as he ignored her and ran past. Strange man. She glanced round and took in a few scattered outbuildings. They must be the Huts where she was to work. Thick smoke spewed from their chimneys and the windows looked solidly dark. Her heart sank. Surely they didn't pull the blackout blinds down in the daytime.

Resisting the urge to see where Hut 6 was located by a sign on the path running both ways and pointing to 'Huts,' she walked a few yards, then turned round to look at the house in daylight now the trees weren't obscuring her vision. She'd glimpsed part of the façade of a Victorian brick mansion in the dusk last night but hadn't realised this was a riot of architectural styles all jostling for attention. The entrance with its columns was Italianate, there were influences of Greek and Gothic decorations, a couple of what looked like Dutch gables were partly hidden at one end and there was a copper cupola at the other end for good measure. She tilted her head upwards. Every window bore another design, some with stained glass. Everything jostled and clashed. Dear oh dear. Who on earth had come up with such a mishmash?

Well, it was not a bit of good standing here criticising what was going to become her new place of work. She needed to meet her landlords and settle in. As there was no sign of Larry Burton, and if the spoilt-sounding Sonia Parsons could walk it, then she'd damn well do the same. Gritting her teeth, she began to limp towards the town.

Chapter Fourteen

Dale's foot began to throb almost immediately. She ought to be resting it, not walking to a town that could be miles away. Larry Burton and his driving had only taken minutes, but at the rate she was going it would take for ever. The road looked deserted of vehicles though a few men and women, some in uniform, were walking towards her. One or two nodded, and an RAF officer smiled and said, 'Good morning', but no one asked her if she knew where she was heading.

The sudden roar of an engine caught her unawares. She pressed herself into the hedgerow as a snazzy yellow sports car with an open top screeched to a halt just beyond her. The driver twisted his head and called out:

'Do you need a lift into town?'

Close up, Dale saw a dark-haired man with film-star looks and twinkling hazel eyes.

'I work at the Park,' he said, 'so I'm perfectly respectable.'

She didn't hesitate. 'I'd love one.'

'Hop in, then.' From inside he pushed the door open. 'Can you manage that case?' She was about to answer when he added, 'I'd better help.' He came round to the passenger side, took her case and placed it in the boot.

'I should tell you my name, so you know you're not going

off with some stranger.' He raised his cap with a sweeping bow. 'Edward Langton – Eddie to my friends.'

He smiled, as though inviting her to be one of the privileged as he settled her in the front seat. Immediately, the luxurious smell of leather wafted into her nostrils as she admired the shining walnut dashboard.

'I hope I'm not being too personal, but you looked a little awkward the way you were walking,' he commented as he put his foot down and roared on.

'I twisted my foot last night on the drive,' she said. 'It's still a bit sore.'

'Oh, bad luck. Good thing I came along when I did, then.'

'Perfect timing,' she said, lightly.

'Where are we off to?' he asked.

'My new digs in Chestnut Street.'

'I know it. It's just off the High Street.'

It was heaven to be driven in such a beautiful little car. She was only obeying Commander Travis's orders, after all. And he hadn't said the driver couldn't be attractive . . . Hiding a smile she stole a glance. He caught her and grinned.

'What is it?'

She was grateful for the breeze cooling her flushed cheeks. Thank goodness he couldn't read her mind.

'Nothing in particular. I'm just trying to take it all in.'

He chatted about the countryside and how lush it all looked at this time of year.

'Only thing is, it's all over too quickly, though I do love autumn as well.'

She listened, liking the sound of his voice, the educated enunciation. He'd obviously gone to a good school – university, more like. She felt a twinge of envy.

'Where are you from?'

Dale was startled from her reverie. 'London.'

'Ah. I'm afraid Bletchley's going to be a bit of a shock for you.'

For an instant she thought he meant her work. He gave her a swift glance.

'The town, I mean. There's not much going on here like there is in the Smoke.'

'It doesn't matter. I haven't come for the culture,' she said primly.

He laughed. 'Actually, there's usually quite a lot going on in the house. And you'd be welcomed with open arms if you can play an instrument, or sing, or act . . . any sort of entertainment.'

'I can't do any of those things,' Dale said, fervently wishing she had at least one of those skills.

'Never mind. We always need a good audience so I'm sure we can count on you.'

'Do you do anything in that line?'

'A bit of acting.'

With those looks, he would.

'Is it your main job.'

He gave a full-throated laugh. 'Not likely. It's a hobby, that's all. In real life I'm a teacher. Languages. Italian and German. Seems like they're pretty useful here.' He gave her a quick glance. 'Which Hut have they assigned you to?'

'Um . . .' She chewed her lower lip. 'I don't think I'm allowed to say.'

He chuckled. 'Security may be tight, but we're bound to run into one another again in the canteen or the library or when we have a party in the house . . . or I just happen to notice which Hut you go in.'

She ignored his last remark and said instead, 'I don't think I'll be doing much partying.'

136

He turned his head towards her. 'Oh, that's a shame. Don't you even dance – when your foot's better, that is?'

She swallowed, the memory of being held close in Glenn's arms so strong she fancied she could, even now, smell the masculine scent of him . . .

'Y-yes. I can dance.'

'Are you all right?' He threw her a swift glance.

'Yes,' she repeated, this time more firmly.

'Good,' he said. 'Good that you're all right, and good that you can dance. That's one of the main things here. Keeps us all sane.' He paused. 'Well, here we are – just coming into the town. It's only just over a mile so it's walkable from the Park, but not with a bad foot.' He sent her a sympathetic smile. 'It's a bit of a dump but you can get most things here – except clothes. There's a small department store but most of the girls go to Watford for anything special like shoes or a party frock that I'm sad you won't be needing. Oh, and there are two cinemas in the town. At least they show all the new films soon after they're out.'

Two minutes later, they turned into a street of terraced cottages. He pulled up and opened her door. She stepped out of the low seat, her skirt riding a little above her knee. She couldn't help noticing his appreciative look.

'You haven't told me your name,' he said, when he'd retrieved her case, amusement dancing in his eyes as he looked down at her. 'I do believe *that's* allowed.'

'Now you're mocking me.'

'Just teasing.'

'Then I'll let you off.' She smiled. 'Dale Treadwell.'

'Mmm. Suits you.' He paused. 'What number are we looking for?'

Dale glanced at the paper, then at the gate near where they were standing. 'Forty-three, and this is thirty-three.'

'Only a few houses along, then.'

Turning to him, Dale said, 'Thank you very much, Mr Langton. You really did come along at the right time.'

'Less of the mister,' he grinned. 'Eddie, to you.'

'Eddie, then. I can take my case now. I don't want to hold you up.'

'Not at all,' he said. 'I was glad to help a damsel in distress. But don't slip away. I've enjoyed our talk and I'd love to see you again.'

And I'd like to talk to you again, but I'm not interested in any other man in the way you're hinting.

Determined to hold herself in check, she said, 'Thank you again, Eddie. As you say, we're sure to bump into one another at one of those dances or you on the stage and me watching admiringly.'

'Now you're mocking *me*,' he grinned, pointing to himself.

'No, I mean it.'

He gave her a final swift look and pressed her hand.

'Good luck, Dale,' he said. 'And I mean that, too.'

He gave a wave and strode the short distance to his car.

Glenn's spoilt my chances of even being remotely interested in anyone else.

But she couldn't help wondering what Eddie Langton's job was at Bletchley Park.

Number forty-three looked the same as its neighbours. A small, neat front garden and a polished doorstep. Dale lifted the iron knocker on the plain front door and heard heavy footsteps. The door opened. A sturdy woman, her hair a dull light brown pulled back from her face, stood there unsmiling. She wore a spotless wrap-over pinafore and shiny brown lace-up shoes and might not have been much more than forty but looked sixty, Dale thought, her own smile fading at the woman's sullen expression.

'You must be Miss Treadwell.' There was not a glimmer of warmth in the pale eyes.

'Yes, I am. And you must be Mrs Draper.'

The woman nodded and stepped aside for Dale to enter.

'We have strict house rules here and I expect you to abide by them. Unlike the first girl, who came in at all hours, running baths, making drinks.' The woman pursed her lips.

'She was probably on night shifts,' Dale said mildly. 'Perhaps I'd better say right now I shall also be working different shifts. Unfortunately, it's the nature of the job.'

'And what might that be?'

Blast. This is a nosy one.

Dale smiled, hoping to lighten the woman's suspicious look.

'I'll be doing clerical work – for the war effort.'

The woman's eyes narrowed. 'What sort of clerical war work?'

'I shan't know exactly until I start,' Dale prevaricated.

'Well, when you know *exactly*, you'll be able to tell *me*.' The woman pursed her lips again. 'The townsfolk are always wonderin' what's goin' on up there. All those uniforms comin' and goin'. The postboy was only saying the other day he heard it's some sort of secret work—'

'If it is, then I still won't be able to say anything,' Dale interrupted, beginning to get annoyed. They hadn't even ventured out of the hallway. 'Would you be so kind as to show me to my room.'

'You'd better follow me.'

Dale hauled her suitcase up two flights of stairs to an attic room, the sloping ceilings offering little space for furniture, let alone the ability to walk around the single bed. Mrs Draper opened a cupboard with three or four wooden coat hangers swinging forlornly inside, and Dale could immediately see that the height was not enough to take her long dress or coat. Besides that, it smelt musty.

'There's some shelves for your other items.' Mrs Draper pointed out a few what looked like hastily fixed pine boards.

There wasn't even a chest of drawers to put away her underwear and private toiletries. She'd have to set them on the wonky shelves for the whole world to see. Dale grimaced behind Mrs Draper's back. The billet fell far short of what she'd expected. She wasn't looking forward to spending even one night here, never mind what might turn out to be months – or even years.

Buck up, Dale. There's a blasted war on. Stop being such a fusspot.

She set her jaw. 'Can you tell me where the bathroom is?'

'On the landing. You'll share it with Mr Draper an' me. Mind you keep it tidy and don't leave no personal things.' She paused. 'The WC is in the outhouse. We're havin' an inside one when this war's over. It'll be our treat for survivin' – if we do, that is.'

Dale's heart sank. It might be bearable in this weather but not the winter at night, stumbling down a garden path to the lavatory.

'An' don't be drawin' water for the bath at night as it wakes up Mr Draper. Baths are twice a week – Tuesdays and Thursdays. And mind you don't fill it above the line.'

'I'm mindful of the five inches of water allowed,' Dale said, 'but I'm used to a bath every night.'

'That's as maybe, but you won't be havin' no bath every night in *my* house, I can tell you that.' Mrs Draper gave a smirk. 'And it's *four* inches, not five.'

'In that case, could the days be spaced out – say, Tuesday and Friday or Thursday and Monday, for instance?'

'No. Mr Draper's worked out everything.' She looked round. 'I'm sure you'll find everything you need. The Bible's in the bedside cabinet.' She sniffed as though she'd done her bit as far as religion was concerned and gave Dale a sharp glance. 'I hope you've not brought a wireless with you.'

'As a matter of fact, I have,' Dale said, 'but I promise I won't disturb anyone. I'll only have it on very quietly to hear the news or a concert.'

'You won't be needin' it at all,' Mrs Draper said. 'No wireless. Rules is rules and we have to stick to them.' She glanced up at a clock on the wall. 'Breakfast is eight o'clock and supper at six. An' no de-vi-a-tion.'

'And lunch?' Dale couldn't resist asking.

'I don't provide no lunch,' she answered.

After her landlady had disappeared, Dale pulled a face as she set down her case. She walked round, carefully bending her head to avoid knocking herself out. The saving grace was that despite being in the attic, her room was free of cobwebs and perfectly clean. You had to give the sour-faced woman that, at least.

Dale awoke from an uncomfortable night on a mattress that felt as though it was filled with straw. She was bursting for the lavatory, but she needed to wash and dress first to face the outhouse. Bending down she pulled the bedclothes aside and looked under the bed. Yes, there was the chamber. She took it out. Sparkling clean though it was, on principle she wouldn't use it. She pushed it back under the bed.

Yesterday evening she'd forced herself to go downstairs and share a supper with her new hosts and soon found that Mrs Draper's meticulous cleanliness was her only good

141

point. Her cooking left much to be desired – at least on hers and Mrs Draper's plates. Surreptitiously throwing a glance at Mr Draper's, she noticed not only did he have a far bigger portion for one so short and podgy, he had something different altogether. Not one, but two sausages – a whole week's ration – a mound of mashed potato, leeks and gravy. By contrast she and Mrs Draper had a small portion of shepherd's pie with more carrot than meat. And what meat there was was mostly gristle.

'Pass the mustard, miss,' he said in a tone as though he was ordering a servant.

He hadn't even had the manners to introduce himself, Dale thought with disgust, after Mrs Draper told him Miss Treadwell would be working at the Big House, as she called it. Mr Draper had merely curled his lip.

'Lot of nonsense goin' on up there,' he said, his voice loud even though he spoke with his mouth full. 'Waste of bleedin' time.' His eyes were slits. 'They say at the station it's the headquarters for Littlewoods Football Pools, but I don't believe it.' He broke off with a sly smile. 'See, I just now told you where *I* work – on the railways – so you tell me what *you're* doing up there. Tit for tat – see?'

'I'm afraid I can't discuss my work with you or anyone, Mr Draper,' Dale said, smiling sweetly and keeping her eyes directly fixed on his, even though his stare gave her the creeps. 'I've signed the Official Secrets Act.'

That ought to shut him up.

'Official Secrets Act,' he sneered. 'Well, well, miss, you do think yourself important for a girl no better than she ought to be. I shan't say nothin' but I've a right to know what's goin' on under my roof. It won't go no further. You can trust me. So just tell us what's goin' on up there.'

Over my dead body.

142

'You must refrain from questioning me, Mr Draper. I find it extremely awkward.'

'I shall find out – mark my words,' he said belligerently. 'Anyway, I'd have thought you'd've joined up if you're so keen to help the war effort. A proper job for king and country. Not some bloomin' typing clerk.' He pulled an ugly face. 'Not that women are much good for anything 'cept cookin' and cleanin' and havin' babies, but it'd keep you out of mischief.'

Under her eyelids, to Dale's delight, she saw Mrs Draper throw her husband a contemptuous look. Not all was well there then. She guessed Mrs Draper wouldn't let that remark about women being good for little go without future comment.

'And what mischief do you think I could possibly get up to, Mr Draper, seeing as you've only just met me?' Dale asked, smiling. How dare he speak to her in such a rude way?

'Boys. Men. That's what I'm meanin'.' He took another huge mouthful. Some of the gravy dripped down his chin. 'I take it Mrs Draper's told you the rules. No men in your room or anywhere else in the house.'

'I wouldn't dream of bringing any friend here – boy or man, girl or woman,' Dale said, springing to her feet, not able to press down her fury. 'So if you'll excuse me, I think I'll retire to my *attic* room.'

Wishing she dared slam the door but not wanting to give either of them any cause for complaint at Bletchley Park, she merely shut it firmly, still hearing Mr Draper's booming voice about how ungrateful the youth of today was. Dale gave a groan of despair. There had to be somewhere better she could be billeted. She wondered where Isobel and Sonia were staying. If there was a spare room in the house at either of their digs it *must* be an improvement.

143

Now, unrefreshed after only a few hours' sleep, but happy to see sunlight fighting its way through the small attic windows, Dale made up her mind she was going to concentrate on the new job, which would be rewarding enough. But first the outhouse – something she hadn't come across since she'd been a small child staying at her grandmother's, when it had been a novelty.

But not now I'm older, she thought, as she opened the scullery door to the back yard and walked down the narrow path, dreading what was in store. To her amazement, no awful smell rose to greet her. The outhouse was just as spotless as everywhere else inside the cottage.

After a satisfactory breakfast of poached egg on toast and a mug of tea, she slung her bag on her shoulder ready for the walk to Bletchley Park. Thankfully, her foot was much better. The bruise had well and truly come out so it was still sore, but the swelling had gone right down and it wasn't nearly so painful. Mrs Jones's bag of ice had obviously done the trick.

Everything this morning looked more normal in the bright sunshine. A bus passed her as she approached the gravel driveway and stopped at the gates of Bletchley Park, joining several more buses which were letting off their passengers. Some of the girls, struggling with suitcases, looked as bewildered as she was. She scanned a few of their faces hoping she'd make some friends quickly to stop the awful feeling of being completely on her own. Then she pulled herself up sharply. She wasn't alone. She and all these other people were here to do an important job for their country to help fight the enemy. That's what would surely bring them together. She couldn't wait to get started.

Chapter Fifteen

At first sight, Hut 6 looked much like the others – a wooden construction of dull black shiplap boarding. As Dale hurried over, she felt a tap on her shoulder.

'Oh, am I pleased to see *you*,' Sonia Parsons said, linking her arm through Dale's. 'It's Del, isn't it?'

'No, it's Dale.'

'Oh.' She frowned. 'I've never heard that for a girl. Is it short for something?'

'No – just Dale.'

A grey-haired man appeared at the door. 'Are you the new recruits?'

'Oh, yes,' Sonia said enthusiastically. 'It's our first day.' She gave a giggle. 'I'm Sonia and this is my new friend, Dale.'

Feeling mean, Dale cringed, praying Sonia wasn't going to be hanging around her from now on. She seemed to act sillier by the minute.

'Then I'd better take you to Mrs Wilcox,' the man said. 'She's gathering a few more for your induction.' He smiled. 'I'm Roger, by the way. Come on in.'

Dale followed Roger and Sonia inside the sprawling wooden building where the stale smell of tobacco hung in the stuffy air. An insistent noise of machinery rumbled and clanged from behind several of the double row of bright green doors in the narrow mustard-painted corridor. Roger opened one of the doors to a room in semi-darkness where the blackout shutters were firmly closed. Dale took in the dozen desks, three-quarters occupied, and all by women. No one looked up. Their attention was focused on what looked like typewriters and scribbling down notes.

Dale stood for a moment riveted, watching the women, hardly believing she was here.

A dark-haired woman with her back to them at the far end stood chatting to two young women. She turned at their footsteps.

'Oh, good,' she said. 'The last two.' She studied her sheet of paper. 'Sonia Parsons and Dulcie Treadwell, I take it.'

Out of the corner of her eye Dale saw Sonia's curious glance.

'Yes, though I'm always known as Dale.'

'Not at the Park,' the woman answered abruptly.

She was a handsome-looking woman, no doubt about that. Her dark hair was pulled into a shining victory roll, which showed off her striking features to perfection. The full lips were painted a ruby red.

'Please all follow me,' Mrs Wilcox said over her shoulder as she led the way through one of the side doors marked 'Administration'.

Inside, a dozen or so chairs were spaced in a semi-circle around an oblong table with a machine placed on the top.

Mrs Wilcox nodded to them. 'Take a seat.'

Sonia immediately sat down and patted the empty chair next to her, gesturing Dale over. When the others had taken their places, Mrs Wilcox stood in front of them.

'Welcome, everyone. I'm Wanda Wilcox, your supervisor in the machine room. Please raise your hand, one by one, and say your name.'

Dale deliberately said, 'Dulcie Treadwell, but known as Dale.' Wanda Wilcox gave her a narrowed glance but said nothing.

After Sonia, a girl with a face full of freckles said, 'Peggy Johnson,' followed by a statuesque woman, her brown hair scraped back in a snood: 'Beatrice Perryman.'

Wanda Wilcox gave a nod. 'Thank you.' She looked round. 'Now you're all here because you have a vital job to do. Everyone is important and equal whatever background you're from. It's brains that count. But don't for a moment think you're going to be cracking thrilling codes all day. No. Hut 6 is probably the busiest one, but ninety per cent of what you do will be boring, mundane, routine and incredibly tiring. But *never*—' she paused to emphasise the word '—dispiriting. Knowing you're working as a team, doing your bit to make up the whole, will be reward enough and keep morale high.' She paused.

'You'll work one of three different shifts of a twenty-four-hour clock, rotating every week as the schedule on the notice board sets out. Make sure you note the mealtimes – very important if you're on the night shift or the early hours of the morning one. You must always take your meal breaks of half an hour. A weak body means a weak performance. The canteen is just beyond the park gates in Wilton Avenue. You can't miss it. WCs are in a separate block near here.'

She looked around.

'You will be assigned a desk and a machine like the one on the table—' she pointed to it '—which is a copy of the one used in Germany, called the Enigma. Before I go into further detail, I want to remind you that you have all signed the Official Secrets Act. Whatever you see or hear or decode in the Hut will not, under any circumstances, be discussed with fellow associates in other Huts, neither friends nor family. Any hint of this, or mention of what we are hoping to achieve here at Station X – code name for the Park – will be treated with extreme gravity. You will be instantly dismissed and it could mean imprisonment. We trust all of you to maintain the utmost secrecy – now, while you remain here, and just as importantly, when you finally leave the Park and return to normal life – after we win the war. Remember, ladies, the smallest lapse of our security could have terrible consequences for our soldiers bravely fighting the enemy.' Her gaze rested on each girl's head. 'Is that understood?'

'Yes, Mrs Wilcox,' three girls chorused.

'Miss Treadwell?'

Dale was startled from the memory of Barking's gun resting on his desk. This constant repetition of never telling anyone anything at all about your work was obviously dead serious.

'Yes, Mrs Wilcox. All understood.'

Wanda Wilcox narrowed her eyes. 'Is anything the matter, Miss Treadwell?'

'Um, no. I was just wondering about the training.'

'I'm coming to that,' Mrs Wilcox said sharply. 'You'll mostly learn on the job, but in a nutshell, the Germans use the Enigma to send messages to their armed forces in the field. Even Hitler uses it to send messages to his generals.' She paused.

A shiver of – was it fear or excitement? – ran up Dale's spine.

'A courier brings the messages to our Hut two or three times a day. They are, of course, not only in German but in code, and it's our job to decipher them into German. That's where this marvellous Enigma machine comes in. The Germans think the enemy could never decode them because they're so complicated and they change the settings daily, but we have some of the best brains here and have already made tremendous strides since May, led by Mr Turing.' Another gaze at the group with those all-seeing dark eyes. 'You'll no doubt bump into him sometime or other – he runs every morning so you can't miss him. Don't be surprised at his unconventional behaviour. He's a little eccentric, to say the least.' She gave a sniff, almost of disapproval. 'But he's an amazing analyst and it's surprising how accurate the boffins can be when the odds are pitted against them.' She paused. 'Now if you'll gather round, I'll give a demonstration on the Enigma, the only machine you'll be working on in Hut 6.'

There was a scraping of chairs. Now Dale could see the machine close up it only resembled a typewriter. She drew a deep breath and concentrated on Wanda Wilcox's words.

'Although there is an on and off switch—' Mrs Wilcox pointed to it '—you will never use it. The machines are to be left to run twenty-four hours a day, every day, and you will always leave your machine on, ready for the next shift. Never turn it off.' She gestured to the top of the machine. 'These three wheels are the rotors. The Germans turn them every day to make the new settings. That's what we have to crack. Before you start each morning, you'll be given the settings, guessed at by the cryptographers, and you'll then turn the rotors on your machine to match them. Any questions so far?' She waited a few seconds, then picked up a piece of paper and passed it around.

Dale peered at it for a few moments before handing it to Sonia. It contained a few lines of jumbled letters consistently spaced in groups of five.

'This is a genuine message,' Wanda Wilcox said as she took the message back, 'which has already been discounted

149

as it didn't give us any lead, but I can use it to demonstrate.' She regarded the group. 'By the way, this is obviously a German keyboard, so if anyone's a typist, you'll see it's not set out quite the same as you're used to.' She paused. 'You press the first coded letter – like so. The decoded letter – in other words, the real one – will light up on the lamp board above – can you all see?'

'So it's a completely different letter?' Peggy said.

'That's right,' Mrs Wilcox said. 'And it will never be the same letter as the key you press first. You'll make a note of the new letter, and simply continue, keeping the letters in groups of five, until you've decoded the entire message. This is very important. You're looking for a German word you recognise. It's what we call "the key". Every day we hope one of you will find one which will then confirm the correct settings the Germans devised for that day. When this happens, you will tell me or if I'm not here, then my colleague, Miss Gibson. We will inform you all so you should be able to decode many more messages coming in that day – which can sometimes amount to hundreds – knowing the settings are correct as the Germans only change them once a day. You will quietly carry on in the knowledge you are doing your vital bit in the war effort. You will also humbly acknowledge to yourself that any individual success – and they don't happen every day or even every week – has been cracked through a team effort.' She gazed at the small group. 'Is that understood?'

'Are the letters in the messages always put in groups of five?' Dale asked.

'Yes.' Wanda Wilcox opened her mouth to continue.

'Why is that?' Dale persisted.

'It's not necessary to know,' the supervisor said, an edge of irritation in her voice. 'The motto here is if you don't need

150

to know, then don't ask. The less you know about the work behind the scenes, the better.'

Dale had the distinct feeling Wanda Wilcox didn't know the reason herself.

'Any more questions?'

'So the message will still be in German but not necessarily make sense,' Peggy said, frowning as though trying to commit it all to memory.

'Yes, it will look like gibberish unless the settings were correct. In that case you might recognise some German lettering which might overlap into the neighbouring group of five. Using that method, you work your way through the pile. You'll understand better when you operate the machine yourselves, so we'll go back to the machine room. I'll show you your desks and give you your day's settings.' She paused. 'The successfully decoded messages are sent to Hut 3 to be analysed by Intelligence. They're put on a tray and pushed through a small tunnel from our Hut which connects with theirs.'

Dale was puzzled. 'How can you push it far enough for them to retrieve it?' she asked.

'By using the handle of a broom,' Wanda Wilcox unexpectedly replied. 'It seems to do the trick.'

Her disapproval at such a primitive way of delivering important messages was plain to see in the down-turned corners of her mouth and Dale smothered a nervous giggle.

No one spoke as they left the room. Dale noticed Sonia looked positively subdued.

'Sonia, you will sit here with Dulcie behind.' Mrs Wilcox pointed to the last two desks at the back, then swept over to the other side of the room to show Peggy and Beatrice theirs.

Tingling with excitement at the thought of decoding the

first message in the pile – maybe one from Hitler himself! – Dale's fingers itched to start pressing keys as soon as she took her seat. But first she needed to study at close range this peculiar-looking machine. It fascinated her. She had so many questions to ask Mrs Wilcox about where the messages came from in the first place, and where did the cryptanalysts work who attempted every day to find the settings? She'd love to know more about what went on behind the scenes, such as what happened to the messages after she and the other women in the room had decoded them. She needed to find out and understand how it all pieced together, but this was only her first day. As usual she was being too impatient. She glanced around. Everyone, even Sonia in front of her, was tapping away. She could feel Wanda's eyes on her as she picked up the first message.

When she'd written down all the new letters on the squared page of the notepad provided, she studied each group of five letters. She couldn't make head nor tail of anything. Surely if the settings were correct some German word or other would have leapt out. But she hadn't done enough serious reading or writing in German, which meant she could easily have missed something. She stared at them again. No, she couldn't see any kind of correlation. Sighing, she picked up the next message.

After what seemed an interminable morning, annoyed with herself at the slow rate she was going, Dale noticed all the women stand up as one, pick up their handbags and make for the door.

'Coming?' An older woman with an elaborately rolled hairstyle caught Dale's eye. 'We're off to the canteen.'

Dale looked at her watch. Exactly twelve noon. At the thought of food, she found she was suddenly hungry.

'Shall we go, Sonia?' she said, but the girl had already disappeared in the crowd.

As soon as Dale passed through the door of a low brick building a short distance beyond the Park gates it felt as though she was entering another world. A cosy warmth emanated from the room; men and women, many in navy and air force uniform, were laughing and chattering, as crockery clattered and cutlery jangled. She looked round, feeling a little confused. People were taking full trays from a long counter to the dozens of tables. Not knowing what the procedure was, she walked up to the counter, amazed to see a display of steaming savoury dishes, sponge pudding and jugs of custard, along with plates and small bowls and mugs.

'Other side, love,' a large woman in a white apron bellowed from behind the counter as she mopped her forehead with a cloth.

Feeling all eyes on her and trying not to think of the woman's sweaty cloth, Dale joined the queue. The girl in front turned to her with a friendly smile.

'First day?' she asked.

'Yes. I'm not quite sure what to do.'

'It's self-service. You take a plate and just point to what you want and one of the dinner ladies will dish it out. Drinks are at the end of the counter with the cutlery – help yourself, then take your tray and sit where you like – there's no hierarchy here. The food's not brilliant but it's usually edible and fills the gap.'

'Thanks for the warning.' Dale returned the smile. 'I'm Dale Treadwell, by the way.'

'Helen Blunt . . . by name and nature,' she said with a laugh.

Dale liked Helen immediately with her short brown curls that framed a heart-shaped face and sparkling eyes. How

153

she longed to ask Helen which Hut she worked in, and what her job was. It was so frustrating not to be able to ask anything at all.

'Have you been working at the Park for long?' Dale asked.

'Only a couple of months. But they're a good bunch of people. You'll soon get to know some of them by sight . . . and some of their eccentricities.'

'Such as?'

'Such as Mr Turing, one of the boffins. He chains his mug to the radiator avec padlock so no one will steal it – though who'd want it, I don't know.' She laughed, but not unkindly. 'And he wears a gas mask when he's out cycling but it's not to ward off a gas attack, it's to prevent him getting hay fever.'

Before Dale could ask Helen to tell her more, the girl had taken her turn at the counter, where two women were serving.

Dale followed and pointed to the potato-covered dish.

'Cottage pie, love?'

'Yes, please. And some cabbage.'

The ample, white-coated woman nodded and dished up the meal, then handed over the plate. 'There you are, love. You help yourself to the sponge pudding and custard.'

'Thank you very much.' Dale gratefully took the plate and when she'd finished serving herself, she glanced over the room. Sonia was chatting at a full table on the far side, but she couldn't see where Helen had gone.

'There's a spare chair here,' a male voice said at her elbow.

She turned to see three men, all in naval uniform, smiling at her.

'Thank you.' She put her plate on the space in front and sat down, then took up her knife and fork.

'You're new?' one of them asked. The oldest one, probably in his thirties.

'Does it show that easily?' Dale smiled. She put a fork of cottage pie to her lips.

"Fraid so. You hesitated when you came in – bit of a clue.' He smiled.

'Oh, dear. But look how confident I shall be tomorrow.'

His companions chuckled.

'So what Hut have they imprisoned you in?' a second man asked. A devastatingly handsome one, probably not much older than herself.

Oh, not again.

'I'm sorry, but even though it's only my first day, I know the rules,' Dale answered, her tone pleasant and her smile warm as she continued eating her meal. The pie was more vegetable than 'cottage' and the cabbage was yellow with overcooking. But as Helen had said, it was just about edible.

He threw her a grin. 'The thing is, it's simple to find out.'

'Well, you won't find out anything secret through me,' Dale said, firmly, hoping to put him in his place.

'It's not exactly secret, just knowing which Hut we all work in,' he said, draining his glass of water and wiping his mouth with a napkin. 'Vernon Bannister.' He winked. 'And may we have the pleasure of knowing *your* name?' He gave her a charming smile.

I bet he's got a girl waiting for him in every port.

Before she could answer, the other two men introduced themselves. She simply nodded and smiled, trying her best to tackle the unappetising plate of food. The men, who had already cleaned their plates, began to chatter about Germany's recent invasion of Jersey. She listened intently, having not dared to switch on her wireless to hear the news this morning after Mrs Draper's warning. Finally giving up on her meal, Dale set her knife and fork together with a determined clatter and rose to her feet.

'But you haven't finished.' Vernon Bannister sprang up. 'I hope it wasn't something I said.' He gave her another of his sweeping-you-off-your-feet smiles.

'Not at all,' Dale said, smiling back. She turned to the other two officers. 'Thank you for allowing me to share your table. It was lovely meeting you all.'

'You haven't told me your name,' Vernon Bannister said.

'It should be simple to find out,' she said, emphasising the last four words with a mocking smile.

'I think she's rather put you in your place, old boy,' was the last thing Dale heard one of his friends say.

Chapter Sixteen

Back in Hut 6, the afternoon passed in a daze of pressing letters on keyboards and making note of the different letters lighting up on the lamp board above. No matter how hard Dale stared at the groups of five letters, they made no sense at all, but no one else announced they'd decoded anything either. She was sure she knew enough German to recognise a word or two if the setting was correct. After three solid hours she got up and tried to stretch her limbs without drawing attention to herself. Oh, what she'd give for a cup of tea. Dale licked her dry lips, then stifled a yawn. She really must have a break soon or she would scream with the monotony.

'You're at work now, so bloody well get on with it,' she muttered as she picked up another message from the never-ending pile.

At four o'clock, as one, everybody in the room made for the door. Dale quickly put her notes together and left the rest of the pile of uncoded messages for the person taking over on the next shift. She felt at a loss. Lonely. Worried about what she was doing and whether her German was up to the job. Wanda Wilcox sometimes disappeared, and she didn't like to disturb the other women, silently fixed

157

to their desks, decoding. Should she go and have a cup of tea at the café in Hut 2 where she might find someone to talk to? Sitting in another stuffy atmosphere with more chatter didn't really appeal. With no ventilation she could discern in Hut 6, and the blackout shutters closed all day, not to mention several women smoking, it had been a strain working in dim lighting on something she wasn't used to, requiring close concentration. She was desperate to see daylight. It would make more sense to go for a walk now she was free until tomorrow morning. She stood and flexed her shoulders, yawning from lack of air, then grabbed her bag and followed the others.

Once outside, she took some deep dizzying breaths.

'Do you fancy a walk to the town? Have a cup of tea?'

Dale turned to see Wanda Wilcox a couple of yards behind her. For a moment, she wanted to say no, she'd rather be on her own. But good manners forbade it. And anyway, she was curious as to why the woman had suggested it. Wanda Wilcox didn't seem to be the kind of woman who sought out anyone's company unless she had a motive.

'Tell me if you'd rather not have company,' she said, smiling, as she eerily tapped into Dale's thoughts. 'I know how daunting it is on the first day . . . first week, even. But then you start to get more efficient and it isn't nearly so bad.'

'Um, that would be nice . . . thank you.'

Wanda Wilcox put a light hand on her arm. 'Sometimes it's nice to talk to someone you can trust.'

Immediately, Dale heard alarm bells. What was that supposed to mean? Was the woman trying to lull her into a false sense of security? Thankfully, the woman chatted about the facilities in the town until they arrived in the centre.

'Here we are then – one of the two cafés and not much

to choose between.' Wanda took her arm and guided her into the smoky interior. 'Let's grab that seat by the window.'

When they were settled and had placed an order for a large pot of tea and two slices of sponge cake, Dale felt Wanda Wilcox's eyes studying her. She really was a very striking-looking woman now her face was more relaxed.

'Do you have a boyfriend, Dulcie?'

The question took her by surprise. She felt her cheeks warm as Glenn's image danced in front of her. She cleared her throat.

'Not exactly,' she said.

'So there *is* someone?' Wanda persisted.

'There was – once.'

Wanda's forehead creased. 'I'm sorry. I shouldn't have probed.' She paused. 'My husband died.'

Dale looked at her. 'Oh, I'm sorry.'

'Don't be,' Wanda said unexpectedly. 'He was unfaithful from the day we married – I'm glad he went.' She looked at Dale. 'Men. Who'd have them?'

Dale shifted a little in her hard seat. She couldn't think how to answer, especially with her father's desertion.

'Anyway,' Wanda continued, 'keep it under your hat.' She gave a short bitter laugh.

'I wouldn't dream of repeating anything so personal,' Dale said, feeling more and more awkward, praying their tea would soon arrive.

'No one understands anyway, unless they've been through something similar,' Wanda Wilcox said with a sigh.

Dale clamped her lips to stop herself from mentioning her own father. To her relief the waitress bustled over with a tray and set the crockery and teapot on the table.

'Shall I be mother?' Wanda Wilcox's tone had changed from bitter to brisk.

'Please do.'

While Wanda poured the tea, Dale ventured, 'Have you been here very long, Mrs Wilcox?'

'Oh, do call me Wanda outside work,' she said immediately, then lowered her voice, though the clattering of cups and cutlery drowned out all conversations around them. 'Yes, I was one of the first, working in the main house before being transferred.' For an instant her expression hardened. Then she said, 'What did you do before coming here?'

'I was a reporter for one of the papers.'

'Oh. Interesting.'

'Not really.' Dale took a sip of her tea. 'I was never allowed to report on anything important.'

'Because you're a woman,' Wanda said matter-of-factly. She took out a silver cigarette case and offered it to Dale, who took one, then flicked her cigarette lighter and lit them both.

'I don't often have one,' Dale said, careful not to inhale as it had a nasty habit of making her cough, 'but today seems to justify it, for some reason.'

'First day jitters, I expect. But I don't bother to excuse myself.' Wanda leant back in her chair and let out a steady stream of smoke from the side of her mouth. 'I couldn't get through the days if I didn't.'

Again, that hint that things weren't right with Wanda's life.

'Where are you billeted?' Wanda asked.

'Just off the High Street.'

'What's it like?'

'They're an awful couple,' Dale blurted. 'The woman told me they'd originally been asked to take in a couple of evacuees, but her husband wouldn't have it. Apparently, he thought a single woman would be less trouble.'

'Truth is, if people don't volunteer to take in our staff, the

160

Accommodations Officer is obliged to force them. They're probably bitter because they couldn't come up with an acceptable excuse not to take anyone.'

'Hmm,' Dale murmured. 'I bet they'll take the money the government gives them quite happily . . . and my ration book.' She looked at Wanda. 'The husband's determined to find out what I'm doing at the Park.'

Dale saw Wanda's posture stiffen.

'Oh?' Her supervisor leant towards her. 'Exactly what sort of things does he say?'

Suddenly, Dale wished she hadn't mentioned this to Wanda. She hadn't yet got the measure of the woman.

'He says there's rumours round the town about what our place is being used for and he has a right to know, seeing as I'm under his roof – under his lousy attic roof, more like.' She grimaced.

'And how did you respond?' Wanda's eyes narrowed.

A warning light flashed. This felt almost like an interrogation. After briefly hesitating, she said, 'I told him I'd signed the Official Secrets Act, hoping that would be the end of it. But I don't think it will be. In fact, I think it's made him even more curious. He gives me the creeps.'

Wanda stubbed out her cigarette in her saucer. 'Why don't you go and see Pauline Patch in the Accommodations Office for a transfer? She would have organised your billet in the first place.'

'I'm not sure I trust her judgement—' Dale gave a rueful smile '—though I'm willing to give her a second chance.'

'You do that.' Wanda called the waitress. 'May we have the bill?' She looked at Dale. 'And I'm paying for this. It was good to have some company.'

'For me, too,' Dale said, 'before facing the two horrors.'

Wanda laughed. 'I'm sure you'll sort them out.'

161

Dale mooched around the small town, but when she bumped into Wanda for the second time, she decided to head out to the country for a walk before supper. Truth was, she wasn't looking forward at all to the second evening spent with her hosts.

Feeling much better from a long walk down the country lanes in the opposite direction from Bletchley Park, Dale reluctantly made her way back to the town and her new lodgings, determined to change her attitude.

But if anything, this evening was worse than the night before. She arrived back at a quarter to six when Mrs Draper opened the door.

'Tea's at half-past five prompt,' she snapped.

'I'm sorry – you didn't warn me,' Dale said with exaggerated politeness as she stepped into the narrow hallway, 'but I must remind you I won't always be able to keep to that as we have to do shift work.'

'What's going on out there?' Mr Draper bellowed through the narrow hallway.

'You'd better come to the dining room straightaway,' Mrs Draper hissed. 'He gets his gander up if he don't get his tea dead on.'

Too bad.

'I need to nip upstairs and have a quick tidy up.'

'No! Please come now!'

Dale hesitated. She hated being ordered around but there was something in Mrs Draper's eyes – was it imploring? – that made her follow the woman into the room where Mr Draper sat, an ugly glare on his face, clutching a spoon and tapping it on the tablecloth.

'That's the last time you keep me waiting, miss whatever-your-name-is. I've put in a proper day's work at the station,

I have, which I doubt you'd understand.' Before she could argue, he added, 'It's not much to ask for a meal to be put in front of a working man on the dot.' His bulging eyes challenged her.

Dale noticed his thick white plate was empty except a smear of gravy and a few stray cabbage shreds. What a horrible man. He'd already gobbled his main meal if the speed he'd eaten yesterday evening was anything to go by.

'I'll get your crumble, Bert.' Mrs Draper scuttled out to the kitchen and brought back a dish with a crumble topping the colour of cement.

Dale's stomach heaved. How different this was to the delicious meals her mother consistently produced.

'Where's the custard?'

'I'm getting it, dear.' Mrs Draper disappeared again.

Dale sat down. She tried not to notice the huge blackheads clustered together on Bert Draper's bulbous nose as she stared back at the hard eyes watching her.

'What've you been up to today?' he said.

'Oh, a bit of filing. General office work,' Dale said vaguely. 'I've been for a lovely walk this afternoon. The countryside is beautiful round here.'

'What's the purpose of that house?' he said, ignoring her change of subject. 'An' don't fob me off. I keep me ear to the ground, I do. Something fishy goin' on and I don't like it.' He studied her with challenging eyes. 'An' you're not tellin' the truth about what you do. Why are you lot all so secretive?'

Dale was just about to repeat yet again that she was not prepared to discuss her work with him or anyone when his wife appeared with a jug of custard and a plate of food for Dale. Throwing her an 'if looks could kill' stare, he said no more, simply swallowing the unappetising-looking pudding

163

in a few enormous mouthfuls, then giving a deep belch and announcing he was going into the parlour to read his newspaper, and that his wife could bring him in a cup of tea, but he'd wait until she'd finished the washing up.

Chapter Seventeen

The first week passed in a daze of routine, only broken up by Dale's time off when she'd go for a walk or get down to studying her German books in the attic bedroom. At least she was making some progress on that. The image of Glenn seemed to be slipping further and further away. Nothing had changed in Dale's heart, but she had to face the fact she was never going to see him again. The idea they'd one day be reunited was growing fainter. All this made her ache so badly that if she was alone she'd burst into tears.

Being shut up for hours on end in the Hut really got on Dale's nerves. Her eyes stung, glued to the Enigma machine. The routine was so mind-numbing that she had to force herself to concentrate, knowing if she made a mistake when she wrote down a letter it could have serious consequences. Something meaningful could slip through from her own carelessness. Struggling to cope with this was bad enough, but the Hut was hot and stuffy, and the permanently blacked-out windows and dim lighting often landed her with a throbbing headache by the time she'd finished her shift.

If only they were told the meaning of any message someone had broken – just occasionally – so they'd have the satisfaction of knowing their work was truly valuable. She just had to believe it, or she'd go barmy. Dale cursed out loud when she glanced at the pile of messages beside her, still waiting to be entered into the machine. The pile looked almost as bad as when she'd begun them last night. She looked round quickly, feeling ashamed in case Chloë, who had taken Sonia's desk in front of her today, had heard her. But the swear word was drowned in the clatter of machinery, constantly in operation, twenty-four hours of every single day. Why hadn't she been able to break a code yet? Surely her German wasn't that bad. But if the settings weren't correct that day it was obviously impossible and not at all her fault, she told herself. Though that was no comfort yesterday morning when Beatrice had broken a message and several girls had quickly followed suit, yet Dale still hadn't spotted anything in German the rest of the day. She gritted her teeth, vowing to speed up her German reading. She must – she simply must – break a code soon.

Her shift this week, midnight to eight in the morning – the worst one, the girls all warned her – had caused a problem at the Drapers'. Mrs Draper had reluctantly handed over a spare front door key, then glanced over her shoulder as though her husband would appear at any moment.

'Don't let Mr Draper know,' she'd said. 'He'd go berserk.'

'I'm sure they must have told you both when you agreed to take me in that I'd be doing shift work. And didn't you have another girl before me?'

'He don't pay no attention at what he don't want to hear,' Mrs Draper had answered, smoothing her apron with nervous fingers. 'All he were interested in were the extra rations.'

Yes, rations meant for *me*, Dale thought, crossly. Was this the time to say something about his meal consistently being better quality than hers and Mrs Draper's? And always more of it. She hesitated, then seeing Mrs Draper's face changed her mind. She didn't want to get the woman into any more trouble with that oaf of a husband. But trying to sleep in the daytime with the traffic noise outside and people shouting, especially when it was market day, and Mrs Draper banging up and down the stairs with her carpet sweeper, was proving impossible. She'd tried hard not to be difficult, not to grumble, even to herself, but the situation was becoming intolerable.

Back in her room she made up her mind. She would find better accommodation and more congenial hosts by the end of August. That gave her a fortnight. She could bear that so long as she had her goal. In the meantime, she'd try to keep cheerful, difficult though it was in the gloomy attic where she tried to spend as little time as possible. Sighing, she opened the letter she'd received that day from her mother. She was relieved to read that Elizabeth Bryant-Taylor, who lived nearby, was proving to be a good friend, though trying to persuade her to join the WVS. Dale hoped she would. It would take her mind off Dad. She mentioned he'd given her the name of his solicitor so things were really serious. Poor Mother.

She's missing me, Dale thought, chewing her lip. It might be some time before she'd be able to see her. Other than that, her mother didn't sound as bad as she'd feared.

Dale slipped the sheet of paper back in its envelope. Wishing there was a desk or table, she sat on the edge of her bed and began her letter to her mother in the vaguest terms, and as usual not mentioning Mrs Draper's dreadful cooking. When she'd finished she'd go for a bike ride. Jennifer in her Hut had just had a birthday and her parents had given her a smart new bicycle. She'd announced she was giving away her old one if anybody was interested. No one else offered to take it so at break time in the canteen Dale had asked her if she could have it.

'Aren't you a London girl?' Jennifer had given Dale a searching look. 'In other words, can you actually ride a bike?'

Dale didn't want to admit she'd never learnt – that she always walked everywhere, or if it was too far, or she'd been on a shopping spree, hailed a taxi. But if her mother was right, they would have to pull their belts in. It would have to be buses from now on. At least the bicycle would give her some independence while she was at the Park.

She nodded. It hadn't seemed quite so bad as telling a fib out loud.

'Then you're welcome to it.'

Confidently, Dale had walked the old bicycle down the gravel drive and through the sentry point, then wheeled it into the lane. She put one long leg over the right-hand side of the frame so her foot touched the ground, then eased herself down to the leather saddle, so worn that she settled into it instantly. She stretched the second foot onto the pedal. The bicycle tipped. For a horrible moment she thought she was going to fall off. Back went her foot on the ground. She took a few deep breaths and tried again, this time managing to hold her balance.

That was several days ago. Now, it was as though she'd cycled all her life, Dale thought happily, even though the bike wobbled as she turned corners while admiring the trees. Their leaves had just begun to change as autumn approached, showing hints of red and gold. Another month and they'd be stunning. Already, the days were getting shorter. She breathed in the clean air, so wonderful after sitting in cigarette smoke for hours on end. Moreover, she was beginning to recognise the various landmarks and hamlets.

A warm breeze lifted thick strands of her hair as she bowled along, revelling in the feeling of being in complete command of the bike. Why had she never bothered to learn to ride before now? She drew a deep, satisfying breath. For the first time since she'd arrived at Bletchley, she felt almost happy.

A group of cyclists passed her, raising their arms and calling out. Without thinking, Dale let go of one of the handlebars to wave in reply and only just managed to keep her balance.

Serves you right for being so cocky.

One cheeky chap with newly shaved short back and sides bellowed, 'What's the weather like up there?'

'Much warmer than where you are down there' – *you little squirt,* she wanted to add. She knew he was referring to the bicycle's old-fashioned curved frame, standing much higher than the more modern bikes, but she didn't mind at all; it suited her own tall figure and she could still put both feet on the ground at either side of the pedals if she felt she was going to overbalance.

He grinned and, taking both hands off his handlebars, threw his hat in the air in front of him, then grabbed it as his bike caught up with it.

She pedalled furiously after them, not wanting them to see she was a novice. It was at that precise moment she heard a hissing sound and the front wheel began to bump and slow down. *Blast! What's happened?* She pedalled a little further, but the bike suddenly jerked and without warning stopped dead. She called out as she was flung to one side, as though in slow motion, landing in a heap in the ditch, the bicycle half on top of her. The cyclists who'd just passed her immediately stopped and turned round.

One of them came running towards her. Eddie! The man

who'd given her a lift when she'd first arrived. It was the first time she'd set eyes on him since then. He immediately lifted the bicycle off her and laid it on the grass.

'Are you hurt?'

'No, I'm all right,' she said, furious with herself for making such a spectacle and struggling to get up, but her knees collapsed.

He stared at her. 'Good God – if it isn't Dale!' He pointed to himself. 'Eddie Langton at your service.'

'I know.'

'Here.' He stuck out his arm and she pulled herself upright. 'You sure you're all right?'

'I'm fine,' she said as she brushed herself down. 'But something's happened to my bike to throw me off.'

'Let me look.' He went over to the verge and set it upright, feeling the front tyre. 'As I suspected. You ran over a nail or something sharp. You've got a tyre as flat as a pancake.' He grinned. 'Know how to change it?'

He knew jolly well she had no idea how to change a tyre. If only she could have shown him there and then. That would have taken the wind out of his sails.

'You know I don't.'

'I don't know anything of the sort,' he said, his grin widening even further. 'Especially with that most efficient-looking leather repair kit you've got.'

'What repair kit?'

'Here . . . that little black bag hooked onto the back of your saddle.' He pointed at it. 'Most bikes have one. If they don't, they ought.' He gazed at her. 'Something tells me you're not a very experienced cyclist.'

'You guessed right,' she said, now laughing. She must stop taking herself so seriously – something Rhoda often accused her of. 'It's my first proper ride in the country.'

'Well, this is your first lesson on changing a puncture,' he said. 'It's never too soon to learn so you'd better come over here and give it – and me – your full attention.' He winked.

She liked the way Eddie rolled up his shirt sleeves and set to with the tyre.

'Here's the little culprit,' he said, showing her a sharp rusty nail before hurling it into the hedgerow.

'So,' he said, stretching up ten minutes later, 'do you think you can repair a puncture the next time?'

'I hope so,' Dale grinned. 'It didn't look all that difficult.'

'It's only temporary, mind. That was quite a rip. You're definitely going to need a new tyre.' He looked at her. 'What shift are you working this week?'

'Midnight 'til eight.'

'I finish at four in the afternoon.' He paused. 'Look, why don't I come for you at your digs day after tomorrow – say, four-forty-five? We'll get the tyre checked, buy a new one if necessary, have a cup of tea and a bite to eat – if you'd like.'

Dale hesitated. Eddie seemed such a thoroughly decent man. She could tell he liked her and was maybe interested in taking things further. He was certainly handsome in a boyish way, but that was not what held her interest. There was much more about him that appealed to her, like his happy-go-lucky manner which belied his thoughtfulness. But her heart wouldn't stop whispering Glenn's name. It wouldn't be fair to Eddie. But what if she'd got it wrong and he was only being kind?

'What is it, Dale? Are you already spoken for?'

Heat rushed to her cheeks.

'Not exactly,' she said, his question confirming her suspicions, 'though there is . . .' She trailed off when she saw the look of disappointment in his eyes.

'Spare me the details,' Eddie said with a short laugh. 'I

should've guessed. Gorgeous-looking girl like you is bound to have the chaps falling over themselves to take you out. Look, if you're in love with someone, then that's my tough luck. But I'd still like us to be friends. You don't have to worry about any more than that. All right?'

'All right,' she said, giving him a grateful smile. 'I'd like that, so long as it's no later than a quarter to. Mr Draper is usually back at five and I don't want him to start questioning me. He's a nasty bit of work.'

'Shall I sort him for you?' Eddie grinned at her.

'No. I'm used to fighting my own battles, but they're both so nosy. Mrs is bad enough, but her husband is a bully.'

'Right-o. I'll be prompt. But I don't like the sound of him. Why don't you change your digs?'

'It's my next job.'

He hesitated, then his eyes twinkled as he looked at her. 'I might be able to help there.'

'Anywhere and any other landlord would be preferable to the Drapers,' she said.

Dale had been listening for Eddie, crosser than ever that there was nowhere downstairs where she was allowed except the dining room. When she heard the doorbell ring, she dashed down the first flight of stairs just in time to hear Mrs Draper say:

'I'm sorry, this is a respectable establishment. No young men allowed. We made that perfectly clear to Miss Treadwell.'

Dale took the second flight at speed as Mrs Draper was about to close the door on him.

'Thank you, Mrs Draper, you can leave the door. I'm just going out.' Dale glanced through the opening to Eddie who looked as though he was about to give the woman a piece of his mind. 'I'll just get the bike from the back yard,' she told him.

Mrs Draper pursed her lips in annoyance that her power had been taken away from her.

'I don't know what Mr Draper's going to say with all this goin' on,' she muttered.

'Your husband's a very unreasonable man, Mrs Draper,' Dale said firmly, and turned away before the woman could argue any further.

The door slammed shut behind them.

Eddie took the bike from Dale. 'You're right,' he said. 'Bloody cheek, excuse my French.'

'Don't mind me,' Dale said, chuckling. 'I've done plenty of swearing at them – in my head, anyway.'

'I'm not surprised,' Eddie said. 'You might like a suggestion I've come up with for alternate digs.'

Dale's spirits soared. 'Oh, where?'

'If it comes off, I want it to be a surprise,' he said with that grin she was beginning to recognise and warm to.

'It sounds very mysterious.'

'You could call it that.'

Chapter Eighteen

'Is it all right if I make my own breakfast tomorrow morning, Mrs Draper?' Dale asked the following Monday, as she helped the woman clear the dirty dishes and take them to the kitchen. 'I'm on an early shift and I'd like to get away really promptly.'

Mrs Draper regarded her with dead eyes. For a moment Dale felt a genuine sympathy for her. What a trap the woman had made for herself in what appeared a loveless marriage. She didn't seem to have anything pleasant going on in her life except to wait on her bully of a husband.

'I suppose you'll have to,' she said through disapproving lips.

'I'll leave everything tidy,' Dale said.

'I expect you will.' Mrs Draper's tone edged on sarcasm. 'Well, I'll leave you out the tea and there's bread in the bin. Just don't use Mr Draper's butter dish or there'll be 'ruptions. And only one teaspoon of sugar, mind.'

Dale pulled a face as she mounted the two flights of stairs to her unwelcoming room.

I can't take much more of this. There's over a week to go before my goal of moving and I've not heard any more from Eddie. Is he another man who can't keep his word?

*　　*　　*

Dale made sure she was up so early that even Mr Draper wouldn't be down at his dead-on seven in the morning. Although it was only just after six, it was fully light out. She'd slept badly and was desperate for a cup of tea. In the kitchen she grimaced at the tea leaves already measured out – the flattest teaspoonful. Hardly enough strength to pull her out of her stupor. She poked around in a cupboard but there was no marmalade or jam to disguise Mrs Draper's cunning mixture of butter and margarine – mostly marge. She cut two thick slices of bread, then lit a match for the grill and popped them under. When they were nicely golden, she put them on a plate and took them to the dining room.

As she sat down, she spotted Mr Draper's butter dish by his place setting – even his wife was not allowed to touch it. With a sly smile she stretched across the table and pulled the dish towards her, then lifted the lid. Real butter. A beautiful yellow. There was nothing like it. Careful not to leave any breadcrumbs on the small mound, she put her knife in and thickly buttered a slice. It spread beautifully, not like that revolting margarine mixture. But just at that moment she heard footsteps on the stairs. Guiltily, she quickly buttered the second slice and was just about to put the lid back on the dish when Mr Draper's short fat body filled the doorway.

'What do you think you're doin'?' His voice was rough.

'Just making my toast,' Dale returned innocently.

'You've been told not to touch my dish.'

Dale made a pretence of frowning. 'It's strange. There are quite a few things I'm not allowed to touch in the kitchen or on the dining room table.' Now she'd started she couldn't stop herself. 'I understand you were given extra coupons for my food so I could eat decently. Yet *you* seem to have all the best ingredients, the best meals – completely different from your wife and me. *We* must do with inferior quality – and quantity. It doesn't seem quite fair to me – does it to you?' she added. 'I just wonder what the Park will have to say when I report you.'

'You cheeky bitch,' he growled, his eyes two shiny black splinters of coal as he came menacingly towards her. He threw up his arm. 'What I have to eat is none of your bleedin' business.'

He was going to strike her!

Dale stood her ground, keeping her eyes unwaveringly on his. Obviously thinking better of it, he let his arm drop, breathing heavily.

'I want you out of here by the end of the week,' he roared. 'That should give you time to find another idiot. Though who would want you, I don't know. You've been more trouble than you're worth. You and your precious secrets. You should be ashamed of yourself.'

'Don't worry, Mr Draper. I shan't stay under your roof a minute longer than I have to . . . which I hope will be *before* the week is up. I just pity the next girl who comes here.'

She grabbed the toast and sped upstairs. The sooner she was out of this miserable dump, the better. Eddie hadn't mentioned anything concrete yet, so she'd go and see the Accommodations Officer this very day before she started her shift.

But she was out of luck.

'I'm sorry, but Miss Patch is away for a few days,' a young girl told her, looking up from her typewriter. 'She'll be back next week.'

Next week is too late, Dale thought grimly.

'It's urgent I change my billet,' she said desperately. 'Can anyone else help me?'

176

'Not really.' The girl gave her a sympathetic smile. 'But I'll make a note that you came in and I'm sure she'll find something for you. If I could just have your name.'

Dale automatically looked up from her desk when the door opened. To her surprise it was Eddie. As soon as he caught her eye he winked, but she turned away, pretending she hadn't seen it. It wouldn't do to be teased by the other girls that he was keen on her. Besides, Wanda had made it clear to them that any romance at the Park was not encouraged, the reason being that the couple might blurt out secrets to one another about their work. Even the pub was supposed to be out of bounds, though no one seemed to take much notice of that particular unwritten rule.

Dale couldn't help watching Eddie out of the corner of her eye.

Wanda glanced up and frowned.

'Morning, Wanda.' He flashed her his charming smile.

'Yes, Edward?' Wanda tilted her head.

So they were on first-name terms. But she calls him Edward.

'I've brought the messages today.'

Wanda deliberately put down her pen. 'I don't believe it's your job to act as courier.' Her tone was surprisingly cool. 'Surely you're more use in your own Hut – apart from the fact you have no business to be in here.'

Every woman stopped working to eye the scene.

Eddie's smile broadened. 'Thank you for the compliment,' he said, with a complete lack of sarcasm, 'but I wanted to say a few words.' He turned to the room. 'Thanks, everyone, for doing such a grand job. Every decoded message is one more step towards saving lives and ending the war.'

He looked across at Dale and gave her a huge wink. She

lowered her head and put a hand to her mouth to smother a giggle. Eddie put a pile of messages on the nearest girl's desk.

'What are you doing?' Wanda asked, her face flushing.

'Just dishing them out.'

'You can leave them with me,' Wanda said, briskly.

'Oh, it's no trouble at all,' Eddie said, wandering round the room, adding a pile to each girl's desk.

Dale could see he was enjoying the attention from all the warm smiles that greeted him. When he got to hers, she had her handbag on her lap, pretending she was trying to find something. He put a pile of messages in her tray and said under his breath, 'Morning, Gorgeous,' then winked again and left the room without a backward glance.

Really, Eddie came close to the mark where downright cheek was concerned. But she couldn't help liking him.

'Cor, what a looker,' Sonia said, turning round to face her when Eddie had disappeared. 'He can park his shoes under my bed any day of the week.' She gave a loud giggle.

One or two other women chimed in, adding their appreciation of such a tall, dark and handsome specimen, until Wanda barked:

'Please get on with your work, everybody. You'd think you'd never seen a man before.'

'We haven't,' one girl said. 'Not as good-looking as him, anyway.'

Several chuckles echoed round the room.

'That's enough. Please all be quiet. There's a lot to get through today.'

Really, the woman had no sense of humour. Sighing, Dale picked up the top message, which had a little red cross marked in one corner. She'd not seen any mark like this before. She opened it, ready to tap in the letters.

D

Meet me outside the gates as soon as you finish at 4 avec bicycle. Do you good to get some fresh air.

E.

How did he know when he wrote the note that she worked in Hut 6? Would she be breaking the rules to go on a bike ride with him? She gave a small sigh. It was so exhausting having to analyse everything she said, everything she did, with the Official Secrets Act and the threat of dire punishment hanging over her head. But, oh, how good it would be just to have some company, cycling along and gazing at the scenery after being cooped up in here all day. She bit her lip. If she was honest, she'd be more than pleased to see Eddie again.

At lunch in the canteen, while scanning the room for a table with a different crowd from those in Hut 6 for a change, Dale noticed Sonia standing up and waving her over.

'Dale – over here. There's an empty chair beside me, so come and join us.'

Gritting her teeth but managing to smile, she walked over to their table.

'Hello, Dale.' It was a woman who Dale recognised from her Hut. 'We haven't really spoken before. I'm Anne – with an "e".' She smiled, though her eyes looked sad.

Anne wore her brown hair in a victory roll. Although her features were plain, she had a motherly expression, even though she was probably only in her late twenties.

'Are you getting on all right with the work?' she asked.

Dale hesitated. 'I think I'm finding my feet,' she said. 'I wish I could speed up a bit.'

'You will when you've been here as long as some of us.' Anne paused. 'And how is it working on the shifts?'

179

'The night one is a bit tricky,' Dale admitted. 'I don't live on the quietest street.'

'Oh, shame.' This was from a girl with short dark curls and sparkling hazel eyes. Dale hadn't seen her before. 'I'm Susan. I'm in Stony Stratford, about five miles from here. It's *too* quiet for me. But they're the nicest couple and treat me like a long-lost daughter. I'm making the most of it while it lasts.'

They chatted about their digs. None of the others lodged in Bletchley itself. Most of them came in and went on the buses Dale had seen, and Susan and two other girls cycled in. It seemed she was also the only one billeted on her own. The others had at least one other girl with them, or even a small group, sometimes from other Huts. For a moment she felt a twinge of envy. How wonderful to have a normal conversation, the camaraderie of other women around her own age, instead of the constant arguing with the Drapers. It was actually a relief to have been given her marching orders by Mr Draper.

'Does anyone know of a spare room going where they're billeted?' she said, looking round at the chattering group.

'Aren't your digs right in Bletchley?' Anne said.

'Yes. Just off the High Street.' Dale suddenly clammed up. She mustn't blurt out anything bad about the Drapers. She didn't want anything to get back to them.

'Is it dirty?'

'No,' Dale said, thankful to answer truthfully. 'Mrs Draper keeps it spotless.'

'I'm jealous,' a pale girl, with eyes made larger by her spectacles, spoke up. 'I have to travel nearly twenty miles each way on a packed bus to get to work. I'd be more than happy if you swapped with me. But why do you want to move when it's so convenient?'

For an instant Dale couldn't think of the right answer. Then she had a brainwave. 'I'm at the top of the house and because of the sloping ceilings and I'm tall, I keep bashing my head.'

'Perfect,' the girl said, standing up and smiling. 'I'm Lilian, by the way. Look, I'm barely five foot. I'd be well away from those pesky beams.'

Dale hesitated. Lilian looked such a frail little thing, her fine hair in a dusty cloud around the earnest little face. She couldn't possibly encourage the girl to move in with the Drapers.

'Is something else wrong with it?' Lilian said.

'Um.' Dale bit her lip. What on earth was she going to say? She'd have to hint something. Why hadn't she kept her mouth shut? 'Mr Draper doesn't hold much to anyone working at the Park,' she said lamely.

'What do you mean?' Sonia demanded.

'He imagines all sorts of things that go on . . . none of them right—'

Careful what you say, Dale.

'Obviously I haven't given him as much as a hint,' she continued. 'I just told him I'd signed the Official Secrets Act, but—'

'No need to say any more,' Lilian broke in. 'Thanks for the warning. I'd rather stay where I am in that case. Mr and Mrs Baldwin might be twenty miles away, but they make up for it in all the important things.'

No one else knew of any spare room going. Dale tried to feel as though she belonged at the table listening to Sonia and Lilian and the others chattering away, but she ate the rest of her meal almost in silence.

Dale went back to her desk with the others after their allotted half-hour for lunch. She picked up the next message to be decoded. Sighing, she transcribed the letters one by one, feeling she'd hardly gained any speed since her first day. It was difficult to concentrate. Glancing at the final letter of the message, she pressed the letter 'K' on the Enigma machine. It lit up as a 'P'. She recorded it on the sheet of paper on the right side of her desk, then stared at the meaningless groups of five letters. If only she was doing something she understood. She blew out her cheeks and picked up the next message from the pile Eddie had brought in that morning. She was getting near the end, but doubtless hundreds more would arrive during the afternoon.

With a start she realised she was feeling lonely. Wanda Wilcox had been quite friendly to her in the café that time, but Dale was conscious not to give it any significance. The last thing she wanted was the others to say there was favouritism going on – and anyway, she wasn't comfortable with the older woman. And she'd never seen Isobel since the morning after she'd arrived, so she obviously worked in one of the other Huts, as did Helen Blunt. Eddie wanted to be more than friends, Dale was sure, but that would complicate things.

The trouble was, her job as a junior reporter had been solitary except when she was in the office. And being the only female, she'd had to put up with constant remarks about her clothes and hair, and smutty jokes. She could only send a dignified look of disapproval and stalk out of the room to the sound of their laughter. Except Bill Thompson. He'd always been a gentleman.

Lost in her thoughts she suddenly felt a grip on her shoulder, making her jump.

'Anything the matter, Dulcie? You've been holding that message for a full minute.'

Dale's head jerked up. 'Er, no, Mrs Wilcox. I was just

thinking how I'd love to know how the decoded messages are used . . . presumably to interfere with the enemy's movements – just so we have an idea of the importance of what we're doing,' she added lamely.

The supervisor's forehead creased. 'It's not for you to think, or to presume, or to know. The work we do in this Hut is *vitally* important. That's all you need to know. Just get on with your job. That's what you're here for. Not to question things.' She moved on.

Dale's cheeks burned with humiliation. She hadn't breached any kind of rule so far as she could see, and surely she couldn't be put in prison for her thoughts. She bent her head to the keyboards and tapped in the next letter on the message. So much for Wanda Wilcox becoming a friend. The sooner four o'clock came and she was let out of this dungeon, the better.

Chapter Nineteen

Eddie was perched on his bicycle waiting for her, a rucksack fastened on his back, when Dale wheeled her bike into the lane leading away from the Park.

'You okay?' he asked as they pedalled off.

'Yes, I'm fine.' She wasn't going to spoil one moment of the time by moaning.

'Hmm.' He gave her a sideways glance. 'You look a bit harassed, if I may say so.'

'I'm sure you'll say it anyway.' Dale grinned.

He chuckled. 'Well, you can relax now. You're not working in the healthiest atmosphere but I've got the answer for right now. After an hour and a couple of hills to get the heart pumping, we'll find a quiet spot and have a cup of tea.'

'And where shall we find a café out here?'

'Ah, I've brought a flask and two mugs. And some biscuits. There might even be a bar of chocolate in the rucksack.'

'You think of everything.'

'It's what I'm here for.'

She chuckled, enjoying their silly banter and this unexpected escape. The tension in her head eased as she allowed herself to enjoy the peace of the countryside. She loved the whir of their bicycle wheels as they ate up the miles, the warm breeze lifting her hair at the back of her neck, and the birds joyfully singing. What a wonderful contrast to the never-ending clattering of the Enigma machines.

When she'd calculated they must have covered seven or eight miles, she began to get a little breathless. Shows how unfit I am, she thought wryly, the vision of a mug of tea sharp in her mind.

'Can we stop soon?' she called to Eddie, who was further in front, his long legs making light work of the steady hill.

'Bit further,' he shouted back. 'There's a perfect little spot half a mile on. We'll stop there.'

The hill became steeper and Dale was forced to pull over and push her bike the rest of the way. Eddie had now gone over the crest without looking back, obviously used to cycling up hills. She grimaced, taking her time and stretching her legs as she finally staggered to the top. Eddie was a dot in the distance. She mounted her bike, then lowered her head and set her chin, and by sheer determination caught up with him just as he was propping his bike against a tree trunk.

'You made it then?' He winked as he took a small, folded blanket from his rucksack and spread it on the grass.

'Course I did. I'm not *that* pathetic.' She laughed as she leant her bike against his. 'On second thoughts, I *am* that weak. But I'll perk up with some well-earned tea.'

'Come and sit down, then.'

He set down the flask and a small packet wrapped in greaseproof paper which he opened to reveal a few biscuits, then poured the tea.

'Just how it should be,' he said as he handed her a mug. 'Good and stewed.'

'Is there any milk?'

His face fell comically. 'Damn. I knew there was something.'

He looked at her. Those dark curling lashes, so wasted on a man. Dale hid a smile.

'Can you drink it without?' he said.

'I'll have to. I'm not turning down a mug of tea for anything. And didn't you mention chocolate?'

'I did.' He delved around in the rucksack and threw a bar of Fry's Peppermint Cream onto her lap.

She wouldn't tell him it was the one chocolate bar she didn't like. The sweet cream was so sickly, but he'd think her an incredible fusspot, especially now chocolate was scarce. No, a couple of squares would melt as soon as she washed it down with the black tea.

'I won't even have a cigarette. But *you* can if you want.' Eddie let his head rest on the tree trunk.

'No, thanks. I only have the occasional one – when I'm nervous.'

'You mean I don't make you nervous?' He bared his teeth and growled.

She giggled. 'Stop it.' Then her laughter faded, and she said truthfully, 'No, Eddie, you don't make me nervous – not at all.'

'I'm glad you feel comfortable with me.' He paused. 'Dale . . .'

'Yes?'

'This war is going to be dirty. We don't know the half of it yet, but I reckon our boys in the sky will have plenty on their hands when it gets going.'

Why is he saying this all out of the blue?

Barely conscious of what she was doing, she broke off a piece of the chocolate bar and slowly chewed it, every sinew alert for what might be coming.

'The Battle of Britain has already started and we're losing large numbers of pilots and aeroplanes,' Eddie went on. 'Hitler will bomb London first, thinking he'll force us into submission as easily as he took France.' He picked a blade of grass and toyed with it for a few moments. 'He doesn't know the British. We've got Churchill now. And we'll fight to the end – just as he says. We'll never be trodden under by the Nazi jackboot. What I'm trying to say is, no one knows how many lives this war will take – how much time we have on this earth.'

Dale's stomach fluttered. She could hear it in his voice. He was going to say something more serious to her – she was sure of it. And she didn't want him to. The piece of chocolate, not properly chewed, went down her throat in a sticky peppermint lump.

'No one ever knows that, war or not, how long they have on this earth,' she mumbled.

'True, but the young will die in vast numbers. You'll see. And that's unusual in peace time.'

She sat quietly, staring ahead at the calm view of the gentle Buckinghamshire dales, hearing a dog bark from far away, and birds taking no notice of any war – simply carrying on being birds. How could it be possible they were at war with such a cultured land as Germany? A country that had produced the most astounding composers, philosophers and poets, and great artists . . . cultured, that is, before that megalomaniac of an Austrian got his hands on it. Now it was filled with people who gathered in huge crowds to listen to his hysterical outbursts. She'd seen him in action on Pathé News. They'd been swept along by his fanaticism.

She couldn't stop Glenn's face flitting into her mind. Was he in danger? Oh, why hadn't he written? Impatiently, she blinked away the threatening tears. What had it all meant?

'I like you so much, Dale,' Eddie was saying as he set his mug of tea down where it promptly toppled over into the grass. He didn't seem to notice.

'I like you, too – very much.'

Please don't say anything more, Eddie.

'I *more* than like you.'

She put up her hand. 'Eddie—'

'You'll say it's much too soon, but I know my own mind and I think you and I would make a great couple. I just wish you'd met me first.' He hesitated. 'I didn't want to know when you first told me, but who is this chap?'

'He's an American,' Dale said quietly.

'How on earth did you meet an American?'

'He's a war correspondent and was here in London.'

'But not any longer.'

'No.'

'I presume he's in Berlin? I hear several British journalists have gone there.'

She didn't answer.

'You know you may never see him again.'

'I know.' She swallowed hard.

'Hmm. It doesn't bode well for a serious relationship, I wouldn't have thought,' Eddie said, not taking his eyes off her. 'But I just hope you know what you're doing.'

The ride back to Bletchley felt distinctly different from when they'd left the Park just over an hour ago, Dale thought. She'd so looked forward to her little escape, knowing how pleased Eddie was that he'd arranged it. Now, feeling awkward, knowing whatever she said might be taken the wrong way, she clammed up. He had quickly gathered the modest picnic remains and pushed them into his rucksack, saying brusquely that he needed to get back to write some memos.

'I'll see you back to your digs,' he said when they reached the High Street.

'Honestly, there's no need. I want a few bits in the town—'

'Dale, why don't you come clean with me so I know where I stand?'

She swallowed hard. 'I'm sorry, Eddie. I don't want to hurt you, but I love him.'

'I see.' He shrugged. 'Well, you've answered my question.' He looked at her and his expression softened. 'I think you could still do with a friend, though, and as I told you before, I'm willing to be that person – if you'll let me.'

'I'd like that more than anything.'

'Right. So as a friend I'm going to get you better digs as promised. I'll be in touch.'

'I hope it's soon.'

'Oh?' Eddie raised his eyebrows.

'I had a row with Mr Draper. He keeps asking nosy questions. Says he's determined to find out what's going on at the Park. I couldn't stand it any more and told him I was looking for alternative arrangements and he said I was to be gone by the end of the week.'

'Hmm. I told you I might have something. I haven't had a chance to talk to the people I have in mind, with all the night shifts I've had lately, and they've never taken a lodger. Be a bit new for them.' He pecked her on the cheek. 'I'll contact you at your Hut, okay?'

Dale thanked him but it didn't sound ideal if they had to be persuaded. She'd feel like a piece of baggage they were reluctant to take in. She presumed they were acquaintances of his and maybe they'd let her stay a week or two until she found something permanent. Well, it would be better than nothing. Within moments Eddie mounted his bike and after a few strong pushes on the pedals he disappeared round the corner.

*   *   *

189

Three days passed and Dale hadn't heard from Eddie. It was Thursday and she was on the second shift – 4 p.m. to midnight. She'd need to sleep a few hours tomorrow, and Saturday she had to be gone. Mr Draper now completely ignored her with not even a glance in her direction. Frankly, she was relieved, but the burning issue of where she would be laying her head on Saturday night was pressing.

After supper in the canteen where she'd swallowed some fish and chips, barely tasting the meal, and talking very little to her table companions, she walked back to the Hut with Sonia, who didn't stop chattering.

'How do you think it's going, Dale?' she said, looking serious.

'Um, all right, I suppose. I don't think they're expecting us to break codes every day.'

'I'm not sure I could break one if it stared me in the face.'

Dale gave her a sideways glance. The girl looked positively worried.

'Why do you say that?'

'I kind of bluffed when they asked me if I could speak German. Most of my German was picked up on ski-ing holidays and finishing school in Switzerland. But we girls used to speak in English nearly all the time.'

Dale had suspected this was Sonia's background. It sounded idyllic and yet Sonia, for all her giggling, never struck her as being particularly happy.

'Well, you must know enough, or they wouldn't have recruited you, surely.' Dale paused when Sonia didn't answer. 'I think the more we worry the harder it will be.'

'I keep getting awful headaches,' Sonia said. 'I'm not used to being cooped up for so many hours with no ventilation. It's a bit of a shock after the beautiful Alpine air.'

'I agree it's not the best atmosphere,' Dale said mildly.

Sonia hesitated as though wondering if she should take it further, but they'd already reached their Hut and Dale felt too worried and tired to listen to much more of Sonia's health issues.

'Maybe you should go to the sick bay,' Dale said.

'What, and have that ghastly Bull woman,' Sonia said emphatically. 'No, thank you. I'll take a couple of aspirins.'

Back at her desk Dale picked up an envelope with 'Miss Treadwell' scrawled across it. This time she recognised Eddie's writing.

Can you meet me over by the lake for a few minutes when we cross over?

E

The hours dragged. The monotony felt as though it was sucking the life out of her. She glanced at the clock. Oh, thank goodness. Not long before packing up and meeting Eddie. Had he arranged somewhere for her to go?

Concentrate, Dale.

She'd already written down what she termed the 'lamp letters' – those on the upper keyboard of her Enigma machine which lit up the hidden letters on the keyboard below – but her vision was becoming a little blurry. She blinked her eyes a few times, forcing them to focus. It was no good. She stared at the short, jumbled message, making neither head nor tail.

Think of it like a crossword puzzle. You're looking for a clue.

Then suddenly something in her brain clicked. Eddie's words on his note. She quickly scanned it again: '*can you meet me over by the lake for a few minutes when we cross over*'. The letters she was staring at on her notepad were in the third group of five: KREUZ. She stifled a gasp. It was a real German word! Kreuz – meaning 'cross'. Ursula Fassbender was always fingering her cross on a chain round her neck and saying how precious it was. It was one of the first words she'd taught Dale.

Her pulse racing, Dale examined the rest of the letters, but she couldn't spot anything else obvious. Her German wasn't up to it. Inwardly cursing herself she stared again, using her finger to trace the letters, in her mind trying to split them up differently. The last two letters of one group of five were **DU**. Her eye roved to the following group. **RCHDE**. Take those letters, DU, and the beginning of the second group, RCH, and you get DURCH. German for 'through'.

The word 'Kreuz' had by chance formed a complete word in the group but this probably didn't happen that often. She needed to break up the letters in their groups before giving up and starting on a new message.

If she was right, she'd transcribed two German words into English from a message of only two lines. Surely that must mean the settings were correct today. She wanted to leap up and announce it, then quickly remembered Wanda's words. But she couldn't still her heart from jumping to her throat, making her almost choke with excitement. She looked around at the other girls, heads bent over their machines. Wanda was sitting quietly in the corner of the room, looking up now and again from writing her notes. Dale stood and wove her way between the desks, ignoring two or three curious glances from her colleagues.

'Mrs Wilcox, I think I've got something,' Dale said in an undertone, trying to contain her excitement as she handed the woman her notepad.

Wanda immediately stiffened and put out a hand. She studied it for a minute, then looked past Dale at the room.

'Dulcie's decoded a couple of German words,' she said. 'Even those two words are enough to know today's settings were correct. I know we're near the end of our shift, but any messages from now on, you'll have a good chance of decoding them.' There was a murmur of approval. 'Right, everyone. You have another hour yet. I'll let the right people know their settings were correct today, though it's a shame no one discovered this earlier. It would have made all the difference.'

Disappointment surged through Dale. If only Wanda had allowed her to be the one to deliver the decoded message. She would have loved to have had a glimpse of what went on in the cryptanalysts' Hut. But Wanda had already torn the page from Dale's notebook and disappeared. Dale gave an inward shrug as she continued working her way through the pile. At least she now knew the settings were correct and that would give her and the others a good chance of decoding more messages between now and midnight.

Chapter Twenty

Dale found herself glancing towards the door, expecting Wanda to appear at any moment. But the clock chimed midnight and Eddie only had a few minutes.

The graveyard shift began coming in. Wanda was obviously not coming back. Dale grabbed her jacket and bag, said a quick goodnight to Sonia and sprinted across the room. Realising this looked a bit conspicuous, she walked more calmly out of the Hut door and into the blackness. She knew her way by now, but she was still glad of the tiny light her torch gave, covered as it was with the regulation tissue paper. People were all leaving at the same time, calling out 'goodnight' to one another, a pair of girls with arms linked tripping towards the bus that would take them back to their digs.

She recognised the outline of the lone figure tossing a cigarette on the path leading to the lake. He turned as she went towards him and took her arm.

'We're going in the motor.'

'I thought you only had a few minutes.'

'One of the chaps owed me a favour.' She couldn't make out his expression in the dark. 'You'll have to trust me on this one. Can you?'

'Yes, of course.'

She walked with him to a large open barn where his bright yellow car, its roof now closed, stood out against all the larger and sleeker black ones.

'It's not far,' Eddie remarked as he spun the tyres on the gravel drive.

'Where are we going?'

'To meet your new hosts,' he said, grinning as they passed through the gates.

'Really?' Dale's mouth fell open. 'What, now?'

He turned his head to her.

'Well, I had to fix you up with something as a matter of urgency. You're going to be booted out tomorrow – and it *will* be tomorrow as it's already Friday. I'm only just going to scrape you in, by the looks of things.' He chuckled, sounding very pleased with himself.

'But it's after midnight,' Dale protested. 'They'll be asleep.'

'Not this couple,' Eddie said. 'He's a night owl and she's just curious and looking forward to meeting you. It might only be temporary, mind, but at least it will solve an immediate problem.'

'So long as it's not like the Drapers' miserable place.'

'I can assure you it won't be a bit like the Drapers.'

These people presumably knew Eddie was also working at the Park and would respect the secrecy they had to maintain. A soft breath escaped her lips.

'You should be able to bike it,' Eddie said as he skilfully took the sharp bends, 'but there's a bus stop just along the bottom of the second drive of the main house and it will drop you off at BP.' He straightened the wheel and glanced at her. 'I didn't ask about your day. Or rather night.'

'The usual routine,' she managed to say casually, her chest tight with what she was sure had been the success of that first message she'd managed to crack.

She longed to ask him exactly what would happen now to the message. Without any hint from him she thought it possible he was one of the cryptanalysts who'd seen the two words she'd decoded not even an hour ago. If only she could ask him.

But she didn't dare.

The message could be of very little importance – or it could be something major. There was just no way of knowing. She couldn't help a frisson of excitement, imagining those cryptanalysts further decoding it, and giving a shout of jubilation that the whole message had sprung to life and therefore the settings had been correct that day. It was such a shame she hadn't discovered it earlier.

They passed a row of cottages and Eddie slowed down. Dale thought he was making for the last one, but he drove by and abruptly turned into a drive, the entrance hidden by thick shrubbery and trees.

Where on earth was he taking her? The car's headlights were so dimmed to comply with the blackout regulations that she could only see the vague outline of a canopy of trees as the car slowly made its way along the drive, now gravel, towards the bulky shape of a house.

Eddie swung the car round a circular carriage drive and leapt out to open her passenger door.

'Welcome to Langton Hall, madam,' he said, giving a sweeping bow, then put out his hand to help her out.

'Who lives here?' Dale asked as Eddie pulled the bell cord.

'My aunt and uncle – answering to Lord and Lady Langton.'

Before Dale could digest this information, the door swung open and a golden Labrador shot out, followed by a tall, upright man in a dinner jacket.

'Good show, Edward,' he said in a beautifully modulated

accent. 'Come on in. Baxter, come here, boy.' The dog licked Eddie's hand. 'I sent everybody to bed – but Hetty's still up.'

He held the door wide, then smiled at Dale as she stepped into an elegant hall. A magnificent curving staircase rose to the upper floor and a crystal chandelier seemed to float from above.

'And you're the young lady Edward's been telling us about.' He put out his hand to shake Dale's, his grip firm yet friendly. 'Hetty's had the kettle boiling on and off for the last fifteen minutes, trying to judge when you'd arrive. I'll call her. Edward, help Miss Treadwell with her jacket. Make your-selves at home,' he said over his shoulder as he went to find his wife.

A short, plumpish lady bristling with energy appeared at one of the doors.

'I told Gresham to show you into the drawing room,' she said, giving her husband a severe frown. Then it softened as she turned to Dale. 'Come through, my dear. You must be tired after the night shift.'

'Yes, it was quite a long night, but I feel wide awake now, and only sorry to have kept you both up at such an hour.'

'Gresham is always late to bed. If I can get him up the stairs by midnight I'm doing well.' She chuckled. 'Just take that seat over by the fire, though it's almost out now, I'm afraid, and I'll make some cocoa.'

'That'd be lovely,' Dale said fervently.

Lord Langton took a stance by the mantelpiece and lit his pipe.

'We haven't taken in anyone from the Park yet,' he said, giving a few quick puffs to get his pipe going. 'But Hetty and I have been discussing this for a few weeks now and we'd like to help the war effort however we can. So when young Edward here said could we do a favour and help you out—' he broke off with a smile at Dale '—we said yes immediately.'

Dale was momentarily stunned. It was hard to take in that this country house might be her new billet. It couldn't be more opposite to the Drapers' at number forty-three if it tried. Then the realisation hit her. She wouldn't be able to afford it. It would be heaps more than she'd paid at the Drapers'. Heat flooding her cheeks, she said:

'I'm afraid Eddie didn't mention rent—'

'No rent,' Lord Langton broke in.

'But—'

'No buts. Hetty and I already agreed.'

'At least I can give you my food coupons.'

'I'm sure Cook will find them very welcome.' Lord Gresham smiled.

'I haven't any letter of recommendation—' Dale began.

'No need to worry. Eddie's recommended you and that's good enough for me.' Lord Gresham smiled, the same smile as his nephew. 'You're probably under the aegis of Commander Travis,' he added unexpectedly, then chuckled. 'Don't worry. He and I are old friends.'

'You know we can't comment on anything,' Eddie put in, to Dale's relief.

'Yes, of course, my boy, but I want Miss Treadwell—' he glanced at her '—or may I call you Dale?' She nodded. 'I want Dale to feel she can relax here, knowing I'm not completely oblivious to what's going on at the Park.'

'Thank you,' Dale said, not sure she'd be able to relax in such sumptuous surroundings. She suddenly thought of something. 'Would I be able to bring my bicycle?'

'Yes, of course,' Lord Langton said. 'Plenty of space to store it in the coach house.'

'That would be wonderful,' she said as Lady Langton came

in with a tray bearing two dainty cups and saucers and a plate of biscuits. Dale noticed she had a slight limp.

'You didn't want one, did you, dearest?' she said to her husband.

'You know I can't stand the stuff,' Lord Langton said. 'Whisky's more my tipple.' He glanced at Eddie. 'Would you care to join me, Edward?'

Dale would have much preferred to join Eddie's uncle with a glass of whisky to soothe her nerves, but Eddie said, 'Better not, Uncle. I need to make sure Dale gets back safely. We won't stay more than a few minutes. Her landlords are bad enough as it is when she does shift work, and we don't want to keep you up longer than necessary.'

Lady Langton handed Dale a cup of cocoa and offered her a biscuit. Baxter bounded up to her, a hopeful expression in his eyes.

'Is he allowed one?' Dale asked.

'Just one.'

She took two biscuits and gave one to Baxter who wolfed it in one bite, then sat by her feet. She took a cautious sip of the drink, thinking it would be boiling hot. But it was barely warm and so weak she couldn't taste any hint of chocolate. She shook herself. It was mean of her to think like that. These people were very kind, and if they'd have her – even for a couple of weeks to give her a chance to find something permanent, she'd jump at it. She swallowed the liquid in four gulps.

'Would you like Gresham to show you the room?' Lady Langton said to Dale. 'My legs aren't that good after the accident, so I try not to do the stairs more than twice a day – not easy when most of the staff have left us to join up.'

'Honestly, it won't be necessary to look at the room right now,' Dale said, at last feeling the sting of tiredness in her eyes. She noticed a quick look pass between Lady Langton and her husband. He gave a slight nod.

'I believe Edward said you were leaving your current billet on Saturday – well, it's already Friday so that's tomorrow. It doesn't give you much time to think about it, but we'd be delighted to have you.'

'Thank you so much,' Dale murmured, following Eddie's move and rising to her feet. 'It really is kind of you both. I should love to take up your offer.'

'Then we'll expect you when we see you,' Lady Langton said. 'The important thing is for you to feel comfortable and at home with us.'

Dale and Eddie said their goodbyes and soon they were on their way back to the Drapers'.

She glanced at his profile. 'Eddie, where do *you* live?'

She knew before he answered.

'All the time I'm working at BP I'm at Langton Hall!'

She sat in silence. She'd see Eddie far more than she did now. She couldn't even rely on him doing different shifts as he seemed to know her own schedule and match his with hers. He was obviously a big cheese in whatever section he worked. Then it struck her. Of course he would be. He was the nephew of the local aristocrats. That's where his posh voice stemmed from. Probably had his own title, she wouldn't be surprised.

As if he'd tapped into her thoughts, Eddie gave her a quick glance.

'It won't make any difference to us, if that's what's worrying you.' He paused. 'You've pretty much told me where I stand and I have to take it on the chin. But you'll be all right with my aunt and uncle. They're a genuinely decent couple who won't pry, though my uncle, as you can probably tell, does have more than a clue than most as to what's going on. He used to be in MI5. A very senior position but now retired.'

'They've made me feel more than welcome,' Dale said, trying to weigh it all up.

They must have supposed she'd gone through the vetting system to enter Bletchley Park and they'd refused to accept any rent. That was the bit she'd been dreading – what they would have expected for offering a room in such a beautiful country house.

Praying she wasn't making a wrong decision that might ultimately hurt him, she said:

'If you're sure they're happy about it, I'm really grateful to you, Eddie. But tell me how I address them.'

'Technically, he's a viscount, so Lord and Lady Langton. But they don't stand on ceremony,' he said. 'Just be yourself.'

The following day was her very last evening at the Drapers'. As was her regular habit she opened Hugo's crammer, *German in Three Months*, that she'd bought in Foyles a couple of years ago and regretfully never got further than the first half dozen pages. Now, after a determined effort these last weeks, she was halfway through.

After an hour of jotting down the answers to the various exercises, already becoming more difficult, but encouraged by most of her answers being correct when she checked the back of the book, she flung down her pencil. Standing up she stretched and immediately banged her hands against the rafters. She cursed out loud. Such a cramped space. That was obviously all the Drapers thought she deserved. She sighed and picked up Hugo's book again, but this time she found it hard to concentrate. Perhaps she should have a change. Read from a proper German book. She jumped from the bed and found *Der Kleine Prinz* – the one she'd mentioned on her interview. It was a sweetly illustrated book, looking for all the world like one for children, but it had some important messages for adults. She opened it and began reading out loud, enjoying the sound of the foreign words on her tongue.

She was quite carried away with her joy at perfectly understanding the story without having to translate back into English, when she thought she heard a noise outside her door. She cocked her head. Nothing. Must be her imagination. She started. Was that a muffled cough? Springing up to open the door, she tripped on the small rug by the bed and would have fallen if she hadn't clutched onto the bedpost as she went. By the time she'd got to the door and looked out on the small square of landing there was no one in sight.

After a moment, she shrugged and turned back into her room. It was time to pack her case, ready for tomorrow.

Chapter Twenty-One

'Shan't be long,' Bert Draper called out to his wife as he opened the front door. 'Me and the boys have important things to discuss.'

Mrs Draper came up behind him. 'It's nearly nine o'clock. What's so important that you're goin' out at this time of the night for? You said you was havin' an early night.'

'It'll just be a quick pint with the lads.'

'*Lads*,' Mrs Draper said scornfully. 'Have any of you looked in the mirror lately?' She narrowed her eyes. 'What's this all about?'

'I'll tell you when I come home. You won't believe it.'

She thinks all we talk about is football and beer and women's tits. Bert stepped out briskly for the short walk to the pub. *Just wait 'til I tell her. But first, I want to hear what the lads have to say.*

He opened the pub door to the sound of the usual raucous laughter and thick smoke – both welcoming him in as his home from home.

'Bit late, aren't you, mate?' Sid Farrow tapped him on the shoulder.

'The wife made me mend the leakin' tap.'

Sid nodded in sympathy. 'Watcha havin'?'

'The usual.' Bert shrugged off his jacket.

'We're over there.' Sid jerked his head to a large round table by the bar where several of his mates were seated. All railway workers. Bert nodded in satisfaction. They were a grand lot. He wouldn't change any of them. But wait 'til he told them the news that had threatened to burst from his chest all day.

When he was settled with a mug of beer in front of him, Bert looked round at his mates and co-workers, his glass raised.

'Cheers, Sid.' He swallowed deeply and breathed out, 'Aaah. That's better. That's hit the spot all right.' He drained the mug then caught the eye of the bartender and nodded for another, then banged the full glass a couple of times on the table, letting it slop over the sides. Everyone stopped talking. 'Yer me mates, right?' Bert said. They all nodded, curiosity sparking in several pairs of eyes. 'Well, I could do with a spot of advice.'

'That's a new one,' Charlie Blackman, one of the engine drivers said, a grin spreading over his large ruddy face. 'You don't normally ask us. You usually give it.'

'That's as maybe,' Bert said. 'But I want to discuss something of the utmost importance.'

'What's that, then?'

'You know I've been forced to take one of them Park women,' Bert began.

'So you said,' Dave chimed in. 'Lucky bloke, havin' a tart wanderin' around the place.'

'You haven't got her up the duff, have you, mate?' Sid said, with a huge wink.

'What, under the wife's beady eye? No chance. She don't miss nothin' and she'd bleedin' kill me.' Bert let his eyes sweep round the circle of men. 'No. This is bleedin' serious.' He

204

took another swig, knowing he had their full attention. 'I've bin harbourin' a German spy!'

He didn't bother to lower his voice. Out of the corner of his eye he saw two heavily made-up women from a nearby table swivel their heads and stare wide-eyed at him. A middle-aged couple briefly turned, then the woman said something to her husband. There was a sudden hush at the bar where several customers were standing, all eyes now fixed on him. Just what he wanted. The more people who heard him the merrier.

'Pull the other one,' Charlie grinned.

'No, really. Listen to this. After I'd finished mendin' the bleedin' tap I heard voices from upstairs in the attic. That's where she sleeps.' He paused to make sure everyone was giving him full attention. 'Voices, mind. More'n one. Who's up there with her? I think to meself. So I creeps up and eavesdrops. She's talkin' to someone in some foreign language. Then I says to meself, "Don't be daft, Bert, no one would slip by the missus."' He shook his head. 'No, Miss *Treadwell*—' he paused, letting the name sink in '—is definitely on her own. Well, if that's the case, then why's she speakin' out loud? I thinks. Now I'm right suspicious. It in't French – I could tell that, all right. So it's got to be German with all that throat stuff they do. And then the penny drops, loud and clear. She were talkin' on a radio. And that call was goin' straight to Jerry – you mark my words.'

He looked round at his mates. For once, they seemed dumbfounded.

'Wot'cher goin' to do about it?' Sid said.

'I've got to work it out. Find out who's in charge up there at the Park. Let them know what's goin' on.'

205

'You'll be lucky.' Dave let the ash from his cigarette fall down the front of his shirt. 'Haven't you noticed all that barbed wire? It's like a prison. Probably is. They won't let you in.'

'Yeah, you may be right there,' Bert admitted. 'P'raps I'll go to the newspapers. I'm sure they'd be interested. Yeah, that might be the easiest way – leave it to them to start nosin' around . . . unless anyone's got any other suggestions.'

There was a silence.

'Then that's what I'll do,' Bert said, looking around and seeing several people still listening. 'Report the snotty Miss Treadwell to the papers.'

'S'long as you tell us what they do to the little bitch,' Charlie Blackman said, tipping back his head and draining his mug.

Bert nodded. 'Oh, yes. You can count on that.' He glanced round the table. 'Well, I do believe it's my round. Who's ready for another pint?'

Chapter Twenty-Two

On the Saturday, after Dale had had a quick snack in one of Bletchley's cafés and walked back to the Drapers', Eddie drew up in his yellow motor. She was waiting in the warm sunshine, her suitcase and extra bag on the pavement beside her. She couldn't help answering his beaming smile with one of her own as he sprang out and grabbed hold of her luggage.

'Good day for moving,' he said, raising his eyes to a cloudless blue sky. 'Oh, and your bike's in the garage.'

When she was settled and they were making their way towards Langton Hall, he said cheerfully, 'I noticed the lovely Drapers didn't come and wave you off.'

'It was quite horrible,' Dale said. 'I'm so pleased to be leaving that place.' She bit her lip. 'I had another row with Mr Draper. I don't trust that man at all.' She wouldn't go over what had happened that morning at breakfast.

Mrs Draper had sat in her usual seat by the side of her husband who was at the head of the table, with Dale opposite her.

'Mrs Draper, you know I'll be leaving today,' Dale said.

'Yes, so Mr Draper mentioned.'

'I'm afraid it hasn't been a pleasant stay for me,' Dale said. 'I had to let the Park know why I wanted to change my billet.'

'Oh.' Mr Draper's eyes were black as they fixed on her.

'It's so they know whether your address stays on their list. I wasn't happy with all the questioning, if you must know, and put it in my report.' She stared at Mr Draper. 'At least you won't be bothered by any of us any more, now my report's gone in.'

'You think you're very clever, don't you, Miss High and Mighty. And it won't be just *you* who's doin' the reportin',' he'd added belligerently.

What was he on about now?

She wouldn't give him the satisfaction of answering. She kept her gaze on him.

'I'll be surprised if anyone else puts up with you and your hoity-toity manner. You think you're so important, but you should be ashamed of yourself.'

Ashamed for not explaining in detail what I do at BP. Blasted little creep.

Now, in Eddie's motor, Dale sighed.

'What's that sigh for?' Eddie put his foot down on the accelerator. 'You're well rid of them.'

It had been pitch-dark when Eddie had first taken her to Langton Hall. Now, as he drew up in daylight, Dale gave a gasp of pleasure at the elegant three-storey building.

'It's beautiful . . . that lovely stonework . . . Georgian, isn't it?'

'Certainly is.'

'And those great beech trees behind, as though they're guarding the house. And the park. I love it already.' She turned to him, beaming.

'You can't prefer this to number forty-three.' Eddie's eyes were wide with mock astonishment.

'Well, I know nothing will be as comfortable as my attic room,' she giggled, 'but I'm willing to make a sacrifice for the war effort.'

This time a maid came to the door and ushered them in.

'Her Ladyship is expecting you,' she said. 'Shall I take the suitcase, Master Edward?'

'No need, Ruth,' Eddie said firmly. 'If you'll just tell me which room has been prepared.'

'The Rose Bedroom,' Ruth said. 'It's unlocked.'

'Right. Up the stairs, Dale, turn right, then it's the second door on the right.'

Dale had longed to walk up the beautiful curving staircase when she'd dimly seen it the first time. Smiling, she straightened her back as she mounted the marble steps. Eddie followed and set down the luggage, then opened the door to allow Dale to go in first. The room was enormous – and beautifully proportioned. Sunlight danced through a very large double window divided into small panes and alighted on a four-poster bed taking centre stage. It was draped in green velvet with a counterpane of cabbage roses and a plethora of pillows and embroidered cushions. Oh, she could just throw herself on the bed and sleep for a day.

She stepped over to the window. It looked over the kitchen gardens to the gentle green contours of the countryside beyond. She thought of her home in Pimlico and wished her mother had such a view instead of more houses exactly the same on the opposite side of the street, with barely a patch of sky in between.

'What a heavenly view, Eddie,' she said, turning to him.

'It is,' he agreed, looking over her shoulder. 'You might notice they haven't taped the windows against any explosions. My aunt said it was too depressing and she'd rather take the risk and see out. But if you're worried—'

'I'm not,' Dale said quickly. 'I'm inclined to agree with her.' She paused. 'Thank you so much for thinking of me and persuading them to take me in.'

'They didn't need persuading,' Eddie said. 'You're to have your meals with them whenever you're here, and I can vouch for Mrs Owens, the cook. She makes miracles from rations. And there's no need to worry about shift work. Someone will be about to let you in, however late. Anything you need, let my aunt know.' He gazed at her. 'Well, if you're sure you'll be all right, I'll leave you to it.'

Dale gave an inward sigh of relief. Dear Eddie. It was all too good to be true. Whatever would Glenn say if he could see her now in such a grand house? A lump rose in her throat.

Annoyed with herself for allowing the moment to be spoilt, she unpacked her suitcase, revelling in the huge oak wardrobe, the cupboards, the fresh flowers in a vase on an embroidered runner on top of the chest of drawers – everything the opposite of her attic room at the Drapers'. But even that, she reminded herself, would have been perfectly acceptable had they been pleasant landlords.

She'd go to the Park early to let them know in the Accommodations Office her change of address.

Eddie was nowhere around when she left Langton Hall an hour later and cycled down the drive for the five miles to the Park. It was a beautiful sunny morning and by the look of the cloudless sky it was going to be a hot day. She wondered if Eddie would pass her in his yellow motor. She didn't want to rely on him for lifts, though it would be nice if they were both on the same late shift and she could ride back to Langton Hall with him. Sailing round a bend, enjoying the feel of the wind in her hair, she couldn't quite believe her luck as she passed fields of sheep and cows, some of them giving her an indifferent glance before continuing their real interest in grazing.

Thirty-five minutes later she was in Miss Patch's office.

The same young girl who'd spoken to her the last time looked up from her typewriter.

'I know Miss Patch is still away,' Dale began, 'but I only want to leave you my new address.'

'Oh, you found something. That was quick.'

'Yes. I moved in two hours ago.'

Dale gave the address and the girl's jaw dropped.

'Langton Hall?' she repeated. 'They're not down on our books as a billet.'

'It's the first time they've taken anyone,' Dale answered.

'Can I add them to the list?'

'No, please don't,' Dale said quickly. 'I think they want to see how it goes with me,' she added with a smile. She was sure the Langtons wouldn't want the news spread around before they were ready.

'As you say.' Losing interest, the girl went back to her typing.

Dale opened the door to leave, nearly knocking over Wanda.

'I was just coming to see whether they had any new billets available,' Wanda said as she stepped back from the doorway. 'Seems like you're doing the same. So have they found you anything?'

'No, but I've met a nice couple and I've just moved in this morning.'

Wanda raised a dark eyebrow. 'Oh. Where's that?'

Dale felt awkward. Eddie hadn't said anything about not mentioning to anyone her new address, and she was obliged to let the Accommodations Office know where she'd moved to, but instinctively she didn't want to broadcast it.

'I don't really want to say unless I have their permission.'

Wanda stared at her. 'You're making them sound very mysterious.'

'It's just that I'm a sort of experiment. They've never taken in a lodger before.'

'It sounds most peculiar,' Wanda said, sounding a trifle huffy. 'You might remember *I'm* not that happy where *I* am.'

Dale took the first message from the pile. She chewed her lip as she tapped the first letter of the message and wrote down the new letter, lit up on the lamp board, in her notebook. She peered at the groups of letters she'd jotted down. Wanda had told them to train their minds to look out for anything a little unusual – the weather, a salutation, an officer's rank. Anything repeated that could be a way of breaking the codes.

'Believe it or not, the Germans are a sentimental lot,' she'd said. 'Think of Wagner and the Romantische Strasse. They have been known to quote from their poets and authors. Once you're on to something like that, you've found the crib.'

As she methodically worked through the pile, she didn't want to be anywhere else but here with her colleagues doing her best to decode the hundreds of messages which poured in every day.

It had been a long session, Dale thought with a sigh. She glanced at her watch. Only five more minutes and they could have a stretch by walking over to the canteen for supper. The buzz of conversation was much louder this evening. To Dale's ears it felt excitable, though tense. She wondered what had happened. Had someone decoded something really big? She saw a face she recognised waving to her to join his table.

'Vernon. Remember me?' he said, with his charming smile.

212

'Yes, of course.' Dale settled herself, ready to tuck into the somewhat overcooked omelette. She realised she was hungry.

'How're you getting on?'

'All right, I think . . . hope,' she added, returning his smile.

'Have you heard the news?'

'No. What?'

'Last night Jerry bombed London – not the airfields as you'd expect, but the West End, can you believe?'

Dale gave a start. The West End wasn't that far from Pimlico. She'd walked it many times. Had her mother heard any explosions? If so, she'd be petrified. Dale swallowed hard. If only she wasn't on the afternoon to midnight shift, she could have rung her. She'd have to wait until tomorrow morning.

Vernon was watching her closely. 'I say, is anything the matter? You've gone a bit pale.'

'Our house isn't that far away from the West End and my mother lives alone.'

'Well, you'd have heard by now if anything had happened to her.' Vernon patted her arm.

She'd have to take comfort in that.

'Do you know what damage it's done?'

'Not yet. It was too late to make the morning papers. But no doubt there'll be some.'

After all the months of preparation, but no actual bombing, it was difficult to visualise any destruction – this time there'd probably be civilians killed.

'They said on the wireless they don't think it was a planned raid . . . that it was an accident,' Vernon went on. 'Apparently, the Luftwaffe was supposed to have aimed for military targets outside the city but overshot them and caught London instead. It was quite cloudy last night so not surprising. They'll probably never know for sure if it was an accident,

213

but I doubt Churchill will take any chances.' He looked at her. 'I reckon he'll retaliate and our chaps will go hell for leather straight to Berlin within the next twenty-four hours.'

Dale froze, her knife and fork in mid-air.

Glenn. Oh, Glenn – where are you? Are you still in Berlin? If you are, please keep safe. Even if we never see one another again, I don't want you to die in an air raid by the RAF. It would be too horrible for words.

First her mother, then Glenn. She couldn't eat another bite. The omelette had been cooked in so much lard it was making her stomach curdle. She couldn't stay a minute longer. She'd go back to her desk where she'd be on her own. Scraping back her chair she tipped her tray over and Vernon only just managed to save her plate from crashing to the floor.

'Sorry, I'm not hungry after all,' she mumbled.

'Hey.' Vernon rose and took hold of her arm. 'This is the second time you've run out on me.'

'Sorry,' she said again, shrugging him off. Let him think what he liked.

Back at her desk her mouth felt dry. She ought to have drunk a glass of water. But all she could think of was that if Vernon was right, Glenn could soon be in danger.

As though on autopilot she went through a dozen or so messages without making any sense. By the time she'd finished and was ready for a new pile that had just been delivered, the rest of her colleagues came in, chattering and laughing as though they didn't have a care in the world.

Eddie was waiting for her at midnight to run them back to Langton Hall.

'How did you get on today?' he asked as he pulled out of the Park's gates.

'It was just routine.'

He turned his head. 'Nothing exciting?' He paused. 'Like the words you uncovered a couple of nights ago?'

She gave a sharp intake of breath. Was he testing her? How should she answer him? She clamped her lips tight, terrified of saying something she shouldn't.

'It's all right,' he said. 'I'm the one who translated the rest of the message from those vital few words.'

So Eddie really was *one of the cryptanalysts.*

She gave him a sidelong glance. His attention was fixed on the road.

But hold on, Dale – this could be a trap.

She sat silently, her hands folded in her lap to stop them shaking.

'So well done.' He paused and turned his head. 'You're not saying anything.'

'You know I can't discuss anything about my work outside our Hut.'

'No, of course not,' he said quickly. 'But I'll just tell you something to encourage you – it's a bloody good start.'

'But others have cracked codes before me.'

'They've been doing it for longer. You've been here less than a fortnight. And some of the women will be bilingual in German.'

How badly she wanted to ask him puzzling questions now she knew his job. But it was deeply satisfying to know what the response had been and that Eddie, and hopefully the others he worked with, acknowledged she'd had at least the one success. But it was enough to spur her on.

'And now you've cracked it once you'll find it gets a little easier to spot – if we've got the settings correct, that is,' he added. He glanced at her. 'I suppose you heard about the bombing on Oxford Street?'

'Yes, Vernon told me when I sat at his table in the canteen though he didn't pinpoint it to Oxford Street.'

Eddie swung his head round. 'Would that be Vernon Bannister?'

'Yes.'

'Hmm. Be careful of him. He's a womaniser.'

'You don't have to warn me. He's not my type.'

'That's not what most women say.'

Dale was beginning to feel irritated.

'Look, Eddie, I've no designs on Vernon Bannister, but I *am* worried about my mother.'

'Oh, yes, you're in Pimlico, but don't worry. The damage didn't go further than Oxford Street.' He paused. 'But if you want to ring her my uncle will still be up when we get back. I'm sure he'll let you use the telephone.'

'I don't think I will,' Dale said. 'My mother's a nervous woman and she might not even have heard about it.'

'That's probably just as well.'

Feeling strange getting ready for bed in such palatial surroundings, Dale quickly cleaned her teeth in the wash-basin, smoothed a few drops of almond oil on her face, shook out her hair from the combs and, without bothering to brush it, climbed into the high four-poster bed. She lay on her back, her mind racing with all that had happened these last two days. The pillow smelt a little musty, as did the sheet. She noticed the velvet drapes around the bed were faded and some of the tassels were missing or frayed. No one could have slept in here for months.

Idly, she wondered where Eddie's room was. All he'd talked about after the mention of the London bombing was Langton Hall and how, as a small boy, he'd loved playing with his cousins in the grounds at every opportunity. And how his aunt and uncle had always treated him like another son, especially since he'd lost both his parents in a plane crash only eighteen months ago.

But even as he'd talked and Dale had murmured her sympathy, Glenn had been uppermost in her mind. The RAF were probably this very moment roaring towards Berlin with a full load of bombs. The thought made her stomach clench so hard she thought she might be sick. She must stop thinking about what might or might not be or she'd go mad.

She'd wanted Eddie to keep talking to take her mind off Glenn, but he'd naturally gone quiet after breaking the news of his parents' death.

The feather mattress enclosed the contours of her body, soothing her overwrought imagination, allowing her to switch her mind to the coded messages. Why were they always grouped in letters of five? Even Wanda hadn't been able to explain the reason. In her head, Dale saw the neat groups of letters in front of her. How she'd discovered those German words. Maybe the cryptanalysts had arbitrarily decided that anything shorter than five letters wouldn't be enough to form any kind of significant word – it would look too 'bitty' – and anything longer would appear even more muddled. Five was probably tried and tested to have the best chance of spotting anything. Such a simple logical decision. With a pleased smile curving her lips she turned over to her side and within minutes she'd fallen asleep.

Chapter Twenty-Three

'Will you please come to the training room, Dulcie?' Wanda said, two days later when Dale was on the hated midnight shift.

Dale glanced at the clock. Just gone four. She badly needed a cup of tea.

Sonia looked round curiously. 'Sounds ominous.'

Dale shrugged. As far as she was aware there wasn't any problem. She was never late. She did her shifts without complaint and rarely got involved in the other girls' conversations at break times.

Wanda waved her to one of the chairs, now set round the table where the Enigma machine still sat.

'How are your new digs working out?' was her first question.

The question seemed innocent enough, given Wanda's recent unfriendliness, but Dale was on full alert.

'Um, fine, thanks.'

'And you still won't tell me where you've moved to?'

Dale shifted in her chair. What was all this about? Before she could think of a reply, Wanda said:

'I know you've gone to Langton Hall.'

Dale gave a start.

'As your supervisor I need to know.' Wanda narrowed her

eyes. 'I knew it would be something special because you were so cagey about it.'

'I was asked not to broadcast it.'

'Rather different from where you were, I should think,' Wanda commented drily, although her eyes gleamed.

'Yes, it is,' Dale said, beginning to feel uncomfortable. This was leading somewhere.

'Well, I haven't called you in to discuss your accommodation,' Wanda said abruptly. 'It's for another matter – rather more serious, I'm afraid.'

Dale's heart jumped.

'Your previous landlord, Mr Draper, has made a serious allegation against you.'

Dale frowned. 'Oh?'

'He said you know the rules that you were not to invite anyone into your room unless you had his permission, and he distinctly heard you talking to someone on your last evening.'

'I've never had anyone in my room.'

'No, he said on second thoughts he realised no one would get past him or his wife.' She looked at Dale. 'So he concluded you were talking on a radio transmitter.'

'What on earth is he on about? I was—'

Wanda held up her hand in that irritating way she had. 'But what Mr Draper was more concerned about was that it sounded like you were talking to whoever it was in *German*.'

Dale let out a peal of laughter. 'Oh, that,' she said, thankful she could explain. 'I was practising my German out loud.' She looked at Wanda. 'Do you know, I thought I heard someone outside my door – in fact, Mr Draper has a nervous cough and I was sure I heard that – but when I went to look, there was no one in sight. He must've been eavesdropping and got hold of the wrong end of the stick.'

219

Wanda kept her gaze on Dale. 'He says he's been harbouring a German spy.'

'What?' Dale's face screwed up in disbelief.

'Yes, they were his words,' Wanda said.

'How ridiculous. I'm so thankful to be out of that horrible place. Well, at least his mates would have told him in no uncertain terms that he was having them on. No one would have believed such a fantastic story.'

'Oh, but I'm afraid they did.' Wanda held Dale's gaze. 'He spread it in the pub that night, telling anyone in hearing distance. As it happens, one of our cleaning ladies was in the pub that night and overheard the whole conversation. She said he was going to inform the newspapers.'

Dear God, this was serious.

Dale felt every muscle tense as she scrambled to understand how something so innocent had escalated like this.

'The cleaner found out which Hut you were in and reported it to me,' Wanda went on. 'You were lucky she didn't go straight to Commander Travis.'

Surely Wanda was intelligent enough to know that nobody in their right mind would think for a second it was true. So why was her heart about to burst from her chest?

'I can assure you I'm not a spy,' she said.

'I don't suppose you are for one minute.' Wanda gave a mirthless laugh. 'But you brought the Park into the limelight to those people in the pub. His mates who believe it will start wondering what the devil is going on here for the Nazis to bother to infiltrate one of their spies. Must be something very important, the pub lot are bound to think.' She looked at Dale and tutted. 'Why on earth didn't you think before you started speaking out loud in German?' She stared unblinkingly at Dale.

'I didn't think anything,' Dale said, forcing her voice to

keep steady. 'Stupidly, I thought my room was private. Seems I was wrong. All I was doing was trying to improve my German. I can show you my books to prove it.'

'Well, however innocent you are, and of course I believe you, I should report this to Commander Travis.'

Dale's temper suddenly flared. 'I'm happy to go and speak to him myself. I'm sure he'll realise Mr Draper's not very bright and that will be the end of it.'

'I wouldn't do that,' Wanda said quickly. 'There's no need to involve him. *I* don't plan to mention it at this particular juncture.'

What on earth was the woman insinuating?

But Wanda's next words sent a chill down her spine.

'There's no need for this unfortunate incident to come out, as at this moment only I and the cleaner know about it. She, like all the other members of staff at the Park, has signed the Official Secrets Act, so she's fully aware she must keep the conversation she and I had firmly under wraps.' She gave a half smile. 'However, it might be a . . . *prudent* gesture if you were to ask the Langtons if they'd offer me a billet.' Keeping her eyes fixed on Dale, she said, 'Would you do that – as a friend, of course?'

Was Dale dreaming? It sounded like a threat. She could feel her heartbeat thudding in her ears. If she didn't ask the Langtons, then Wanda was giving no guarantee that she wouldn't take what she called an 'unfortunate incident' any further. Dale hesitated. What should she do? It was an imposition to ask them. Should she go to Eddie? No, she couldn't involve him. He wouldn't want to bring any hint of suspicion to his aunt and uncle after asking them such a favour to take *her* in. The alternative was staring her in the face. If she explained to Commander Travis, surely he'd believe her. But dare she take the risk? Furious that Wanda should put her in such a position over something so patently ridiculous made a spurt of anger rise in her throat. She looked straight at Wanda whose smile now registered regret.

'It might put them in an awkward position.'

'I think you'll persuade them with your charm.' Wanda glanced at her watch. 'Good. Mrs Jolly should be round with the tea urn at any moment and I'm sure you could do with one. Oh, by the way, I collected everyone's post this afternoon before the mail room shut.' She handed Dale a couple of envelopes.

Dale was about to retort that she preferred to pick up her own post, thank you very much, but the gleam in Wanda's eyes stopped her. She glanced at the envelopes. One from Mother and a typed one from London which she'd forwarded on. But there'd be no chance to read them until she was back at the Langtons'.

For the rest of the shift, Wanda acted perfectly normally. All Dale could hope for was that Draper had been bluffing about the newspapers and there wouldn't be any further ramifications. She put a hand to her head. It felt fuzzy and her stomach was protesting against the strange mealtimes on the night shift. But she needed to think what to do about Wanda's demand.

Perhaps she could have a quiet word with Eddie to get his reaction. Make out Wanda was more of a friend than she actually was. Yes, that's what she'd do. If Eddie said he was sure they wouldn't mind at all, then maybe things could get back to normal.

And if they didn't, her inner voice said. *If Eddie said not to approach them, or indeed if the Langtons said no – what then?*

It was just possible Wanda might not be making an idle threat. And next thing, she'd be defending herself to

Commander Travis against that little twerp Draper. Which meant she'd be tossed out of the Park, and her reputation in tatters. No company would want to touch her after that.

She certainly didn't know Wanda well enough to guess which way the woman was thinking. Was it a real threat? Or was she just joking to let her know if there was a chance Lord and Lady Langton would accept her, she'd love to live there? No, Wanda never cracked a joke. She was deadly serious.

By the time Dale had gone outside for a breath of air, dawn was breaking.

'It's a perfect time of the day, isn't it?' Sonia said, coming to stand by her side as Dale watched the ducks and swans on the lake. 'Watching nature. It's so peaceful. And knowing we're doing something important to help our soldiers.'

'Mmm,' Dale agreed, not really wanting to chat to Sonia.

'You're very quiet.'

Dale shrugged. 'Tired, I expect.'

'I wish we could spot something important now and again to keep us going,' Sonia said. 'What do you focus on when you're looking at the new groups of words you've written?'

'I suppose I'm looking for any repeat pattern. Seeing if there's a German word that stands out. That night I had my first break I saw a word that was exactly in the five letters and it jumped out at me.'

'I need that to happen to me.' Sonia sounded rueful.

'What made you come to Bletchley?'

'Daddy. He had connections with the military. I'm pretty good at maths and apparently that helps you see things differently – solve things.'

'Why don't you have a word with Mrs Wilcox,' Dale suggested. 'Maybe she could transfer you. Put you somewhere you could use those skills.'

Sonia stared at her. She seemed to hesitate. Then she said: 'Dale, what do you really think of Wanda Wilcox?'

Was this a trap? From Wanda herself to see what I might disclose to Sonia.

'She's okay,' Dale said, making her tone as non-committal as possible. 'I suppose she has quite a lot of responsibility keeping us motivated.'

'Just okay?' Sonia repeated. 'Nothing more?'

'I don't know her that well.' Dale hesitated. 'Why do you ask?'

'People say I'm a bit psychic,' Sonia said. 'So maybe I'm being unfair. But there's something about her I don't trust.'

Dale felt a prickle of anxiety. Had Sonia suspected anything about her and Wanda's conversation a few hours ago?

'Any reason for thinking that?' she asked casually.

'Yes. Did you know she has her eye on the chap I've seen you with a couple of times in that yellow motorcar?'

'What, Eddie?' Dale laughed. 'What's that got to do with not trusting her?'

'Everything.' Sonia paused, almost as though for effect. 'Apparently, he and Wanda had been dating for several weeks. That is, until *you* came along.'

She wasn't prepared for this. Nor was she prepared to feel a little piqued at the image of Eddie with Wanda.

'And I've heard through the grapevine he's dumped her. You can imagine Wanda's not amused. And you know something?' She looked up at Dale, her baby blue eyes wide. 'I'd say she's the sort who'd be out for revenge if things didn't go her way.'

Chapter Twenty-Four

Dale couldn't stop thinking about Sonia's innocently prophetic words when she went back to her desk. The girl obviously thought she was warning her that Wanda had her claws in Eddie, and Dale had better watch out. That would explain why she was so upset, having already had an unfaithful husband. And underneath her seemingly friendly exterior lurked Wanda's determination to move to Langton Hall, almost as though she were competing.

Though a little hilly, it was a pretty country ride to her new billet, Dale thought, wobbling a little as she cycled along, hoping the fresh air would help pull her round from the long, stuffy night in the Hut. She gave a wry smile. Even though she'd only been at Langton Hall for a few days she never thought of the elegant country house as her digs. That word had only applied to the Drapers'. Her smile faded and a bubble of anger took its place. What a foolish, ignorant man Mr Draper was. What on earth was his game? Surely no one in the pub would have believed such nonsense. Who would have thought that reading her German book aloud to become reacquainted with the language would have led to his thinking she must be a German spy? Or was he brighter than she'd given him credit for? Had he simply searched for any excuse to get her into trouble because she'd refused to tell him what she was doing at the Park? Dale bit her lip. That was probably more like it. Even if someone like Wanda had pointed out to him the futility of the accusation, he only had to say it was better to be safe than sorry by reporting anything that could possibly be deemed suspicious. That he was an upstanding citizen who only wanted to do his duty. By then, he would have achieved exactly what he'd set out to do.

Stevens, the Langtons' butler, opened the door.

'Welcome back, miss,' he said, standing aside to let her pass by. 'His lordship said if you haven't eaten, to join him at breakfast. He's in the dining room.' He ushered her in, and Lord Langton half rose from his chair.

'There you are, my dear. Do help yourself to the buffet.' He nodded towards a table draped in a white cloth by the French windows. 'Then come and join me.'

Dale gingerly took the silver dome off one of the platters. Four pairs of kidneys looked up at her and she quickly put the lid back on. The second one, to her relief, contained a mound of buttery, bright yellow scrambled eggs. The chickens she'd heard clucking were doing their bit, she thought, grinning as she spooned a serving onto her plate, then inspected the third platter from which an enticing salty smell of several rashers of bacon wafted upwards. She helped herself to two rashers though she could happily have wolfed the lot, it had been so long since she'd tasted bacon. She took half a grilled tomato, fluted round the edges, and a slice of pre-buttered toast, then went back to the breakfast table, her mouth watering with anticipation.

'May I pour you a coffee,' Lord Langton said, smiling at her.

'Please.' She'd rather have had a cup of tea at this time of the day but perhaps the coffee would wake her up enough that she wouldn't fall asleep over the table and embarrass herself, let alone his lordship. She grinned at the image.

He picked up a silver coffee pot and half-filled her cup, then passed her the jug of hot milk. She poured some in and took a sip. Oh, it was good. Not the awful coffee they frequently served at the Park, made from dandelions or acorns, or something equally foul.

Lord Langton silently finished his breakfast and dabbed his mouth with a spotless napkin.

'How did the night go?' he asked.

'Fairly routine,' she answered, taking a bite of the delicious breakfast. She didn't want to talk – didn't want even to think. Her mind was numb from the long night and Wanda's bombshell.

'Well, just relax and enjoy your breakfast. And if you don't mind . . .' He indicated his newspaper.

'No, not at all.'

Minutes later she smothered a yawn as she put her knife and fork together on her empty plate.

'You poor girl.' Lord Langton stood. 'While we've been sound asleep in our beds you've been working like a Trojan.'

'I think I will try to have a few hours,' Dale said, rising.

'You do whatever you like. It's your home while you're with us.'

Should she broach the subject about someone she worked with who was looking for a billet? Dale hesitated. But it wasn't the right time when her head felt like cotton wool. And anyway, she hadn't had enough time to think it through.

Upstairs in her room she took off her jacket and lay on the bed, fully clothed. Then she remembered her letters. She got up and fished them from her handbag, and opened her mother's.

My dear Dulcie,

I hope you are still enjoying your job whatever you're doing. I wish you could tell me more about it. I try to picture you, but I have no idea what to picture.

Did you hear about the bombing the other night in Oxford Street? Thankfully, it was too late for anyone to be about but some of the department stores were damaged.

Have you heard from your father? I've heard nothing from the solicitors.

Elizabeth is still trying to persuade me to join her on the van, but I keep busy making her biscuits and cakes and she says they go down very well with the boys. And I have my sewing to get on with. I've made myself a new skirt and blouse. I'm trying to smarten myself up and lose a few lbs.

Well, dear, that's all for now. Oh, rather a thick letter came for you with a typed envelope. I've no idea what it was but I've forwarded it on to you, so you should get it with the same post as this. Write when you can. I miss you very much.

Your loving mother X

Dale puffed out her cheeks in relief. Her mother sounded as though she was coping quite well. Propping a pillow behind her head she sat up straight and glanced at the thicker, typed envelope. It had been sent to her home address but was now firmly crossed out and the PO Box number inserted in her mother's neat handwriting. Curiously, she slit it open. Inside was a sheet of typed paper and a second typed envelope addressed to the *Kensington Evening Post*. Frowning, she glanced at the signature on the letter: Bill. Feeling a little guilty that she hadn't bothered to have that coffee with him, she quickly scanned it.

Dear Dale,

I hope this finds you well. I expect by now you've been snapped up by another newspaper. If so, I do hope you're happy, but it hasn't been the same around here since you left. I miss your smiling face and our chats. Franklin is forever in a bad mood. When he saw a letter with your name and addressed to the KP he lost his temper, saying the newspaper was not to be used as a post box, particularly by someone who didn't even work here any longer and threw it in the wastepaper basket! But I retrieved it for you!

If you ever need to contact me, my address is at the top. I think you know by now I have a soft spot for you, but you've always made it clear you only wanted to be friends. So I'm your friend – all right?

All the very best,

Bill

With hands that shook uncontrollably, she opened the enclosed envelope, knowing with the most wonderful certainty who it was from. She removed the two sheets of paper covered on all sides in small handwriting. Her heartbeat pounded in her ears. She began to read:

September 8, 1939

Dear Lord, this was written nearly a year ago – just days after the last time she'd set eyes on him. She swallowed.

My dearest, most darling Dulcie,

Darling, I'm so very sorry I couldn't meet you on that last day as we'd arranged. You can't imagine how sick I felt at the idea of you waiting for me on the bridge, thinking

I'd stood you up, and what a jerk I was. You must have been furious. Then later maybe wondering if I'd had an accident. But when I left you that last night I was instructed to catch a very early morning flight and had to leave immediately for the airport with no way of letting you know. We were going to exchange addresses the following day!

I will do everything I can to see that this letter reaches you. But it might be some time arriving as it will have had a circuitous journey. I intend to take it to the American Embassy who I hope will send it on to a colleague and friend of mine, Don Murphy, at CBS Studios, 485 Madison Avenue, New York. It will go via Washington and then be redirected. I'm sure Don will then do everything possible to see that it's forwarded to you in England.

When I walked you home that first night in London's new blackout you said you lived in Pimlico but didn't mention the street, least of all the number. I just walked with you without taking much notice of exactly where we were going – it was hard to see anyway, and I don't know London. Besides, I was already captivated!

I don't know if you're still at the Kensington Post, but I think there's a better than average chance you'll get this. Even if you're no longer there, the editor (or his secretary) will have your address and will surely forward it to you.

You wouldn't believe the situation here. The city goes into blackout every evening and the streets are deserted. There's not much sign of rationing but there's a sense of unease that this is going to be a protracted war and things are bound to get worse for the civilians. I've not talked to many yet but the few I have didn't want this war. A terrible situation.

We're allowed to record our news bulletins and news-paper articles in full. I wonder how long that will last!

Darling Dulcie, I'm praying you'll receive this letter. I long to hear from you that you are keeping safe and are happy. If you can forgive me and write back, you should write to Don who will then send it on to Washington and it will eventually arrive at the Am. Embassy. It may take some time before you receive my answer as it's not a normal way of sending a letter and is asking a favour each time. But Don's a pretty good guy.

My hope is that by the time you get this letter, which may take weeks or even months, you won't have forgotten me. I keep imagining the worst – you will have given up hope of hearing from me and met someone else. If this is the case, darling, then with my whole heart I wish you every happiness but will curse this war for tearing us apart.

I love you and I always will.

Glenn XXXXX

She started to read it again, slowly this time. But the words blurred on the page. Automatically, she brushed her fingers across her eyelids. They were wet with tears. Glenn still loved her.

She closed her eyes. All this time she'd listened to her head, telling herself he'd forgotten her so she must forget him. She'd tried to give herself permission to meet someone else, even when her heart never wavered from insisting something had happened as to why he'd not been able to write. Her eyes tightly shut she whispered, 'I'll wait for you as long as it takes, my darling.'

For the first time in nearly a year, the yearning ache in her heart lifted.

*   *   *

Dale awoke and stretched out her arms. She looked at the bedside clock. Oh, my goodness. It was four o'clock. She'd slept all through lunch without even undressing. Quickly, she swung off the bed and tidied her hair in the mirror above the washbasin, marvelling at her eyes that sparkled with happiness. Glenn was alive. He loved her. A warm blanket wrapped itself around her heart. But with her next breath, she suddenly shivered and her mouth went dry. He was alive a year ago, but what had happened in the meantime? The RAF and the Luftwaffe were fighting it out in the skies over Kent to tremendous losses on both sides, so the papers said. And when the Luftwaffe had dropped bombs on London last month the RAF had immediately retaliated and done the same to Berlin. This was just the start – she was sure. But she couldn't lose him now – she just couldn't. She'd write to him today.

But first she was desperate for a cup of tea.

'I've just made a pot, love,' Mrs Owens said as Dale tentatively put her head round the kitchen door.

'How did you know that's what I was after?' Dale said as she came in and closed the door behind her to keep the warmth in.

'Stands to reason. His lordship said he'd packed you off to bed after you nearly fell asleep over the breakfast table.' She took another cup and saucer from the cupboard and poured out the two cups.

'He was right,' Dale grinned. 'I was exhausted, but I feel much better now.' She hugged herself at the thought of Glenn's letter. 'Thanks, Mrs Owens. Is it all right if I take it to my room?'

'Why don't you come and sit with me,' Mrs Owens said, easing herself down at the pine table. 'I don't have much company these days what with nearly all the staff leaving to join up.'

She'd answer her mother's letter later, Dale thought guiltily, as she sat at Cook's pine table and let Mrs Owens rattle on about her family until she was able to make her excuses and leave.

She needed to write to Glenn.

Chapter Twenty-Five

August 1940, Berlin

Sitting at his desk in the airless room which served as an office for three other American correspondents as well as himself, Glenn reread his notes, then put down his pen. He gave a deep sigh before lighting what must be his fourth cigarette in a row. What a night! He'd hardly slept two hours. Hearing the RAF flying overhead all the way from London had given him real hope for the first time they were showing Hitler that whatever he dished out the British weren't going to take it without strong retaliation. He'd certainly have plenty to talk about this evening over the air – that is, if they allowed him to mention the bombing.

To think that Göring, Hitler's Commander-in-Chief of the Luftwaffe, had boasted to Hitler that his air force would wipe out the RAF in less than a week, preparing the way for the invasion. Well, with Britain's superior Spitfires and Hurricanes, that hadn't happened, thank God. Göring's latest boast was that it was impossible for the RAF to reach Berlin. Hitler had believed him and had repeatedly assured the public in his many manic appearances that Berliners were safe from ever being bombed. Now *that* myth was shattered, too.

He'd been in Berlin long enough to know that Hitler would fly into one of his rages when he ordered Göring to report to him this morning. Glenn shook his head. He wouldn't want to be in his shoes. He'd met Hermann Göring once and found the creature utterly repulsive. He couldn't help a satisfied grin imagining the scene. But the situation was dangerous and ready to boil over at any minute, and with France having capitulated, Britain was standing alone. If only he and his colleagues, reporting as strongly as they could get away with under the suspicious eyes of the censors, could persuade Roosevelt to enter the war.

Glenn inhaled deeply. He had to bring the truth to the American people. Let them know that Hitler was determined to have domination not only over Europe but also the world, and to hell with democracy. He blew out the smoke through his nostrils, then cleared his throat. He should cut down on the cigarettes. His mouth felt stale. He needed several coffees and breakfast. He stubbed out his cigarette and ran down the apartment steps.

The neighbourhood appeared to be untouched. His stomach rumbling, he made his way to his favourite café where Stefan, the waiter, immediately brought him a double espresso.

As always, Glenn's thoughts turned to Dulcie. That tip-tilted nose, her mouth just made for kissing. The thick, gold-streaked hair. As though it were yesterday, he remembered how he'd removed the combs that first time they'd made love and her hair had tumbled around her shoulders like a shaft of sunlight in the dimly lit room. A quiver ran through him at the thought of the way she had given herself to him. Had seemed to hold nothing back. And in return he'd given her his body and mind, heart and soul as he'd floated on a cloud.

But he'd heard nothing from her. He'd sent several letters to the *Kensington Evening Post* but they must not have forwarded them or surely she would have answered. If only they'd had a chance to meet on what they'd thought would be their last day, he would have had her proper address and not be going through this torture.

She'd think he'd forgotten her. Didn't care about her. Had used her. She'd never know how sick at heart he'd been to leave without any word. But deep down he was certain, as far down as his very bones, that their love was so strong they would one day be together. Even if they had to wait until the war ended. Which wasn't going to be soon, by the look of things.

Momentarily, he closed his eyes against the warm rays of sun that already promised another hot day when suddenly a thought struck him, making him jerk from his slumped position at the café table. The tea dance at that hotel! Except for those staying there, everyone had had to sign in with an address. It was probably a long shot, but he had to try.

The thought cheered him immensely as he swallowed his coffee – nearly cold now – in three gulps, before a glum-looking Stefan set a plate of eggs and a white sausage in front of him with two hunks of rough brown bread.

'*Dankeschön,*' Glenn said, eyeing such a feast. Exactly what he needed to set him up and clear the fug from his brain.

'It is a sad day for Berliners,' Stefan remarked, as usual in English. 'A sad day for all Germany. No one will win.'

Glenn nodded his agreement as he peppered and salted his breakfast.

'Many German people do not want war,' Stefan went on, as though bursting to talk to someone who would listen. 'We have not recovered from the last one.'

'But your Führer has persuaded the people that other countries started the hostilities,' Glenn couldn't help commenting.

'Not all Berliners believe everything,' the waiter said, his mouth tightening as he looked beyond Glenn.

Glenn turned his head a fraction to see four highly decorated Nazis heading for the café.

'*Guten Appetit,*' Stefan said to Glenn in a louder voice, then gestured the newly arrived customers towards a nearby vacant table.

By now Glenn knew enough German to gather the gist of their conversation, mainly against the weakness of the British forces, said in loud, derisory tones followed by bursts of raucous laughter. It made him feel uncomfortable, especially when one officer glanced his way more than once and murmured to the others, who in turn looked across at him. Presumably the bastard was telling his slimy friends that the man in civvies, sitting on his own, was an American broadcaster.

Suddenly, the meal didn't look so appetising. He managed the eggs and toast, then asked for the check. As he passed by their table with a curt nod, he was aware of their upturned smirking faces as they acknowledged him.

Much later in his bedroom, Glenn scribbled his impressions of the day's events in his diary, as he did every evening unless he was too exhausted. He knew he was taking a huge risk. But he felt compelled to keep it up – to tell the truth. One day, after this was all over – please God, don't let it drag on – he'd smuggle it out of Germany and back to the States. That is, if the Gestapo didn't discover it first. And if by that time America had declared war on them, he knew he would be interned for the duration. The thought of a German internment camp filled him with horror.

Glad he'd got everything down while it was fresh in his mind, Glenn lit a cigarette and inhaled deeply. Rereading his words, he replayed the afternoon when he and some other journalists had gone along to one of Berlin's squares to listen to Hitler's latest rantings. He hadn't known how to contain his fury when Hitler screamed to the thousands in his audience that the British were killing innocent German men, women and children *on purpose*. Glenn gave a deep sigh. He'd made a broadcast only yesterday to the States announcing Hitler's latest order to the Luftwaffe to bomb London to smithereens and to take as long as necessary to break the morale of the citizens.

London. Glenn raked his fingers through his hair. As far as he knew, Dulcie still lived there with her mother and would no doubt soon witness the horrors the bombing would unleash.

Sweat trickled down his chest. He tore off his tie and loosened his collar. He stubbed the rest of his cigarette into a tin lid that served as an ashtray. For the first time it hadn't helped him to calm down. To do that he needed to think about Dulcie. Going to his bedside table he picked up the framed photograph and, feeling more than a little self-conscious, kissed it before propping it on his desk so he could see her lovely face as he wrote to her.

August 26, 1940

My beloved Dulcie,
All this time has gone by and I haven't heard from you. I pray you are safe and well. I'm doing OK but

Glenn stopped in mid-sentence. Should he tell her about Berlin being bombed last night? He sighed. Maybe not. It

238

would only worry her, though she'd probably hear it soon enough. He crossed out the word 'but' and continued:

I keep busy with regular evening broadcasts to the US and have gotten to know a whole bunch of folks – American correspondents and regular Berliners going about their business who like to practise their English with me. It's interesting to hear their view of developments, but no one is enthusiastic any more about further conquests. They just want to get on with their lives and have enough to eat. Me, too!!

Darling, I've written several times to your old work address at the Kensington Evening Post where I thought they'd surely forward them to you – but maybe you've never received them. The only other address I can think of is the Grosvenor Hotel. So this time, that's where I'll send it.

One day, God willing, I'll hold you in my arms again and this time I'll never let you go. But for now I only want you to know that I will love you forever.

All my love, my darling, and sending kisses,
Your Glenn XXXXX

Feeling as excited as a schoolboy having his first crush, Glenn folded the letter and tucked it in an envelope. Surely the hotel would forward it to her, especially when the manager read his letter pleading he do so in the name of love. Glenn gave a sheepish grin. His buddies back home would call him a sentimental fool. Little would they know he'd take it as a compliment!

Chuckling, he hid his diary in the usual place.

Chapter Twenty-Six

September 1940, London

Dale picked up the *Observer*, one of several that Lord Langton read with regular habit. She quickly scanned the headlines that took up practically the whole of the front page, bracing herself for the worst.

**BIG AIR BATTLE
OVER LONDON**

**'REPRISAL' FOR ATTACKS
ON BERLIN**

**SIXTY-FIVE RAIDERS
SHOT DOWN**

**98 MINUTES OF FIERCE
FIGHTING**

**FIRES STARTED IN THE
EAST END**

Another newspaper reported:

Children sleeping in perambulators and mothers with babies in their arms were killed when a bomb exploded on the ventilation shaft of a crowded shelter in London's East End . . .

Dazed, she put the paper back on the sideboard. She couldn't read any more. Try as she might, she couldn't hide her relief that most of the bombs had dropped in the East End of London. That meant Mother was safe. But for how long? She swallowed the guilt, her heart going out to the people who'd lost their homes, their jobs and worse – their lives.

Although she realised the RAF would have to retaliate, she couldn't bear to think of hundreds of planes bound for Berlin, where she was sure Glenn still was, though he'd not mentioned the name in his letter. She supposed he couldn't. He'd be too worried it would get into the wrong hands and some Nazi would report him.

She blinked back tears. More innocent civilians would be blown to pieces. She mustn't think like that. Germany was the enemy and Glenn was trying to bring the news to Americans about what was happening and force them to realise it was a war from which they couldn't escape. She couldn't even imagine the risks he'd be facing. Did he have enough food? Had he made any friends – other American reporters and radio broadcasters? He wouldn't be the only one, she comforted herself by thinking. They were all in it together.

But she couldn't know anything for certain. Glenn had written the letter a year ago. He might have already gone back to America. If he had, at least he'd be safe. But his job was to report on the war and he'd be so frustrated if he'd been sent home. No, she was sure he would still be in Berlin. She sighed. If only there was a quicker way to receive an answer. She'd hardly had a moment to think what she should say to Glenn. This was no time for subtlety, playing games or reproach. In the end she simply listened to her heart and attempted to keep up with her teeming brain as she poured out her love and longing. Then following Glenn's instructions, she addressed it c/o Don Murphy and the address in New York. There was nothing to do now but wait.

Grateful to be on the morning shift, Dale wheeled her bicycle out of the coach house and swung onto the saddle like a professional. She couldn't help smiling. Then her smile faded. Wanda was on the same shift and she knew she wouldn't be able to stall the woman any longer. She'd changed her mind a dozen times as to whether she should kowtow to Wanda's threat or call her bluff. She just didn't feel comfortable begging her hosts to extend their hospitality any further. She fought down the constant irritation since Wanda had broached the subject. Her hair blew loose as she pedalled along, breathing in the autumnal air.

What should she do?

By the time she'd parked her bicycle in the cycle shed she'd made up her mind. She'd tell Wanda she wasn't going to ask. And if Wanda started the nonsense about going to Commander Travis – well, she'd beat her to it. She'd take a chance and see him herself.

Feeling better that she'd come to a definite decision, she entered her Hut. Wanda pounced the moment Dale walked through the door.

'Dulcie, there you are. I need to speak to you urgently. Please come to the training room immediately.'

The woman really was a drama queen, Dale thought scornfully. *She won't like what I'm going to tell her.*

242

She followed her in, her back straight, her chin determined.

'Sit down, Dulcie.'

There was something about Wanda's expression she couldn't fathom.

'I'm afraid I have some bad news.'

Dale's stomach jolted. Had the woman already reported her to Commander Travis? Was she about to be sacked?

'Wanda, please—'

'Listen a minute. You heard about the bombing last night – in London?'

'Yes. I read it in the paper this morning.' *What had that got to do with her job?*

'You live in Charlwood Street, don't you?'

'Yes.' A feeling of foreboding crawled over her.

'Several houses were bombed – in your area.' Wanda paused and looked directly at Dale.

She had to hold herself together. She must.

'My mother . . .' Dale choked on the words.

'They're trying to find the whereabouts of some people. I don't know any details.' She gazed at Dale. 'I'll get you a cup of tea.' She disappeared.

Dale's head swam. She pulled in her stomach, desperate not to faint. She swallowed hard and nodded.

Please be alive. Please don't have died.

A thin stream of bile came up in her throat making her cough. She pulled out her handkerchief and quickly got rid of it. Would they allow her to go home? She caught herself. Home? She might not have a home any more. She closed her eyes as nausea enveloped her.

Oh, Mum, I'm going to find out where you are if that's the last thing I do.

She didn't realise she'd reverted to calling her mother 'Mum' as she had as a child.

'Here, Dulcie, drink this,' Wanda said as she came in and set a cup of tea on the table.

Dale sipped the strong sweet brew, conscious of her supervisor's eyes on her.

'I need to find out if my mother's all right.'

Wanda's eyes narrowed. 'Dulcie, I'm sympathetic, but we don't know any information that would justify your simply rushing off. You're doing a very important top-secret job here which is vital for the country, and messages we uncover could save hundreds, maybe thousands of lives. The very next message you decode could have a major impact on the direction of the war.' She paused. 'If and when there's some definite information that's distressing regarding your mother, I could allow it for compassionate reasons.'

Dale's mouth fell open. Had the woman no heart?

'I worked seven days last week with no day off,' Dale said. 'If I go right away, I can be back for the night shift.'

There was a long pause. By Wanda's creased forehead it seemed she was going to say no. But to Dale's relief Wanda gave her a brief smile.

'All right. I should be able to report this as an emergency, even though we still don't know if your house has been affected.' She hesitated. 'Just make sure you're back for the midnight shift, then neither of us will be in trouble.'

'Unless anything really bad has happened – if my mother was injured or—' Dale sprang to her feet, splashing the rest of the tea down the front of her cardigan. Impatiently, she brushed the drops away. 'Thank you, Wanda.'

She grabbed her bag and rushed from the room and out of the Hut, conscious that several pairs of curious eyes turned to watch her. She wheeled her bicycle out of the coach house and jumped on it, pedalling as hard as she could towards

244

the station, her overriding thought to get on a train that would take her to London as quickly as possible.

'The train's about to leave,' the ticket man said. 'You'll just make it.'

She saw the conductor put his whistle to his lips as she flew along the platform.

'Don't let it go!' she shouted.

He turned, letting his whistle fall to his chest, and opened the nearest door.

'Thank you,' Dale said, her breath coming in painful gasps as she scrambled into the corridor.

The conductor nodded and slammed the door behind her. He put his whistle to his mouth and the train began to rumble out of the station.

Dale opened the nearest carriage door and thankfully spotted the only available seat in the corner. She opened her book but the words blurred. It was no good. She couldn't concentrate.

Oh, Mum, please be found. Don't let anything have happened to you. I couldn't bear it. I do love you even though I don't tell you.

Dale half ran, half walked up Lupus Street – the street before her own – looking out for any bomb damage. It appeared intact. People were going about their business normally. It gave her hope. Maybe the damage wouldn't be as bad as Wanda had indicated. Things tended to get exaggerated when they were passed from one person to another. She turned the corner into Charlwood Street, her heart thumping in her chest, mentally bracing herself.

But nothing – even Wanda's brief warning – had prepared her for the sight that met her eyes. Rushing past the crowd that had already gathered, she blinked in disbelief. Where there should have been a row of eight elegant Victorian houses, two were now reduced to shells and the one on the end was a pile of rubble, smoke still curling upwards. Dale stepped further towards the roped area, the terrible smell, not just of smoke but something even more shocking – she couldn't bear to think what it might be – nearly knocking her back. For a few seconds, holding her breath, she stood motionless, hardly getting her bearings as she tried to work out which house was hers. A long low garden wall which had originally been shared by several properties in the street had smashed onto the pavement and people were picking their way round it. But her parents' home, she now saw, was still standing next to the three which had taken the brunt of the explosion. Jerkily, she expelled her breath. She had to go inside and see if her mother was there. Ignoring the rope, Dale swung one leg over it and was just about to bring up the other one when a loud voice stopped her.

'Move back from the rope, miss. This is a danger zone.'

She dropped back and looked round to see an ARP warden striding towards her. Thank God. She flew up to him.

'I'm looking for my mother . . . Mrs Treadwell. She's . . . we live at—' she gulped '—at number 57. That's our house.' She pointed. 'Please let me make sure she's all right.'

'Sorry, miss, you're not allowed. A few houses across the street caught it, too. Look at them windows.' He pointed. Dale followed his eye. 'There's not one left whole. No, miss, it's not safe. The repair squad are on their way and they'll assess when it is.'

'Our house looks all right.' She swallowed hard. 'Please – I must find my mother.'

'I'm afraid you'll have to be patient. You can't see all the damage as some is at the back.'

'How long will the repair people be?'

'Goodness knows. It's the worst ones they'll see to first. They probably won't turn up here until tomorrow.' He flipped through a notebook. 'What did you say your name was?'

'Treadwell. My mother's Patricia Treadwell.'

'Mr and Mrs Treadwell?' he repeated, his head bent. 'The name's here but it's not yet crossed off.'

'My father's away in Scotland. It would only be my mother.'

'We're still trying to account for everyone. And your mother's not been accounted for. But we do know a whole family copped it in that end house.' He jerked his head towards the pile of debris. 'Name of Winslow. Do you happen to know how many in the family who would've been home last night?'

'No.' Tears streamed down her face. 'I don't know them.' And at this moment she didn't bloody care. Her eyes stung as she looked at the ruins where once there were people's homes.

Where is my mother?

Her spine buckled with the fear of not knowing.

'They brought out another body early this morning,' the warden said. 'Terrible business. And we're going to see a lot more of it. Jerry'll mainly go for the docks, I reckon, but this won't be the first time London gets it and—'

'My mother,' Dale interrupted, panic rising in her voice. 'Where can I find out about her?' She bit her lip hard to stop herself from screaming.

'You'd best go to the First Aid post. They've set up a centre at the local primary school – in Lupus Street. Can you let me know if you find out anything . . . for the records?'

'Yes,' Dale said, calling 'thank you' over her shoulder as she turned and ran.

Three minutes later she arrived, breathless, at the small

Victorian red brick building that was once a school, but now the children had all been evacuated. A hand-made sign outside stated: FIRST AID POST. Parked outside was an ambulance. Two men were carrying someone in on a stretcher. She saw a sheet had been pulled over the body.

Her stomach gave a sickening lurch. *Don't let it be Mum.*

She waited until they'd gone inside, then followed. Several Red Cross nurses were tending to white-faced patients. The atmosphere was charged with activity, yet calm, and Dale could immediately tell that here things were properly organised. A middle-aged woman with a kind but tired face looked up from a makeshift reception desk where she'd been writing notes in a large book and smiled.

'What can I do for you, my dear?'

Forcing herself to ignore the thundering in her chest, she answered:

'I'm Dulcie Treadwell, looking for my mother, Patricia Treadwell. We live at 57 Charlwood Street and some of the houses were bombed late last night. I'm working away from home and only arrived in London just now and there's no sign of her.'

'Let's see.' She turned the page of her record book to the previous one and glanced down. 'Treadwell, you say?'

'Yes.' *Oh, please hurry.*

'Samuels, Thornton, White . . .' She gazed at Dale with an apologetic look in her warm grey eyes. 'I'm so sorry, dear, there's no mention of a Mrs Treadwell here.' She hesitated, chewing her lip as though thinking what to say next. Then seeming to decide, she said, 'We do have two bodies from the demolished houses near you and don't have any idea who they are – they're both ladies in their forties, I would say. I wonder if you might be able to identify them, but of course if you don't feel you can, I quite understand. You'd have to prepare yourself – it's possible one of the ladies might be your mother.'

A wave of nausea attacked Dale's throat. She couldn't do it. But she had to. She couldn't turn away and out of the door without knowing for sure.

'All right,' she whispered. 'I'll look at them. But I only know the nearest neighbours' names, and the other ones just by sight.'

'Any identification would be very helpful to us, but especially if we can put a name to them,' the woman said, rising from her desk. 'Let me take you over. I'm Mrs Brooks, by the way.'

'Will they . . .' Dale gulped. 'Will they be . . . recognisable?'

'Yes, my dear, they are. Often people are quite intact when there's a raid. It's the shock and blast that usually kills people.'

A curtain had been hurriedly pinned across a section of the room where several shrouded bodies were laid out. Mrs Brooks walked over to the wall by a window where two forms lay side by side. Gently, she drew the sheet away to show a woman's face. Swallowing the threatening bile, Dale steeled herself and peered closely. She shook her head. Mrs Brooks drew the sheet up over the poor woman's head, then turned down the second sheet. Dale looked closely, and gasped.

'I know this person,' Dale croaked. 'She's Mrs Dennett, our neighbour.'

'Are you certain?'

'Yes.'

'Do you know her first name?'

'No. She and my mother weren't on first-name terms.'

'Was she married?'

'Yes, there is a Mr Dennett. And two sons – both in the

Army. I don't know anything more about them.' Dale suddenly clapped her hand in front of her mouth. 'Is there a lavatory?'

Mrs Brooks grabbed her arm and quickly led her to a door marked WC. Not stopping to bolt the door behind her, Dale knelt over the pan and was violently sick.

Finally, she hauled herself up and reached for the chain, washed her hands in the sink, rinsed her mouth under the cold tap, then drank greedily. Oh, that was better. She glanced in the small mirror over the wash basin. Dear God, she looked dreadful. Her face was as white as some of the survivors waiting to be assessed, her lips a red gash. Greasy strands of hair hung around her perspiring forehead. Using her fingers, she raked it back and dabbed at her mouth with her handkerchief, leaving the blood-red stain of her lipstick. She couldn't muster the energy to do anything more. Besides, Mrs Brooks would wonder what on earth had happened to her.

She made her way to the reception desk.

'Are you all right, my dear?' Mrs Brooks said, her expression one of concern.

'I'm better now.' Dale licked her lips, her mouth still tasting sour.

'It's all a shock,' Mrs Brooks went on, 'but it's really good of you to brave it by looking at the two ladies.' She paused. 'Take a seat a moment while I write down the details. Did you say Mrs Bennett?'

'Dennett,' Dale said shortly. She needed to get out of this place.

'Oh, yes, Maureen Dennett.' She glanced at Dale. 'Can I get you a cup of tea, Miss Treadwell?'

'No, thank you.' She'd been here long enough. Every moment might count.

'You said you're working away from home so I'll need your address where we can contact you.'

'It's a PO Box number.'

Mrs Brooks raised her eyebrows. 'What about your father? Is he at work?'

'Yes – in Scotland. I can give you his telephone number.' Dale fished in her handbag and looked in her address book. She wrote his name and the phone number on a scrap of paper.

Mrs Brooks lifted her head. 'Is there anyone else who lives nearby and knows your mother? Preferably another neighbour.'

Dale thought quickly. 'Mother's friend, Elizabeth Bryant-Taylor. She's only five minutes away – 38 St George's Drive. I'm sorry I don't have her telephone number. Stupid of me.'

'Don't worry, my dear, now we've got the address.' She gazed at Dale. 'I think that's all we need.'

'Can you suggest anywhere else I can go?' Dale asked.

'You might try St Gabriel's church near you. They'll probably be doing refreshments and you never know. Someone might have seen her.'

'Thank you,' Dale said, rising to her feet. It was all she seemed to be doing – thanking people but not getting anywhere. 'You've been very kind.'

Once again, Dale ran – this time along Cambridge Street towards the church. She suddenly stopped. St George's Drive where her mother's friend lived, was the next street. She'd go there first. Why hadn't she thought of it before? Taking in a few jerky breaths and feeling her twisted foot beginning to ache, she started to run again. Minutes later she was outside number 38, a similar-looking house to her parents'. Picking up the iron knocker in the shape of a dolphin, she let it fall loudly and waited. There were no answering footsteps. She banged the knocker down harder this time. But there was nothing. No sound except the wild hammering of her heart. Don't say something had happened to Mrs Bryant-Taylor as well? Dale took a few steps back and stared up at the house. It didn't seem to be touched by any bomb damage; nor did any other houses in the street. She blew out her cheeks and sprinted to Warwick Square.

St Gabriel's Gothic-style church with its elegant tower stood like a beacon of hope in Dale's eyes. A few people were emerging from the entrance and she waited until the last people, an elderly couple, came through. The husband put his hat on, then took hold of his wife's arm. They turned and walked towards her, the woman's eyes streaming with tears. The man nodded as they started to pass by.

'Excuse me,' Dale said, hating to disturb them, 'but do you know if the church is helping people from last night's bombing?'

'It'll be in the big hall they use for the children on Sunday afternoons,' the man said. 'We've just come from there. They gave us a cup of tea.' He glanced down at the shrunken woman by his side and patted her arm. She looked up with dull wet eyes. 'The wife's heard some dreadful news. Her sister was killed in the raid last night.'

'Oh, I'm so very sorry,' Dale said, briefly touching the poor woman's arm, feeling the nausea sweep over her again.

'Are you looking for someone, love?' he said.

'Yes.' Dale swallowed hard. 'My mother.'

'There're quite a few people there,' he said, 'and even if she's not there, you may find someone to help you. We wish you luck, don't we, Hazel?' He tipped his hat at Dale.

The woman gave a sad smile. Dale felt she would never forget it.

She shot into the church to hear the murmuring of voices

and the clatter of cups and saucers coming from the rear. Following the sounds, she saw a door with a notice: *WVS here. Please enter.*

She gazed around at people seated at tables, all looking as shocked as those at the First Aid post – except two women who were pouring teas and handing out biscuits and cakes. Her pulse quickened when she recognised Mrs Bryant-Taylor carrying a large tray of cups to a table in the far corner. Dale crossed the room, hoping against hope her mother's friend would know where she was. At a trestle table several women sat silently, though one rested her hand on the shoulder of a woman who had her head buried in her hands and was sobbing.

Dale's heart leapt into her throat.

Chapter Twenty-Seven

'Mum!' Dale exclaimed, rushing to her side.

Her mother lifted her head, staring with dull eyes wet with tears.

'Dulcie! Oh, I'm so glad to see you.' She pressed her lips together as though to stop a fresh bout of weeping. 'How did you find me?'

Mrs Bryant-Taylor put the tray down so hard that tea slopped over the edges of some of the cups. 'Well, this is a surprise,' she said before Dale could answer her mother. She looked at Dale. 'Your mother's had a bad shock with the bombing last night. I expect you heard. She was lucky not to have been killed. If she'd been next door she would have.'

'I've seen it,' Dale said, her stomach churning. 'Thank goodness ours is still standing but some of the neighbouring houses weren't so lucky.'

'*We* weren't let off the hook completely,' Patricia said with a shudder.

'Were you asleep when it happened, Mum?'

'Yes. I didn't hear the bomb come down. It was the sound of smashed glass that woke me, with the rain pouring through my window. It's the back that's taken the brunt. Most of the windows have gone and everything's sodden.

The sculpture of the angel your father bought me from that antiques auction is shattered.' Her mother began to cry.

'Come on, Patricia, don't take on so,' Mrs Bryant-Taylor said, putting an arm around her friend. 'Everything will turn out for the best.' She looked at Dale. 'But until such time as they tell us the extent of the damage, I've told your mother she's to come and stay with me until it's safe to go back.'

'It's very kind of you—' Dale began.

'Patricia would do the same for me,' Mrs Bryant-Taylor said. 'That's what we have to do – help one another, especially when she's got no one here.' She looked pointedly at Dale. 'No husband . . . and no daughter, it seems, with you working away from home.'

A rush of guilt swept over Dale. She didn't know how to answer the woman, as it was true.

'But I expect you'll give up your job wherever you are and find somewhere to rent nearby for the two of you – just temporarily until you get your house repaired,' Mrs Bryant-Taylor carried on. 'I'm afraid I won't be able to keep Patricia indefinitely, much as I'd like to. I've got my own girls still at home and my son who's a pilot in the RAF—' She broke off and Dale was sure it was to let that snippet of information sink in. 'He comes home on leave every now and again. It's lucky he's not home at the moment or I wouldn't know where I could put Patricia.'

Mrs Bryant-Taylor was speaking as though her mother wasn't there. And talking about her so-called friend as though she were a parcel that she could deal with for a bit, but there was a limit. Dale fought to hold back a retort. Whatever she said would sound rude and her mother would be furious.

'It's not as though you've joined one of the forces to do your bit, is it, dear?' Mrs Bryant-Taylor added.

Dale swallowed. She cursed the fact she was under oath,

even though her cool brain understood and entirely agreed. How dare Mrs Bryant-bloody-Taylor assume she wasn't doing anything to help the war effort. Her mother opened her mouth and instinctively Dale sent her a warning signal – a tiny shake of her head – not to mention anything about the Foreign Office or signing the Official Secrets Act. To her relief, her mother closed her mouth again, but not before a warm feeling enveloped her. Mum had been about to stick up for her – she was certain.

It was getting dark before Dale was on the train heading for Bletchley. She'd hated having to leave her mother and had even been tempted to ask Mrs Bryant-Taylor if she could possibly sleep on the sofa. But her mother had assured her she would be fine, and insisted she catch the next train so as not to be back too late.

For once, the train was only three-quarters full. Exhausted, she leant her head back on the seat of the second-class carriage, trying to block out the chatter of two WAAFs in their smart air-force blue uniforms, as she went over again in her mind the events of the day.

'Have you heard from your Steve?' one of the WAAFs said, her face so full of freckles they almost blurred her features.

'No, but he always tells me not to worry,' the one opposite said.

'I should think you do worry though, what with him liable to get shot down at any moment.'

'Don't remind me. But he's a brilliant pilot, so his mates say.'

'Doesn't have to be his fault,' came back the first girl. 'Betty's young man was terribly injured. Face half burnt when his plane caught fire. He'll never be the same again. I wouldn't

blame Betty if she couldn't face him with his face all funny—'
She stopped short and gave a nervous laugh. 'I shouldn't
have put it like that. I meant—'

'I know what you meant. It makes me shudder at the
thought.'

Please shut up, both of you. I can't take much more of this.
Dale's eyelids fluttered until they closed, going back to her
mother's plight again.

It had been a difficult hour in the church hall, to say the
least.

'I'm glad my daughter's got her own place to go to,' her
mother had said, sounding a little cool after her friend's
avowal that she couldn't keep Patricia at her home indefinitely. 'At least I know she'll be safe out of London.'

'Is it far?' Mrs Bryant-Taylor had asked Dale curiously.

'Just a train ride away,' Dale said noncommittally. 'But
now I know Mother's going back with you I feel much better
so I ought to get going. I'm on a late shift tonight.'

'You're doing *shift* work?' Mrs Bryant-Taylor's voice rose.
'Do you work in a factory or something?'

She said 'factory' as though it was a dirty word. Dale
bristled. The girls who worked in factories were to be
commended, not derided.

'No. It's clerical work.'

'So as it's nothing important, I expect you'll be handing
in your notice?' Mrs Bryant-Taylor said.

Dale momentarily closed her eyes. Maybe the woman was
right. Maybe that's what she should do. But it had been
instilled in all of them at the Park what important work they
were doing. She swallowed hard, not knowing how to answer.

'An intelligent girl like yourself – don't you think you're
wasting your time when the war needs you?' Mrs Bryant-
Taylor persisted.

Patricia shook her head at her daughter, then cut in:

'Elizabeth, Dulcie's not able to tell *me* any details so I'm sure she can't *you*. But I can assure you it's war work.'

Mrs Bryant-Taylor pursed her lips. 'Hmm – it's very strange she can't say what.'

Dale struggled not to put her in her place. After all, the woman wasn't a bad person, the way she did her volunteer work on the mobile van, but really, she could have been a little more gracious about taking her mother in.

After their tea the three of them had walked back to Charlwood Street to see if they'd be allowed to collect any items from the house. The same ARP warden was on duty but told them it was still declared unsafe to enter until the local authority had been given the go-ahead.

'Trouble is, miss,' he said, his eyes focused on Dale, 'so many builders and carpenters have joined up, and there's a shortage of materials, I can't say when you can expect them. It could be weeks, it could be months. But it certainly won't be days.'

'I think we'd all better go back to mine,' Mrs Bryant-Taylor had said, taking Patricia's arm. 'You can come and see her settled in and we'll have a bite to eat. I expect you're hungry.'

It had all taken longer than Dale had anticipated. Mrs Bryant-Taylor's phone had rung several times and the woman spent an inordinate amount of energy relating to whoever was at the other end the trauma of the night before and how it had affected her friend's house and how she was giving her a home for the time being.

Patricia rolled her eyes as the two of them listened to these conversations and for the first time Dale grinned. Her mother wasn't completely taken in by her friend.

'That was Mrs Jordan, one of the ladies I play bridge with,'

Mrs Bryant-Taylor said after the third call. 'She knows how close I am to the raid and was asking if I was still in one piece. So of course I told her about you, Patricia. She sent her best wishes even though she's never met you. And says why don't you join the group for bridge next week.'

And so it went on.

Mrs Bryant-Taylor had given her mother a single bedroom, apologising but reiterating about the lack of bedrooms.

'But I was always taught by my own mother that if there's room in the heart, there's room in the house,' she finished, shrugging off Patricia's gratitude.

The sudden jerk of the train made Dale's eyes flick open. She overbalanced and it was only the WAAF's outstretched arm across Dale's chest that saved her from pitching over.

She turned, but before she could open her mouth to thank the girl there was a terrific bang. The compartment was plunged into blackness. The squeal of brakes and a scream from a woman opposite. No one moved. Dale jumped up from her seat and felt her way to slide open the door to the corridor, pulling up the black-out blind only to find bursts of steam obliterating any view from the filthy windows. Had it been a bomb? If so, there could be more. Her heart beat wildly. The train finally juddered to a halt, belching out more steam. It was too dark to see her watch, but she guessed they'd only been travelling for half an hour. She needed to be back by eleven to quickly freshen up at Langton Hall before cycling back to the Park ready for the night shift. Sighing, she returned to her seat.

Time dragged for what must be an hour. The lights still hadn't come back on. So far, no one had told them why they were being held up and people in the carriage were beginning to mutter.

Dale rose for the second time. 'I'm going to see if I can

259

find a conductor anywhere,' she said as she picked up her bag and jacket.

The corridor was packed with passengers all trying to peer out to see what had happened. Dale squeezed by as she made her way towards the front of the train. People were thinning out now, but she was only able to make out the conductor by the weak light from the lamp he held. He was talking to someone with his back to her. As she approached and said, 'Excuse me,' the young man turned his head and she looked into the startled eyes of Eddie.

'Dale! I heard the news about the raid in London.' He caught her arm. 'Is that where you've been?' Before she could answer, he said, 'Come and sit down in my compartment – you look worn out.'

'Right. If you can both move aside, I'll let the other passengers know why there's a hold-up,' the conductor broke in.

'Sorry,' Eddie said, sliding open the compartment door and ushering Dale in.

'Do you know why there was that awful bang and now we've stopped?' Dale asked.

'It's not very nice,' Eddie said. 'If you're squeamish.'

'I'm not.'

Was it true? She remembered the two dead women in the First Aid post when she'd been asked if she could identify them. Although their faces had been untouched, she still couldn't bear the fact that they had been alive only hours before and the same fate might have befallen her own mother. Eddie was watching her curiously. She felt a sharp pricking behind her eyes.

'Tell me,' was all she said.

'Someone fell onto the tracks at the next station platform,' Eddie said, taking out a packet of cigarettes. 'The driver wouldn't have stood a chance of braking at the speed we were going.' He looked at her. 'It was more than likely suicide.'

'Dear God.'

He offered her a cigarette, but she shook her head. After hesitating a moment, he stuffed the packet back in his jacket pocket. 'It'll take them a while to remove the body.'

Dale swallowed hard with the image of some poor person lying mangled on the railway tracks, probably now unrecognisable.

'Do they know if it's a man or a woman?'

'No, the conductor didn't know any more details.'

What must they have been going through to have wanted to end it all?

'Oh, Eddie. The war has hardly started . . . and to think—' She put her hands to her eyes and brushed a tear away.

Eddie gently took one of her hands in his own, and she let it rest there.

'Now tell me if your house was intact,' he said.

'It looked all right from the front but Mum said there was some damage at the back. I don't know the extent but apparently the windows were all smashed in. What was much more worrying was that Wanda had told me they hadn't located everyone. That's why I dashed to London.'

'Dear Lord.' He stared at her. 'How did you find her?'

'After going to the First Aid post I found her in our church.'

She filled him in on some of the details and he listened without interrupting.

'She's staying with her friend now,' Dale finished, 'but neither of us are allowed back in the house – even to get personal items – until the local authority says it's safe. And who knows how long that will be. I haven't even had time to think about my things – or my mother's and father's. But the most important thing is that she's alive and not injured.'

'You know, you never mention your father,' Eddie said.

Dale's face clouded. 'We haven't seen him much lately. He's in Scotland.' She paused. 'I don't even know if he's been told about the raid, but I'll go into the town tomorrow and ring him.' She lowered her voice. 'He's met someone there and has asked Mother for a divorce. You can imagine how that went down.'

'Like a lead balloon,' Eddie said, grimly. He squeezed her hand. 'It must be awful for you both, but especially for your mother.'

'She's very bitter,' Dale admitted. 'But she's stronger than she thinks. She'll come through – although the raid has certainly set her back . . . as it would anyone.'

She suddenly remembered.

'Eddie, if the train doesn't start soon, I'm going to be late. I told Wanda I'd be back for the midnight shift. She was reluctant to allow me to go as we didn't have any real news that something bad had actually happened to my mother – or the house.'

'You won't be doing anything of the kind tonight,' Eddie said. 'We'll probably not get back until the wee hours. I'm taking you straight to Langton Hall – and no arguments,' he added when she opened her mouth to protest. 'Your eyes are drooping with exhaustion so you wouldn't spot anything anyway. You need to sleep as soon as we get back. Then I'll run you in in the morning. I start at eight tomorrow so that'll work perfectly.'

'But Wanda—'

Dale stopped short when she saw Eddie's eyes narrow.

'She'll understand when you explain about the hold-up.'

* * *

262

Eddie was right. The train didn't move for a good two hours but there was no point fretting. If anything, she must think about the one who'd lost his or her life by falling on the rails, and what the family would be going through when they were notified. And what if the person had changed their mind at the very last split second? But it would be too late. They would have already toppled onto the tracks.

Dale gave an inward shudder. It was all too horrible to contemplate. She found herself not able to keep awake and Eddie put his arm round her, drawing her to him. She allowed her head to fall on his shoulder.

'Have a nap if you can,' he whispered, but she didn't even hear him. She was already asleep.

The next thing she knew was that Eddie was gently shaking her.

'Come on, Dale. We're just coming into the station. Grab your things and let's get off this damn train.'

He helped her onto the deserted platform, and just as when she'd first arrived at Bletchley, no one else alighted. Eddie guided her to where he'd parked his car and gratefully she sank into the passenger seat, happy for the time being to let him take over.

When Eddie had safely put the motorcar in one of the garages he kept hold of her hand until he unlocked the scullery door.

Feeling awkward, Dale said, 'Thank you, Eddie. I can't thank you enough for your kindness. If you hadn't been on the train—'

Without warning he stopped her flow of words by pulling her into his arms and kissing her. For a few moments she held back, then to her surprise found herself returning his kiss, her arms sliding round his neck. Oh, it had been so long . . . And here was Eddie. So warm, so inviting, so damned good-looking . . .

It was several seconds before they parted, Eddie still holding her.

'Well – that was a surprise,' he said.

She could imagine his grin in the dark.

'I don't know why. You're the one who kissed *me*.'

'But you were the one who responded,' he said, his voice gleeful. He made to kiss her again but this time she put her hands on his chest to gently push him away.

'Eddie, you're a dear, but I'm dead beat.'

'Sorry, love. I'm not thinking straight any more.' He briefly kissed her forehead. 'It's cold in here. I think we'd both better get to bed – just a bloody shame it won't be together.'

Chapter Twenty-Eight

No matter how hard she tried, Dale couldn't sleep. She supposed it was because she'd dozed on the train. But no, that wasn't it. It was because everything was turning over in her mind: Wanda giving her the devastating news of the bombing raid, the rush to London, the shock of seeing her home roped off and being unable even to retrieve any of their valuables, the overwhelming relief that her mother was unharmed, seeing Eddie on the train, and then their kiss. A wave of guilt consumed her, making her cheeks flame at the way she'd kissed him back. Had they merely been flirting with each other? After all, he'd only just broken up with Wanda and still not told her. Or did she care for him more than she admitted? And if so, what about Glenn? She'd thought right up until now that he was her love. If only she could shake her head hard to dislodge all that had happened and let it settle, rather like the snowman in a plastic ball Aunt Faye had given her one Christmas. She'd loved shaking him so vigorously that the snowflakes flew, almost obliterating him, until they stopped falling and all was calm again.

Thinking of snow, Dale turned over once again, this time pulling up her knees, trying to get warm. She hadn't noticed until this minute that there was no heating at all in the room.

It wasn't all luxury at Langton Hall, Dale imagined herself telling Wanda.

Seeing Wanda in her mind's eye reminded Dale of Sonia's remarks about Eddie and how Wanda would be out for revenge now Eddie had apparently set his sights on another woman.

I wonder if he'll ever come clean and tell me. Dale shut her eyes tightly. *Don't think of them. It's Mum you should be thinking about.*

With a start, she realised she'd only begun calling her 'Mum' and not 'Mother' since the bombing raid. She wondered if her mother had noticed. Even whether she liked it. But Dale sensed a change and felt closer to her mother today than any time since she was a child.

What about Dad? Had anyone notified him? She had his telephone number to be used only in emergencies, he'd warned, but as soon as she had the chance she'd ring him. Though what could he do anyway? Mum was safe and they weren't allowed in the house, so she couldn't imagine him coming all the way from Scotland, breaking off from his important work and leaving the new woman in order to comfort his soon-to-be ex-wife.

She couldn't stop it – Eddie sprang to her mind again.

Desperate now to get some sleep before her shift started in the morning, Dale dragged the eiderdown up to her chin. If only she had a hot water bottle to warm her, though Eddie's last remark hadn't mentioned hot water bottles to snuggle up to. She couldn't help a wry smile at his cheek as she finally fell into a restless sleep.

At the breakfast table Eddie was grinning at her from ear to ear when Dale came into the dining room.

'Morning, Dale. Did you sleep well?' He emphasised the 'sleep well' bit.

'I always sleep well here,' she echoed. She wasn't going to ask him about *his* sleep habits.

'Yes, me, too, though it took a while. You see, I had this gorgeous girl playing on my mind—'

'Stop it,' Dale admonished. 'Your uncle will be in at any minute.'

He looked at her, still grinning. 'You're right. He doesn't need to hear any hanky-panky going on under his roof. He'd—'

'What's this about hanky-panky?' Lord Langton demanded as he came through the door, as usual perfectly groomed.

'Just a joke, Uncle,' Eddie said.

'I should hope so,' Lord Langton returned. 'You'll have your aunt to deal with, if not.' He sent Dale a saucy wink which brought the blood flying to her cheeks, but she wasn't going to let Eddie's nonsense go unremarked.

'Eddie is telling tales like a naughty schoolboy.'

'You behave yourself, young man.' Lord Langton turned to Eddie. 'Dale's a lovely young woman and you've made her blush.'

No, it was you who made me go red, Lord Langton.

Dale ate her breakfast in near silence. His lordship was deep in his paper, but Eddie looked thoughtful as he wolfed down his bacon and eggs, then left the table, abruptly saying he'd be outside at quarter to eight to drive her back to the Park.

Lord Langton put down his newspaper. 'Is he making a nuisance of himself, Dale? The truth, now.'

'No. Not at all.'

'You're sure?'

267

'I'm positive. And if it were true, I'd tell him myself. I'm perfectly capable of doing just that,' she added.

He gave her an intense look. 'Yes, I imagine you would be.'

'All set?' Eddie asked, his smile back in place, as Dale settled in the seat beside him. He turned the key and did his usual skidding on the gravel.

Dale wondered who raked it every day, cursing at Eddie's arrivals and departures.

'The leaves are beginning to turn,' she said, more for something to break the silence, feeling a little embarrassed about last night. How she'd momentarily forgotten all about Wanda and Eddie going out together when she'd unexpectedly enjoyed the sensation of his mouth on hers and kissed him back. She gave him a sidelong glance. He caught her looking and her cheeks warmed.

'Thinking about anything in particular?' he asked in a mischievous tone.

'I don't know what you're talking about.'

'Oh, yes, you do. You haven't forgotten our snog any more than I have.'

Glenn would never use such a juvenile word.

'It was only the heat of the moment,' she retorted.

'Pull the other one,' he said, grinning.

'It's true.'

'Well, if it's not that – and I don't believe you – then you've got something else on your mind.' He slowed down as he approached a particularly sharp bend. 'Do you want to tell me about it?'

Dale hesitated. This would be the perfect time to mention it. See if he told her the truth.

'There *is* something. It's about my supervisor, Wanda

Wilcox. She's unhappy in her digs and I was wondering what you thought of the idea of her coming to Langton Hall.'

'Did you tell her where you'd moved?' Eddie said, turning his head sharply to narrow a glance at her.

Sonia was right. He looked as guilty as could be.

'Not at first. She found out through the Accommodations Officer and said how lucky I was and could I put in a word on her behalf.'

'To be billeted there, do you mean?' His tone was overly casual.

'Yes.'

'It's out of the question.'

She turned to him. 'Why do you say that?'

Eddie kept his eye on the road. 'Let me explain. My uncle made an exception for you because I vouched for you. I told him how well you're doing at the Park – that sort of stuff. And I assured him you could keep mum. So they were both quite happy about having you, but offering a billet to another person they don't know would be out of the question.'

'She must have signed the Official Secrets Act the same as everyone else,' Dale said. 'We're all very aware of not talking about anything to do with our work outside our own Hut.'

Irritably, she remembered that vile little man, Mr Draper, had already reported her. Heaven knew what Eddie and his lordship would think of that.

'It's not that simple,' Eddie said. 'I think my uncle's hinted to you he's not totally ignorant of the work we're doing at the Park. I didn't go straight to bed last night. Didn't have any excuse.' He paused and gave her a brief smile. 'My uncle was still up and we had a whisky and a chat. He's asked me to tell you that he and my aunt have to move.'

Her mouth fell open. 'Do you mean they're forced to?'

'More or less,' Eddie said. 'The War Office wants their house and land for an army training unit. They often take over these sorts of estates.'

'I see.'

Eddie's news was deeply disappointing. Just when she'd settled and very much liked her new accommodation, particularly her new hosts. 'Will they be going far?'

'Not exactly,' he smiled. 'It's just on the other drive. They're planning to move into the Dower House. It's obviously much smaller – very few bedrooms – but it's part of my uncle's plans to do his bit in the war effort.' Eddie cleared his throat. 'Anyway, he asked me to pass on the message to you.'

'When will they move?'

'I believe in the next few days. Just enough time for the cleaners to give it a thorough going over as it hasn't been lived in for years.'

'In a few days?' Dale squeaked, not able to quell the rush of alarm. 'But I don't have anywhere to go.'

He chuckled. 'You *are* an idiot. We're going with them. But there's definitely no place for Wanda Wilcox, either in a spare room or with the extra security precautions he has to abide by.' He gave her a quick glance before watching the road again. 'Just keep what I've mentioned under your hat.'

'What should I tell Wanda?'

'You'll have to make some excuse, but for God's sake don't mention they're moving into the Dower House. It's all top secret. Comes under the Official Secrets Act as far as you and I and everyone else are concerned. But get it nipped in the bud right away with her.' He hesitated, then added, 'I'd just be careful what you say to her.'

'Oh, I will,' Dale replied, and decided to add, just to see his reaction: 'Do you remember when she was rude to you that time when you brought in the messages?'

'Did she? I didn't notice.' He changed to a lower gear as he approached the Park.

She was just about to say of course he'd noticed and that she knew about their affair when he said:

'None of us is that keen on her, but I'm told she does an excellent job. And I have a feeling she does more behind the scenes, though I don't know for certain. But that's probably why they keep her on. It's just a shame she's always so ready to pounce on anyone.'

So he wasn't going to mention his personal relationship with Wanda. She would have thought more of him if he had.

Soon they were through the sentry gates and she was walking to her Hut, ready to face Wanda and apologise for not getting back in time as she'd promised.

But it was a different supervisor who sat at her desk. An older woman with a greying bun, stray wisps escaping at the neck and sides of a stern face. Dale's heart sank even further. At least she was early. Only a few girls had already arrived.

'Your name, please?' the woman's voice was thin, like her colourless lips.

'Dale Treadwell.'

'Is that *Dulcie* Treadwell?'

'Yes.'

'Ah.' The woman, her glasses sliding down the narrow nose, peered at her notes. 'Mrs Wilcox left a message. She's not in today but passed the message on that she hoped all was well with your mother.' She removed her glasses and looked myopically at Dale. 'I hear the area where you live in London was bombed.'

'Yes. Our house has been hit but thankfully my mother is safe and staying with a friend.'

'Excellent. So you'll be able to carry on without leaving us in the lurch again today.'

271

'I'm sorry, Mrs—' Dale started. She didn't know the woman's name.

'*Miss* Gibson,' the woman corrected her.

'Miss Gibson, I've been working seven days with no day off at all, and Wa – Mrs Wilcox told me they hadn't located everyone whose houses had been bombed. All I knew was that it had happened right where we live. I was frantic. And then coming home there was a terrible accident on the line which held the train up—' She broke off, holding back the tears at the thought of the person who'd wanted to end their life.

'You must understand how difficult things can get here without the full complement of staff,' Miss Gibson said, 'so we can't keep swapping shifts at any time we like with no notice.' She studied Dale. 'However, this was an emergency, so we'll say no more about it.'

I should bloody well think not, Dale fumed as she went to her desk and changed the rotor positions on the wheels according to the day's instructions. She worked through several messages, but as usual nothing stood out. Chewing her lower lip with frustration she picked up the next message on the pile, carefully pressing each letter on the machine and jotting down the alternative one lit up on the lamp board. When she'd finished, she stared at the new groups of letters. There was nothing significant that she could fathom, and yet . . . She screwed up her eyes in concentration as she sometimes did when searching for a clue in the *Telegraph* crossword. The letters danced before her eyes. After what was probably a whole minute, she opened them and gazed at the letters for several more seconds. Yes, there was some- thing about them, but it was eluding her. She chewed her lower lip in frustration. She couldn't spend any more time on it. Maybe she'd have better luck on the next one.

Reluctantly she put the message to one side to begin what would become the pile that had got the better of her, when almost without thinking she snatched it back and crossed out the first four letters of the groups of five she'd been puzzling over to give:

D ERFUE HRERI STIND ERWOL FSSCH ANZE

If it wasn't for that blasted 'E' coming after the 'U' it would have read *Der Führer* – the Leader. Herr bloody Hitler. Dale's heart began to hammer. If she was right it would mean she would have cracked this message and she could confirm to Miss Gibson that the rotors were set correctly for the day. Maybe she'd made a mistake and had tapped the wrong letter to start with. But she knew she hadn't. No matter how tired she was she always checked every key on the board twice to make sure she'd have an accurate decoded letter light up. Damn. She was so close. So could the 'E' be a mistake by the German operator at the other end? Wanda had warned that sort of thing did sometimes happen. But instinct told her it wasn't the case in this message. And then something clicked. In her mind's eye she saw her book of poems – by Goethe. The way his name was pronounced always sounded to her as though it should have an umlaut. The sound of 'o' and 'e' together made the same sound as an 'o' with the umlaut.

Of course! She swallowed her excitement. *They can't put umlauts into code! The 'E' stands in place of the umlaut – to give the same sound.* She'd almost forgotten.

Oh, why hadn't she remembered this before? She might have missed several vital messages. She gritted her teeth. She needed to accelerate her German studies.

Out of the corner of her eye she saw Miss Gibson curiously watching her. Quickly, she bent her head to see if she could work out any of the other groups of letters in the same message. 'I', then 'ST' together made 'IST'. The Fuehrer is . . . The next letters were easy. 'IND' and 'ER' beginning the next two groups of five letters – meaning 'in the' – and ending with 'WOL'. And the very next group of letters started with an 'F' to make 'WOLF'.

Wolf. She frowned. It was exactly the same word as in English! But what did it mean? Was 'Wolf' code for something? She stared at the letters following WOLF, running the two groups together. SSCHANZE. And then something in her brain clicked. Could it be Wolf's Lair? Hitler's headquarters? That's what the rest of the letters must translate to – Wolfsschanze. She'd not come across the word 'Schanze' before but it must mean 'lair' or something similar. Dear God, she'd uncovered what might be a really significant message.

With shaking legs Dale walked over to Miss Gibson and handed her the open page in her notebook. After the supervisor had studied it for a few seconds she nodded to Dale and rapped her fist on the desk for everyone's attention.

'Miss Treadwell has already ascertained that the rotors set for today are accurate.' She paused while there was an enthusiastic clapping, beaming round as though she'd decoded the message herself. 'So you will all be extra vigilant now you know it's confirmed.'

'Can I just say how I realised I had something?' Dale said. 'In case it helps anyone else.'

Miss Gibson nodded. 'By all means.'

'I hadn't remembered until just now that the Germans sometimes use an "e" after a vowel which normally has an umlaut,' Dale began. 'That's what threw me, at first – that extra "e".'

'I thought we were all picked because we could read and speak good German,' a newcomer called Belinda said with more than a hint of sarcasm.

'It doesn't hurt to remind everyone,' Miss Gibson said firmly. 'I will now notify the cryptanalysts.'

She disappeared.

'Well done,' Sonia said, turning round. 'Maybe now we know the settings are right, I'll have a chance of decoding my first message of the day.'

Chapter Twenty-Nine

'Dad, it's me.'

'You've caught me at a rather difficult time, love. I'm with someone.'

Dale rolled her eyes.

'No, not who you're thinking – it's a work colleague. Can it wait?'

She gave a heavy sigh. Though she'd dropped him a line telling him where to write before she'd even left London, she hadn't heard from him.

'No, it can't. I'm ringing from a phone box where I work to tell you our house has been bombed.'

'Dear God.' There was a silence. Then he said, 'Are you both all right?'

'Well, I'm not in London but Mother was and—'

'She's not hurt, is she?'

Dale could hear the alarm in his voice.

'Dale, tell me . . .'

'No, Dad, she's not hurt, she's—'

'Oh, dear Lord, she's dead.'

'She's not dead.' Dale snapped. 'She's perfectly all right, but the authorities won't allow us to go into the house. It was horrible, Dad. One of the neighbours a few doors along – I don't know if you know them – the Dennetts – and the woman . . . I had to identify her.' Dale felt her eyes prick as she relived that awful moment when the woman at the First Aid post had folded back the sheet, praying it wouldn't be her mother.

'I'm sorry I wasn't there . . . when she needed me,' he said, his tone sounding contrite. *Did he mean it or was it merely a platitude?*

'I'm sorry, too,' she said.

'Where is she now?'

'Just round the corner – staying with her friend Elizabeth.' The line crackled. 'I'm hoping you can go down to London to see what damage there is, and how you can help Mother. She can't do it all on her own.'

'No, of course not. Elizabeth's on the phone, isn't she? Can you give me the number?'

Dale told him and was just about to add, 'Dad, are you really going ahead with this divorce?' when the pips went. 'I don't have any more change,' she said hurriedly. 'Dad, be kind to her. She—'

There was a resounding click as the operator disconnected them.

What was her father doing that was so important? He'd implied he wasn't with his fancy woman, as her mother called her. She couldn't bear to think of her father, so clever, so steady, so *unchangeable* – that was the word – whom she'd admired so much as a child, wanting to show him she was clever, too. And all the time he had it in him to be unfaithful. An adulterer, her mother called him. She swallowed hard. It couldn't be *all* his fault. The thought occurred that maybe she and Mum had simply taken him for granted. Not given him enough attention. And this woman obviously had. But she'd never be able to make such a suggestion to her mother.

Wrapped in her thoughts Dale jumped as a woman outside the kiosk banged on the window. She pushed open the stiff door, glad to escape from the stink of the stale beer and tobacco in the cramped space.

'Sorry,' she smiled, but the woman pushed past her and into the kiosk without a word.

The sun was shining on the puddles in Bletchley. Black clouds that had gathered earlier had all dispersed although rain still dripped through the long line of trees dividing the High Street. Dale took in a few deep breaths. It was turning out to be a fine afternoon. Shame she'd been stuck in the Hut for most of it.

'Are you going to the show this evening?' Jennifer asked Dale a few days later as they finished the lukewarm stewed tea in Hut 2's café.

'I hadn't really thought about it.' Dale glanced at her watch and rose to her feet. 'We'd better be getting back.' She paused. 'What time does the show start?'

'Eight. That'll give us time for some supper.'

Eddie had mentioned it last week, but she hadn't given him a definite answer. Apparently, he had a major role, though she couldn't for the life of her remember the name of the show.

'Remind me what it's called,' Dale asked Jennifer when they were outside.

'"Everything is Rhythm". It's a musical. Your bloke is playing the lead – a conductor who falls in love with a princess.'

'Who do you mean – "my bloke"?'

'Eddie Langton, of course.'

'I wouldn't exactly call him "my bloke".'

'*We* would,' Sonia said, catching them up, and giggling.

'It's all over the Hut that he's mad about you. He's always making excuses to pop in with the messages. You must've noticed. And aren't you billeted together at some grand country house?'

Dale felt her cheeks burn. How did Sonia know that? Worryingly, it sounded as though everyone in the Hut knew. She supposed they'd seen her go off with him in his bright yellow sports car when he was giving her a lift.

'He's been in our Hut *twice* to leave our messages,' she corrected. 'And for your information we're just friends.'

'Yeah, that's what they all say.' Sonia laughed and linked her arm through Dale's. 'Come on, Dale. Don't take yourself so seriously. Give yourself some time off from all that dreary German studying and come with us this evening.'

Dale hesitated. She was moving to the Dower House tomorrow. But what difference did it make? She'd only got a few belongings to pack and that would take all of ten minutes. She hesitated. Then without thinking further, she linked her other arm through Jennifer's and turning her head to each girl, smiled broadly.

'All right,' she said. 'Count me in.'

The musical was to be held in the main house. Dale hadn't been in the strange-looking mansion since her interview with Commander Travis. The three women trooped in with several others where they were guided to the magnificent ballroom, doubling as a teleprinter room, though tonight the desks and machines were stacked along one wall. Dale twisted her neck up to admire the gold and white plastered ceiling, then took her seat near one of the graceful wooden columns where Sonia and Jennifer sat. Dale recognised several women from her Hut who smiled, and saw quite a number she'd never set eyes on before. More and more people seemed to be coming to the Park to work every day. She spotted Vernon with the same group he hung around with. He caught her eye and sent her a wink but she pretended not to notice.

It was an amusing play enhanced by a small band to accompany the songs. To her surprise she noticed Eddie had a fine voice. He also had perfect timing for the comic scenes and she felt some of the tension drain away from her neck and shoulders as she joined in the laughter.

There was a short interval and most of the audience rose to stretch their legs and head for the makeshift bar. Mrs Peters, who usually brought round the tea when they were on the midnight shift, was already pouring from a large steel urn.

'Let's go mad and have a glass of wine,' Sonia said, eyeing the upturned glasses.

'And I'll treat,' Dale said quickly.

When they'd all been served, Dale raised her glass.

'To us at BP.' She clinked her glass with the two girls. 'May we crack Jerry's rotten stinking codes so fast it'll make their heads spin.' Sonia and Jennifer grinned and repeated her sentiment as they clinked glasses.

'To us,' they repeated.

Dale felt a sudden glow of kinship. Friendship might come later but for now she was content. Just then she spotted Vernon. He caught Dale's eye and immediately broke away.

'Are you enjoying the play, ladies?' Vernon said, his charming smile in place as he sauntered up.

'Yes, it's wonderful,' Sonia said, treating him to one of her giggles.

Vernon raised a dark eyebrow at Dale. 'Do introduce me to your friends, darling.'

Ignoring his uncalled-for endearment, she noticed the

sudden spark of interest in Jennifer's eyes. In the girl's quiet way, she was just as captivated with Vernon as Sonia evidently was. Quickly excusing herself after making brief introductions, Dale wandered round the room, holding her glass, then instantly wished she'd kept with the others. Wanda was making straight for her.

'They're pretty good, aren't they?' Wanda said, jerking her head towards the platform. 'Especially the Honourable Edward Langton.' She watched Dale closely. 'Did you know he was an honourable?' When she didn't answer, Wanda said, 'I'd have thought you'd have guessed by his voice and his relation to Lord and Lady Langton. Rather out of your league in the marriage market, don't you think?'

Dale felt a bubble of irritation. Wanda obviously didn't think Eddie was out of *her* league, even if he *was* titled. She decided not to rise to Wanda's bait. She wished to high heaven she could escape.

'Nice singing voice, too,' Wanda commented. She gazed at Dale. 'Don't you think?'

'Very nice.'

'So have you asked about my coming to Langton Hall?'

Dale held her gaze.

'Actually, I did speak to Eddie. I'm sure you know he's billeted there with his aunt and uncle.'

Wanda nodded, her eyes not wavering from Dale.

'He explained they only live in one of the wings,' Dale continued, 'so there's no available bedroom for any guest.'

Wanda's eyes were slits. 'Don't tell me they're so poor they can't afford to run the whole house.'

'No, it's not that.' She met Wanda's disbelieving glare. 'The main part of the house has been sequestered.'

'By whom?'

'I'm sorry, I'm not able to say.'

'Look, Dulcie, I've signed the Official Secrets Act the same as you. I'm your supervisor. I think you can trust me with this mysterious take-over.'

Dale shook her head. 'I'm sorry, Wanda,' she repeated. 'You'll have to ask the *Honourable* Edward Langton yourself if you don't believe me.'

'Don't go on, Dulcie,' Wanda interrupted, her mouth thinning. 'It's obvious you don't want me cramping your style.' She stalked off.

At that moment the bell rang for the second act and Dale went to find her seat. But she couldn't concentrate on the play, even though people around her were roaring with laughter – mostly at Eddie's part. When it came to a close she clapped loudly with the others. What would have been an enjoyable evening had been spoilt by the awkward encounter with Wanda.

Eddie was waiting for her in the small bar that had been set up.

'Did you enjoy it?' he said as soon as he spotted her.

'I did . . . very much.'

'I could hear you clapping at the end.'

'Course you couldn't,' she said, laughing. 'One clap is the same as another.'

'No. I was looking at you.' He paused. 'By the way, I noticed you talking to Wanda Wilcox before we started the second act. Did you say anything about how it's not possible for her to come to Langton Hall?'

'Yes. And I tried to explain why.'

'And?'

'She wasn't pleased.'

He grimaced. 'Hmm. I'm afraid she's in for a shock if she thinks she can take this any further. My uncle is the last person she wants to run up against.' He glanced at her. 'Sorry, Dale. I haven't even asked what you'd like to drink.'

'Nothing, thanks. I had a glass of wine in the interval.'

'Good for you.' Eddie downed his beer and turned to her. 'Then shall we go? We're going to be busy moving tomorrow.'

'I'll get my jacket,' Dale said.

As she and Eddie turned to leave the ballroom, she was aware of Wanda staring after them with such venom it made Dale shiver.

Chapter Thirty

Dale fell in love with the Dower House the instant she set eyes on it. It was an elegant Georgian building with a stone façade and a two-storey bay topped by stone finials, with climbing roses adorning the small-paned windows. Beautiful though Langton Hall was, the Dower House looked more inviting and homely.

'What do you think, Dale?' Eddie said.

'It's perfect.'

'You haven't seen inside yet. It's not been lived in for years. And I've only been in it once when I was a child and a barmy old great-aunt lived there.'

Dale stepped into the hall cluttered with sculptures and paintings that Eddie told her his aunt had insisted upon bringing over from the main house.

'There you are,' Lady Langton smiled as she bustled in and out. 'I've set two rooms aside for you.'

'You choose which bedroom and I'll take the reject,' Eddie said with a grin.

Lady Langton glanced at her nephew. 'When Dulcie's unpacked you can show her the reception rooms and say hello to Mrs Owens who's getting the kitchen sorted out.'

There were seven bedrooms and three bathrooms, Ruth the maid explained, as she showed Dale a bedroom at the side of the house. It was rather gloomy despite the sunny day. She went over to the window, but the view was mainly a coach house and some other outbuildings looking in dire need of repair. Disappointed, but telling herself off for even entertaining such a thought, she followed Ruth to another door. This one was very different. The sun beamed in through the almost floor-to-ceiling pair of Georgian windows. Dale walked over to see the view. It looked onto the Dower House's own private gardens, though she could glimpse the gardens adjoining the main house, partly hidden by tall trees, now in full leaf. As she gazed out she noticed a slight movement. A figure dodged in and out of the trees. A dozen or more followed. This must be the reason the Langtons had been obliged to give over Langton Hall to the War Office. There was obviously some kind of training going on already. She pressed her lips together and stepped away from the windows, then looked round the room.

'Hmm. I can't see Master Edward in here,' she chuckled, glancing at the brightly flowered wallpaper that even covered the ceiling. It felt both summer-like and warm and welcoming at the same time.

Ruth shyly smiled in agreement. 'Have you decided on this room then, miss?'

'Yes, this is perfect, thank you.'

'The bathroom's opposite, just for you and Master Edward,' Ruth said as she set Dale's suitcase down near the double bed. 'So if there's nothing more, miss . . .'

'Thank you, Ruth, very much for helping me decide.' She sent the maid a conspiratorial wink.

Ruth grinned and disappeared.

Dale wandered over to the windows again and opened one, letting in the clean country air. She put her head out, feeling it brush her cheeks. Beaming with delight as she heard the birds twittering and singing, she couldn't help a stab of guilt that she'd nabbed the best room. Not enough to change my mind though, she thought, still smiling. Peering to the right she saw another movement in the distance in between the trees. It was Lord Langton with Baxter, his beloved Labrador, who rushed in front, then retraced his run to take his place at his master's side.

Relieved that Wanda would not be joining them, Dale ran downstairs. Eddie was nowhere in sight, so Dale peeped into the rooms by herself. She found a dining room, music room and drawing room, and a small library that didn't look as though it had been cleaned yet. Closing the door, she heard the clattering of pans and the smell of baking but decided not to disturb Mrs Owens in her new domain. There'd be plenty of time later.

To say that Wanda was a bit off with her would be an understatement, Dale thought. She hadn't said anything specific – it was merely the atmosphere between them. It crackled like electricity. Dale couldn't understand it. She'd had a successful fortnight, breaking the codes at least three out of every five days by thinking in the same way she'd always done when faced with a particularly tricky crossword clue. On every occasion Wanda hadn't made any comment – just pursed her lips and nodded before she informed Dale's colleagues that the rotors were set correctly and taking the message to wherever they were to be decoded.

Dale was aware that Beatrice Perryman, who'd started the same day as Dale, was managing to crack codes once or twice a week, but some of the others – even those who'd been there before Dale – were having difficulties. Sonia had still not had much luck.

'My Italian is far better than my German,' she confided

to Dale one evening when they were in the canteen having macaroni cheese, warmed up for several hours from the lunch menu, or so it tasted.

'Why don't you ask Wanda or Miss Gibson if you can have a transfer? I'm sure one of the other Huts would be able to make use of your Italian.'

'Maybe I will.'

But it wasn't Sonia who was transferred.

Two days later, on the midnight to eight shift, Wanda made an announcement.

'One of the cryptanalysts has been taken ill so they're short. They're looking for someone on a temporary basis – maybe a few weeks, maybe longer. Believe me, it's a real honour as the position must go to someone outstanding, whom I deem worthy. But first—' she looked round the room '—do we have any volunteers?'

Dale immediately shot her hand up, her heart beating fast at Wanda's words. It was exactly the opportunity she'd been looking for. Not only because she wanted to be challenged even further, but quite frankly she was getting fed up with Wanda's attitude.

'Anyone else?' Wanda said. Beatrice raised her hand. Wanda nodded. 'Well, then . . . I will recommend *you*, Beatrice.'

Sonia looked round at Dale.

'You're much better at this than Beatrice,' she hissed.

'Please get on with your work,' Wanda said sharply. 'Beatrice, collect your things and come with me.'

Beatrice stood and picked up her bag, throwing an apologetic smile to Dale as she followed Wanda. Dale watched her retreating back, bewildered that it wasn't herself who was being temporarily promoted. It wasn't Beatrice's fault, she had to admit. Beatrice was a solid, reliable worker with a steady success rate. But not nearly the number of successes *she'd* had.

Dale fumed as she picked up the next message. It was clear that Wanda had deliberately chosen someone other than herself. Someone who hadn't cracked as many codes. But someone whom the supervisor, as far as she knew, had had no trouble with. She let her breath out in a quick angry puff of air. Was there really something in Sonia's remark that the woman was miffed because Eddie apparently only had eyes for herself? Dale rolled her eyes. Making any complaint would look like sour grapes.

Dale peered at the next message. Forgetting everything except the task in front, she scrutinised the string of letters, as usual neatly grouped into fives.

DIENS TAGAN DIEGR UPPEH EUTEI STDER

Excitement fizzed through her. *Dienstag An die Gruppe Heute ist der* – she couldn't read the next words. They looked like something technical. But the German words definitely translated as: 'Tuesday To the group today is the . . .'

She raised her hand.

'Mrs Wilcox, the settings are correct today.'

Everyone clapped. Wanda came over to her desk and nodded.

'Good,' she conceded and looked around the room. 'Well, girls, there shouldn't be any difficulty in translating many more messages tonight.'

It was four o'clock in the morning when Dale had made up her mind. She was going to tackle Wanda about Eddie. Everyone was making for the door to walk over to the canteen, but Wanda was still at her desk making notes. The perfect opportunity.

Dale quietly cleared her throat, trying to think what she

wanted to say, then decided it was best to be completely natural rather than come out with a rehearsed piece.

'Wanda, are you going to the canteen for supper?'

Wanda raised her head. 'In a few minutes. Why do you ask?'

'I'd just like to have a word with you.'

Wanda nodded. 'Yes, I thought you might.'

Dale quelled her irritation. 'What I want to say is not what you think.'

'Oh.' Wanda put down her pen and fixed her eyes on Dale.

At least that's caught Wanda's attention.

'And what did you suppose I was thinking?' Wanda's tone had become sarcastic.

'You might have thought I was going to ask you why you didn't choose me to join the cryptanalysts even though I've had more successes with decoding than anyone else in the room . . . and I put my hand up to volunteer.' By the tightening of Wanda's lips Dale knew her guess was right. 'But that's your prerogative,' Dale continued, pretending to be oblivious to any reaction from her supervisor.

'Well, then, what is it?'

'Someone recently remarked that you were annoyed with me about something personal.'

Wanda blinked but said nothing.

'To do with Eddie Langton,' Dale said. 'Isn't that it? That he and I are friends?'

'I'm afraid I don't believe you're just friends.' Wanda's eyes flashed. 'If you must know, he and I were going out together – quite seriously. Then you come here and a week later he says he's met someone else. Love at first sight for him, apparently.' She curled her lip.

Dale raised her eyes to the ceiling.

'That doesn't mean it's reciprocal.'

'Are you saying it isn't?'

'I'm afraid, Wanda, that's my business.' She looked straight into Wanda's eyes. 'I'll see you in half an hour.'

As it was, Beatrice was back in their Hut after only a fortnight, looking sheepish.

'We thought you'd be gone much longer,' Jennifer said. 'Did he make a miraculous recovery?'

'I can't discuss it.'

'What's that supposed to mean? We know you can't discuss the work, but Mrs Wilcox indicated it was going to be several weeks or longer before he was fit enough to return.'

'It didn't work out,' Beatrice said, her face flushing. 'That's all I'm saying.'

It sounded to Dale as though Beatrice had either clashed with one of the cryptanalysts or she simply wasn't up to the job. How Dale longed to be given the opportunity to work with them and understand how Hut 6 fitted in to get a sense of the big picture. Share some of the excitement they must feel when they'd cracked the settings for the day so Hut 6 could decode the messages.

She wondered if she should have a word with Wanda about whether they were going to replace Beatrice. But on second thoughts she knew what Wanda's response would be.

Dale sighed. She wouldn't risk the humiliation.

Chapter Thirty-One

16th November, 1940

Dear Dale,

You're not going to believe this but I've joined up!!! It was a toss-up between the WAAFs and the Wrens, but the sea beckoned – if they send me abroad, that is. If they do, I'll get a chance to see the world before doing the marriage and babies thing and the naval uniform was the most flattering and makes me look positively sylph-like. I'm thrilled to bits. All those handsome sailors! I'm in training and you should see me marching and saluting. It's a scream but I love it. Our billet is in a castle, but not at all as grand as it sounds – it was filthy when we arrived and we've had to muck in – literally! – to be able to fancy it. We have to say <u>deck</u> and <u>porthole</u> for floor and window as if we're on a real ship. All good fun but I can't wait to finish the training and be sent on a real ship to who knows where.

You wouldn't recognise the London you knew. Some whole streets are just a mass of rubble. So depressing. That's why I wanted to get out of here. You left at just the right time. I'm glad to hear your mother's back in her house.

I suppose you've heard the terrible news night before last – poor Coventry was smashed to pieces, and the beautiful cathedral copped it as well. Bloody Nazis!

I've not heard from you for ages. It all sounds a bit hush-hush where you are and what you're doing when no one can reach you by telephone and you've got this Box No. for your post. I expect when we meet next time there'll be plenty to talk about. But I can see this war going on longer than some people think.

Well, that's all for now. Write when you can. I do miss you and Jane but am making some nice friends here. We sometimes have a grumble but then we laugh and remind each other that we're all in the same boat, haha!

Lots of love,
Rhoda XXX

Dale read the letter again, a wry smile on her lips, before she folded it and put it back in the envelope. Joining one of the forces was not the first choice Dale would pick for Rhoda – her friend was too rebellious and always assumed rules and regulations were for other people only. At school she'd been the same. Dale supposed the Navy would be the more likely one to offer some adventure. Whether it would open the door to a life of glamour and excitement, Dale was doubtful, but maybe it would give her friend what she was craving.

For a moment Dale envied her. The thought of the open sea was such a sharp contrast to the airless Hut she was buried in six days a week. She'd had to put up with the stuffy atmosphere during the hot summer months, but now, with winter approaching, the same Hut was miserably cold and damp. She could hardly believe the summer had disappeared so quickly.

Hearing from Rhoda made her realise how much she

missed her and Jane. She hadn't made a close friend at the Park though Helen Blunt had partnered her at tennis a few times. This was thanks to Prime Minister Churchill ordering two new tennis courts because the old one was too far gone to repair and they'd had to play rounders instead. But Churchill had soon altered that. She and Helen had met up for a drink in the bar occasionally and Dale liked her very much, but it was so frustrating that they couldn't discuss their work. It might have made all the difference if she could understand where her own decoding slotted in.

'Some of the musicians are putting on a concert this evening,' Helen said one day after they were sitting having a drink after an early morning game. Dale was feeling particularly pleased she was improving under Helen's expert tuition and had won a few sets. 'Do you fancy it? It's classical, if you like that.'

'I love it,' Dale said at once.

'A lot of musicians work here,' Helen said. 'Apparently, it was one of the criteria they were looking for when they set up BP.'

'Really?'

'Same with mathematics,' Helen said. 'That's how I got in. And maths has a strong connection with reading music.'

'I didn't know that,' Dale said, intrigued. 'It sounds fascinating.'

'What about you? How did you come to be here?'

'I won a crossword competition,' she said. 'I've always loved doing them. My dad could do them in his head.'

Helen nodded. 'Yes, I've heard people good at crosswords look at words and letters in a different way. That's obviously useful for a cryptographer.' She paused and looked at Dale. 'What about languages? Do you speak German or anything?'

Suddenly, Dale caught a glimpse of the 'Be Like Dad – Keep

Mum' poster pinned on the wall behind the bar. Even though she was certain that Helen was a thoroughly decent woman, you just never knew. This could lead on to how she knew German. And that might lead to Ursula Fassbender. Dale bit her lip. Was she becoming paranoid? Oh, this was all so difficult. She and Helen might have had a better chance at friendship if they'd at least worked in the same Hut.

Helen followed Dale's eyes to the poster.

'No need to say, if you feel uncomfortable,' Helen said cheerfully.

'I feel awful we can't have a natural conversation,' Dale said, 'but I suppose it's better to be safe than sorry. I'd hate to get hauled up by one of the bigwigs for blabbing.'

'Thank goodness music is a common language that won't get anyone into trouble,' Helen said, draining the last of her orange squash. She glanced at her watch. 'Well, we'd better get to work. I'll meet you at the hall just before seven.'

Before Dale went back to her Hut, she popped into the mail room as she did most days when she wasn't on the midnight shift. There was just one typed brown envelope. Disappointed it wasn't from her father in answer to one she'd recently written, it was stamped with the Grosvenor Hotel. Her typed address at home was crossed out and her mother's neat handwriting forwarded it to her PO Box number.

It could only be to remind her that she'd never collected her gloves, she decided, with a flash of irritation. They must have got her address when she'd signed in that time for the tea dance. Instantly, her whole being flew back to the event. When Glenn had unexpectedly walked in. How the room had lit up. How suddenly, gloriously happy she'd been. She swallowed hard. She'd heard nothing from him since that one and only letter although she'd written back many times. Was he still in Berlin? Was he still alive? Her eyes pricked with tears. His letter had been so loving yet there'd been no further word. It had been over a year since he wrote it.

Sighing, she put the envelope in her bag and hurried to her Hut.

'I've saved a seat for you towards the front for the best view,' Helen said as soon as she spotted Dale, 'as it's not arranged *quite* so well as the Royal Albert Hall,' she laughed.

Dale grinned. 'I'm sure the music will more than make up for the venue.'

She looked around seeing several familiar faces, though there was no sign of Eddie. She wasn't sure whether to be relieved or disappointed. She was becoming fond of him – she couldn't help it. He was everything she'd thought possible she'd want in a man – decent, reliable, fun to be with and, on top of that, extremely attractive.

But he wasn't Glenn. She bit her lip, willing the music to start so she could lose herself and her thoughts. She was surprised to count as many as a dozen musicians on the platform, and to her astonishment she saw Jennifer at the piano.

A tall thin young man holding a baton stepped forward. 'Good evening, ladies and gentlemen. Tonight we'll be playing Rachmaninov's Piano Concerto Number Two. There'll be a short interval. Sorry we can't provide a printed programme for you all, but there's a certain reason why there's a paper shortage.' There were several chuckles from the packed hall. 'So without further ado, we'll begin.'

Dale leant back on the hard upright chair, wishing she'd brought a cushion as some of the others had. But soon she forgot about any discomfort as she let the strains of the composer's magic wash over her, soothing her. But when it changed to the slow movement, for some unaccountable reason, the tears rolled down her cheeks. She swallowed, desperate to blink them back but still they flowed. Helen glanced at her, then handed her a handkerchief. Dale gave her a wan smile and wiped her eyes.

'Are you all right?' Helen whispered.

Dale nodded. Somehow, she managed to get through to the end, Rachmaninov's dying strains only enhancing her emotions.

'Shall we stretch our legs?' Helen said at the interval.

'Helen, I know I'm acting like a wet week, but I think I'd like to leave.'

'It's a man, isn't it?'

Dale gave a start. 'Is it that obvious?'

'Yes.' Helen studied her a few moments. 'Are you sure he's worth it?'

Dale remembered the woman who'd stopped her on the bridge when she thought she'd been stood up by Glenn that time. She'd said in no uncertain terms that no man was worth a woman's tears. But Glenn was different.

'I thought so once,' she said, shakily.

'And now?'

'Now I don't even know whether he's alive.'

The miserably cold bike ride to the Dower House in the pitch dark except for the regulatory dimmed front lamp seemed to go on for ever, but eventually she was wheeling the bicycle into the shed and a few minutes later she was back in her room. Now, thoroughly frozen, she switched on the electric fire Eddie had managed to find for her in the attic. There were two bars but only one worked. With all the appearances of luxury, the Dower House was bitterly cold, she thought, as she got ready for bed.

She smeared a few drops of almond oil on her face,

wondering what Glenn was doing at this very moment. His position as a broadcaster must be terribly dangerous. He'd mentioned they didn't censor his scripts, but that could all change if America entered the war. That's what Churchill was aiming for. Then the Nazis would see things take a different turn.

By then, Glenn would be the enemy.

She swallowed the lump in her throat. There was still talk of an impending invasion. Look what had happened in Jersey. Those poor people had already suffered several months of jackboots marching all over their island and no one had come to their aid.

A shiver ran through her. It was too dreadful to imagine what it would be like to hear Germans marching through London with their hateful swastika flags. People cowering in doorways, so they didn't have to give that ridiculous Nazi salute. She shook her head. No, the British wouldn't cower. Hitler had underestimated the British if he thought he could ride over them roughshod. According to the newspapers and the wireless most of the public were behind Mr Churchill, who never doubted they would win. She must have faith and do the same and hope the very small part she was playing was useful.

Oh, Glenn, where are you? Why haven't I heard? I miss you so terribly. I still love you. I'll wait for you for ever if I have to. But do you still love me?

Trying to picture him brought all her emotions to the surface. She smothered a sob. She needed to know what had happened to him once and for all. Had he received *any* of her letters? Was it futile to keep writing to him when he never responded? She turned from the mirror, tears of anger and frustration pouring down her cheeks, and climbed into bed.

But no matter how she tried, she couldn't stop thinking of him. She tossed from one side to the other, willing herself to lie still and drift into sleep but she heard the clock on the coach house chime every hour. Twelve . . . one . . . two . . . through the night.

Dazed with exhaustion and a throbbing headache, in the morning she forced herself from her bed, having only slept the last two hours, knowing she must be alert for the day's work or Wanda would have something to say.

It was only as she was about to leave her room that she remembered the letter from the hotel. She was never going there again. She'd have to make some excuse to her mother as to why she no longer had her gloves. Retrieving it from her bag and without another glance at the envelope, she tossed it into the wastepaper basket.

PART THREE

Chapter Thirty-Two

March, 1941

It was strange, Dale thought, how each shift crawled by, yet the weeks flew. How different her life was these past eight months. She and the other girls in Hut 6 were having a steady stream of successes – even Sonia frequently contributed, especially when they worked in pairs, though Dale preferred to work on her own. Her German had vastly improved due to her diligence in studying almost every day. She'd found plenty of German books and novels in the Mansion's library with its plaster ceiling and panelled walls and imposing carved fireplace. It wasn't a quiet room like most libraries as there were half a dozen desks occupied by women typing and the constant noise of teleprinters in a nearby room, but to Dale's delight Lady Langton encouraged her to use the library at the Dower House, now clean and welcoming.

She'd begun reading German poetry, getting to grips with more vocabulary and appreciating the rhythm of the choice of words. She still had her eye on a promotion to one of the Huts where the cryptanalysts worked, but no more was ever said about their needing extra help. It had not dampened her determination, but all she could do at present was demonstrate to Wanda that she was an exemplary worker.

It would all be so much more bearable if she'd heard from Glenn. She'd written again – several times – being careful when posting the letter to follow exactly the route he'd outlined that would reach him.

Maybe something's happened in the set-up, her inner voice suggested. *Someone – Don, perhaps – could have been transferred somewhere and the new person wouldn't be in on the arrangement.*

No, she was just making excuses. Dale's lips tightened. Glenn would have been notified of any change and used a different method. She should have wiped him out of her mind a long time ago. But just thinking that conjured up his face. That crooked smile. The cleft in his chin. His eyes that showed his every emotion.

Should she tell Eddie she couldn't see him tonight after all? She hadn't seen much of him lately as they'd been working different shifts for the last three months or so. She had to admit she missed his company. But this last week had been gruelling with hundreds of messages every day pouring in. At least the worst of winter was over. But the freezing cold Hut had begun to take its toll on her and she'd started sleeping badly. It would be such a nice change to escape for the evening and have Eddie's company.

In the darkness of the cinema Eddie held her hand. It felt warm and comforting. Every so often she felt him glance at her but she kept her eyes fixed on the screen. She'd been wanting to see *Rebecca* but somehow she couldn't concentrate. All she could think of was when she'd gone to see *Wuthering Heights* with Glenn, followed by their night of love-making . . . How tender and loving he'd been when

302

she'd confessed it was her first time. Dale closed her eyes, her body tingling at the memory.

In the car she chatted about the film, but she could tell his mind was elsewhere, the way he kept his eyes fixed ahead but saying nothing. Maybe he was feeling the pressure of his job today more than usual. It had begun to rain. She watched the wipers swish backwards and forwards, almost hypnotised with their movement, not able to break the silence. It was after eleven when they arrived at the Dower House, Eddie taking the gravel drive slower than usual.

'I'll put the motor away while you get in before you catch your death.'

Heaving a sigh, Dale opened the scullery door. There'd been no heat in the car and she was cold and tired. She'd make some cocoa. Maybe Eddie would have one. It'd warm them up. She put the kettle on and it was whistling by the time Eddie appeared.

'What're you making?'

'Cocoa, but I know you don't like it—' she smiled '—so would you like tea?'

'I'd prefer something stronger.' He opened the scullery door again and shook out his wet mackintosh. 'It's vile out there.' He turned to her. 'But cocoa'd be fine.'

She put the filled mugs on Mrs Owens' pine table. Eddie was pacing up and down.

'You're making me dizzy,' Dale said. 'Come and sit down.'

He went over to the table and took a few swallows, then purposefully set his mug down before pulling Dale to her feet.

'I can't stand this any more,' he said. 'I want you. You know that. You've known it for a long time. But you're still carrying the torch for that Yank who might be dead, for all you know.'

Dale swallowed hard. She hadn't the heart to push him away. She could tell by his angry words he was deeply upset.

'Dale, listen. You – we've only got one life. Let's make the most of it. Don't waste your precious youth hankering after someone who's not even in this country. He comes from a different world. A different culture altogether. You'd have to up sticks and move to America as he would never stay in England after the war. You'd have to leave your family and friends. You'd be making a huge mistake.' He gripped her shoulders. 'Take a chance with me, Dale. I love you and I think you have feelings for me, too.'

'Of course I do, Eddie, but—'

He stayed her with his arms. 'No "buts". I love you and I don't care that you don't love me in the same way. Because one day I think you'll grow to love me in return. But until then I've got enough for both of us. And if you're worried about losing your independence, I promise not to hold you back. I know you're a determined career woman but I'd like to think we'd have children one day – to carry on the family tradition.' He kissed her forehead. 'I'm asking you to marry me.'

Her head spun. He was rushing too fast, not taking into consideration anything she'd tried to tell him – that she was in love with someone else and always would be. And as far as children went – good God, there was a war on. She didn't want to think that far in advance with anyone, let alone Eddie. She had to stop him.

'Eddie, please—'

He let her go.

'All right,' he said, 'but don't turn me down before you think about it.'

In bed that night she tossed one way and then the other, wondering what to do about Eddie. Had she led him on that it had come to such a head? She'd tried so hard to make him understand. When she finally dragged herself out of bed, her head fuzzy through lack of sleep, she was grateful for once that she was on the afternoon to midnight shift. How she felt at this minute there was no way she could pull round and concentrate on codes. But at least the rain had finally stopped. Helen, whose shift coincided with her own this week, had suggested if the weather improved they'd have a game of tennis before they started work. Dale grimaced. She felt no more like playing tennis than flying to the moon but maybe being out in the crisp March air would help the fog in her brain to clear. Besides, she hated letting anyone down – particularly Helen, who'd lately become a real friend.

Helen was smiling as she bounded up to Dale.

'Do you mind a foursome?' she said.

'No, though I haven't played a foursome since school days.'

'It doesn't matter. I've got two others signed up. Kathy, who works with me, and a new girl – one of that group of Wrens who arrived yesterday.' She paused and looked towards the drive. 'Oh, here they come.'

Dale's hand flew to her mouth in shock.

'Dale!' Rhoda squealed, her face one enormous smile as she ran over, her arms outstretched. 'I can't believe it! What're *you* doing here?'

'Same as you,' Dale said, still reeling as she hugged and kissed her friend. 'I thought you were abroad.'

'I was . . . in Gib. They said they wanted some of us to do important work for the war in England. But they never said what. So I hope it's going to keep me interested. I've been enjoying a marvellous life and I don't want anything dull and boring.'

If she's in our Hut she's in for a shock.

'Helen was one of the first people I met.' Rhoda turned

to smile at Helen. 'She said as I'm not starting work until tomorrow I might like a game of tennis. So I jumped at it.' She pulled Dale into another bear hug and kissed her soundly on each cheek. 'But am I glad to see you, old friend.'

'Less of the old,' Dale chuckled.

Dale and Helen managed to beat Rhoda and Kathy, who was as short and slight as Rhoda was tall and big-boned. Rhoda put it down to being shattered after the month-long voyage and Dale didn't have the heart to tell her she was probably going to get just as exhausted at the Park without any sea voyage.

Although it was wonderful having a quick chat with Rhoda if they met in the canteen or on the tennis court, it wasn't the same as a real heart-to-heart with her friend, Dale thought.

'Where are you billeted?' Rhoda asked when at last they were able to have a cup of tea in the town's café the day after she'd begun work.

'I'm not allowed to say.'

Rhoda's large brown eyes flew wide.

'What! Has security gone completely mad?'

'I know it sounds like it. But the house isn't certified for BP workers. I was lucky and got it through one of the crypt-analysts I met on my first day here.'

She filled Rhoda in a little with Eddie but decided not to mention he also lived at the same house.

'Sounds to me as if this Eddie is important to you,' Rhoda said. When Dale didn't comment, she suddenly darted a look at her. 'Is he in love with you?'

'He says he is.'

Rhoda stared at her. 'Did you ever hear from that American chap you were so crazy about who never turned up that time?'

Dale swallowed hard. Desperate to control the sudden hammering of her heart, she managed to look steadily at her friend.

'Once. One letter and that was written just days later telling me he'd been sent abroad with no chance to let me know.' She looked at Rhoda. 'But I didn't receive it until last September – a year later. I don't know whether he's still there.'

'What does he do?'

'He's a war correspondent.'

'Could he be in Germany?'

Dale nodded. 'I think so.'

'So how did he get that letter to you?'

Dale began to feel uncomfortable. She didn't dare explain the circuitous route the letter had to take in case Glenn got into trouble.

'I'm not sure,' she said. 'He hasn't managed to get anything else through. That, or he's not written any more.' She bit her lip.

'I doubt that. It must be very difficult for him being in enemy country, trying to do a simple thing such as getting a letter out. Even though he isn't considered the enemy at the moment, I bet he'll still be watched closely.'

Dale's chest squeezed.

Rhoda stared at her. 'You're still in love with him, aren't you? It's not Eddie at all, is it?'

'You know me so well,' Dale said, trying to laugh it off.

'Yes, I do. And you need to sort yourself out where Eddie's concerned.'

'I know.' Dale paused. 'The trouble is, Eddie's the nicest, most decent, thoughtful, intelligent, good-looking—'

'Stop!' Rhoda raised her hand. 'All those things – but no mention of love.'

'Strangely enough I *do* love him . . . for all the things I've just told you. But not in the same way as he does.'

'Or as you feel for Glenn. I'm right, aren't I?'

Dale nodded miserably.

'Then you have to tell Eddie the truth.'

'He already knows about Glenn.'

'And?'

'He always reminds me Glenn might have gone back to America by now, or maybe not even—' she swallowed hard '—be alive. But in any case, he's willing to take the chance.' She hesitated, then said, 'He's asked me to marry him.'

'Dear God, you can't. You're not in love with him.'

'He thinks with time I'll feel the same as he does.'

Rhoda vehemently shook her head. 'You won't. And you'll be bloody miserable. And so will Eddie. Even if it's not Glenn – if by any chance something awful *has* happened to him – you still have to wait until you feel that same kind of spark with someone else. And that might never happen again. Glenn might always remain the love of your life.'

'I didn't know you were such a romantic,' Dale smiled.

'I'm not where *I'm* concerned,' Rhoda said, unexpectedly. 'But where *you're* concerned, I know that nothing else will do.'

Rhoda's words reverberated in Dale's head as she sat at her desk the following morning on a coveted daytime shift. Was her friend right? She seemed to understand her better than Dale did herself. She sighed. Why did life have to be so complicated? And made so much worse since the war.

She picked up the first message. No luck. Nor the second or third. But in the fourth message she noticed something a little odd after she'd transcribed it from the lamp board. It

308

was only short but it was the beginning which puzzled her. She peered at the nine groups of letters.

H H WEN NICHW EISSW ASLIE BEIST SOIST ESDEI

NETWE GEN H H

Why were there two sets of double H H's? One at the beginning and one at the end. And then with a little thrill she realised there was a rhythm . . . was it poetry? Something nagged at the corners of her mind. Something Wanda had said about the Germans being sentimental and liked quoting poetry. That could be a crib they were all supposed to be looking for, like an officer's rank or the weather. She studied the letters again, her brain teeming. Could HH stand for Hermann Hesse? In her head she took the double HH's away leaving WEN. She added another 'N' from the beginning of the second group to form the first German word: 'Wenn'.

The rest of the message fell into place, giving her one of the most beautiful lines in poetry. She'd always loved it but had never fully understood it – until this moment.

'*Wenn ich weiß, was Liebe ist, so ist es deinetwegen*'.

There it was, staring at her. Not only had she decoded the line which confirmed the settings were correct today, but it was as though the sentimental German operator, showing off his literary knowledge, had unknowingly given her the answer to her own dilemma. She needed to report this straightaway, but Glenn's image floated in front of her . . . and that famous line:

'*If I know what love is, it is because of you.*'

Rhoda was dead right. Glenn was the love of her life. Anyone else would be second best.

Chapter Thirty-Three

Daffodils were in full bloom, nodding their heads in the light breeze at Bletchley Park. The countryside was beginning to wear all the shades and tones of green and even the birds were singing their approval. Fluffy ducklings followed their mothers on the lake and all seemed right with the world. Except it wasn't, Dale thought grimly. But at least nature's magic had lifted the spirits of everyone in this interminable war – well, everyone except Rhoda. And today was no exception.

'I don't know how you stand it,' Rhoda said when she and Dale were on the bus after having been to an afternoon showing of *The Wizard of Oz* in Bletchley. 'I'm getting bored sick. I think my job would be more interesting if I was a telephone operator – though on second thoughts I wouldn't like that either, sitting all day getting the wires mixed up and putting the caller onto the wrong person.'

She gave a hoot of laughter, but Dale knew she was serious about not being very happy at work. It was a shame, but Rhoda had always craved action and from the snippets Dale had gathered over the months, most of the work in the other Huts sounded tedious too.

They were sitting upstairs at the front of the bus, which was gradually filling with mostly Bletchley Park staff. Before she could warn Rhoda, her friend had turned to her.

'My work was so interesting at the Foreign Office in Gib,' she complained in her clear voice, 'and then, of course, there was the fantastic social life.' She pulled a face. 'I'd go completely bananas if you weren't here, Dale. You've no idea how dreadfully confining it is, working in the dark all day. It's like being permanently on night duty, but with no lighting.'

Dale longed to tell her she was working in a very similar environment.

'I don't do anything exciting like you code-breakers,' Rhoda went on, ignoring Dale's frown. 'All I do is work on a bloody great machine—' she rolled her eyes '—keeping it going day and night. You wouldn't believe the noise they make.' Dale sent her a warning glance, but Rhoda carried on. 'I think it ties in with that machine you work on, but I feel like a robot and it's taking its toll on me, I can tell you.'

'Rhoda, shut up!' Dale hissed. 'I've never mentioned my machine. You're not supposed to discuss anything about work with me or anyone. I'll pretend I haven't heard.'

Rhoda glanced at her. 'I haven't given any secrets away. And anyway, they're all BP people on this bus.'

'It makes no difference,' Dale muttered. 'We're not allowed to discuss anything about our work with someone who works in another Hut – or one of the cottages – never mind when we're off the premises.' She paused. 'I just don't want you to get into trouble.'

'Oh, well—' Rhoda shrugged '—if someone reports me, it'll be good riddance.'

Dale changed the subject. It was simply too risky to continue. She just wished her friend understood the responsibility she'd taken on by signing the Official Secrets Act.

But nothing was going to get Dale down. For the first time since the bombing of Charlwood Street, she was going home tomorrow afternoon, straight after finishing her shift – and Miss Gibson had given permission for two whole days.

'Dulcie!'

Her mother stood at the door beaming. How good it was to see her smile. Dale gulped as she thought how easily she could have lost her.

'Hello, Mum.'

'Come on in, dear,' she said, kissing her. 'I'll make some tea. Take your coat off. I've put you in the guest room as I had to clear your room. The curtains never looked the same when they dried out and the carpet was ruined after the explosion. But we do have nice new windows,' she said, laughing.

Something had changed in her mother. Not just seeing me, Dale thought, as she unpacked her small travel bag, but there was a lightness about her. She looked younger and was wearing a little make-up which she hadn't lately. Maybe that bombing had made her realise how fragile life was and she was really going to make the most of it now.

'Come and have your tea,' Patricia called up the stairs. 'We're in the sitting room.'

Dale was touched to see that her mother had brought out the best china, usually reserved for guests, and a variety of cakes.

Dale took a bite of Dundee cake. It was delicious. But then her mother was a superb cook. She sipped her tea. Oh, it was good to be back.

'You've got a new hairstyle,' she remarked.

'Mmm. Do you like it?' Her mother touched it briefly.

'I do. It suits you.'

'I needed a change.' Patricia pushed over the cake trolley.

'Try one of these ginger biscuits. It's a new recipe. The boys love them.'

'You mean the soldiers who come to the mobile van?' Dale enquired.

'The very ones. I help serve them now. I couldn't not, when Elizabeth had been so kind to me.'

'How did the two of you get on when you lived together?' Dale asked curiously.

Her mother gave a rueful smile. 'Let's just say I'm pleased to be in my own home although the bombing's still going on and I'll never get used to it. At least volunteer work makes me feel I'm doing something worthwhile for those boys. Sometimes they're missing a hand, or an arm or leg but they're always cheerful.'

Dale couldn't put her finger on it but her mother seemed to be holding something back.

'Are the chaps all young?' she asked, hoping her tone sounded innocent.

Patricia hesitated. 'No . . . most . . . but not all. There's an ARP warden who turns up quite regularly. He's about my age.'

Ah, that accounted for the new hairdo and the lipstick.

'He's a nice man, Jim. Lost his wife to cancer five years ago. She was only forty-six. I think he finds a bit of comfort in talking to me.'

Normally Dale wouldn't have been that interested, but with the warmth in her mother's eyes, she wanted to know more.

'Does he have children?'

'Yes. One daughter and one son. They're both away. The daughter's in the ATS and the son's in the RAF. I think he's lonely as he loves hearing about you.'

Dale was suddenly alert. 'You don't tell him what I'm doing.'

'No, dear, seeing as I don't even know where you live, let alone what you do,' Patricia said mildly. 'I just told him you're doing war work. That's all you've told me anyway.' She paused. 'And you don't need to worry about him. He's as decent as they come.'

So that's how this has started.

Impressed that her mother seemed to be gaining some independence, Dale decided she wouldn't probe further. Mum would tell her in her own good time if there were any developments.

She finished her tea and wiped the crumbs from her lips in a most unladylike fashion with the back of her hand.

'That was absolutely perfect, Mum,' she said.

'I'm pleased you enjoyed it . . . and by the way, I like it that you've started to call me "Mum",' she added, then suddenly looked towards the fireplace. 'Oh, there's a letter for you on the mantelpiece. Another one from the Grosvenor Hotel.' She glanced at Dale. 'Why do they keep sending you letters, dear?'

'I don't—' Dale broke off, her heart thumping madly in her chest. Dear God. She knew. Oh, she knew. She touched the base of her throat to still the sudden pain and gulped. That letter she'd thrown away last year. It was nothing to do with leaving her gloves behind. She shot up and grabbed the brown envelope with the hotel's distinctive mark.

'You sit there and read what they have to say and I'll just clear these things,' her mother said.

Dale hardly took in her words. Ripping open the envelope she pulled out the hotel's letter. And there, as she knew it would be, was another envelope hidden inside. Glenn's letter.

314

Dearest beloved Dulcie,

This is the second time I've sent a letter to you via the Grosvenor Hotel. I don't have any idea whether they forwarded the first one as I've had no reply.

I'm being sent to London!

Dale gasped. Swiftly she read on.

I'll be there in two weeks' time for five days. I arrive on April 12 and leave April 17.

Dale gave a start. *He's already here! And he leaves the day after tomorrow! That only gives us one day.* The words danced in front of her.

I'll be staying at the Lansdowne Club again so if there's any possible chance you can get away and meet me there, even if it's only for an hour, I'll be the happiest guy in all London. The phone number is Mayfair 9408.

I think this will have to be the very last letter I write to you, darling. It's not fair to you that I keep writing if you're happy with someone else. But I'm still hoping this letter will find you so at least you'll know that I've never stopped loving you and I never will.

Your Glenn XXXXX

Tears welled in Dale's eyes. She could hardly take it in. He was alive and well. All this time he'd never stopped writing. But the only other one she would have received if she hadn't been so irritated with the hotel and so bloody stupid would have been collected by the maid at Langton Hall and thrown into the rubbish bin long ago. If only . . . Heaving a sigh she read the letter from the hotel.

315

Dear Miss Treadwell,

We trust this finds you well.

We believe this is the second letter we've forwarded on to you, and whilst people are sometimes moving around and might prove difficult to contact, we must ask you to refrain from using the hotel as a post box.

We do hope you understand.

Yours sincerely,

J. H. Moore (General Manager)

P.S. May we remind you again that you still haven't picked up the gloves you left here last September. If we hear nothing in the next fortnight we will send them to the WI for their jumble sale.

Dale chewed her lip as she skimmed the letter. Her first response was a flicker of annoyance with this Mr Moore, but then she pulled herself up sharply. It was her own fault that Glenn had felt the need to try one last time with the Grosvenor Hotel's address. They'd been more than kind to forward on the two letters. She would pick up her gloves and thank them while she was in London. That is – if there was time. Every moment would be precious.

'Is everything all right, dear?' her mother asked as she came into the room. 'You look a bit flushed. You haven't got a cold coming, have you?'

'N-no. I'm fine.'

'What was the hotel on about this time?' Patricia said.

Dale hadn't prepared herself for the obvious question.

'I left my gloves there when I went to the tea dance that time,' she said. At least it was the truth. 'I'll call in and collect them while I'm here.' She hesitated. 'Mum, may I use the telephone?'

'Of course, dear. I'll go and start supper.'

Heart beating wildly, Dale picked up the receiver.

'Oh, operator, could you put me through to the Lansdowne Club in Mayfair?'

'Putting you through . . .

'I'm afraid there's no answer from his room, Miss Treadwell,' the receptionist told her. 'He may be in the dining room. But I'll leave him a message that you called.'

Every bone, every muscle, every sinew shouted for her to leap into a cab and go straight to the Lansdowne Club. But he might well have gone out to a restaurant. And anyway, it wouldn't be at all fair to her mother. After all, she was hoping to spend the whole day with Glenn, so her mother wouldn't see much of her at all at this rate. No, she had to settle herself in for the evening.

It was one of the nicest evenings in her mother's company that Dale could remember. Patricia had made a special supper and poured the last of the sherry. The two of them laughed together, and Dale came clean about meeting Glenn all that time ago.

'I knew there was something more going on besides gloves,' her mother had chuckled.

'It's the sherry making me talk.' Dale joined in the laughter.

How her mother had changed. She'd gained some confidence since she'd had to manage on her own. Maybe it had allowed her to find some pleasures in life, particularly in her volunteer work. She'd lost some of those bitter lines around her mouth. Or was that mostly down to Jim? Well, good for him, if it was. She gave an inward smile.

When the telephone rang she almost jumped out of her skin. Glenn. She forced herself to stay sitting while her mother got up to answer it.

But it was her mother's friend, Elizabeth, who kept

her talking on the phone even though Dale heard her mother say more than once, 'I must go, Liz – I've got Dulcie here.'

It was a good half-hour before she returned.

'She never listens when I say I have to go. Just keeps on. But I can't be rude – she was so kind to me when I couldn't go back to the house.'

'I know, Mum. You don't have to explain.'

'Now, tell me more about your American.'

The following morning Dale dressed with extra care, her heart singing with the thought that maybe in a few hours she'd be in Glenn's arms. The weather was much colder than normal at this time of the year. There was a stiff breeze but at least it was dry today after a spell at the beginning of the month when it had done nothing but rain. To be on the safe side, though, she'd have to wear her raincoat.

At least she had more to choose from in her wardrobe at home. Dale picked a jade-coloured wool dress with elbow-length sleeves. She slipped it on and looked in the full-length mirror. The colour suited her, bringing out the deep turquoise of her eyes, and the belt emphasised her slim waist. She fastened the string of pearls round her neck that her parents had given her on her twentieth birthday and gave a last glance in the mirror. She smiled, and her reflection glowed with pent-up love.

Glenn hadn't phoned back. Either he'd been late in or never got the message. She was beginning to think that since the war nothing seemed to work smoothly. Well, she'd surprise him. She was nice and early. It was only half-past seven. If she hurried, she'd be there by eight. Maybe they could have breakfast together. But just as she was about to leave the telephone rang.

'I'll get it,' Dale called out. She picked up the receiver,

not believing she was just about to hear his lovely voice. His Southern accent. And she would tell him she'd soon be there.

'Hello, sweetheart. How are you?'

She smothered a sigh. 'I'm well. Is everything all right up there in Scotland?'

'It was when I was there yesterday. But I'm in London and want to see you. Your mother told me you'd be here for a couple of days, so I've timed my trip with yours. I'm staying at my club. When will you be here?'

Dale's heart could not have sunk any lower. All she would have was this one precious day with Glenn. And then he'd be gone and she'd be on her way back to Bletchley. Oh, it was too bad.

'Can't you come over here this evening?'

'No, I'd rather not come to the house.'

'Why not? I thought you and Mother were getting on better now she's accepted the divorce.'

'It's not that. I want to discuss something important with you. I need your opinion. So come now – for breakfast. I'll order some extra coffee.'

'I can't,' Dale blurted. 'I'm meeting a friend.'

Her father snorted. 'Not all day. Surely you've got some time for your own father.'

Why did everything have to revolve around Dad? She was beginning to understand her mother better.

There was a crackle on the line and his next words were distorted.

'Sorry, Dad, I didn't catch what you said.'

'It sounds like you're meeting a boyfriend. Would it be the American?'

'Yes.' How on earth did he remember about Glenn? 'He goes away tomorrow.'

'I'll forgive you, then . . . that is, if you come over right away.'

'Aren't you going to see Mother at all?'

'Yes. When you've gone back to wherever you work.' He paused. 'But don't tell her you're meeting me. I'll tell her later.'

He didn't sound quite himself. As though he wasn't quite sure where he stood with her. Well, he was in for a surprise if her mother told him about her new friend, Jim.

'All right. I'll come now.'

She slammed down the receiver. She'd give him half an hour.

Her mother came downstairs.

'Have you had breakfast already?'

'Yes.' She'd managed to swallow a half slice of toast and jam.

'Then have a lovely time, dear. I suppose I'll see you when I see you.'

'It might not be until this evening,' Dale said. 'Do you mind much?'

'Not much.' Her mother smiled. 'You just enjoy yourself. And you look gorgeous.'

'Thanks, Mum.' She bent to kiss her mother's cheek and to her surprise her mother put her arms round her and gave her a hug. It felt natural and comforting.

Dale tried to force down the burst of resentment that her father had picked today of all days to ask her opinion. Something he'd never done before. Well, the sooner it was over, the sooner she'd see Glenn. Her heart skipped with joy at the thought.

At least her father's club was in Mayfair – not far from the Lansdowne, Dale thought, as she was ushered in by the doorman. It would only take her fifteen minutes if she ran. But for now she had to be the dutiful daughter and listen to what her father had to say that was so important.

'Mr Treadwell's expecting you,' the perfectly groomed receptionist told her. She looked up and smiled at Dale. 'He's having breakfast in the dining room. I believe you've been here before so you know where to go.'

As Dale quickly made her way to the dining room, she was hardly aware of its grandeur in the brightly painted red walls, the gold-trimmed cornice and the sparkling chandeliers which hung over the central aisle. She scanned the crowded tables.

'Ah, there you are, darling.' Harry Treadwell stood and gave her a bear hug. Then he studied her. 'You look beautiful.'

Immediately, she regretted her churlish thoughts. It was good to see him after all these months. She'd forgotten how alike they were. The same mouth. Same determined chin.

'Hello, Dad.' She removed her hat and set it on one of the other chairs.

'Come and sit down. I'll pour you some coffee.'

His eyes looked anxious. She wondered why. Maybe the divorce wasn't happening quickly enough and he was going to ask her to encourage her mother to press along with the proceedings. Well, she wouldn't interfere. Her mother was entitled to go at her own pace.

When they were settled, he said, 'I'd better get right down to it, Dale. I know your mother and I have had our difficulties. But I've always cared for her.'

She bit back a retort. She would remain silent. Let him speak before she said anything.

'I know what you're thinking. I can't have cared that much if I abandoned her for another woman,' he said, reaching for the butter.

His hand's trembling. He's nervous. He must want this other woman very badly.

Dale took a sip of the delicious hot coffee and waited.

'Well, you'd be right,' he said, looking down as he buttered the toast. 'The trouble is, I didn't realise how much I thought of her until you telephoned that the house had been bombed. At that moment I really thought I'd lost her for good. And it was terrible.' He raised his head. 'The thing is – I realise I've made a dreadful mistake.'

Dale's jaw slackened. This wasn't at all what she was expecting.

'I want her back, Dale. I'll do anything. You have to tell me what's the best way.'

Chapter Thirty-Four

So many possibilities whirled in her mind, but Dale couldn't think of one answer to her father's bombshell. How could she sit here and say that her mother had lost all trust in him? Or that Mum was more confident since she'd joined the Women's Voluntary Service, whereas before she'd been made to feel no more than a housewife and mother – what she'd thought her husband wanted until someone more glamorous and obviously younger had appeared on the scene. Dale's lips tightened. Or worse – that her mother appeared to have found someone else? It wasn't her place to be some go-between.

Resentment for her father putting her in such a position flared.

'Dad, you've been unfaithful to Mum, bringing her untold misery, and now you want her back.' A thought suddenly occurred. 'Has the other woman kicked you out?'

Her father hesitated. So that was it.

'No, she hasn't done that. But I realise we're not really suited.' He gazed at her. 'She's a lot younger than me – only a few years older than you, actually. But she's not as sensible as you. All she wants is a good time. And I can't give it to her. There's a war on and my work is pretty intense. She needs to grow up and I'm not prepared to be her father.'

Everything he was saying somehow made it worse. Dale bit her lip hard to stop herself from giving him a well-deserved dressing down in a public place. Draining the rest of her coffee, now gone nearly cold, she sprang to her feet. She wanted to let him stew a bit. Let him wonder how he was going to approach her mother. She wasn't about to help him in any way. All that was on her mind now was to see Glenn.

'Sorry, Dad, you'll have to work that one out for yourself. I don't want to interfere. It's too important and I'd hate to say anything behind Mum's back. So as there's nothing more I can say, I'll let the two of you get on with it. My concern now is to see the man I love whom I haven't set eyes on for more than a year.'

Her father stood up. She noticed his eyes were wet with tears, but she steeled herself against them.

'I've been a selfish swine, haven't I, love? But I'm going to make it up to your mother if it's the last thing I do.' He kissed her cheek. 'I do love you, darling, even though I've neglected both of you these last months. I haven't even asked about your job, but you wouldn't be able to tell me anyway, would you?' She shook her head and he smiled. 'It seems like both of us are doing secret work. Maybe one day . . . but now you must go and see that young man of yours. And tell him if he doesn't treat you properly, he'll have *me* to answer to.'

She ran until her chest ached. Until she had a stitch in her side. Until she was breathless. And still she kept running. All she could think of was Glenn, and how if she was only one minute later arriving at the Lansdowne Club, she might miss him again.

Please let him be there. Please don't let him be gone already. Please let him have left me a note if he has.

324

She didn't know to whom she was appealing. Maybe it was to the fates. Or simply to herself. But thirteen minutes later she'd arrived at the club and was at the reception desk, her breath coming in short gasps, her hair loosening from under her hat.

'I'm meeting Mr Reeves.' She drew in another breath, slower now. It was as though all she desired had culminated in this moment . . . here at the reception desk of the Lansdowne Club. Her breath escaped in a sigh. 'Mr Glenn Reeves.'

The tall, bald-headed receptionist with a sandy moustache sent her a curious glance, then checked the register. He nodded and glanced at the keyboard.

'Ah, yes. He's in his room. Would you like me to ring and tell him you're here, Miss—'

He was here. In this very building. She swallowed hard.

'I'm his cousin.'

'I'll let him know his *cousin* is waiting in Reception.' He gave the word extra emphasis to let her know he didn't believe a word of it.

'Oh, please, I'd like to surprise him – so if you could just give me his room number.'

'Room nineteen,' the receptionist said with a disapproving sniff. 'Take the lift to the third floor.'

She thanked him and pressed for the lift. Inside the small space her heart thudded so hard she barely heard the clunk that it had reached his floor. Number nineteen was at the far end. He was behind this very door. It was unbelievable. She was just about to knock when it struck her what a sight she must look from all that running. She should find a cloakroom. Tidy herself. No. She wouldn't wait a moment longer. Adjusting her hat, and with a tiny jangle of nerves, she gave a soft knock. She heard footsteps. The door opened. And there he was, his eyes wide.

'Well,' he said, gently bringing her inside. 'It's about time.'

His face was thinner than she remembered. But his lapis-blue eyes twinkled with his wide smile, as he sat her on the only easy chair.

'I thought this day would never come,' he said, removing her hat and setting it on the arm of a chair. His eyes roved over her face, then flicked to her legs, her ankles.

She could smell the scent of him just those few feet away, perched on the edge of the bed. *Why didn't he sweep her into his arms?* But he seemed perfectly content simply to gaze at her when all she wanted to do was lean against his broad chest, to run her fingers through his freshly washed hair, to feel his lips on hers . . .

Perhaps he was no longer attracted to her in that way.

No, she was sure that wasn't the reason.

'Tell me how you've been,' he said. 'I want to know everything since I last saw you.'

She gave a small sigh. 'Well, today I've come from seeing my father – the first time in months. He's decided he's made a mistake and wants to go back to my mother.'

'That's great news,' Glenn said. 'You must be very relieved.'

'Not really.' She quickly filled him in. When she mentioned Jim he gave a slight frown.

'Oh, boy. Your dad's in for a nasty shock. I wouldn't want to be in his shoes when she sends him away. But perhaps it's not too late.'

Dale shook her head. 'I think it is. She's changed a lot since she's busy with her voluntary work and met Jim.'

There was a silence. Why didn't he come to her? Why was she still sitting in a chair?

A prickle of tension filled the space between them.

'Dulcie,' he said, 'I never received one letter from you – waiting, not knowing, was the worst time of my life

– nineteen lonely months. All I could think of was that you'd never forgiven me for not being on the bridge that day. And picturing what you must have felt. Completely betrayed, I imagine. So I couldn't blame you. Yet there was something so special between us. That's what I clung on to.' He fixed his eyes on hers. 'Did you ever write?'

'Of course I did,' she said, fiercely. 'I got the first one you sent when you'd just arrived in Germany, but not until a year later. My old boss threw it in the wastepaper basket. It was lucky that Bill, one of the journalists, saw it happen and retrieved it for me. Mother forwarded it to my work. I wrote back that same day and followed all your instructions to get it to you. But there was never a reply. I wrote several more letters but still nothing. It was only when I went home yesterday that my mother gave me an envelope forwarded by the Grosvenor Hotel. And I realised this was your second attempt to find me by using that address.'

'What made you think that?'

'I did something unutterably stupid.' She looked at him, her eyes serious. 'The same marked envelope came to me at work. Mum had forwarded it on. I thought it was the hotel telling me I'd left my gloves behind that time at the tea dance. I was so upset, remembering how we danced and were so happy—' She gulped. 'I never wanted to go back to that place again. I was in a bit of a state, so I threw it in the wastepaper basket, not dreaming your letter was inside.' Her eyes welled with tears. 'I'd given up hope.'

'*I* never gave up hope,' Glenn said as he stood up. He held out his arms. 'Come to me, my darling.'

In one heartbeat she was in his arms. He didn't kiss her at first. Just put his hands at either side of her face, brushing away her tears with his fingertips.

'You're even more beautiful than I remembered.' He gave

a tiny disbelieving shake of his head, then brought her close to him, stroking her hair. 'We're together now. Nothing else matters.'

I'll go mad if you wait any longer. Just kiss me. Please, Glenn, just kiss me!

Slowly, tantalisingly, he kissed her forehead, then the tilt of her nose, each eyelid, along her jaw, her neck, sending quivers of delight along her spine, down her legs, making her draw short jerky breaths . . . and then when she thought she would burst with longing his tongue softly licked the corners of her mouth, then followed the curve of her lips . . . little light feathery touches, making her thrill with desire for him. She couldn't stand it any longer. She brought his lips to hers and he softly laughed against her mouth as he kissed her back, until their kisses became more urgent . . .

'Will you come to bed with me, Dulcie?' he said, his voice husky when they finally drew apart. It wasn't a question.

She nodded.

As though he had not a moment to lose, Glenn quickly undressed her.

'You're so very beautiful,' he said when she was standing in front of him naked. 'Your face, your perfect body.'

He stripped off his own things and threw their clothes on the chair she'd been sitting in only minutes before. Then he drew back the blankets and sheet from the bed.

Afterwards, they lay entwined, revelling in their joy in one another. Dale propped herself on one elbow gazing down at him. Nothing about him escaped her attention. The cleft in his chin which she bent to kiss, his well-shaped ears where her lips lingered, the golden hairs on his chest and forearms, his hands – broad and strong and warm as he idly caressed her naked breast . . . it was almost too much after so many empty months.

'I don't want this to end – ever,' she whispered.

'It won't,' he said. 'Not now we've found one another again. But we need to sort out a better mailing address to keep in touch.' He looked at her. 'You haven't told me where you're living now. I'd prefer to write to you there rather than your home as you'll get it sooner.'

'I'm not allowed to give out the address.'

Glenn frowned. 'Why not?'

'Because the people – a lord and lady – who own the house – don't want it publicised.' Glenn's frown deepened. 'It's a grand country house and it's been taken over by the War Office. We've all had to move into the Dower House.' She wouldn't mention Eddie.

'What's a Dower House?'

'It's when one of the family becomes a widow. Then she's called a dowager and has to move out to make way for the younger generation and their families. So it's big by normal standards but not if you're used to living in much grander surroundings.'

'Did you ever live in this grand house?'

'Yes, for a short time.'

'So you've had to come down in the world as well,' he said, grinning.

She laughed. 'It would have been the height of luxury at the time, but it needs money spent on it. There's no heating to speak of, and neither is there in the Dower House. I would have frozen to death if Eddie hadn't found me an electric fire to plug in.'

'Who's Eddie?'

Chapter Thirty-Five

Dale could have bitten her tongue out. She hadn't done anything disloyal. But the blood rushed to her cheeks as her brain replayed the scene when she'd wound her arms round Eddie and kissed him. And enjoyed it.

'You're blushing, darling,' Glenn said, half laughing, half serious.

'Eddie's the lord and lady's nephew.'

'Ah. Tell me more.'

'There's nothing to tell. Only that he works at the same place as me.'

'Which is . . .?'

'I can't say.' She looked at him. 'Glenn, please don't question me. I've signed the Official Secrets Act. I'm doing war work which we've been told is vital. If we are ever caught blabbing it could be imprisonment – or worse.' She shuddered, once again picturing Major Barking's gun on the desk.

Glenn blinked. 'My goodness. That sounds ominous. Are you allowed to tell me what part of Britain you're living in?'

She shook her head. 'It's a small town in Buckinghamshire . . . that's all I can say, but I'll give you my PO Box number and you can write to me there.'

'And you say this Eddie works in the same place.' Glenn

gave a small grunt. 'That's bringing you into a lot of contact with him. I don't like the sound of it.'

'He works in a different department,' Dale said, 'so I rarely see him at work.'

'But after work?' Glenn's eyes narrowed.

She might as well be truthful. 'Sometimes. And we sleep under the same roof – but it makes no difference.'

'So he's not attractive to you then?'

'He's quite handsome, but that's beside the point.'

'The point is, is he in love with you?'

She hesitated.

Glenn's forehead creased. 'Right . . . he is. And are you with him?'

'No.'

'And you've never been tempted to fall in love with him? Even though you didn't hear from me.'

'Glenn, stop it. Eddie and I are friends. I think he'd like to be more. But if I've ever been tempted to waver, I always think of us. Eddie's not you. No one else is you. Anyone else would be second best. And I'm not in the habit of settling for second best.' She kissed him. 'Have I made myself clear?'

'Perfectly,' he said, grabbing her to him and kissing her back.

The day whirled by in a dream. Hand in hand they walked along the Serpentine, sometimes in silence, content to be together, but mostly they talked. She wanted to know about his life in Berlin so she could imagine what he was doing when he was no longer by her side. He told her how sickened he was by Hitler's lies when he was invited to attend various briefings and some large public events as one of the American correspondents. How he was regularly broadcasting to CBS in America, but unfortunately the

Nazis were beginning to look more closely at his script and censoring anything they didn't like. Sure, he could say something off his script, but then his broadcast would be cut and he'd be given a severe warning. Next time he'd likely be sent packing. This assignment was far too important for that to happen, as it had already with three of his colleagues. No, he needed to be there. To report as best he could not only on the developments of the war, but on the everyday horrors that the Germans were facing daily because of Hitler's madness.

'Most of the other foreign journalists are disgusted but they can't do any better than me,' Glenn concluded. 'Their newspaper reports are under the same scrutiny. But we do try to get the truth out in a roundabout fashion, though by the response we get from the US, it seems to fall on deaf ears.'

'It sounds awful,' Dale said. 'Do you think Hitler still intends to invade Britain?'

'He did,' Glenn said, unhesitatingly. 'But since the RAF won the Battle of Britain, as your Mr Churchill calls it, he seems to have changed his tune. At least from what I hear, he never mentions it. The Luftwaffe doesn't control the skies and they can't invade without air superiority.'

'A lot of people are still worried about the possibility,' Dale said.

'There's always a possibility – but it didn't work in the Blitz when he hoped to bomb y'all into accepting terms of a peace agreement.'

'No, Churchill would never have given in to that,' Dale said firmly. 'Our freedom is far too precious.'

'Same as in the US,' Glenn said. 'And Hitler has plenty of other battles to deal with at the moment. He and the Italians have only just invaded Yugoslavia and Greece.'

'Something I want to ask you,' Dale said. 'How did you manage to leave Berlin and come to England when we're the enemy?'

He hesitated, then said, 'I have connections in London. They arranged for me to take the same route that I went out – through Switzerland, which is still neutral.'

'Do your broadcasting people in Chicago know you're here?' She paused. 'Or shouldn't I ask?'

'Probably best not.' Glenn gave her a rueful smile.

He was obviously doing something more than broadcasting to America.

She swallowed. He'd be at even greater risk if the Nazis got to hear of it.

Dale insisted he was not to see her home, so Glenn suggested they have an early meal at the Lansdowne so as not to waste time searching for a restaurant. They could say their goodbyes privately in his room.

They hung their coats in the large open cloakroom and a waiter found them a quiet corner and handed them a menu.

'My feet are killing me,' Dale sighed.

'You shouldn't have worn such glamorous shoes for all that walking.' Glenn grinned. 'Not that I'm complaining. You look absolutely gorgeous.'

'I get fed up with looking sensible and drab every day as though there's nothing to get dressed up for.'

'You! Sensible and drab?' He chuckled. 'I don't think you've ever been sensible and drab in your life.'

She couldn't help laughing. How lucky she was to have such a lovely man who'd told her he was in love with her. Had been at first sight, so he'd said.

'We'd better look at the menu.' Dale smiled at him.

333

The fish pie was tasty, but Dale found it difficult to eat. Every mouthful seemed to stick in her throat.

'What's the matter, darling?' he said, when she put her fork down. 'Don't you like it?'

Dale's eyes pricked with threatening tears. She was *not* going to spoil their evening – their last hour together.

'It's not that,' she said.

He took her hand warmly in his own.

'I feel the same,' he said, 'but we need our strength. I wish you'd finish your meal.'

'I'm all right, but I'm glad you've eaten yours.' She studied him. 'Are you getting enough to eat?'

'I don't do too badly,' he answered, but she knew it wasn't the truth. She loved him for not wanting to worry her.

'Could you manage a dessert?'

Dale shook her head. She wanted to get out of the restaurant. Feel his arms round her. Have him reassure her that everything would come right. That one day they'd be together. She wouldn't think further.

'Let's go,' he said.

Back in his room Glenn put one of the bedside lamps on, then pulled open the blackout curtains. He beckoned her over.

'Just take a look at that.'

She drew in a gasp of pleasure. 'It's a full moon.'

'Not quite,' he said, putting his arm around her. 'It's what's called a waning gibbous moon – means the full moon's getting smaller and will eventually become a crescent shape.'

'How do you know all that?'

'I've always been interested in the sky. Loved it since I was a kid.'

There was a shout from below. 'PUT THAT RUDDY LIGHT OUT!'

Glenn immediately drew the blackout curtains together and giggling like a pair of children they fell onto the bed.

He could not have been more gentle, more tender, more loving . . . But afterwards reality rushed at her with such force she began to sob.

'I don't want anything to happen to you. Berlin's dangerous with all the bombing.'

'Don't cry, my darling.' Glenn wiped her tears with his fingertips. 'You're getting plenty of unwelcome action in London.' His mouth tightened. 'We both have to keep safe for each other.' He brought her face to his and kissed her. 'Will you promise that one thing?'

'I promise.'

'I promise, too,' he said. 'I have something for you, so you can't forget me.'

He threw on a dressing gown and opened a small suitcase, then brought out a narrow cardboard box.

'Sorry it's not wrapped properly,' he said, handing it to her. 'I didn't have time to ask them in the shop. It was all a little rushed.'

Dale opened the lid. A heart-shaped locket on a silver chain gleamed up at her. She gave a gasp of pleasure as she removed it from its cotton-wool nest.

'Does it open?'

'Try it.'

There was a tiny catch on the edge. She put her fingernail underneath and the two halves sprang apart. And there inside was a tiny photograph of Glenn in one half and one of herself in the other.

Immediately, she kissed Glenn's photograph. 'I love it,' she said, her eyes shining. 'You couldn't have given me anything more precious. I can believe you'll come back to me every time I look at your photograph. You'll seem real and not a dream.' She looked at him. 'You took this of me when we first met.'

'Yes.' Glenn grinned. 'You looked so cute. And remember when I asked that guy to take a picture of us together?' She nodded. 'I cut round the photograph so I got into the locket as well!' He chuckled.

'That's the most important one,' Dale said seriously. 'What about the others you took?'

'They turned out real good,' he said. 'I would have gone crazy without your pictures to look at.'

She couldn't stop gazing at her locket and the tiny photographs.

'Would you like me to put it round that elegant neck of yours?'

She nodded, completely overcome.

Where his fingers touched her neck as he did up the clasp caused a quiver to run through her – up her spine, across her shoulders, to the top of her head.

'There,' he said. 'Go take a look.'

'I don't need to. I can feel it.'

The locket seemed to settle against the warmth of her skin.

'Thank you for such a wonderful present.' She turned to him. 'I might have to kiss you for that.'

Glenn clicked his tongue and shook his head, then grinned. 'Okay, if you must.'

'I must.'

All too soon it was time for them to get dressed.

'What time are you leaving tomorrow?' Dale asked when they were in the lift.

'First thing.'

He walked with her to the reception desk and ordered a taxi.

'I wish you'd let me come with you.'

'No,' she said. 'We'll keep to our arrangements. You need a good night's sleep before the long journey ahead.'

'I'll be dreaming of you – and our togetherness.'

She swallowed hard. 'When will the war be over?' She knew it was a stupid question.

'No one knows – not even that bastard in Germany.'

When the taxi arrived, he stepped outside with her. The doorman opened the passenger door, but Glenn ignored it. He took her in his arms, murmuring against her hair.

'I love you, Glenn.'

He kissed her, his lips still warm from their kisses. 'I love you, too, my darling dearest Dulcie. One day this damned war will be over and we'll be together . . . for always. But for now, you must get back to your mama. She'll be wondering what's happened.'

'She knows I'm seeing you,' Dale said, smiling in the darkness. 'So does Dad.'

'And . . .?'

'I think I can bring them round.'

She climbed into the back of the cab and the doorman slammed the door. She could hardly make out Glenn's figure in the blackout, but she waved through the window in case he could see her. Then she settled back in the seat, her fingers automatically going to her locket. She had a lot to think about. Their day had to last them for who knew how long before they saw each other again. Maybe not until the war was over. She'd dreaded this goodbye – yet deep down, she'd never been happier.

Chapter Thirty-Six

Dale quietly let herself into the house, hoping she wouldn't wake her mother. Her stomach felt empty and churned up from not eating much supper and then leaving Glenn. She'd go and make herself a cup of hot milk.

She switched on the light and took a small saucepan from a shelf and poured in some milk and lit the gas ring. Just as she was reaching for a cup, the kitchen door opened and she swung round, ready to apologise to her mother for disturbing her. But to her astonishment it was her father.

'Dad! What are you doing here?'

'Hello, sweetheart. I heard you come in. I was waiting up for you.'

Dale's heart sank. She didn't feel like listening to her father or talking about Glenn. All she wanted was to take her drink upstairs and hop into bed and lie there reliving their day.

'I'll make myself a cup of tea and join you,' her father said, putting the kettle on the stove.

'I'm quite tired, Dad. If you don't mind, I'd really like to go to bed.'

'I just wanted to tell you something – it's important.'

Dale sighed and took her drink to the sitting room. What now?

He joined her a few minutes later, sitting in his favourite armchair by the dying embers of the fire.

'Did you have a nice time?' he said when he'd swallowed his tea in the usual three or four gulps, no matter how hot it was.

'Yes, but I don't want to talk—'

'No, I know. You've said.' Her father's tone was a little irritable, but when he looked at her his gaze softened. 'Have you been crying?'

'I've just said goodbye to the man I love,' she answered. 'And I don't know when I'll ever see him again – so yes, I've been crying.'

'I'm sorry, love. I shouldn't have said anything. I'm sure it'll all work out.'

'Dad, you said you had something important to tell me. What is it?'

'Your mother and I have been talking. I told her I'd made a mistake in leaving and that I didn't want a divorce. She just laughed. "Did the other woman throw you out?" she said. I told her it wasn't like that, but she doesn't seem interested in listening to me. I wanted to tell her how sorry I am. But she shook her head and said she wouldn't take me back if I was the last man on earth. I thought that was a bit steep. And then she mentioned someone called Jim.' He fixed his gaze on her. 'Do you know anything about him?'

Oh, God.

'I think he's an ARP warden.'

'Is she in love with him?'

'Dad, I don't know. She's only just mentioned him to me since I've been home this time. Maybe he's just a friend who Mum enjoys having a conversation with.'

'A friend!' Her father practically spat the word. 'I don't believe that for one minute.' He sent her an imploring look.

'Dale, darling, will you please talk to your mother. Tell her how sincere I am.'

'I really don't want to get involved,' she said, once again resentment rushing in. 'I have enough on my mind. It's not fair of you to ask me. She has to speak for herself.'

'She does – did. And that's the trouble. I didn't like what I heard.'

She wanted to say that was his fault. But what good would it do.

'Dad, please let me go to bed. I'll try to talk to Mother in the morning.'

'I'm going back to my club now. But will you promise?'

It was the second time that night she'd made a promise.

'Yes,' she said, 'I promise.'

By the time Dale went upstairs carrying her milk drink a skin had formed on the surface. Pulling a face, she skimmed it off with the spoon and swallowed a mouthful, but it was almost cold. When she was finally in bed she lay on her back, her hands behind her head, and went over the day in her mind, frowning at the way it had begun and ended with her father's pleas. She didn't hold out much hope for him, but she would speak to her mother at breakfast on his behalf. Maybe there was still something to salvage in their marriage.

Marriage. She closed her eyes. It hadn't worked very well for her mother, who had married when she was only eighteen and Dad had been twenty-two – Dale's age now. Had Mum married for love – or infatuation? Or for convenience? She remembered her mother hadn't had a particularly happy childhood, always told she wasn't as clever as her two older brothers. Then Dad came along. He must have been extremely good-looking when he was young, Dale mused. He still was, now she came to think about it. He was also clever and charming and would have easily fallen for Mum, a natural beauty. She must have been captivated. They had only known one another a few months before they married but it was the one time her grandparents were unanimous in their blessing for their daughter Patricia. Harry Treadwell was known in the area to be quite a catch with his looks and brains and respectable family background.

So where does that leave me? Dale thought. She hadn't spent more than a few days with Glenn, let alone months, but she knew if he asked her to marry him, she wouldn't hesitate. And anyway, was he *really* serious enough to want to spend the rest of his life with her? He'd never talked of marriage and children. And she must never forget he was an American and would surely one day want to go back home. If he asked, would she be willing to give up her country? Leave her parents and friends? Yes, her heart said. She nodded in agreement and turned onto her side, pulling the blanket up under her chin. They were both still young and more importantly there was a war on. No one knew from day to day what was going to happen. Who would even still be alive when the war ended. She shuddered. It didn't bode well to make too many plans. They could be blown apart as easily and with the same force as one of Hitler's bombs.

As Dale came downstairs the next morning, she could hear her mother singing in the kitchen, as the smell of toast wafted through the open door.

'You sound happy,' she said as she kissed her mother's cheek. 'I haven't heard you sing like that for ages. You should do it more often.'

'I haven't felt much like singing this last year but I think I've turned a corner.' Her smile lit up her features. 'There's tea in the pot – I've only just made it.'

Dale poured herself a cup of tea and sat at the kitchen table watching her mother with curiosity.

'I'm having a boiled egg – the one egg a week we're allowed.' Patricia turned from the stove. 'Would you like one, Dulcie?'

'I don't want you to go short. I realise how lucky I am when I hear about all the rationing. At least we get plenty of food where I work – and more than one egg a week if we want it.'

'I'm pleased to hear that, dear. But don't worry, I shan't go short. Jim brings me a few extra bits now and again. Sometimes even joins me at the breakfast table.' She laughed a little self-consciously, then flashed a look at Dale. 'And it's not what you're thinking,' she added swiftly.

'You don't know what I'm thinking.'

'Yes, I do. You're my daughter, don't forget. And no, he hasn't ever stayed the night. He's a decent man and a very good friend to me.'

Dale was relieved her mother's new friend had come up in the conversation naturally instead of her having to force it.

'You've mentioned Jim a few times now,' she said, keeping her tone casual. 'He sounds nice.' She looked in her mother's eyes. 'Are you sure he's only a friend?'

Patricia hesitated as though wondering if to elaborate. Finally, she said, 'At this moment Jim's a dear friend, but who knows where it might lead.'

'Be careful, Mum. Some men prey on divorced women if they think they're well-off. And we're not in the same financial position we once were.'

'Jim's not like that,' she came back quickly. 'He's as genuine as they come. By a strange coincidence we were at the same school together, though he was in the year below. He's kind

342

and generous and completely down to earth. He looks out for me and has time to listen to *my* opinions and interests. Your father worked all the hours God sent so we could buy this house in a good area and we hardly saw one another. When I was having you he was away. I was left on my own with a young baby and too far for your grandparents to visit much.' She put a couple of slices of buttered toast in front of Dale. 'But you know something, Dulcie – a lovely home isn't everything. It's who you share your home with that counts.'

Her mother had never been this candid. It was a new side to her mother and a lot to digest.

When Dale had finished her egg and the last piece of toast and marmalade, she said, 'Mum, do you ever hear from Frau Fassbender who used to be our maid? You used to keep in touch with her?'

A shadow passed across her mother's face.

'No. Ursula was Austrian, you know, not German—' She broke off and looked at Dale. 'She was a Jew, you know.'

'Since the war started I suspected it,' Dale said.

'So when Austria was annexed in '38 I was terribly worried,' her mother continued. 'I keep hoping she's safe. But she hated the Nazis and wasn't above saying so. And this was years ago, long before Hitler took control.' She poured them both another cup of tea. 'After this war, whenever that is, I'd like to go to Austria and see if I can find her.' She looked at Dale with tearful eyes. 'I don't suppose you'd like to come with me, would you, Dulcie? Your German would come in handy . . . and of course I'd love your company.'

'Good job you quickly added that,' Dale chuckled, then became serious. 'You know, I'd quite like to use my German after the war – for work, I mean. I always wanted to be a journalist, but the war has changed everything.'

343

'If it's anything like the Great War there'll be plenty to do afterwards to pick up the pieces. I imagine your German would be welcomed by the Foreign Office.' Patricia regarded her daughter. 'Now I know you can't discuss your work, so we'll talk about your father. I'm sure he waylaid you last night to try to persuade me to take him back.'

'He was in a bit of a state,' Dale admitted. 'Are you sure you can't give him another chance? I know it's no excuse, but it *is* the first time.'

'Is that what he told you?' Patricia rounded on her.

'Um, yes – well, not exactly, but I assumed—'

'You assumed wrong,' she said, the familiar bitterness hovering around her lips. 'He's a womaniser, through and through. He had another woman before *Claudia*—' she let the name hang in the air '—and I had my suspicions there were one or two more. But he always came back because of you. He thinks the world of you and has always been very proud of his only child – a clever daughter.' She looked at Dale. 'As *I'm* proud of you.'

Dale swallowed hard. 'You never tell me. Even when I was a child—'

'I didn't want you to get too big for your boots – like your father. I was always admiring him and telling him how clever he was and it went straight to his head. I didn't want you to turn out the same. He made me feel inferior about so many things. According to him, my role was cooking and super-vising the staff and the house and looking nice when he came home. And, of course, bringing you up which he always considered *my* job. His job was to make sure you had the best education, and his big disappointment was that you didn't go on to university.' She looked at Dale. 'I never really knew why?'

'I wanted to be a journalist,' Dale said, stunned by her

mother's outburst. 'That was my dream. But I ended up a junior reporter with a boss who refused to acknowledge that women could do the job as well as men. Because of that he wouldn't let me report on real-life situations, which is why I was sent on that unending round of children's parties, church jumble sales and the Women's Institute. When I was on Westminster Bridge, the night of the blackout—'

'Was that when you met your American?'

'Yes.' Dale momentarily closed her eyes. 'Anyway, I wrote what I thought was a really good article catching the mood of the nation – he told me it was a load of sentimental twaddle. But Bill – the chap who retrieved Glenn's letter and forwarded it on to you – thought it was really good and that I'd spoken from the heart. Which is what I wanted. Franklin thought differently and told me to run along and take lessons from Bill.'

'You never told me all this,' Patricia said.

'You were never really interested in my job.'

'I was – I am.'

They looked at one another and suddenly they broke into a peal of laughter. Dale sprang to her feet and kissed her mother.

'I'm sorry I—'

'We don't need to explain anything,' Patricia said, smiling. 'But I do know one thing—' she kissed Dale's cheek '—I've got my daughter back.'

Chapter Thirty-Seven

Happy though Dale was that she and her mother had become more understanding and more confiding in one another, sending a warm glow round Dale's heart, she was relieved to be going back to Bletchley. She'd already overheard a murmur from two of the passengers in her compartment, a middle-aged couple, about why she wasn't in uniform. How badly she wanted to tell them she was doing secret work for the Foreign Office. Inwardly, she sighed.

Just ignore them and read your book. Or think of Glenn and our reunion.

Think of Glenn. She'd never stopped thinking of Glenn. A smile curving her lips, she put her bookmark to one side and was soon absorbed in *Cold Comfort Farm*, and a few minutes later trying to smother her laughter.

Thankfully, there were no hold-ups and an hour and a half later Dale alighted from the train. She braced herself against the April wind, wishing she'd worn her winter coat. There was no sign of a taxi. She'd have to wait for the bus.

Fifteen shivering minutes later it finally came in sight and soon she was back at the Dower House. She looked round her room. It was becoming as familiar to her as her own bedroom at home – or rather the guest bedroom while hers was drying out. Her stomach rumbled and she glanced at her watch. Well after lunchtime. She'd go downstairs and see if Cook would be kind enough to rustle up a sandwich, then a quick tidy-up and she'd cycle to the Park ready for her four o'clock shift.

Wanda was in her usual position at a desk near the entrance of the Hut when Dale entered.

'Commander Travis asked to see you, Dulcie, as soon as you return.'

'Oh.' Dale looked at Wanda's neutral expression, her heart giving a little skip. She was finally being acknowledged for her code-breaking. This was her promotion to the cryptanalysts' Hut. She'd be more than happy to work with Eddie, if that's where Commander Travis intended to put her, or anywhere he saw fit. She needed a change. More than that, she needed to get away from Wanda's constant penetrating gaze. 'I'll go now, then.'

Wanda nodded.

Outside Commander Travis's door Dale took a deep breath. This was it. Once more she rehearsed the words to tell him how grateful she was, and how determined to carry on doing her very best, and with his faith in her she wouldn't let him down.

'Come in.'

He was sitting behind his desk jotting notes in his pad like the first time she'd stood there. He looked up and nodded for her to be seated but gave no sign of a smile. Well, he held a serious position and couldn't be expected to beam whenever she appeared. She grinned at the thought, then quickly composed her expression to match his.

'You've been away the last two days, I understand,' he said.

'Yes,' Dale smiled at the memory. 'I went home to see my parents – the first time since the house was bombed.'

347

'Ah, yes.' The commander put his pen down. 'Mrs Wilcox mentioned it. I was sorry to hear about that.'

'Thank you. But we were lucky we didn't have to wait too long for it to be repaired.'

'There is another matter I wish to discuss with you. A serious one.'

She held her breath. She needed to let him feel her promotion was a total surprise.

His eyes were fixed on hers. 'I believe you were on a bus coming back from the town recently – sitting upstairs at the front with your friend, Rhoda Hamlyn. Is that correct?'

The blood drained from her face. She grasped both sides of her seat, feeling she might float away. Her mouth dried. She licked her lips.

'Yes, sir.' She forced out the two words. Dear God, what was all this about? But she knew. It was Rhoda's loud voice complaining about the work, and how boring it was.

Blood rushed to her face. She must look as guilty as hell in the commander's eyes.

'Mrs Wilcox happened to be sitting a few seats back and heard every word. She did the right thing and reported it to me.' He rapped on his desk making Dale jump. 'Our work here is top secret. You knew that from your first interview and from your second interview with *me*. And again, in your induction by Mrs Wilcox. How many times do you need to be told? Men have died by dangerous gossip and we will not *tolerate it.*'

Dale opened her mouth but shut it again. If she said anything it would only be that she'd tried to warn Rhoda. She gulped. She would never be disloyal to Rhoda but at this minute she could wring her friend's neck.

'Neither of you appeared to take any notice of the fact that you'd signed the Official Secrets Act.' His voice was cold.

'I took . . . take it very seriously,' Dale said, her voice choking. She had to say something. 'My friend's new here and—'

'No excuse at all,' Commander Travis snapped. 'I'm afraid the conversation was serious enough to warrant dismissal. Miss Hamlyn has already been discharged. Furthermore, I warned her that as soon as she leaves the premises she is not to mention anything to anyone, including family, about the work we're doing here, or her particular job, and that we will be keeping a close eye on her. And I say the same to you, Miss Treadwell. The Official Secrets Act remains in place for the rest of your life. As for now, you are hereby dismissed.'

Dale gasped. This was far worse than she could have imagined. Oh, why had Rhoda been so impetuous and not heeded her warning? This would be a terrible black mark on their work record. Any employer would think twice about hiring either of them in the future.

'I am particularly disappointed in *you*, Miss Treadwell.' His eyes met hers. 'I had high hopes for you with the great number of successes you have had in Hut 6. In fact, I had in mind to move you where you would have used that fine brain even more fully.' He shook his head, his mouth in a hard line. 'Such a waste for a foolish, thoughtless indiscretion.'

Oh, it couldn't be – just when she was on the verge of promotion. What she'd longed for. She felt she would explode with frustration.

'Please, sir, let me tell you the exact conversation—'

He held the palm of his hand towards her. 'There's nothing more to say, except to go to the office and hand in your pass to Mrs Jones, then sign out.'

In disgrace. Dale felt her eyelids prick. No, she would *not* cry in front of him. She *had* to say something – try to explain.

349

'Sir, this has been grossly exaggerated. Rhoda didn't divulge any secrets or anything and neither did I . . . I swear it . . . and—'

'You may go, Miss Treadwell.'

Dale rose and crossed the room, which felt a mile away to his office door. She opened it and without glancing behind her, shut the door quietly, even though she felt like slamming it off its hinges. What should she do next? For a few moments she stood there dazed. Then she remembered – she had to retrieve her handbag in the Hut. She'd have to face them all. Face Wanda. That would be the worst part. Well, Wanda had finally won. She'd got rid of her. She'd had her revenge. But nothing Rhoda had said could surely justify their dismissal. Wanda must have exaggerated. Even made up a few choice bits. Oh, it was too humiliating. And Rhoda had already gone. She couldn't even ask her what Commander Travis had said to her and what she'd said back. She'd bet Rhoda hadn't taken her dismissal meekly.

Slowly Dale walked down the stairs, as dignified as she could act, nodding and smiling to a handful of the staff, but then she had to dash to the cloakroom. Sitting on the toilet seat she put her head in her hands, the tears flowing between her fingers. She loved working here. Yes, it was often mundane, the room was stifling in the summer and freezing in the winter, and she'd found it difficult to get close to anyone because of the worry not to say the wrong thing. But it was so satisfying when she cracked the setting for the day and decoded messages. She was almost as pleased when the others did because it was teamwork. They all needed each other. And now her part had ended abruptly and unfairly.

She couldn't stop the harsh sobs that racked her chest. The disgrace. The humiliation. The promotion that had been in her grasp. Oh, it was unbearable. The gossip which must by now be circulating around the Park. In her own Hut. And Eddie. He would probably already know. She'd let him down. Most of all she'd let down Lord and Lady Langton who'd taken a chance and been so kind to her. She gave a last shuddering sob and pulled herself upright.

Catching sight of herself in the mirror above the wash basin, she splashed her face. There was nothing she could do about her reddened eyes. She ran a comb through her hair. She looked a sight. But what did it matter. Everyone would have forgotten her in a few days' time and be on to the next juicy piece of gossip. Someone else would sit at her desk, trying to work out the codes. Dale drew in a jerky breath, then defiantly squared her shoulders. She wasn't guilty and she wasn't going to act as though she was.

Her poise crumpled the moment she saw Wanda. But then she noticed the triumphant gleam in Wanda's eyes. Dale bristled. She'd bloody have her say.

'Mrs Wilcox, may I have a word with you in private?'

Several of Dale's colleagues looked up.

Wanda sucked in her cheeks, but Dale's glare seemed to do the trick. When they were in the training room, Dale remained standing.

'You can take a seat, Dulcie,' Wanda said, sitting down and coolly lighting a cigarette.

'I don't think that will be necessary.' She had nothing to lose now. 'I've gone over and over in my mind the conversation I had with Rhoda and she said absolutely nothing that could possibly get anyone, or herself, into trouble. She gave no secrets away, as you well know.'

'I'm afraid that wasn't how Commander Travis saw it.' Wanda blew out a stream of smoke as she relaxed back in her chair.

'You obviously embellished it then.'

Wanda shook her head and tutted. 'So you're calling me a liar.'

'I didn't say that. But I do believe Commander Travis is a fair man. He wouldn't have dismissed us if he'd been privy to the conversation – of which I remember every word.'

'Then your memory is failing you.'

'How dare you!' Dale exploded. 'My memory is what got me here in the first place.' She shook her finger at Wanda. 'And you know perfectly well Rhoda and I said nothing out of order.' She paused, her eyes flashing. 'I intend to take this further.'

'I shouldn't if I were you,' Wanda said, a little flushed. 'I might have to bring up the German conversation.'

'This is becoming more ridiculous by the minute,' Dale said. 'I'm already dismissed so you can't make it any worse.'

She turned to leave when Wanda said, 'Before you go, your friend left you this letter.'

Dale practically snatched it, hurried back to her desk and picked up her bag.

'I'm sorry to see you go,' Sonia said, turning from her desk in front. 'We'll miss you.'

Dale shook her head. 'Not the way Mrs Wilcox was talking,' she said, glancing round at the others. 'I just want to tell you, so there's no doubt in anyone's mind, that the other girl who's been dismissed happens to be a close friend of mine. And she didn't give away any secrets at all or hint to me what her work was, only that it was monotonous, and she hadn't been prepared for that after the excitement of joining the WRNS and working abroad. And I didn't mention my job at all.' Dale bit her lip, just managing not to say it had been a witch-hunt led by Wanda Wilcox. There was a hush. All eyes were on her, then swivelled round as Wanda came into the room.

Dale ignored her. If the woman had heard her last remark, then good. Smiling round, she said:

'Good luck, everyone. It was lovely to meet you all and I'm really sad to be leaving under such unfair circumstances.'

She couldn't utter another word. If she did, she'd burst into tears. And she wasn't going to give Wanda the satisfaction of seeing her beaten. Without a glance at the supervisor Dale swept past and walked up the drive, past the sentry and across the road to the bus stop. She just hoped a bus would come along soon before she completely broke down.

Chapter Thirty-Eight

A yellow sports car drew up at the bus stop and Eddie jumped out.

'In you get,' he said, opening the passenger door. 'I've been looking everywhere for you.'

Dale practically fell into the seat. Her head felt it had been pressed through a wringer.

'I heard,' he said, pulling out into the road so sharply the tyres protested loudly. 'But I don't know what reason.'

'Who told you?' Dale demanded.

'The giggly girl. I don't know her name. I'd just finished my shift and ran into her in the corridor. She told me you and another girl have been dismissed for blabbing.' He gave her a sideways glance. 'That's all she knew. So I've been trying to track you down.'

'Do *you* think I blabbed?'

'I doubt it. You wouldn't even tell me which Hut you were working in.'

Dale folded her hands in her lap, staring ahead at the road. 'That's how I've always been – extremely cautious in answering questions. Why I wanted to get away from the Drapers.'

'Look, Dale, tell me when we get back. My aunt's at home but Uncle had an appointment in London and he's not

354

expected back until late tonight. Why don't we include her, so you get it over in one go?' He looked at her. 'Don't worry. I know you wouldn't have said anything you shouldn't, but I don't know the other girl.'

'Rhoda,' Dale said. 'She's a close friend of mine and hadn't told me she was coming to work at Bletchley, the same as I hadn't told her. She didn't say anything that broke the Official Secrets Act and certainly nothing to warrant being dismissed.'

'Then let's go and find my aunt.'

Ten minutes later Ruth brought a tray into the drawing room with tea and shortbread biscuits.

'Dale has something rather difficult to tell us, Aunt,' Eddie said.

Lady Langton sent Dale a sympathetic smile. 'Drink your tea first, my dear. Whenever I'm facing a problem, I always find a cup of strong tea with two sugars does the trick – well, I allow myself only one sugar now we're rationed,' she added with a rueful smile.

A cup of tea. If only it were that simple.

Gratefully, Dale sipped her tea, but she couldn't swallow anything solid. After a few moments she said, 'Lady Langton, I don't know how to tell you, but I've just been dismissed – and my friend, too – for breaching security. But we didn't break any rules.'

Lady Langton put her cup down in the saucer so abruptly that it rattled. 'Oh, my dear, how dreadful for you.'

Dale could tell by the way Eddie had his ear cocked that he was listening intently.

Quickly, she recounted the conversation with Commander Travis.

Eddie shook his head. 'Who reported you?'

'Someone heard us on the bus.' Deliberately, she left Wanda's name out of it.

355

'If that's all he had to go on, it's pretty flimsy,' he said to his aunt, then turned to Dale. 'And I've known you long enough to believe you.'

'But Commander Travis doesn't.' Dale's voice was bitter. 'So there's nothing I can do.'

'Oh, but there is,' Lady Langton said, rising from her chair. 'I want you to promise not to do anything, say anything, to anyone bar my nephew for the rest of the day.' She paused. 'Will you do that?'

'Um . . . yes, but I was going to pack—'

'Don't say another word,' Lady Langton said imperiously. 'Eddie, take her into town this evening. There's a new Bette Davis film showing at the picture house. It'll take her mind off things. We'll speak again in the morning after breakfast.'

Eddie looked at Dale. 'What do you say?'

A tiny spark of hope lifted Dale's mood. She was with people she liked and respected. They believed her and it seemed they weren't going to let her go without a fight. But then she came down to earth. There was nothing that would alter Commander Travis's mind. She'd been made very aware of that. He hadn't needed to rest a gun on a desk like Major Barking. She'd seen the steel in his eyes.

In her room, Dale opened Rhoda's letter, dreading to read the lines.

Dear Dale,

I'm so very sorry I've been the cause of your dismissal. If only I hadn't opened my big mouth. But I still can't believe Travis made such a mountain out of a molehill. I wish I could have had the chance to tell you in person how sorry I am but I was more or less marched off the premises. You must be feeling so shocked to lose your job and furious with me. If you are I don't blame you. But who would believe that bitch Wanda was sitting behind us? Why didn't we see her? She must have rushed down the stairs before the driver stopped at the gates and then shot off to do her dirty work. And we wouldn't have been any the wiser. Until we were hauled up in front of Travis, that is.

It's you I feel sorry for. I couldn't care less for me. I'd already decided to pack it in. But I know how you love your work and being at the Park. I tried to tell Travis, but he wasn't having any of it. I wanted to speak to that despicable woman, but I wouldn't have been allowed into your Hut if I'd tried.

I'm sure to be chucked out of the WRNS but I'll find other war work as I know you will – where we'll be appreciated.

Please telephone as soon as you're home. Jane and I have missed you so let's all meet soon. I only hope you'll forgive me.

Love,

Rhoda XX

Dale read the letter again. Rhoda was right in her analysis of her own self. Her friend was quick to pick herself up and plan the next adventure, but *she* was different. She'd taken her work very seriously and now she had no idea what to do. Commander Travis had made it clear that her reputation was finished as far as the Park was concerned. All she could do now was to keep her word to Lady Langton and spend the evening with Eddie – forget it for a few hours.

But she knew she wouldn't.

*   *   *

'Eddie, I'm not in the mood to watch a film,' Dale said when he was turning into the country road.

'I don't intend to take you,' he said, glancing at her. 'We haven't had a chance to have a proper talk – and I don't mean about what happened this afternoon.'

He means us, Dale thought, mentally bracing herself.

'We're going to have a nice relaxing meal,' he went on. 'I'm taking you to the Swan Hotel. They run a decent kitchen. It should be quiet as we're fairly early and you can relax with a glass of wine.'

'I need to keep my head.' Dale turned to him. 'The Swan – that's in Fenny Stratford.'

'Yes. You've probably cycled there.'

Eddie prattled on until he abruptly came to a stop outside the hotel. There were only half a dozen couples in the dimly lit dining room, the blackout blinds already pulled firmly down, even though it was still light outside.

'May we have that table in the corner?' Eddie motioned to the waiter.

'Certainly, sir.'

He saw them over to their seats and laid a white linen napkin on each of their laps. Eddie scanned the wine menu, then pointed to the list. 'We'll have a bottle of white,' he said to the waiter. 'Whatever you have left in stock.'

'Thank you, sir.'

'Okay with you, Dale?' Eddie said, barely glancing up.

'Yes, lovely.'

She looked across at him, his head bent as he made his choice. He certainly liked to take control. Immediately, she felt mean. Eddie was only being kind. Probably thought she wasn't fit to make even a small decision.

When the waiter had disappeared, Eddie caught her eye. 'You've had a horrible shock.'

She shrugged. 'It's hard for it to sink in.'

He nodded. 'I know I said we weren't going to talk about it, but I just want to say one thing. I don't believe for one minute you leaked anything. Or your friend, from what you tell me. And even if she'd started to say something, I'm sure you would have stopped her.'

'I did,' Dale said, 'before she said anything she shouldn't. The trouble with Rhoda is that she's been working abroad as a Wren, enjoying a good social life, but when they offered her an important job for the war effort in England she was intrigued. She didn't realise it was going to be so monotonous. But all she said out loud was the size of the machine she used. She didn't name it. I had no idea what it was or what she did on it, and I doubt anyone else would have had any idea if they'd heard.'

She broke off as the waiter poured two glasses of wine, feeling some relief to have got that off her chest. If only Commander Travis had given her the same courtesy.

'Do you know who reported us?'

Eddie frowned. 'You said someone on the bus.'

'Yes. Wanda Wilcox.'

Dale watched as Eddie visibly startled.

'That woman has a lot to answer for. She—'

'Used to be your girlfriend,' Dale interrupted. 'Isn't that true?'

He flushed red, lowering his head to fiddle with the cruet. 'How did you find out?' he mumbled.

'She told me herself. More or less said to back off. She's had it in for me ever since she discovered I was living at Langton Hall where you were. I think she thought if she could muscle in, your attentions would turn from me back to her.'

'Well, she has another think coming.' He gave a deep sigh. 'I should have told you.'

'Yes, you should have been honest. And I would have understood why she was so awful.'

'I'm so sorry, Dale. I was never in love with her. And she began getting very possessive. Do you forgive me?'

Dale shrugged. 'There's nothing to forgive. But the sooner I'm back in London the better.'

'I'm not so sure about that,' Eddie said, picking up the menu. 'But for now, we'll change the subject while you relax and let me order for you.'

Perhaps Eddie was right. Perhaps she was too feeble to make any decision. She suddenly realised from the enticing smells from nearby diners' plates that she was hungry and soon they were tucking into a delicious curry.

'That's better,' Eddie said, wiping his mouth with his napkin. 'Any problem always makes me hungry. I can think better on a full stomach.' He drained his glass and glanced over to hers which was still half full. He poured himself another.

The waiter came to collect their dishes and as soon as he'd disappeared Eddie reached over and took her hand.

'My problem is much more easily solved,' he said, 'but it needs your complete cooperation.' He grinned and gave her hand a quick squeeze. 'I think you know what I'm saying, dearest Dale.'

'Eddie—'

'Just let me finish.' He took another swallow of his drink. 'I know you think you're in love with someone else but he's not here – and I am.'

'I'm sorry,' Dale said, gently pulling her hand away. 'The answer is no – I can't marry you.'

Eddie drove home in silence, only cursing when he caught the kerb twice as he left Fenny Stratford. Once inside the Dower House he said:

'We'll go in the drawing room. There should be the remains of the fire, at least.'

The room was chilly and Dale kept her coat on. When they were sitting on one of the sofas he said:

'It's still that Yank, isn't it?'

She turned her head to him. 'This is hard for me to explain, and I don't want to hurt you, but even if I hadn't already given my heart to him, I would still say no.'

'Why? We get along well. We have a good laugh together. We're working on the same side, doing our bit for the war.'

'That's just it. The war has brought us together. It's drawn us close, I admit. But it's because of that – don't you see?'

Eddie shook his head. 'No, I don't see at all.'

'If I'd met you and there'd been no war, and even though I'd find you very attractive, it would soon be obvious to both of us that we could only be friends. We're from a different class. I've heard that you're called the Honourable Edward Langton.'

Eddie snorted. 'Don't take any notice of those idiots. They're just teasing you and even if it were true, it doesn't alter my feelings for you.'

'So you don't deny it,' Dale rushed in.

'I don't deny or agree,' he said. 'I told you, none of that nonsense makes any difference.'

'Maybe not now, but it would later,' Dale said. 'You'd see it more clearly after the war, moving in different circles. It's natural for you to take control – you've been brought up to do it – but I have to be in charge of my own destiny. Not from a man who believes he's doing what he thinks is right for me – taking control without even asking.'

'I'd never—'

'You've done this sort of thing several times.' Dale smiled, trying to soften the tension. 'Tonight even. And sometimes it's nice and comforting. I don't have to think.' She turned further towards him, so she was facing him. 'You're a dear friend, Eddie, and I value your friendship – you don't know how much. If you remember, we've had a similar conversation before, and you said then you'd be my friend even if it didn't turn out to be more serious.' She gazed at him. 'I hope you still feel the same.' When he didn't answer she patted his arm. 'It's late. I'll see you at breakfast tomorrow.'

Without waiting for a reply, she stood and left the room.

Chapter Thirty-Nine

Dale entered the dining room just before seven the following morning. No Eddie. She bit her lip. Had she been too cruel to him last night? She'd gone to bed shortly after their conversation, his protestations still sounding in her head.

She hadn't fallen asleep until the early hours and it hadn't been easy to make herself climb from the bed and into the bathroom this morning to wash and dress. She went downstairs to find only Lord Langton at the breakfast table.

'Good morning, sir,' she said quietly, not wanting to disturb him from his newspaper.

'Good morning, Dale. Did you sleep well?'

Dale gave a start. Had Lady Langton already told him what had happened yesterday? But Lord Langton's smile was just as frank and cheerful as usual. Should she say something, or leave it up to her ladyship?

'Not quite as well as usual,' she answered.

'I would think that's to be expected after yesterday.'

So he did know.

'I spoke to Eddie last night . . . and then I rang your commander.'

Dale's jaw dropped. 'Wh-what? Goodness, that was late.'

'You know I'm always up late and I know he's a night owl

as well, so I thought I'd have a word. He wants you to report to him this morning at 10 a.m.'

She gave a sharp intake of breath. 'Sir, I do appreciate your speaking to him, but he's told me in no uncertain terms that there's nothing more to be done. I have to respect that.'

'It may not change anything in the slightest,' Lord Langton said, 'but I told him it's a bit unfair if you haven't at least been given the opportunity to defend yourself.' He looked at her. 'Will you go?'

Dale hesitated. To be seen at the Park by people who'd heard of her dismissal for so-called blabbing . . . was it worth it? To be spotted by any of the girls who worked in her old Hut and see their look of surprise or, worse, their pity? To face Commander Travis and his grim demeanour again after she couldn't get out of his office quick enough yesterday? Momentarily, she closed her eyes. No, she couldn't. It was useless. Let Travis think what he liked about her.

Lord Langton was waiting for an answer. When she didn't speak, he said:

'It's not easy to face a difficult situation and it will take courage to knock on his door. But for your own peace of mind, I think you should do it. If you don't, you'll always regret it.'

Commander Travis thought she was a blabbermouth. She wasn't. She'd been so careful, always. Dale drew herself up and stuck out her chin.

'All right, sir. I'll do it.' For the first time since that awful interview, she felt a fraction lighter. If she could convince him she was telling the truth she'd feel a hundred times better when she walked out of the gate later today for the last time. She turned to Lord Langton. 'And thank you.'

*   *   *

Commander Travis's beautifully groomed secretary looked up as Dale approached her. She raised a pencilled brow. Dale took in a breath.

'Dulcie Treadwell,' she said. 'I have an appointment at ten o'clock with Commander Travis.'

The secretary glanced at the appointments book. She frowned.

'I'm sorry, but Commander Travis isn't in until this afternoon. Why don't you come back and I'll see if he can see you for a few minutes then.'

Dale's chest tightened with anger. Why had he told Lord Langton he would see her and then not be here?

'I can't wait that long,' she said, her tone abrupt. She turned to go.

The secretary put her hand in the air. 'Just a moment, Miss Treadwell . . .'

Dale paused. What now? The secretary was peering at the appointments book.

'My apologies. Commander Travis has left a note that you're down to see Commander Denniston at ten thirty.'

Dale whirled round. 'There must be a mistake. I was specifically told it was ten and it would be Commander Travis. He alone knows the situation. It wouldn't be any use speaking to someone else.'

She knew she sounded curt, but she couldn't help herself. She wished Eddie hadn't interfered, and Lord Langton hadn't taken things into his own hands. This was worse than a dignified exit.

'I'm not sure what you want to talk to Commander Travis about, Miss Treadwell, but it appears that Commander Denniston will be seeing you instead.'

'I'm sorry, I'll already be gone,' Dale said, 'so I'd be grateful if you'll cancel it.'

Had she done the right thing? Dale thought, as she went downstairs. Yes, she had, her brain told her. So why did her stomach feel so leaden?

On her way out she bumped into Helen.

'Dale! I heard on the grapevine you've been dismissed. What on earth happened?'

Without warning, Dale's eyes filled with tears. Helen took her arm.

'Come on, love. Let's go and have a cup of tea.'

Dale hesitated. She didn't want to be seen by people she knew.

'I'm with you,' Helen said, as though she'd read Dale's mind. 'You're not on your own. I'm your friend – remember? So dry your eyes and come with me.'

She couldn't speak. Helen was being so kind. And she could do with a cup of tea.

Luckily, there weren't many people in the café and although a few heads turned in their direction, Dale couldn't discern any hostility. She took a few calming breaths.

'I'll get them,' Helen said. 'You go and sit down. Do you want anything to eat?'

'No, thanks. Just the tea.'

Helen was back in a jiffy with two steaming mugs and a small plate of biscuits.

'Now tell me what all this is about – from the beginning.'

When Dale said how it had started on the bus that evening Helen suddenly interrupted.

'Was that when you were with your friend, Rhoda? Who we played tennis with?'

'Yes.'

'Ah. It all makes sense. Rhoda was complaining about her job, wasn't she?'

Dale spluttered on her mouthful of tea. 'How do you know that?'

'I was on the other side, about three rows behind. You two were at the front. Rhoda has quite a carrying voice and I heard her. You told her to shut up.'

'Yes, I did. I was terrified she was going to go into more detail about her work.'

'So now it all fits into place.' Helen's expression was thoughtful. 'Wanda was sitting across the aisle from me, so if she was like me, she heard everything.'

'Apparently so.'

'And for some reason she has it in for you.'

'Yes,' Dale admitted.

'Any idea why?'

'Apparently she and Eddie were going out before I came on the scene. She's livid because he broke it off with her when he met me.'

Helen grinned. 'Serve her right. I don't know what he ever saw in her. But about you—' she looked at Dale '—it's preposterous to dismiss you for nothing. All right, Rhoda mentioned the machine she works on, but she didn't name it. And some of us know that much anyway, even if we don't work in that Hut. You can hear the terrific noise of several loud machines going just walking by.' She looked at Dale. 'I presume Commander Travis dismissed you. Didn't you tell him the exact conversation?'

'I tried, but he wouldn't listen. He's apparently changed his mind and I was supposed to see him this morning but he's not back until this afternoon.' Dale quickly explained what the secretary had said. 'I'm not going to hang around hoping the great man will see me when he deigns to appear. Which might not be for the rest of the day.'

Helen gave her a steady look. 'Commander Denniston is willing to hear your side. Why don't you see him?'

'It wouldn't do any good. Commander Travis isn't the sort of person to change his mind – once it's made up.'

'Maybe not . . . but in any case, dear Dale, you're going to keep that appointment with Commander Denniston. He happens to be the Director of the whole Park and would have the final say. And I'll come with you! I can tell him exactly what I witnessed.'

Dale's eyes widened. 'Are you sure?'

'Most definitely.' Helen drained her tea. She looked at her watch and stood. 'Come on. It's nearly half past.'

Dale couldn't believe she was walking into the entrance of the main house yet again. On the first floor she was a little embarrassed to see the same secretary, and even more so when Helen marched up to the desk.

'I'm Helen Blunt and I believe my colleague, Dulcie Treadwell, asked you to cancel an appointment with Commander Denniston,' she began. 'Could you please reinstate it, and allow me to go in with her?'

The secretary frowned as she glanced up at Dale. 'It's lucky for you I've been busy on the phone and haven't had a chance to cancel it.' She dialled a number on the switchboard. 'Miss Treadwell is here, sir, with Miss Blunt,' she said, then paused. 'Thank you.' She turned to Dale and Helen. 'You can both go in. Second door on the left.'

Helen took Dale's arm, but Dale gently removed it.

'I can't thank you enough for your offer, Helen, but actually I think I have to do this on my own. I don't want him to doubt my word and need your report to convince him I'm not guilty – or my friend – of giving away secrets. I won't be staying anyway. If he doesn't believe me nothing you say will make the slightest difference – if he does, then

I'll have the satisfaction of assuring him on my own.' She paused. 'Can you understand?'

Helen nodded. 'I think so.' She hesitated. 'Well, if you're really sure, I can only wish you good luck. I'll wait here for you just in case you need me.'

'Don't do that, Helen. I'll catch up with you later.'

Dale glanced at the brass plate with Commander Denniston's name engraved. Taking a deep breath, she knocked.

'Come in.'

A small, slight man, Commander Denniston had a completely different demeanour from Commander Travis. As soon as she entered, he smiled and rose from the chair, then came from behind his desk, extending his hand.

'Is Miss Blunt coming?'

'No, sir. I preferred to see you on my own.'

He nodded. 'Now, Miss Treadwell, come and sit down and tell me what all this is about.'

Dale gave an inward sigh. How she hoped this would be the last time she'd have to repeat that dreaded conversation.

Commander Denniston leant slightly forward behind his desk listening intently without any interruption. When she'd finished, he said:

'Thank you for explaining. I don't think there's any need for me to say any more.'

So he didn't believe her. Well, she'd done her best.

'I understand your friend Rhoda Hamlyn has already left,' Commander Denniston continued.

'Yes, but she wasn't happy in her job. I was hoping to change her mind.'

'We can't have anybody here who doesn't put their back into it and give whole-hearted loyalty.' He tapped his pen on the desk. 'But I'd like you to tell me how *you* felt in the job.'

'There are periods when you feel mentally exhausted, mainly when you've not cracked a code for several hours . . . or sometimes days. But when you do – oh, my goodness. The surge of adrenalin knocks you flying. It's incredibly exciting and satisfying. There's no feeling like it.' She swallowed. 'I always felt really privileged to have been chosen to work here.'

Commander Denniston's eyes dropped to an open file.

'You've certainly had a good share of successes,' he said, still reading. 'Miss Gibson always put in an excellent report about your conduct as well.'

Dale bit her lip. She knew what was coming next.

'Mrs Wilcox, who reported the incident on the bus, wasn't quite so forthcoming, though she did acknowledge you were one of the best decoders.' He looked up. 'By your record, you *were* the best.'

Dale sat silently, his last words sounding in her ears. Past tense. You *were* the best. His next words took her completely by surprise.

'I believe everything you've told me, my dear, and I would like you to go back to Hut 6 today, after you've had some lunch, taking up exactly where you left off. I'll put a message through to Mrs Wilcox, who is on duty today, that you are to be reinstated with immediate effect.'

Dale's heart jumped. And then she thought of working in the same Hut as Wanda. She couldn't do it. She couldn't face that spiteful woman. Wanda would make her life a misery. Was this the time to mention Commander Travis had had it in mind to move her to another Hut? She couldn't think straight. Her mind was going in jerky fragments of thought.

'Mrs Wilcox—' she started.

'I think I know how you feel,' he interrupted. 'But in life we have to get along with all kinds of people. We're facing exceptional times. This is war and we need people like you to help us win it.' He fixed his eyes on hers. 'So tell me, Miss Treadwell. Are you still with us?'

Chapter Forty

When Dale left Commander Denniston's office she felt a mixture of relief and trepidation. She wondered if she'd been too hasty to tell him she would go back. Maybe she should have had time to think about it. All the ramifications. Not only Wanda but Eddie and the Langtons. Would they still allow her to live under their roof? Would Eddie see it as a sign that he'd put himself out to help her regain her job and maybe she'd change her mind on his proposal? There were so many things to consider. But then she shook herself. Glenn would encourage her to go back. Look how brave *he* was – in Berlin amongst the Nazis day after day, not to mention the persistent bombing. Commander Denniston was right. Nothing was so important when there was a war on and the possibility they could yet be invaded. She set her jaw. If her help really counted, she was ready to carry on.

It was coming up to noon and she was hungry. She'd have a quick snack in the canteen and be back before the others so she could be at her desk before everyone arrived. The canteen was crowded. It seemed everyone had decided to take an early lunch. The first person she set eyes on was Vernon. He waved her over, but she simply smiled and nodded, then made for a table with only one person sitting there. Helen.

Helen sprang to her feet. 'I was hoping you'd stay for a bite,' she said. 'I'm dying to know what happened.'

'I've been reinstated,' Dale said, almost humbly.

'That's wonderful.' Helen threw her arms round her. 'You must be thrilled.'

'I'm really pleased he believed me, but I don't relish working under Wanda's malevolent eye. Commander Denniston wants me to go back after lunch as though nothing's happened.'

'I think that's the right way to handle it,' Helen said. 'You'll do it.'

'Thanks for your faith in me,' Dale smiled, biting into her cheese sandwich.

Wanda was at her desk near the entrance to Hut 6 when Dale walked in, her head high. No one else was in the room. The supervisor looked up with a cold expression.

'So you're back.'

'Yes,' Dale returned. 'And I intend to do my job as well as I can.'

'You have Commander Denniston to thank for that,' she said, with a curl of her lip.

'Then I thank him.' Dale looked round the room. 'Can you tell me which desk is available?'

'That one,' Wanda gestured. 'Right opposite me.'

Later that afternoon a young girl came in and gave Wanda a half-sheet of paper.

'It's to go on the notice board,' Dale heard her say timidly. 'And another one for the canteen.'

Wanda glanced at it, grimaced and got up to pin it on the board, then left the room. Several girls crowded round.

'It's about you,' Sonia said with a giggle as she glanced at Dale.

'*Me?*'

'Well, it doesn't actually mention you by name.'

Dale shrugged and carried on tapping the letters.

'I'll read it out.' Sonia cleared her throat.

18th April, 1941. Regarding the suspension from duty of two members of staff, the order has now been cancelled and one girl has returned to duty today.

All members of sections should be warned once again to avoid any talk about their work in the presence of their colleagues from other Huts, their billetors, family, friends, or any other person at all times and in the future.

'It's signed "Commander A. Denniston, Director", Sonia finished. She looked across at Dale. 'Welcome back, Dale.' She began to clap.

Before Dale could say a word, several girls joined in and soon the whole room echoed to the sound of a dozen pairs of hands enthusiastically clapping and cheering.

Dale rose to her feet. 'Thanks, everyone. You've made me feel as though I'm truly a member of the team and might be doing a bit of good here.' She paused and smiled. 'But we'd all better get our heads down before Mrs Wilcox returns. I think I've had enough excitement for one day.'

'So you saw Commander Denniston – the top man?' Eddie said as soon as he entered the dining room at the Dower House the following day for bacon and eggs before he took to his bed after a midnight to morning shift. 'And by the notice on the canteen board you're back in your Hut.'

Dale quickly updated him.

'Bloody good show,' he said. 'Denniston has a much more lenient attitude to a small error of judgement such as Rhoda's than Travis. And, of course, he's Travis's senior.'

'He was very nice and listened without interrupting,' Dale said, feeling much lighter now she'd got the afternoon with Wanda out of the way. Tomorrow would be easier. She smiled at Eddie. 'Afterwards he encouraged me to believe I was doing an important job and was needed back at work. So I said I would. And all the women welcomed me back – well, all except one.'

Eddie rolled his eyes. 'Don't remind me what a fool I was.' Then he smiled. 'I'm really happy for you, Dale. It would have been awful to see you leave under some false cloud.' His hazel eyes met hers. 'And about that conversation we had . . . I won't go back on my word. You can always count on me as one of your closest friends.'

'You couldn't have told me anything nicer,' Dale said, giving him a peck on his cheek.

'What was that for?'

'For being so damned nice.'

'Well, of course if you ever change your mind . . .'

'I won't,' Dale said quickly. 'But thanks for giving me the opportunity.'

Lady Langton bustled into the room.

'There you are, my dears. Dulcie, you must feel very relieved this morning.'

Dale had told Lady Langton about her interview with Commander Denniston as soon as she'd gone back to the Dower House when her shift had finished that afternoon. While the two of them were having tea, Dale had asked her ladyship a burning question.

'Is it still all right for me to stay here?'

375

Lady Langton had broken into a wide smile.

'We love having you here, Dulcie. This is your home all the time you're working at the Park.'

'And his lordship?'

'Gresham?' She chuckled. 'He's tickled to bits. He thinks it's all his doing that finally the powers that be saw some common sense.'

'Well, it was Eddie to begin with,' Dale said truthfully, 'and then it was you telling his lordship . . . and he took action. Then Commander Travis put me on to Commander Denniston who listened.' She paused. 'So it was teamwork,' she added with a smile.

'No,' Lady Langton smiling back. 'When you've been married as long as I have, you'll know that men like to take all the credit. And Gresham is no different.'

'I'll remember that,' Dale grinned. 'If I ever get married, that is.'

Lady Langton gazed at her. 'I had a feeling you and Eddie might be doing something in that direction. I know Eddie lights up every time he's with you.'

'He's a very dear friend,' Dale said. 'But I'm in love with someone else – before I ever met Eddie.'

'Well, my dear, I'm happy for you but disappointed for Eddie. He's like a son to us.'

'Eddie will meet someone one day who'll be perfect for him,' Dale said quickly.

Lady Langton held her gaze. 'You've never mentioned this man. Is he away serving in the military?'

'He's away, but not in the military,' Dale answered, her heart beating more rapidly. 'He's an American war correspondent working overseas.' She swallowed. She mustn't give any more details. But it was such a relief to say even this much to this kind, sympathetic woman.

'Oh.' Lady Langton's eyes widened in alarm. 'That sounds like a dangerous job if he's reporting from the heart of the Nazi regime.'

'I know.' Dale swallowed hard. 'I simply can't imagine what he's going through.'

Chapter Forty-One

September, 1941

There was a knock at the door of Hut 6 and a courier appeared. Dale looked up. Something was going on by the looks of the chap's excited expression. He handed Miss Gibson a note and Dale watched as the woman's jaw dropped. Then she nodded and the courier disappeared. Miss Gibson rapped on her desk.

'Your attention, everyone. A marvellous piece of news. The Prime Minister, Winston Churchill, is in the Park and will visit our Hut shortly. When he arrives, you will all stand in silence facing your machines.'

There was a delighted murmur amongst the girls. Sonia turned round from her desk and beamed at Dale.

'Isn't this exciting? Something to write in the diary tonight.'

Dale shook her head in warning as Miss Gibson's eyes bored into them.

'Until then, please resume your work.'

Nearly half an hour passed before Dale heard voices outside. Someone put their head in the door.

'The PM's going to give an address outside,' he said. 'So this is your chance to witness history in the making.'

'All right, girls, you may go . . . in an orderly fashion,' Miss Gibson warned as she rose from her desk.

Everyone shot to their feet.

'Come on, Sonia,' Dale said, grabbing the girl's arm.

There was not a hint of sun and the wind was chilly, but Mr Churchill's presence was electric as he stood on a piece of higher ground to be more easily seen. He was not so immediately recognisable without his hat or his famous cigar but the instant he began to speak there was no doubt who the great man was. It was a magnificent performance and sent shivers along Dale's spine. What an inspiring human being.

'I bet Wanda will be furious she was away today of all days,' Sonia giggled, and Dale couldn't help grinning at the thought.

The Prime Minister finished his speech by thanking everyone for the vital work they were doing.

'To look at you, one would not think you held so many secrets, but I know better and I am proud of you.' He beamed at the crowd as he put two fingers in the air forming the V for Victory sign. The applause was thunderous. Dale's hands stung from clapping, and she couldn't help thinking that everything would turn out all right so long as Mr Churchill remained in charge.

PART FOUR

Chapter Forty-Two

November 1941, Berlin

Dear God, how long had he been here? Except for those few days in London – those wonderful, magical days when he'd seen Dulcie, made love to her – he felt the familiar tingle down his spine at the memory – he'd been in this city of propaganda and brutality for over two years. Why had he stayed so long when so many of his colleagues had gone back to the States? Several of them had urged him to do the same.

His mother always said he had an obstinate streak, just like his father, but she said it with pride and love, not with any criticism. But if she knew how dangerous the situation had become, she'd tell him to get the hell out of there. Well, she wouldn't have sworn – Glenn couldn't help smiling at the idea – but she would certainly have made her sentiments known.

But until he was pushed out – again, as other journalists had been forced to leave for being too explicit with what the German censors considered not to be in their interests – he still wanted to stay. If only he could influence Roosevelt to for God's sake respond to Churchill, who must be getting quite demoralised by now, wondering if America would ever come to his country's aid. Britain didn't just need material goods under the Lend-Lease scheme, which had worked well supplying military aid to the allies but still letting the US remain neutral, Glenn thought. No – what they needed was for the US to declare war on Germany without further delay.

He lit a fresh cigarette from the stub of his old one, and signed off a letter to Dulcie. Feeling a little foolish he kissed his forefinger, then pressed it onto her name before folding the sheet of paper and putting it in the envelope. After a couple of puffs on his Lucky Strike, he glanced at his watch. Jackson and Bentley, two of his closest friends, were leaving today on the Berlin train to Switzerland along with Donna Price, one of the few female war correspondents. Glenn was particularly sorry she'd be going. Donna was a woman who wouldn't allow herself to be intimidated by anyone and would probably make a member of the Gestapo think twice if they came up against her. Nor was she shy in offering her personal views to anyone who'd listen – American or German. But in the end, it had got her into trouble. She'd been arrested once and let go after a miserable twenty-four hours in prison. They were closing in on her, Donna had said only a week ago, as casually as if she was saying it was going to rain at the weekend. But like him she'd tried to hang on. It was only Jackson and Bentley who told her in no uncertain terms they would not leave Berlin without her.

'Anything you'd like me to take to that mysterious girl-friend of yours?' she'd said, her almond eyes sparkling with mischief. 'A letter, or anything?'

'Would you?' Glenn said. 'That would be great. It will get there quicker than my usual method.'

'Don't forget to give it to me. And make sure you don't write anything to incriminate me or you'll see me sooner than you'd thought,' she'd said, and laughed.

Glenn grinned. Donna was incorrigible. In a way she reminded him of Dulcie – impetuous, clever, brave. He scrawled Dulcie's Post Box address on the envelope, still none the wiser about the work she was doing. Whatever it was, he guessed it was top secret, or she would have told him. He tried to imagine her engrossed in her work, the thick golden hair smoothed back into a victory roll, showing off her long slim neck. He ached for her. Just to see her beautiful face. Those amazing eyes. And then the most terrible thought seized him. Made him feel his whole world was collapsing. It was a month now. She'd promised faithfully to write twice a week as he had promised her. Could she have been caught by a goddamn Nazi bomb? Was she . . . could she be . . .?

Don't even think of it. Don't even think of that heart-breaking word.

He shook himself.

I'd know it if it were true.

He glanced at his watch. Time to go to the station to say goodbye to his friends.

The station was packed with people departing and arriving. Hissing steam, piercing whistles, booming voices over the tannoy – everything assaulted his senses, causing his nerves to prickle. He was overcome with relief when he spotted the three of them just inside the entrance.

'We thought we'd have a quick beer over there—' Bentley jerked his head '—before we go.'

'Sounds good,' Glenn said.

There didn't seem much to say after all. They were going back to the safety of a neutral country and he would be left in the thick of it. *But it's your choice*, his inner voice said. *You could just as easily board the train. Even now. There wouldn't be any problem. You've got your papers with you. It's not too late.*

'Do you have your letter to your girlfriend?' Donna asked as she took a mouthful of beer.

'Yes.' Glenn regarded her seriously. 'And you're sure you're happy to do this? I don't want the police to come after you.'

Donna gave a knowing grin. 'It's a love letter, right?'

He nodded.

'Then I'll take a chance – for the sake of love.' She chuckled. 'Come on, give it to me.'

'I'll do it when you're safely on the train,' Glenn said, his eye on the station clock, 'which is very soon. I think we should go.'

Glenn helped his three friends to gather their luggage. They pushed their way along the crowded platform where the train was waiting, its engine already roaring, impatient to leave.

'I'll be sure to call your ma and pa,' Jackson said, his head poking out of the train window.

'Thanks, Jackson.'

'The letter, Glenn.' Donna's head was close to Jackson's.

Glenn took the envelope from the inside of his raincoat pocket and handed it to her. She glanced at the address.

'Didn't you say she lived in London?'

'Yes, why?'

'If you give me her address, I could go see her. Hand it to her in person.'

'She lives away, near her job. It's a bit secret so that's why it's a Post Box number which is preferable – just in case it got into the wrong hands.'

'It's only *my* hands it's getting into,' she said, putting it in her bag.

386

She looked up and grinned. A split second later he saw her expression freeze. His blood curdled.

'Run!' she hissed. 'It's the—' The rest of her words sucked up in a belch of steam and smuts as the train began to rumble and slowly move.

'*Halt, Amerikaner!*'

Glenn spun round.

Holy Moses. The Gestapo.

'Your papers,' the taller one demanded in English.

Glenn took them from his inside coat pocket and handed them over.

Keep calm. You're perfectly entitled to be here. They can't get you for anything . . . unless they've already ransacked my room. He froze. *Dear God, the diary . . .*

'We are very interested to know what papers you handed your colleague,' the second one spoke in perfectly enunciated English. 'You will come with us to explain.'

Chapter Forty-Three

Early December, 1941

On her afternoon teabreak, Dale walked over to the main house to see whether she had any post. Some of the staff had already decorated a Christmas tree in the dark panelled hall and fixed swags of coloured paper chains, criss-crossing them over the superb plastered ceilings.

'Two for you, Miss Treadwell,' the clerk said, handing her the envelopes.

She glanced at them. One was from her father, only the second she'd received. She shook her head, hoping he'd finally come to terms with the fact that her mother wasn't prepared to have him back. In her last letter her mother had written that she and Jim had been out together several times and she was enjoying his company. Dale sighed. Her parents were both adults. They'd have to sort out their problems without any interference from her. The other handwriting, she didn't recognise at all. It was postmarked Geneva. She frowned. She didn't know anyone from Switzerland.

The café was crowded as usual, and the buzz of chatter loud. Dale took her mug of coffee and joined a table where Jennifer and Sonia were reading their letters. They looked up as Dale took a seat.

'We're not much company.' Sonia gave a giggle. 'Do you mind?'

'No, it means I can be just as bad-mannered and read mine,' Dale chuckled. She couldn't wait to see who was writing to her from Geneva. She glanced at the date: November 22, 1941. It was from someone who wrote the date the other way round as Glenn did.

Dear Dulcie (if I may),

I'm an American journalist and knew Glenn well when we were both in Berlin but am now staying in Geneva.

Oh, my goodness. This was wonderful. Someone who knows Glenn. Dale smiled as she read on.

I left Berlin on November 20 with two of my colleagues . . .

Oh, they'd be the friends Glenn mentioned, Dale thought happily. This woman was filling in the picture. How kind of her.

Glenn came to say goodbye at the station, as is our habit amongst our group when anyone leaves permanently. I wish he had come with us. But he said he had to stay longer. He had several more broadcasts planned but he promised he wouldn't leave it too long before he packed his things and left.

This next part is going to be terribly difficult to write.

Dale's smile faded. What does she mean? Anxiously she skimmed the next lines.

389

Our train was just about to leave. He gave me a letter to mail to you, thinking you might get it quicker from Geneva. I must own up to doing something bad. I've held it back. I wanted to be sure you read mine first.

What on earth . . . Who did this woman think she was, holding back Glenn's letter?

I hid the letter Glenn gave me for you and put my head out the window to wave goodbye as the train pulled out. Two Gestapo men waylaid him and took him away. They must have seen Glenn hand me your letter. That's all I can think of.

I will be sure to put your letter from Glenn in the mail tomorrow. Please forgive me. I only wanted to let you know what had happened first before you read Glenn's letter as his would not give you an indication as to what happened after we left.

I am so very sorry to be the one to give you such upsetting news. A few words I hope you find of some comfort to see you through a difficult time – Glenn loves you with all his heart. It's in his eyes, his expression, his words – he never stopped talking about you.

Yours very sincerely,

Donna Price

Dale clutched the edge of the café's table, her face drained of blood. *The Gestapo.* Those wicked, cruel, evil men. Where had they taken her darling Glenn? Would they torture him? Had they thrown him in prison! A nauseous lump came up in her throat.

'Have you had bad news?' Jennifer said.

'What?' Dale stared at the two girls, numb with shock.

'You look as though you've seen a ghost,' Sonia said, studying her. 'Are you all right?'

'I don't think I'll ever be all right . . . ever again.'

She scrambled from her chair and rushed to the door, then over to the Hut with the WCs. All six were occupied.

'Please come out, someone,' she called, trying to stop the bile from spewing out.

A door opened and a woman came out. Dale shot in and bent her head over the pan just in time.

'Dale.' It was Sonia. 'I'm outside waiting for you.'

'You go on,' Dale said, her legs shaking as she hauled herself upright.

'No, I'll wait.'

Dale wished she wouldn't. She put her mouth under the washbasin tap, rinsed it and then swallowed several gulps of water, hoping Sonia would give up. But when she emerged, Sonia took her arm.

'It was that letter, wasn't it?'

Dale looked at Sonia through a blur of tears. 'I'm sorry – I can't talk about it.'

As the American woman had promised, Glenn's letter came the next day, full of love and tenderness and hope for their future. He'd asked CBS if he could be sent to London for a few months to cover the war from there and had had a promising response – all he was waiting for was confirmation, so it was only a matter of a couple of weeks before he'd be with her again. Dale swallowed hard. He'd had no idea when he wrote these lines that he'd be marched off by the Gestapo.

She was grateful now that Donna had posted her letter first. If she'd read Glenn's letter without this knowledge – unbearably painful though it was – she'd be sailing on a cloud of false hope. That would have been far worse. But how was she going to survive the not knowing where or how he was? She wouldn't let herself think of the ultimate agony.

Dale read the letter a dozen times, tears streaming down her cheeks. How could she get through her work knowing Glenn . . .? She swallowed hard. Was he at this moment in prison? Would they shoot him? She hated that she had no idea of what the Gestapo did in this situation – only that they were cold and heartless. Oh, it didn't bear thinking about. If she could, she would march into the Gestapo's office and demand his release. Show them what was bound to be an innocent letter containing nothing detrimental about their stinking regime.

She didn't even know if she should write to him. Would it get him into even worse trouble? What should she do for the best? In her room she threw herself onto the bed and broke down in sobs.

It was many minutes before she stopped crying. She had to pull herself together. There was still a job to do.

On the evenings when Dale was on a day shift, Lady Langton would invariably insist she must not be on her own but to join her and Gresham in the drawing room of the Dower House. Work helped keep her sane, but the evenings in her room alone would have been unbearable.

This evening Eddie was there chatting with Lord Langton about the developments of the war.

'Time to put the news on, dear,' Lady Langton addressed her husband. He rose and switched on. Lady Langton put down her embroidery, and Eddie and Lord Langton fell silent.

'This is the BBC World Service Nine o'Clock News. Today,

Sunday the 7th December, at 7.55 a.m. Japan launched a surprise strike on the American naval base at Pearl Harbor in Hawaii. Thousands of American servicemen were killed or injured in the attack, which severely damaged the US Pacific Fleet. Four US battleships were sunk and nearly two hundred aircraft destroyed. Japan has declared war on Britain and the United States. The US president, Franklin D Roosevelt, has mobilised all his forces and is poised to declare war on Japan. We await more details . . .'

'Winnie will be delighted,' Lord Langton remarked, lighting his pipe. 'It's all he's wanted since the war started – and rightly so. America will declare war not only on Japan but Germany and Italy within days.'

Dale sat silently, her thoughts flying. What would that mean for Glenn? She caught Lady Langton watching her.

'Is everything all right, Dale?' she said. 'You look worried. But it will turn out to be the best news now America will be with us.'

Before she had time to reply, Eddie said, 'Just a minute—' he stared at her '—that means your American won't be broadcasting – from Germany, isn't it?' Dale nodded. 'They'll boot him out now the Americans are their enemies.'

'I wish that were so.'

'What do you mean?'

'Glenn's been arrested by the G-Gestapo.'

'Oh, my dear.' Lady Langton glanced across at her husband, who was already engrossed in his newspaper. 'Gresham, darling, can you go and see Ruth – ask if she'll bring us some cocoa. And I'll go and fetch my shawl. It's getting cold in here.' She stared at him pointedly.

'Oh . . . yes, of course, my dear.'

When they'd both disappeared, Eddie said, 'How do you know that?'

Tears streaming down her cheeks, she told him about Donna's letter.

He shook his head. 'Let's get this into perspective. They'll ask him what it was that he passed to his colleague. If he has any sense, he'll tell the truth – that it's a love letter to his girl.' He put his hand under her chin and turned her face towards him. 'Don't forget, love, he's an accredited journalist with the Nazis. They've only got to check his papers are in order. I'm sure they'll let him go. You mustn't think the worst.'

'How can I help it?' Dale snapped, brushing her tears away. She looked at his stricken expression. 'I'm sorry, Eddie. I know you're only trying to help.'

The following day, 8th December, the Americans declared war on Japan. Dale's colleagues discussed endlessly, whenever they got the chance, that surely now the Americans would come into the war against Germany and Italy.

'You've gone very quiet, Dale,' Sonia remarked in the canteen the following day. 'What do *you* think will happen?'

'President Roosevelt may still try to keep out of Europe – unless, of course, Hitler or that equally ghastly Mussolini decides to declare war on *them*. Then the Americans will be forced to come in.'

The newspapers, Lord Langton and everyone at the Park said it would be the turning point of the war. It was what the public was desperate to happen. But all the time Dale's burning question was where Glenn could be at this moment. If he hadn't managed by now to get out of Berlin, and if the United States declared war on Germany, he would be interned until the end of the war. At least that's what Eddie had told her would probably happen – if Glenn was lucky, he'd added. Her blood ran cold as her mind flew to the worst possibility.

Four days later, almost every newspaper screamed out the same headlines:

US NOW AT WAR WITH GERMANY AND ITALY

Yesterday, 11th December, 1941, Herr Hitler declared war on the United States and six hours later President Roosevelt declared war on Germany and Italy.

'Isn't it marvellous news about America finally coming in?' Helen said when Dale bumped into her at the chemist in the town that afternoon.

'Yes, it is.'

Helen studied her. 'What's the matter, Dale? You don't seem that happy about it.'

'I am, but—' Dale swallowed the threatening tears.

'But what? Something's bothering you?' She linked her arm through Dale's. 'Why don't we have a cup of tea in the café. It might help to talk to a friend.'

'I'm fine, really.' Dale sniffed and felt in her bag for her handkerchief.

'Come on, Dale. I'm dying for a cup of char even if you're not.'

Inside the café Helen asked the waitress for a pot of tea and two Chelsea buns. When they were sipping their tea, boiling hot as a change from the canteen at the Park, she glanced at Dale.

'What's on your mind? Is Eddie playing up?'

Dale shook her head. 'It's nothing to do with Eddie. But he's the only one who knows – I haven't told anyone at the Park.'

'Knows what?' Helen asked with raised brow.

'That I'm in love with an American,' Dale blurted. 'He's a foreign correspondent, a war broadcaster.' She gazed at Helen. Helen was someone she trusted completely. 'He's in Berlin. And the last I heard was that he'd been taken off by the Gestapo at the railway station when he was seeing off some of his American colleagues. Heaven knows what's happened to him now America's declared war on them.'

Helen's mouth fell open. 'Oh, my goodness. You poor thing. You've been worrying all this time.' Her brow furrowed as she drank her tea. 'Well, I can't give you any advice, only that you're going to have to stick it out. Concentrate on your work until you hear some news.' She paused. 'It's going to come to a head now with what's happening in the world.'

Chapter Forty-Four

'Commander Travis would like to see you in his office,' Wanda said when Dale walked into Hut 6 the next morning.

Not again. Dale bit her lip, desperately trying to think what she'd done this time to cause Wanda to rat on her. She'd kept her head down, she'd made herself concentrate on the job in hand, maintaining a steady stream of successes even though her heart was breaking. What more did the woman want from her?

And why couldn't it have been Commander Denniston, who from the outset had been so much fairer and kinder? Why did it have to be Travis? These days her nerves were constantly on edge and she knew she was swinging between despair and anger.

'He wants to see you right away!' Wanda said, her eyes boring into Dale's.

Outside his door Dale took in some calming breaths. It wouldn't do to antagonise him. She knocked.

'Enter!'

He glanced up from his desk, the same as before. He was dressed in full military uniform adorned with more medals than she could count. He looked the very epitome of a commander and immediately she felt herself shrink under his gaze.

'Ah, Miss Treadwell, take a seat.'

He took several moments shuffling papers and flipping through a file where she read her name – upside down from her viewpoint. This time he studied her. Not to be intimidated, she sat a little straighter, trying to picture what was going on in his mind.

'You seem to be doing well since you were reinstated,' he said, almost as though he were surprised.

'I'm doing my best, sir.'

'Yes, well, that's what we expect.' He frowned.

Dale's heart beat fast. *For goodness' sake tell me the worst instead of all this prevarication.* She swallowed.

'I'm transferring you.'

She almost jumped from her seat. Had she heard right? A transfer. What kind of transfer?

'You will report tomorrow at 8 a.m. to Hut 3.' He paused, then to her surprise added, 'I believe you live under the same roof as Lord and Lady Langton.'

'Yes.' She almost blurted out, *and their nephew, Eddie.*

He sent her the glimmer of a smile. He knew.

'What will I be doing, sir?'

'You'll be known as a clerk – one of the few female clerks.'

Her shoulders drooped in disappointment. It didn't sound very interesting at all. A *de*motion instead of the promotion she'd longed for.

'But it's much more than clerical. Thing is,' Commander Travis averted his eyes and cleared his throat, 'we don't have a title for female cryptanalysts. That's the only reason you'll be called a clerk. Hut 3 works closely with Hut 6 and your knowledge of the Enigma should hold you in good stead.' He brought his eyes to hers again. 'Every single success we have will help to shorten the war and thus save thousands of lives. So see you bear that in mind.'

'I will, sir. It's something that spurs us all on.'

'I'm glad to hear it.' He half rose from his desk. 'Oh, by the way, about the matter involving your previous landlord, Mr Draper.'

Dale held her breath.

'That spy business.' Commander Travis regarded her.

Dale's stomach churned. So Wanda had ratted on her after all.

'But surely you don't—'

'Let's just say we've given him the fright of his life. I don't think we need to worry about him any more.' This time he smiled. 'That'll be all, Miss Treadwell. Well done and good luck.'

'Thank you, sir. I'm very grateful.'

Once outside Dale hugged herself. She'd done it! A clerk might not sound exactly like a promotion, but she now knew it was. She set her chin. And no one, including Wanda, was going to stop her from doing her level best to beat those damnable Germans and their bloody codes.

Tomorrow couldn't come quick enough. At five minutes to eight Dale, desperate not to look too excited, forced her eager walk to a stroll as she passed Hut 6 and approached the door to Hut 3 located right next to it. Tentatively she opened the door. The next moment a familiar figure bounced over to her.

'Hello, Dale. Welcome to Hut 3!'

Dale chuckled. 'You knew I was coming here, didn't you?' she said to the grinning Eddie. 'You could have mentioned it this morning when you gave me a lift.'

'Well, last night you refused to tell me where you were being transferred so I thought I'd surprise you.' He took her arm and brought her inside. 'Here, come and meet some of

399

the chaps who crack the settings on Enigma.' He glanced at several young men who were eyeing Dale appreciatively. 'They're not a bad bunch,' Eddie went on, 'though you need to look out for—'

'For the charming Honourable Eddie, more like,' a tall gangly man with a pipe cut in as he thrust out his hand. 'John Wilkins. Pleased to meet you.'

Dale threw Eddie a knowing look at his fellow cryptanalyst's mention of being an 'honourable' but Eddie simply gave her a wink.

The rest introduced themselves, all making cheeky, good-humoured remarks about one another.

'The boss isn't here today,' Eddie said. 'Just as well, so you get a chance to settle in. You'll meet him tomorrow. He's a good bloke. You won't be actually working in this room – we need you more for translation purposes. So you'll be in the Watch Room.' He saw her puzzled expression. 'It's just along the corridor. I'll take you there and introduce you. They'll explain everything, but in a nutshell the German messages you've decoded in Hut 6 are translated into English, making any corrections such as typing errors, filling in gaps that sometimes occur in the transmission, sorting out anything that's muddled – again, often from the transmission or the transmitter.' He caught her eye. 'It's where your knack of solving cryptic crosswords will come in handy,' he grinned. 'Finally, the messages are turned into intelligence.'

The days flew by. It was a completely different atmosphere to what she'd been used to, under Wanda's vigilant eye and working with all women. But even though the men she now worked with were much less formal, they were completely focused. Sometimes she'd hear a cheer ring out along the corridor where Eddie worked, confirming Hut 6 had cracked the day's settings of Enigma. Their shouts of delight never failed to thrill her. In turn, Dale found her work was far more varied, being able to use her newly acquired confidence in her German.

It was what she'd longed for. What she'd aimed at. She was already treated as a new but valued member of the team. If only there wasn't that constant ache in her heart for Glenn.

Chapter Forty-Five

The Nazi propaganda machine was closing in on him. Only last week when Glenn had gone to the studio to do his regular broadcast to America, the German Broadcasting Company had changed the microphone. Instead of speaking into it, he'd had to hold this one to his lips. This meant that American listeners would not be able to discern any background noises. Until now, Glenn had been satisfied that even though he'd been banned from mentioning any British bombing, the roar of RAF planes overhead dropping bombs onto the city would have been clearly heard by CBS. Not any more. He'd always known that as soon as his broadcasts were strictly censored he would leave. He'd decided there and then to book his train ticket for Switzerland in three days' time.

This evening had been his last broadcast, though he'd made no hint of it. Back in his room, Glenn reached under his bed and pulled out the pile of notepads which made up his diaries and laid them on the counterpane. There were eight full notepads. Should he burn them? He glanced at the small black fireplace. It would take a while, but it was a necessary undertaking. He flicked through the first one. My

God, he hadn't spared the Nazis in any way. If he was caught and the Gestapo read his descriptions of the situation in the city: the haunted faces of the Berliners, the lack of food, his own anti-Nazi comments . . . hell, there was enough in this one notebook to put a noose round his neck, let alone all eight of them.

He laid a couple on the grate, but just as he was about to strike a match, he changed his mind. He must get these notepads out of the country. They were a testimony of the truth from an accredited eye-witness by the name of Glenn Reeves, who'd made a mockery of Goebbels' propaganda machine. He caught sight of his suitcase, empty and ready to pack. Could he really get away with it?

He'd gotten away lightly that time at the railway station when he'd handed Donna the letter for Dale. When those two Gestapo bullies had asked what it was, he'd answered:

'A birthday card to my girl in America.'

'Any letter inside?' one of them barked.

'No. Just a note telling her I'm thinking of her on her birthday.'

They'd given him a hard stare, glanced at each other, then handed back his papers. With a click of their heels and a Nazi salute they'd vanished.

Glenn snapped back to the present. He set the notepads flat out on the bottom of one of the cases, then placed a thick stack of his broadcast scripts on top. They'd been officially stamped with approval by the military and civilian censors. If he was lucky the Gestapo would glance at these papers and assume they represented the rest of the contents and wouldn't bother to dig deeper. He hesitated, then threw in a few General Staff maps he'd obtained from friends in the High Command on top of the pile for good measure. The Gestapo would immediately pounce on them as maps were strictly forbidden to be taken out of the country. He knew they loved to demonstrate to the foreign correspondents their absolute power, such as discovering items like maps and making a song and dance of removing them. Hopefully it would be another distraction from the diaries. It was risky, but daily life under the Third Reich had been risky, he reminded himself. It was worth taking a chance.

Feeling better that at least he'd made a decision, however dangerous, he lit a cigarette, letting it dangle from his lips as he packed his clothes and other items, leaving out only the few pieces he needed for the morning. His heart lighter as he thought of Dulcie and that he'd soon be seeing her, he left the room to walk the short distance to the restaurant where he and the last two journalists were meeting before they all left on the night train in an hour's time to neutral Switzerland. Please God, let nothing go wrong with his plans.

Mid-December 1941, Langton Hall

Dale declined Lady Langton's invitation to join them for supper the following night. These first two days at work had been thoroughly absorbing but there was so much to cram in, she needed to be on her own for a bit. She would listen to the wireless. There was a Mozart concert coming on after the seven o'clock news. A perfect antidote to what was going on in the world now that America had finally declared war on Germany and Italy.

How lucky she was to be allowed to have her wireless set in her bedroom – unlike those hateful Drapers who said it was against their rules. This evening she wouldn't even open her *Teach Yourself German* book. She'd have a night off and relax for a change.

She switched on the wireless. It wasn't quite half-past six

but there was usually an interesting programme about this time. At the moment some man was droning on about stamp collecting which didn't interest her in the least. She turned the volume down and made herself comfortable on the small velvet bedroom chair.

As usual, when she was on her own, her thoughts turned to Glenn. If only she knew what had happened to him at the railway station when the Gestapo got hold of him. A shiver crawled up her spine. *Was he still alive?*

I just want to know – however awful, I need to know. But please God let him be safe.

Almost unconsciously, she fingered the chain of her silver locket, tears threatening. She mustn't cry – she wouldn't cry. There couldn't be any more tears left. Realising she was now pressing down hard on the locket's heart, she unclasped it and edged her nail underneath the seam, then laid it open on her dressing table. She peered at Glenn's photograph. Even though the image was so tiny, the little black and white picture was sharply defined, down to the twinkling eyes and the cleft in his chin as he smiled out at her. She glanced at herself. How happy she looked – in love for the very first time. And the last, she was certain. She closed her eyes imagining him. Imagining his voice. She could almost hear him. As if he was softly speaking in her bedroom. Closer than that. His voice was in her ear.

Oh, Glenn, if only you were here, safe and sound.

That voice. The sound of his voice *was* in the room! It couldn't be. She was imagining things. She had to stop this or she'd go mad. She opened her eyes and still in a daze, glanced towards the wireless. Then springing from her chair she turned the volume on full to hear the announcer say:

'Tell us, Mr Reeves, how you escaped from Berlin and arrived in London.'

She gasped, her hand flying to her mouth. She kept her eyes glued to the set, not quite believing . . .

'Things were heating up and I decided I should make tracks . . . literally.' He chuckled. She could visualise him. It was Glenn! Her dearest beloved Glenn. He was safe! And miraculously here in London! Her head swam. She put a hand on the bedpost to steady herself.

'And am I glad. I found out yesterday I was on the last train out. Two days later Germany declared war on the US. If I hadn't left when I did, I would have become an enemy alien . . . interned in Germany for the rest of the war.' He paused. 'Sure not a pleasant thought.'

Dale could hardly concentrate on the rest of his account. All she could think of was that he was alive. Safe. In London. After a few minutes, when Glenn had painted a fuller picture, the presenter said, 'I imagine you'll be busy settling in now you're in London for the foreseeable future, broadcasting to America.'

'Yes, sir. Today's been real busy.'

'I expect you've had to contact your family – let them know you're safe and sound.'

She held her breath.

'I've manged to speak to my folks. But the most important thing right now is to phone my beautiful English girl. Let her know I'm safe and that I love her.' He broke off. 'If you're listening, darling, I'm staying at the club.'

Dale felt the heat rise to her cheeks. Glenn had made it sound as though they were the only two people in the world instead of tens of thousands of people listening in, wondering who this woman was that Mr Reeves was so in love with.

'Let's hope your girl is listening,' the presenter said. 'And thank you very much for sparing the time to give us such a vivid picture of Berlin.' He paused for a few seconds. 'You have just heard our special guest speaker, Mr Glenn Reeves, all the way from Georgia in the United States, telling us the situation in Berlin when he left just four days ago.' Another pause. 'And now for the seven o'clock news.'

Dale's legs shook as she stumbled the few steps back to her chair, her heart beating wildly. He was in London. A train ride away. If only tomorrow had been her day off. But she was down for the afternoon shift at four o'clock. She wouldn't have a full day for another five days. She flung herself on the bed and thumped her pillow, swearing at the unfairness that she wouldn't be able to see him. By the time she had a day off he could be back in America. All because of duty. And how could her trivial contribution count for anything in this damned interminable war?

She couldn't – wouldn't – wait that long. She leapt up and paced the room trying to think. She must work something out.

Maybe it was just possible to travel to London very first thing in the morning and get back to the Park in time for her shift. She'd go. And to hell with Bletchley Park. Glenn came first. All the worry about him, not hearing, then that nightmare letter from Donna that the Gestapo had arrested him . . .

By the time she'd calmed down after giving in to her tears of frustration, her stomach was left in knots, but she'd made up her mind. She would go very first thing in the morning. They'd have a few hours at least.

For now, she'd go downstairs and join her hosts. It might help take her mind off Glenn . . . waiting for her . . . hoping.

But as soon as she entered the drawing room and saw Lord Langton and Eddie sitting in the far corner at the card table, both heads bent over the chess game, and Lady Langton sitting in her armchair that had been drawn closer to the fire and concentrating on her tapestry, Dale wavered. How could she let these people down? They had taken her in because she was doing her bit for the war effort, and there she was, about to throw it back in their faces. They wouldn't think too kindly of her after that. They'd all been brought up to do their duty to their King and country whatever the cost. She took in a shuddering breath recalling Wanda's words when she'd asked for a day's leave to see her mother on that terrible day after the bomb had exploded in Pimlico.

You're doing a very important, top secret job here which is vital for the country, and messages we uncover could save hundreds, maybe thousands of lives. The very next message you decode could have a major impact on the direction of the war.

Dale closed her eyes, trying to still the turmoil in her head. She couldn't do it. She couldn't let them down, especially now she was working in a smaller group and Eddie was one of the cryptographers. Even if she went early in the morning, she could get held up on the train like that last time. Mr Welchman wouldn't be so lenient when he discovered it was all for just a boyfriend. Not even a fiancé, let alone a husband. He might decide it was a serious enough breach to throw her out of the Park. And this time it would be real. She swallowed. No, she had to be professional at all times.

She opened her eyes to find Lady Langton sending her a warm smile.

'How nice to see you, my dear. Have you finished your studies?'

'I didn't start them,' Dale said, forcing her mouth to smile back. 'I decided to have an evening off.'

'Good for you.' She gazed at Dale and frowned. 'You look a little flushed. You're not sickening for anything, are you?'

Dale shook her head. 'No. It's just that—' She broke off. Now, in front of Eddie, was not the time to speak about Glenn.

'Come and sit with me.' Lady Langton gestured towards the opposite armchair. 'You look as though you have something on your mind. It wouldn't be your American, would it?'

Dale's cheeks grew even warmer.

'How did—'

'How did I guess?' Lady Langton packed her tapestry into a carpet bag by her side. 'Call it women's intuition.' She paused. 'I'm a good listener if you'd like to tell me about it.'

Dale glanced over at Eddie who was still immersed in the chess game, feeling the familiar stab of guilt that she couldn't love him as he deserved. She drew in a deep breath.

Lady Langton listened quietly while Dale told her how Glenn had been a guest speaker on the programme and that he was now back in London – and had actually spoken to her on the programme. How she longed to go to him, but she was due at work at four tomorrow and daren't take the risk of being delayed.

'So that's why your eyes are so red. You've been crying.'

Dale nodded.

Lady Langton glanced at the clock on the mantelpiece.

'You know, my dear, it's not too late. If you hurry you could catch the 7.53 to London and if there aren't any hold-ups, be there by ten. That's not too late to have a night-cap with him.' She sent Dale a mischievous wink. 'Then you could make an earlier train tomorrow morning to give you plenty of time for any delays to be back for your afternoon shift.'

Goodness, she'd never have thought it of Lady Langton.

Dale gazed at her. She would have been beautiful in her day, though she was still lovely now, with her creamy skin and cloud of silver hair. But it was her true compassion and affection that shone out of those clear blue eyes.

Dale didn't know how to answer. It was a crazy idea, making her heart jump beats.

'I would if it were me,' Lady Langton said softly. 'If I loved him enough.' She paused. 'I'm sure Eddie would run you to the station.'

Dale stood outside Glenn's door. There hadn't been time to ring him to tell him she was catching a train tonight. He'd be tired from his long journey. He might be asleep. She hadn't thought of that. She shouldn't have come. He'd think she was fast. No, she should have waited until tomorrow morning. They weren't married . . . not even engaged. Glenn had never mentioned it. But he'd told her tonight that he loved her – in front of the presenter and all the listeners.

Stop being such a coward, Dale. For God's sake knock on the damned door.

She brought her knuckles up and knocked louder than she'd meant to. If he was already asleep, he would definitely be awake now.

She heard the scrape of a chair, then muffled footsteps.

The door opened.

Glenn stood there. His eyes widened. He stared at her for a full ten seconds.

'Dulcie! I can't believe it!'

He drew her into his room. She put her bag down inside the door and he switched on the overhead light.

He stood in front of her. 'Tell me you're not just a beautiful vision that will float away.'

'No, it's really me,' she said, laughing at his nonsense. 'I thought that's what *your* voice was this evening . . . a figment of my imagination. I thought I was going mad. There you were in the room with me, but that was impossible.'

'You heard it then.' Glenn kept his eyes on hers. 'I had a feeling you were there when I spoke directly to you. But it's so late. And you still decided to come right away. You didn't wait until tomorrow when I hoped you'd be here.' When she didn't answer, he said, 'Darling, do you want to rest for a bit?'

'No, I've been sitting on a train.'

'Shall I order you a hot drink? A sandwich . . . or something?'

'I prefer the "something",' she said mischievously, 'if it's the "something" I want more than anything in the world.'

He nodded. 'Come here then.' He jabbed his fingers at the space in front of his feet.

She edged forward.

'Closer,' he ordered.

She moved another inch.

'And again.' He caught her arm. 'As close as this.'

And then he gathered her to him. She was aware of a fresh smell of lemony soap. She put her hands through his damp hair.

'You smell wonderful,' she whispered. 'Exactly as I remember.'

'I just got out of the shower,' he whispered back. 'I must have had a premonition you were coming here tonight.' He nuzzled her neck. 'Mmm. You don't smell so bad yourself.'

She laughed softly.

'You can kiss me if you like,' she said.

'Not just yet. I want to savour everything about you.'

'I've waited seven months and seven days and seven min—'

411

Before she could finish, he took her face between his hands and pressed his lips to hers.

After such a long wait his kiss was everything she'd dreamed – tender, then turning to passion as she felt the tip of his tongue. She kissed him back in the same way.

'My goodness.' Glenn drew away after a long minute, catching his breath. 'You've been practising since I've been gone.' His eyes were teasing.

'Well, you set such high standards for kissing, I didn't want to lose my technique.'

'You've bewitched me,' he said with a mischievous grin. 'I'm no match for such a little minx.'

She laughed and kissed him again. He held her to his chest so tightly she felt the breath would be squeezed out of her for ever.

'I never want us to be apart again,' he said, gently setting her a little distance away so he could look at her. His face took on a serious expression. 'I want us to be together always. You know what I'm saying, don't you, darling?'

'I'm not sure,' Dale said lightly, though her heart was hammering in her chest. 'I say that you have to ask me properly as I could be answering the wrong question.'

He smiled that lovely, crooked smile. Then to her surprise he dropped to one knee and took hold of her hand, raising it to his lips, all the while gazing up into her eyes.

'Dulcie, my darling, would you do me the honour of marrying me?'

'Oh, dear, that's a big question.'

'You must have known—'

'Of course I did,' she interrupted him, 'and yes, dearest Glenn, I'd love to be your wife more than anything in the world.'

'You would?' He laughed with delight as he shot to his

feet, lifting her up and swinging her round in his arms, making her dizzy as she laughed with him. 'That's settled then.' He kissed the top of her head. 'And tomorrow we'll make it official and choose the ring. What do you say?'

'I say that I have to work tomorrow.'

'Oh, that's too bad.'

'But not until the four o'clock shift.'

She'd tell him later that she'd been promoted at work. With the Official Secrets Act embedded in her brain, that was all she dared say, but she couldn't help hugging herself that it was so different now at the Park, her skills being taxed to the limit, enjoying it immensely and being part of a team who not only had brilliant minds but loved to tease and joke to release the tension. She wanted to let Glenn know that his words had come true when he'd once told her she was the kind of girl who'd want to play her part in the war – no matter how difficult.

'You don't have to be back until four?' Glenn repeated, watching her face for a few seconds. 'I don't suppose there's any chance of your staying the night then?' His bright-blue eyes were wistful.

'No chance at all.'

Dale hid a smile. She'd let him know much, much later that she'd deliberately chosen a bag to bring all she needed for a night in the Lansdowne Club. Best of all, she'd even brought with her Lady Langton's blessing!

Acknowledgements

Anyone who imagines a writer is huddled in an ivory tower – translate to kitchen table, attic room, spare bedroom, home office – scribbling away with no one to interrupt them, has completely the wrong image. I do have a writing cabin in the garden which I love, and I do spend hours there most days typing my stories straight onto the computer. But writers need people, or else where do they get their characters? And because I write historical romance I need to do a huge amount of research which brings me into contact with the most interesting people.

However, because of the various lockdowns we've had when I was beginning to write this novel, talking to anyone face to face was out of the question, so I had to rely on a number of non-fiction books (reading every single one cover-to-cover). Luckily, I'd already been to Bletchley Park. The first time was with my late husband, Edward Stanton, and a good friend of ours, Richard Milton. This was some twenty years ago and since then I've been twice on my own. Now restrictions have eased I was fortunate to go on a day trip to Bletchley Park with a group led by a military historian, Paul Beaver. This turned out to be an excellent refresher course, particularly wandering through the rooms in the Huts to differentiate the various roles each one played in the war.

Richard Milton is a mine of information on the two world wars, and when I asked him if he would read my manuscript, he accepted the challenge immediately! Being a published writer of both fiction and non-fiction, and having a keen interest in Bletchley Park, he was invaluable, explaining very patiently over Zoom how my heroine would operate the Enigma machine, and even get inside the head of a German encoder!

Regarding the vocabulary for my American hero, I knew just the person to consult – an American southerner and life-long friend, Don Bohannon. We met when I lived in Atlanta half a century ago! I think he was secretly flattered to be asked, and not only spotted the mistakes I'd made but also reminded me of the right expressions and tone.

If you've read any of my previous novels you will know I make up the fourth person in two writing groups: the Diamonds and the Vestas. We're all published writers in different genres and firm friends, bringing our particular skills to the table. We never shy away from critiquing each other's chapters but always with plenty of laughs along the way. Zooming sessions have been a lifeline for us, but we're now able to meet in person and it's wonderful. The Diamonds are: Tessa Spencer, Sue Mackender and Terri Fleming. The Vestas are: Carol McGrath, Suzanne Goldring and Gail Aldwin.

Alison Morton, thriller novelist with the long-running and successful Roma Nova series, is not only a good friend but my critique writing partner whose historical and general knowledge is phenomenal. We edit one another's finished manuscripts, our red pens hovering. Neither of us holds back with our comments but she calls it 'brutal love'. We usually have a weekly chat on Skype (she and her husband live in France) and have just begun to meet in person again.

Then there is the professional team who are involved in the creation of this novel and its journey to publication and beyond. I'm proud to have Heather Holden Brown of HHB Agency as both my agent and delightful friend. She treats me with unfailing humour and enthusiasm, plus a good dose of common sense.

In my opinion, Avon HarperCollins are the dream publishers. They consistently win the Imprint of the Year which is no surprise when I see what they achieve on my behalf. My new editor, Lucy Frederick, has joined the team and is highly talented with a lovely positive and encouraging manner, along with the graphic art, digital, marketing and sales departments, all who make my stories into a beautiful book. Thank you all so much.

Historical Note

I have taken the liberty of mixing my own imaginary characters with a handful of the many remarkable figures at Bletchley Park. They are as follows: Alan Turing, Commander Alastair Denniston, Commander Edward Travis, and last, but of course, not least, Prime Minister Winston Churchill.

Just for the record, Winston Churchill really did pay a visit to Bletchley Park in September 1941, and he made a speech with an ending much as I described in the novel. This is a little different from the common belief about Churchill telling the staff at the Park they were his golden geese who never cackled. Apparently, there is no record at all that he said this, although you will probably agree it does rather have the ring of a Churchillian expression.

Reading List for Wartime at Bletchley Park

The Bletchley Girls by Tessa Dunlop

Secret Postings: Bletchley Park to the Pentagon by Charlotte Webb (A memoir)

Codebreaking Sisters: Our Secret War by Patricia and Jean Owtram (A joint memoir)

The Secret Life of Bletchley Park by Sinclair McKay
  The Lost World of Bletchley Park by Sinclair McKay

Enigma Variations: Love, War & Bletchley Park by Irene Young (A memoir)

My Secret Life in Hut Six by Mair and Gethin Russell-Jones (Part memoir)

Thirty Secret Years: A.G. Denniston's work in signals intelligence 1914-1944 by Robin Denniston, Alastair Denniston's son

Last Train from Berlin by Howard K. Smith (A memoir)

The Codebreakers of Bletchley Park by Dermot Turing (Alan Turing's nephew)

Enigma: The Battle for the Code by Hugh Sebag Montefiore

Read on for an exclusive extract from the next novel in the Bletchley Park series . . .

Chapter One

Rosie entered the front room, normally only used by her parents or on special occasions. Her father's *Daily Mirror* was tucked under her arm, as she carefully carried her cup of tea. She sank into his armchair, dead tired having been on her feet all day. How much longer could she bear this relentless routine? The tea-break chatter from her fellow workers, usually about boys, clothes and the scarcity of both, only occasionally broken by the sobbing of someone who'd just lost a friend or relative in action. She scolded herself for being so intolerant as she thought back on the day.

'Did you hear the latest, Rosie?' Gloria had said while their team was eating lunch.

'What's that?'

'We won't be able to add a bit of nonsense to our under-clothes,' Gloria answered with disbelief. 'Everything's got to be under the new Utility Clothing Scheme from now on. Bad enough to have clothes rationed let alone haberdashery, but a bit of lace here and there is the only thing that keeps my Sid interested for you know what.'

Several girls giggled. The edges of Rosie's mouth barely lifted.

'You all right, duck?' Martha, an older woman in her usual brightly coloured turban, asked.

'Bit of a headache,' Rosie said. 'It'll go.'

But it wouldn't. It would remain with her for the rest of the day.

The others threw her sympathetic looks, then continued their conversations until the bell rang for everyone to resume work.

I hate living like this, Rosie thought as she packed boxes of Caley's chocolates ready to be put on the delivery lorries. She'd asked many times if she could work in Accounts. But Mr Lane always turned her down, even when they'd had a couple of vacancies these past two years when one of the bookkeepers and an apprentice accountant both left to join the Army. Mr Lane likely thought she was only bound to get married and then he'd have to train someone else.

Fine chance of that, Rosie now thought bitterly. She opened the newspaper to skim the front-page news. The war was dragging on. It was all very well remaining cheerful here in Norfolk, but Norfolk folk hadn't faced the merciless bombing that London and Liverpool people had. Those cities were far away but it would surely only be a matter of time until the Luftwaffe picked on Norwich. The beautiful cathedral, the castle, the medieval buildings. She closed her eyes for a few seconds, trying to imagine the destruction. It was an awful thought. Even worse was the constant discussion of invasion. It was enough to freeze the blood in your veins. She bent her head to read the main headlines.

All Single Women Must Go To War

New Parliamentary Act decrees by Spring all single women and childless widows between 20 and 30 must join the armed forces, work in industry, or join the Land Army, unless in a reserved occupation.

It went on to state what the reserved occupations were, such as teaching and nursing.

Rosie bit her lip and the pulse of her headache became more insistent. She was twenty-three. High time she did something definite to help in the war effort. But where did she stand? Her parents would never let her join the WRNS, which she'd longed to do ever since war broke out. It would take her away from home and her mother needed all the help she could get looking after the two young ones, Roddy and Poppy. But surely her two sisters, Heather and Iris, now nineteen and seventeen, were old enough to pull their weight.

For goodness' sake, Iris is the same age now as I was on when I thought I was getting married.

But she mustn't be unfair to her sister. Iris had just started as a munitions worker at Lawrence and Scott's, finding factory work physically exhausting after having just left school. And Heather was in for a shock next spring when *she'd* be conscripted because a salesgirl wasn't considered a reserved occupation. Rosie couldn't help smiling at the thought of Heather toeing the line. Then her smile faded. Mum would argue they were both at work all day so couldn't help with all the cooking and washing for seven people, seeming to forget her eldest daughter was also at work.

With a sigh Rosie stood and left the newspaper on the

chiffonier in the parlour. She'd known conscription for women was bound to happen. And it was right. Women *should* play their part as much as the men. But the only way she could obey the new act was to continue the lie she'd been keeping up for some time now. And no doubt the guilt about that would only worsen. But even that thought couldn't stop the frisson of excitement that this might just be the opportunity she'd been longing for.

She went upstairs to change out of her overalls.

'Rosemary, where are you?' her mother called up the stairs.

'In the bedroom, Mum.' Rosie looked round the room she shared with Heather and Iris. Heather, as usual, had thrown her belongings on every conceivable surface including the floor, her excuse being that the single wardrobe allocated for the three of them simply wasn't big enough. Scattered on an old desk serving as a dressing-table was a hairbrush tangled with all three shades of hair and Heather and Iris's few toiletries. Rosie was always careful to hide her own precious pot of Pond's cold cream and Armani shampoo, but even though she'd labelled them 'RF' and hidden them in different places every few days, Heather always found them. She sighed. The room was a permanent mess.

'It's hard for you being squashed in with Heather and Iris,' her mother said, glancing round at the double bed the girls shared, next to Rosie's single one. 'You should have your own home by now, let alone a bedroom to yourself.'

Don't bring that up again, Mum. It was six years ago.

Rosie swallowed. It might have been six years, but it didn't make her feel any less bitter.

Her mother sent her an anxious look.

'What's the matter, love? You look as though you've got something on your mind.'

Before she could answer, Rosie heard the back door open.

'Shirl? Where are you?'

'Oh, that's your dad home already.'

She hurried downstairs, and after a moment of hesitation, Rosie followed. Her mother gestured towards the back kitchen door. 'I'd better put the kettle on as he'll be wanting a cup of tea.'

Her father was outside holding onto the door frame of the scullery with one hand, the other tugging at his fireman's boot.

'You're early, Dad,' Rosie said. 'It's freezing out there. Come into the kitchen and I'll help you get that boot off.'

He looked up. She saw the lines of exhaustion on his face, enhanced by streaks of filth. His eyes were bloodshot and expressionless, as though the life had been sucked out of him.

'What's happened?' Rosie asked, dreading the answer when he sat at the kitchen table and finally pulled off one boot.

'There's been a bad fire over at one of the warehouses. Weren't even a bomb this time, only some twerp who didn't stub his fag out. One of the lads died and another went off to the hospital in an ambulance with bad burns. I don't know if he's going to make it, poor sod.' He let out a long breath. 'We've bin goin' non-stop. No tea break, no nothin', so when a few of the lads on the next shift turned up early the boss sent us home.' He grunted as he yanked the second boot. It didn't budge.

Rosie grimaced at the news. But the others would soon be home from school. This might be her only chance to talk to her parents in private. While her mother made the tea, Rosie managed after a tussle to free her father's other boot.

'I can see why it was difficult to pull off,' she said. 'Your ankles are really swollen.'

'I'm not surprised. Braddy boots don't fit right and even if I had the money to get another pair, they're almost impossible to come by these days.'

It was true. Clothes rationing had started in June, and it took too many coupons for shoes and boots that were scarce anyway. Even if you found a pair in one of the shops, they were often the wrong size. The children wore one another's cast-offs and her mother constantly worried their feet would be ruined in years to come. But with a large family to provide for and only her father's modest wages, her mother had struggled to make ends meet all the years before her daughters went out to work.

Rosie shut her eyes, trying to block out the reason why the money had to stretch further than it ought. She swallowed hard. When Poppy was born she'd promised she'd be completely responsible for the baby until she was old enough to go to school. Poppy had started in September and at that point Rosie had gone to Caley's so she could finally contribute to the household. But now with this latest news . . .

'I think I'll go in the front room and read the paper,' her father broke into her thoughts. 'Can you bring my tea in, love?'

Rosie went back to the kitchen. Her mother poured a mug of tea and added two teaspoons of sugar.

'You should cut him down to one,' Rosie said, 'now sugar's rationed.'

'Oh, he has mine,' her mother said. 'I gave it up in tea last month.'

'You're getting thin,' Rosie observed. 'You shouldn't keep giving Dad your rations. And don't argue,' she said as her mother opened her mouth to reply. 'I see you doing it. And not only Dad, but you give yours up to Roddy as well.'

'I've probably had a snack you haven't seen,' her mother said mildly. 'Anyway, you'd better take his tea in before it gets cold.'

Rosie picked up the mug.

'Thanks, love.' Her father took his tea and nodded to the other armchair. 'We don't ever find time for a chat, do we, girl?'

'I thought you liked to be quiet and read your paper.'

'I do. But now you're here—' He broke off and lit a pipe, then glanced at the front page. 'Well, well, conscription is to be mandatory for girls and widows without kids,' he said without looking up, 'and you're in the right age bracket.' He stroked his chin. 'I doubt they'll make working in a chocolate factory a reserve occupation with a war on, even though we like a square or two ourselves when you bring home the odd bar.' He smiled, but it quickly faded as though he'd thought of something. 'You realise what this means, don't you, love, if you join the forces? Though I can't see you knuckling down to the discipline . . .'

'I would if I thought it was helping the war effort,' Rosie protested.

'Have you thought which one you'll join if you still get the choice?'

She didn't hesitate. 'The WRNS.'

Her father rolled his eyes. 'You can forget that. The Navy is the snobby one. They want the cream of the crop – which we're most definitely not – and I'm sure that will go for the WRNS as well.' He looked her directly in the eye. 'No, my girl, it'll be the Army for you.'

'I don't want the Army,' Rosie said. 'You know how I love the sea. When we used to go to Hunstanton every year I loved watching the waves when there was a storm and—'

'You're living in cloud cuckoo land,' her father interrupted.

'Women aren't allowed to serve on ships. I'd have thought you knew that.'

'Yes, but if it's abroad, you'd have to get there on a ship,' Rosie argued, then lowered her tone. 'Anyway, much as I want to see the world, I know it's not practical now.'

He looked at her, puffing on his pipe. 'How will your mother cope if you leave home?'

'Heather and Iris are adults,' Rosie said, 'so Mum won't have to look after them. Heather always moans that she's tired after a day on her feet in Woolies and leaves me to help Mum when I come home, but I've worked just as hard in that blasted factory all day. Iris helps Mum when she can, but I know her munitions boss is very strict. Heather's on the lazy side but she'll just have to buck up and give Mum some help with the younger ones. And whatever I earned I'd send Mum most of it, as I do now.'

He settled back in his chair. 'She's getting too thin. I'm worried about her.'

So her father *had* noticed.

'I was going to talk to you about that, Dad. Do you realise she gives you half her rations most days, and if she knows you've eaten well at the canteen she'll give it to Roddy.'

Her father's jaw dropped. 'I didn't know that.'

'Well, you do now, so can you keep an eye on *her* plate?'

'Course I will.' He shook his head. 'Blasted war and blasted Germans.' He paused. 'Mind you, they must see their own people are gettin' killed and cut to pieces as well. For what? An Austrian maniac who don't care tuppence for them, only his own vanity to conquer the world. Well, he's got another think coming if he thinks we'll let Blighty go in a hurry.'

Rosie couldn't help smiling. She gazed at him with affection. What a brave man he was, never complaining about his job, even on that terrible night eighteen months ago when there was a raid of high explosive bombs on Colman's mustard factory. Five young women were killed. Several mills had burnt to cinders. There'd been three huge fires roaring and at the same time one of the water mains broke and a warehouse fell into the river just where he and the other firemen were drawing out the water. To cap it all, the ambulances hadn't been able to get down the main roads to pick up the injured as they were blocked by the bomb damage.

Things had quietened down a little since, but you never knew when the next raid would start. Her mother was permanently on edge, bracing herself for the next tragedy to occur.

'I was thinking that if I *did* join up, Dad, I'd probably get a better wage which would help the family.' She hesitated. 'As you say, with the conscription news I'll be called up anyway by one of the forces – most likely the Army – and sent too far away to come home every day.' She hesitated.

Should she . . .

Before she could stop herself, she blurted, 'Unless I tell them the truth. Then they can't make me.'

Now you've finished Dale's story,
why not check out Raine's wartime tale of hope
and friendship in the Victory Sisters series?

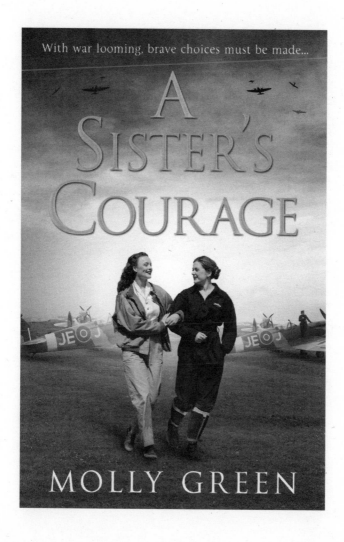

Available in paperback, eBook and audiobook now.

In the darkest days of war,
Suzanne's duty is to keep
smiling through . . .

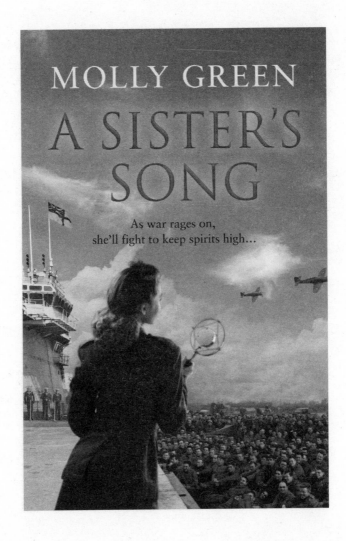

Available in paperback, eBook and audiobook now.

Ronnie Linfoot may be the youngest
sister, but she's determined to do
her bit . . .

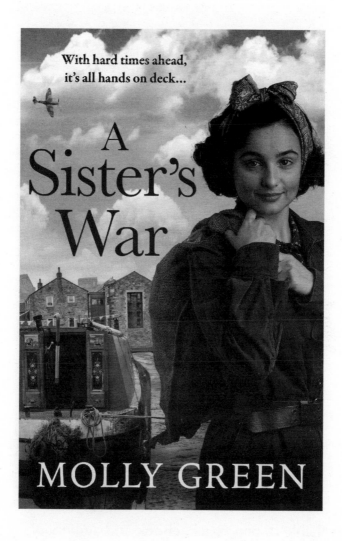

With hard times ahead,
it's all hands on deck...

A
Sister's
War

MOLLY GREEN

Available in paperback, eBook and audiobook now.

And then curl up with Molly Green's
heart-warming Orphans series...

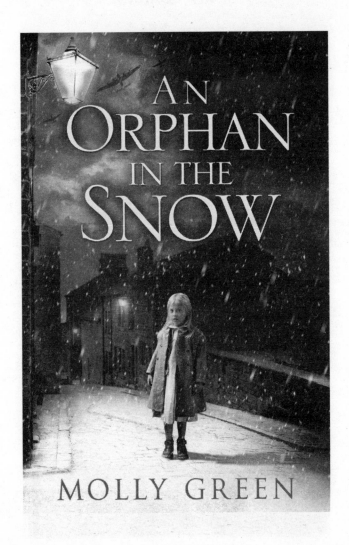

War rages on, but the women and
children of Liverpool's Dr Barnardo's Home
cannot give up hope . . .

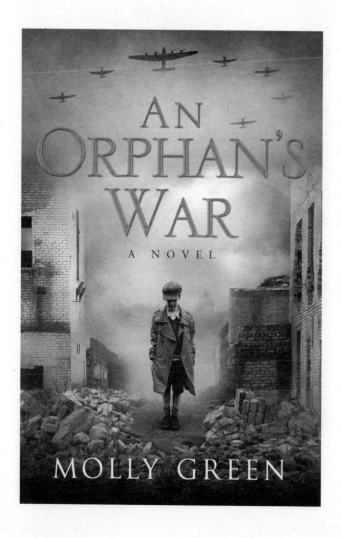

Even when all seems lost at
Dr Barnardo's orphanage, there is always a
glimmer of hope to be found . . .

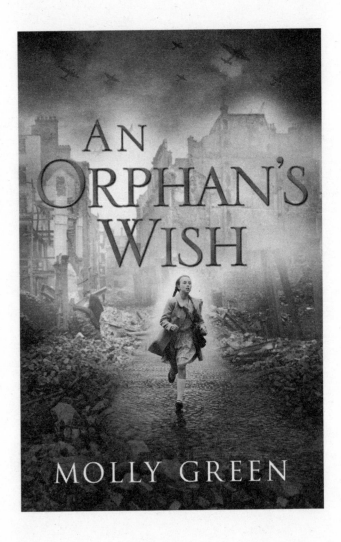

Available in paperback, eBook and audiobook now.